PINK CARBIDE
Aluminum Opus

By E.S. Wynn

PINK CARBIDE: ALUMINUM OPUS
ISBN: 978-0-6151-7983-4

Pink Carbide series copyright © 2005-2008 by Earl S. Wynn
Cover Art by Earl S. Wynn

First Edition: 2008, Thunderune Publishing
www.thunderune.com

For information address:
Earl S. Wynn,
ATTN: Aluminum Opus
P.O. Box 3902
Sonora, Ca,
95370

PRINTED IN THE UNITED STATES OF AMERICA

10 9 8 7 6 5 4 3 2 1

Special thanks to:

Alexia Retallack and Jonathan Langsam for proofreading, deep critique and incredible feedback, among other things. Thanks! You're both awesome beyond all reckoning!

I'd also like to thank the following Deviant Art artists for their support!

The awesome miss Cassy (~M4dLeprechaun)
Max Dunbar (~Psycho-fish)
Kong Chho (~Captkiro)
Sonya Hale (~Dannonlee)
Rasmus Gunnarsson (~Raz42)
Dylan Odom (*lwcldylan)
Catherine Brezniak (~Bubbamesa)
Colin Hamilton (~Cjhonline)
Alex Karagiannopoulos (~Vaitylos)
Erin Walsh (~Muffin-Wrangler)

And of course all the boys (and girls) at {CCB}, WC and D341.

Thank you!

Chapter 1: Grey Synaptic Requiem

It was Wednesday, late Wednesday.

As Cylea made her way through the airport terminal, people surged past on either side of her, pushing and shouldering, hefting bags and coats like weapons against the cold and the light drizzle of rain that played along the sidewalks outside. Her black leather boots padded silent across dull grey carpet worn smooth by the footsteps of thousands of passengers over the last century and a few spare decades beyond that, stepping lightly past clusters of obese, stereotypical tourists that clung to the walls in noisy knots. Most of them were Chinese, men and women from the East chattering happily or descending upon the gift shops and restaurants that lined the walls in tight clumps, sweaty fingers eagerly pressing cash cards into those glorified vending machines. In a way, it was almost entertaining to watch them, wealthy and oblivious– nothing like Hok and his family, *her family*, the family that had taken her in and treated her as one of their own, working to secure her sanctuary with the stark, no-nonsense Triads... She swallowed quickly, pushing the thoughts away, trying not to think about the sacrifices they had made, the sacrifices that had gotten her as far as they had, allowed her to be here, now, on the edge of an almost phantom-like safety that waited for her somewhere in Hong Kong with the Golden Koi. Thinking about all the terrible twists and turns she'd endured that day, about all the brushes with death and hot cacophonic explosions of lead and fire and the outright shattering of a way of life she'd finally grown accustomed to brought a bad taste to her mouth, a bad taste that had the nasty tendency to linger.

Sighing, she ran one lithe hand absently through her short, wild blond hair, then let it drift back to the top of a worn, olive-drab commuter bag slung loosely over her shoulder. Her vibrant, clear blue eyes drifted absently ahead of her, distant and aloof over her distinctively Germanic nose and gently curving, painfully pink lips. At her neck, a small silver chain stretched down her chest to a single Japanese character, kanji for "Tsuki," –she'd long since forgotten the translation– that rested between her breasts, just over the top of a white, stylized eye of the Egyptian god Ra emblazoned across the front of her loose, black tanktop.

With the quiet clink of metal on metal, the kanji bounced lightly against something that was an even bigger mystery to her– a small brass key marked with a single word: "Gramercy." She knew both were important, significant in some hidden way, each keys to mysteries in their own right– but how she knew was another story, one she still had yet to discover, an elusive thread that she kept grabbing at and that kept unraveling more mysteries than answers with each desperate attempt. It was like deja vu, but stranger, much stranger, almost like sifting through someone else's memories.

Pulling her free hand from the pockets of her worn out and stained blue jeans, she gently touched the kanji and the key, almost superstitiously, as if she were the last priestess of some long forgotten faith touching the last sacred talismans in the last short hour before the end of everything– there was still a lot she didn't know about herself, a lot of strange, dark potential she felt buried somewhere within her, potential that scared her, though she couldn't say exactly why. More of those strange feelings. Shivering against the memories, against the images of her bloodied fists and the edge of Walt's neural matrix sticking out of the crushed and beaten caricature of a smiling butler that had served as his face, she forced her eyes forward, to the tourists and the sprawling, windowed waiting area. It was all in the past now, she told herself– everything that had happened in Los Angeles was behind her now, everything except that damned bounty.

Closing her eyes briefly and breathing a sigh, she glanced absently to the left, watching as an elderly man, body merged into a roughly chair-like, motorized amalgam of cybertechnology that was more life-support hardware than flesh, shakily conversed with a tall Korean woman whose bold figure was all sleek, hard lines encased in the stiff folds of some kind of dark green running suit. Her dark, jade-green eyes, as wary and severe as any snake's, met Cylea's gaze instantly, silently and solidly urging her to look away and mind her own business. Not that it mattered– the old man reminded her too much of Smash, the hacker-turned-government tool from her not-so-distant past and the woman was a vague echo of the Golden Koi Triad rep she'd known as Shang, both of those thoughts bringing on a whole new wave of painful memories she had to struggle to repress. Again, her eyes darted back to the happy, chattering flood of tourists, and again she breathed a tired sigh.

As the concourse dropped away on either side of her, replaced by huge plate-glass windows that looked out over a seemingly endless sea of light-spotted tarmac, she glanced once at her ticket –an aisle seat on flight thirty-eight forty, service to Hong Kong through gate B fourty-four– and stepped onto the angled gridmesh of the gravway. Based on the same suspensor technology that made hoversedans possible, gravways were expensive strips that served as a more modern version of the movable walkway, using an artificially-generated gravity field to push passengers along at a speed roughly equivalent to walking.

She looked up slowly, forcing a smile as her eyes followed a huge liner pulling out of a gate at the far end of the airfield. It looked like one of the newer extraorbital products of some legacy manufacturer like Boeing or Ellison Conway, a craft that could circumnavigate the earth in four hours pushing the redline with a full complement of close to five hundred passengers plus baggage. It had been all over the news when a new law had come across in the re-envisioning of the old FAA codes requiring every older, petrol-based liner to be retrofitted with the newest engines and fuel systems, but the impact on the huge extraorbital liners had been the most talked about– running only a pair of underwing nacelles that wasted so little fuel they could run for weeks without needing to be replenished with EX-2 –a highly concentrated and compact form of atomically altered water-- the largest and fastest liners had suddenly become almost dirt-cheap to run– not that it had driven down the price of seats any. If anything, the prices had actually risen. Now considered the transportation of the elite, every seat aboard these liners was first class– the upper lounge, complete with a full-service bar, a pair of synthskin lovebots for every seat, and wireless access to every Neuroline channel available on the planet was simply upgraded to the "Penthouse."

As she watched the plane taxi off into the darkness, another absent sigh escaped her lips and she looked away. Her destination was getting close now– just beyond a comparatively new desk of some sort of dull grey plastic manned by the same kind of legless servedroid that filled almost every niche and alcove where any kind of business was conducted, half a dozen people were already seated in the waiting area outside the gate for her flight. Forcing another smile, she stepped off the gravway and pushed forward, quickening her pace in a desperate attempt to shake the past from her heels, to think about something pleasant for a change. Not that the idea of flying "Penthouse" wasn't pleasant, but she doubted she'd ever get the chance to do so, and even then the lovebots would probably get old before too long. Neuroline still sounded interesting... she'd always wanted to see Neoclassic Electrorock goddess Arizona Alhambra perform in Neuroline.

Taking a seat three chairs down from an elderly woman in some sort of teal, flower-print dress with a little boy, maybe two or three years old sitting on her lap, Cylea glanced around the waiting area. Across from her, a man in a disheveled, stained suit skimmed through a handheld newsfeed and absently sipped his coffee next to an emaciated, butch-looking young man absorbed in some sort of meditation. A tiny holographic Jesus rested in his hands, whispering something monotonous she couldn't hear, but after a moment he looked up, smiled, and gave her a slow, silent nod which she absently returned.

But it wasn't the other passengers that drew her attention in the end. Glancing around briefly, looking past the scattered, groggy masses and the Chinese tourists, her suspicions were quickly confirmed–the airport was almost completely automated, but the security was still human, though even they showed signs of some kind of heavy cybernetic augmentation or another. The older, grizzled veterans with patches of worn chrome and hard grey plastic showing on sagging, age-tanned skin seemed to stand out more than the sleeker new recruits, but it was still easiest to spot the long-term personnel who actually lived at the airport, kept in an endless cycle of half-consciousness by bulky EverWary systems and breaking only for coffee or some cheap airport food every few hours to keep their bodies from indulging in outright rebellion.

Half a century ago, when seemingly half the world's security personnel had jumped at the chance to test out the first EverWary systems put out by Duke Industries' highly controversial neural restructuring division, the units had been large and clunky to say the least, sacrificing nearly the entire back of the skull for a thick, direct-interface band of chrome that effectively eliminated the need to sleep. Unfortunately, it also had the nasty tendency to keep its owner in a permanent state of groggy grumpiness that only got worse with age, and often shaved years off a person's life expectancy to boot. Even the latest models weren't pretty– the hardware itself was hard to compress into something even half-sized, especially after the whole project was shelved and research had gone completely underground following a series of spectacular lawsuits. These days, new EverWary systems were a quasi-legal black market commodity that left a thumb-thick, plastic wraparound stretching across the back of the skull, one that stood out even under some of the most expensive nanocosmetic hairstyle jobs. Still, considering the consequences of having your brain rewired to avoid the need to sleep, or at least, to keep your whole brain from slipping into unconsciousness at once, it was one hell of a sacrifice to make just for a bigger paycheck.

A peal of squealing laughter caught her ear and she looked over, smiling softly as the toddler and the older woman met her gaze with happy grins. Silently, she grinned back, waving. It was refreshing to see something that didn't remind her of anything unpleasant, but such things rarely lasted, and this was no exception. The Korean woman she'd seen earlier took a seat at the end of the row, her face as cold and emotionless as a rock, with the old man wheeling up beside her, wheezing unhealthily.

Turning away, Cylea let her eyes drift to the windows. Overhead in the cold, starless night sky, clouds roiled fitfully like boiling mercury under the light of the full moon. The tarmac glowed a faint blue under the quilt-like sea of cloud cover, brightening slightly at the base of the plane that waited at the gate like a silent ferryman for someone's last journey-- one she hoped wouldn't turn out to be hers. Inside, people skittered past the windows, walking briskly along the aisle, making sure everything was prepared and clean, ready to receive the next load of passengers.

On the whole, the plane itself wasn't anything spectacular, just a small jet liner, a cheap Mexican knock off of something the Pakistani had reverse-engineered from a design the Chinese had based on god only knew what, plastered with cheap, peeling decals of the Chinese flag and the logo for GKI air wherever the paint had worn off. Its engines were obvious retrofits, something shoddily done that looked like a couple of archaic turbo-boosted hydrogen systems had been jammed haphazardly into housings that had been intended for something far smaller-- originally, they'd probably housed an even older set of turbine engines, but now they were forced and stretched over what was probably a technician's nightmare held together with duct tape and more of those already overused decals.

When the call to begin boarding finally came and the gate doors were opened, Cylea stood with the rest of the tourists. The old woman let the toddler stumble and run near her feet, and the Korean woman turned stonily toward the gate, the chair-bound old man watching her with a soft smile. Ten minutes later put Cylea on the plane, ten rows down from the front and on the left side of the aisle, sitting in the outermost of the two seats next to a teenage girl with dark hair that flared out at odd angles just past her collar, brushing against her shoulders when she moved. She'd been only too happy to show Cylea that the image spread out across the front of her shirt was a full-motion capture of some popular band, the "Screaming Scarlet Dundlemen," complete with a touch-activated thirty-second soundbite from one of their latest songs, a jumpy number and a top-ten hit titled "Sweden." It wasn't bad music, something like a cross between downtempo darkwave and ambient salsa with all the keening bagpipes of traditional Celtic mingled with the same overused beat she'd heard on countless pop songs in the past, but hearing the same condensed thirty second strip over and over again got old fast.

Smiling politely and pulling a silicon magazine out of the seat in front of her, Cylea shifted toward the aisle and thumbed the dull grey strip of metal and fabric to life, soft silicon lighting up with the brilliant cover and all the glossy, full color pictures of GKI air's shopping catalog. As the soundbite started again, she flicked the language preference settings from Chinese to German and triggered the activation for the first page, giving the girl another polite smile and nodding absently before burying her eyes in pages of shiny, kitschy useless junk with price tags only a corporate suit might find reasonable.

Chapter 2: State Of The Union

The stewardess welcomed the last few passengers onboard, smiling politely at each in turn until the last sweaty tourist came jogging down the ramp and started for his seat. She cast one last glance out the hatch, absently hoping to catch sight of the Captain, then turned and started helping the few people still milling in the aisle with their carry-on baggage and seatbelts. Inside the cockpit of the liner, the co-pilot was already running through the preflight checklists and singing distractedly to a catchy tune that lilted quietly through the flight deck, something almost wholly synthesized and rich with vocals that bordered somewhere between Soul and Bhangra, complete with a chorus of backup singers belting out punjabi couplets in a distinctively operatic manner that still, somehow, managed to fit in perfectly with the song's decidedly disco edge.

"Not this crap again." The Captain grimaced, shouldering open the door. As he stepped into the cockpit, a brown paper bag marked with a bright, friendly and faintly glowing logo in one of his beefy hands, the smell of greasy, cheap Chinese food followed him in, instantly soaking the flight deck with its rich aroma. "Peterson, if you're gonna use the GLATS to pick up LiveSat radiocasts, the least you can do is choose something decent to listen to."

"What's wrong with K-Velos?" He asked quickly, pushing a potato chip into his mouth. He was significantly thinner than the Captain, but it was clear that his diet and his profession were taking their toll on his doubtlessly once-sleek figure. "I mean, they've got all the latest music. You know, Boatswain Carpenters, Tactile Malfunction, Arizona Alhambra..." He tapped a screen on the control panel lightly, chewing in the pause. "Mmhh, this song is Tatro Rassad's number one hit," Peterson swallowed, adding: "and he's the king of Electrosynth Bollywood Disco."

"Yeah? Well, my ass is the king of this seat." The Captain plopped down with a grunt, then leaned over to the Copilot with a grin. "But that doesn't mean it can sing worth a damn."

Peterson opened his mouth to say something, but the Captain cut him off so casually it seemed almost like it was little more than second nature. "No, you see, what we need to listen to is some talk radio." His fingers darted across the small, lightly green glowing screen. "Pat Davis is on right now, and he's the best damn talk show host since David Helzer, Ken Harrington or even Rush Limbaugh."

"Yeah... so you've said," Peterson turned away, reaching for something on the other side of his seat, "and only about every time we've ever made a flight."

"That's all? I figured it'd have been more." The Captain laughed, trailing off as the familiar sound of Pat Davis' brusk voice, lightly accented in a decidedly New Englander fashion, echoed across the speakers, already sounding as irritated as it did amused.

"*...and he actually tried to tell me –me, of all people– that not only is Ted Solomon secretly supporting FLAIL, but that he's doing it under the guidance of some alien overlord. The guy actually had a name for it too, something like Klaxu or Kalahan or Killus or something with a 'K' in it. Anywho, somehow, Solomon is 'supposedly' doing this because he's planning to pull a profit out of the whole thing that he can then turn around and immediately invest into time travel! Can you believe that? Of all the conspiracy theories I've ever heard, this one takes the cake, Sandra. What a kook.*"

The Captain laughed, turning to Peterson with a wide grin plastered across his face. "Now this is entertainment–" his face soured instantly; Peterson had already pulled on a broadband broadcast headset and was gently bobbing his head to some unheard music.

"Hey. Hey." The Captain grimaced, leaning over and quickly tapping the Copilot on the shoulder. "Hey, Peterson."

Flipping up the visor with an irritated sign, Peterson's eyes met the Captain's, his features dominated by a mild, tired look of annoyance. "What?"

"Finish the checklist." The Captain stated immediately, bushy eyebrows making it clear he expected nothing but strict compliance. "We haven't got time for you to watch some fairy dance around stage in tights singing about how much he loves women's clothing. Once we get in the air, you can do whatever you want, but right now, we need to get this piece of crap ready for flight."

"I wasn't watching–" the captain cut him off again.

"I don't really give much more than a half a damn, Peterson, I really don't." He managed, trying to sound as gentle and detached as he could manage. "Come on now, it's checklist time."

The Copilot sighed quietly and set aside the headset, turning to the control panel and flicking switches as he silently mouthed each step in the process. The captain swivelled back toward the panel, laughing heartily as Pat Davis delivered another witty remark. The caller's response came quickly.

"*... I'm not saying I agree with mister Hatfield, I'm simply pointing out the fact that the FTL project might not be the main reason Solomon bought up Minerva. Mark*

Gutierrez was a brilliant man, a modern day mad scientist, if you will. He was an inventor, above all things, as you well know, and he tinkered around with a lot of controversial theories. I would not be at all surprised if he shelved an experimental gene sequence or a chronometric device of some sort that Solomon's just been itching to get his hands on since long before the commercial accords."

"Chronometric? Come on, everybody knows that time travel is impossible. Oh sure, the theory has waffled now and again since the eighteen hundreds, but that doesn't change the fact that it is impossible. Now, a gene sequence, maybe, but I'm still a strong believer in Solomon's sense of duty. Mark my words, Sandra, he's gonna take us to the stars someday. Next caller..."

"Y'all up for some coffee?" The sweet, heavily accented voice of the Stewardess cut through the obligatory, and yet no less excited "hi pat!" of the next caller. Instantly, both men swivelled toward her.

"Honey, you read my mind." The Captain grinned. "You know how I like it, right?"

"Two lumps, no cream, Cap'n Stevens." She smiled. Instantly, she had a pair of white Styrofoam cups in her hands, both filled to the brim with steaming coffee. "And the whole nine yards for Gary."

As she handed off the cups and turned to leave, Peterson caught her hand, heaping on the charm with a wide, ivory grin. "Thanks, Betty."

"Sure thing sugar." She smiled back. "I don't mind keeping healthy boys like all y'all awake and alert. Don't wanna end up in the sea, after all." The three laughed, and Peterson let her go. They shared a wink, and then she was gone, the door closing softly behind her.

"She's great, you know." Peterson shook his head, grinning.

The Captain managed an amused smile in between careful sips. "She's a stewardess, Gary. A gold digger through and through."

"Nah, Betty's different." He sighed dreamily. "She's real, you know?"

Stevens guffawed. "Yeah, and I'm sure for the right price, she'll–" Instantly, there was a burst of static from the radio, interrupting him. Grimacing, the Captain set down his cup of coffee with obvious disgust and sucked in a tired breath as the call came in. "GKI air zero-five-three-tango, this is Los Angeles ground; you've been painted by authorities for a criminal extraction, over."

"Ah, not this crap again." He grumbled. "Why do the lawbreakers and liberals always have to choose my flights?" Peterson glanced worriedly out the cockpit window. Sighing, Stevens quickly keyed the mike. "Roger that, ground control, holding position."

He turned slowly toward the copilot, still grimacing. Peterson's eyes flicked back, meeting the Captain's– his face was blank, withdrawn, but his eyes betrayed silent nervousness.

Stevens smiled. "You mind handling this one, Peterson?"

The other man watched him carefully for a moment, then nodded once, fingers fumbling slightly as he set down his coffee and pulled on his hat. In the next instant, he was up and out of the cockpit, the door closing noisily behind him.

Clearing his throat, Stevens quickly flipped back over to the intercom. "Passengers, this is your Captain speaking. Please stay seated. It shouldn't take long before we can get underway."

Emerging into the aisle just outside the door, the copilot traded a few quick words with the stewardess and her smile instantly faded. She nodded once as he finished, then quickly pointed out a single passenger reading a newspaper, a silent, reserved looking man with oddly parted hair and a black leather coat that hung open to reveal a plain, white, button-up shirt. Glancing quickly at the man, the copilot gave her one quick, nervous nod, licked his lips, and started down the aisle.

Chapter 3: Heart of Darkness

"Wow! Look at that!"

Absently, Cylea turned toward the window, silicon magazine held loosely in her hand. Something was making the teenager excited, something outside the plane in the hazy darkness of the strobe-lit tarmac. Flashing lights flared blue and crimson, playing off the engine's dull housing.

The instant she saw it, she swallowed. Before the nervous murmurs started rippling up and down the aisle, before the sound of the Captain's voice came over the intercom again, gently informing them that the Bureau of Terran Defense had arrived, would be coming on board shortly, but only briefly, and needed their full cooperation for a fast and safe operation, she had known exactly what was going on. It hadn't taken long, but they'd caught up to her; they'd caught up to her when she had been so close, and it didn't seem like there was any way she could manage to escape this time. She was trapped, trapped on the very plane that was supposed to take her to safety, and this time she doubted Jack, the bartender and long time friend who'd pulled her out of a few tight scrapes in the past, or even her Silent Savior, that strange man who'd appeared seemingly out of nowhere earlier the same day and rescued her from certain death at the hands of a couple of FBI agents looking to cash in on the bounty being offered for her, would be able to come to her rescue.

She looked away quickly, an unpleasant knot forming in her stomach as she stared nervously forward– it was all happening too fast. All day, she had been running from the law, corporate soldiers, bounty hunters, and god only knew what else. She couldn't let it end this way, refused to let it end this way– the plane was probably surrounded, there was nowhere to run. She licked her lips and peered nervously into the aisle, eyes darting once over the co-pilot and the stewardess. There really was only one option left. It was time she stopped running, time she stood up and made a stand... somehow.

She swallowed uneasily, eyes darting around the cabin– she had to find a weapon of some kind, something to use to defend herself or threaten others with. Briefly, she considered taking a hostage, but that would probably only have made things worse, and she didn't have the heart, much less the nerves to hold some terrified and innocent civilian under the imminent threat of death while she waited for the BTD to get a sniper into place. What was the saying? "We don't negotiate with terrorists?" If the BTD was involved now, they probably considered her a terrorist of some kind or another. Best to fight until they finally managed to subdue her– it wouldn't take long once they were inside the plane. Even nerve-blocked gene-hulks of vat-grown muscle that were capable of lifting hovertrucks collapsed eventually under the effects of stunsticks and mace-gel. One or two hits would probably be all it would take to leave her writhing in pain on the floor of the liner, unable to fend them off as they cuffed her and dragged her away to whatever fate awaited her in the seedy guts of the legal system. She bit down hard, gritting her teeth– they had to get into the air!

As she frantically searched for something to use as a weapon, struggling with the seatbelt and trying to bend the silicon magazine into some kind of even remotely threatening edge, the chair-bound man wheeled past, steadily moving down the aisle with the Korean woman at his heels. The co-pilot, quietly conversing with a man in an aisle seat four rows down from the front, looked up slowly at their approach, but stayed rooted to his spot, eyes wary, confused, and only slightly frightened.

"Excuse me, young fellow," the older man's voice rang out, as cordial and clear as a silver bell, and only lightly accented in a distinctively Irish fashion. "I don't mean to be rude, but my life support systems are on their last legs– I have barely enough time to make it to my physician's office in Hong Kong as it is," He smiled softly, one thick, gnarled hand shakily reaching back and grasping the Korean woman's. "My wife worries so, about me... Would it be possible to perhaps forego the apprehension of whatever member of the criminal element we're carrying until we've at least reached our destination?" The co-pilot opened his mouth, ready to shake his head, but the chair-bound man cut him off. "I'm certain that the BTD has personnel in Hong Kong that are apprized of the situation..." He smiled again, gently squeezing the Korean woman's hand enough that she cracked a smile of her own. "Please, do it for my wife, will you?"

Already shaking his head, the co-pilot managed a quiet "I'm sorry, but I can't–"

"I strongly urge you to reconsider." The chair-bound man's voice took on a suddenly ominous quality. Slowly, steadily, the man the co-pilot had been speaking with let his hand stray toward the edge of his coat– it was a gesture too absent and careful to be noticed by most, but the Korean woman didn't miss it. Her muscles tensed with apprehension.

"Sir, I'm afraid there's nothing I can do about it." The co-pilot shrugged helplessly. "The BTD will be aboard any minute now, and as soon as they have whoever they've come for, we'll be able to get clearance to leave." The chair-bound man's features darkened slightly. "It shouldn't take more than fifteen minutes... with a little luck, we'll pick up a strong tailwind and–"

Instantly, an oddly ridged, creamy-white blade shot between them, followed quickly by a sickening crunch and a startled yelp of pain. The co-pilot's eyes widened, darting toward the man in the aisle seat, his hand pinned to his chest through the black leather of his coat by the tip of a fearsome-looking, telescoping blade just over three feet long that had sprung from the heel of the Korean woman's palm. A single, dark pistol slipped from underneath his jacket and came to rest in his lap.

"Sky martials, hmpf!" The old man quickly snatched up the pistol and it disappeared into a fold on his chair. "No respect for the elderly." He cackled, and the sound was hollow, disturbing. Slowly, he turned in the aisle, half-facing the Korean woman, who watched him out of the corner of her eye, blade still fully extended. "Keep an eye on them for me, would you, Kyoung-Mi? I think I need to go and have a little chat with the captain."

"Shouldn't you change first, Brock darling?" Her voice was strange, silky, oddly perfect, with no accent or inflection of any kind– from the sound of her voice, she could have been from anywhere, spoken nothing but English her entire life, and likely have made a career doing audio advertising of some kind or another. If it was a synth job, it was an extremely good one, designer work in the hundred thousand dollar range.

Wheeling around the rest of the way and shooting Kyoung-Mi a wide grin, he nodded once, his eyes drifting to the confused, anxious passengers mumbling fearfully among themselves like a gaggle of geese facing a hungry wolf. Even Cylea had taken an interest in the two, stopping her search for some kind of weapon the instant the blade had been drawn. She licked her lips apprehensively– maybe there was hope for escape yet.

What happened next seemed almost surreal– a crease formed down the center of the older man's balding head, progressing to an even crack with rubbery edges that slipped steadily down his face, neck, and chest, disappearing into his sweater an instant before his entire body quaked unnaturally, arms flailing. His sausage-like fingers pulsed with dark potential, vibrating as something smooth and ashen stirred within his prostrate flesh, surging like a trapped demon an instant before it rose, before *he* rose, ripping off woolen clothing and sloughing off the skin and chair alike, bearing the smooth, even pegs of some shiny black metal that served as his teeth in a feral, maddening grin.

A shocked silence gripped the cabin as the remains of the old man quivered sickeningly in the motorized chair, disconnected life support equipment hissing quietly. The new man, the new Brock, let his eyes drift slowly across the passengers. Someone in the back of the plane retched, then vomited noisily.

Brock's changed form was nothing like the old man that had wheeled up the aisle only a moment before; rather, he was a lanky, almost emaciated-looking man, all thin, pale, unhealthy-looking skin stretched taut over the hard, smooth, defined shapes of artificial bones, actuators and harsh, angular techware. Where hair should have sprouted from his long, oddly angular skull, there was only an amalgam of plastic, chrome and thick dark cables that rejoined his skin by plunging into of his hairless back at grotesque angles. His eyes were pupiless polished chrome, his teeth the color of sleek, midnight steel with a pale, blue tongue that pulsed eagerly against them. He wore no clothes, and his sleek, bizarre frame was completely unadorned but for his obvious cybermodifications and the faded blue, tattoo-like strips of high-yield direct-link neural interface points that stretched across his arms, legs, chest and neck like the markings of some long forgotten tribe. Throwing back his head and flinging his spindly, ashen arms wide, he screamed at the ceiling with all the angry fervor of a god gone mad.

"And thus I did clothe my naked villainy with odd old ends stolen out of holy writ, and seemed at first a saint, when most I play the devil!"

With that, he plucked the sky martial's pistol from the chair, whirled around, and disappeared into the cockpit, his face stretching with the sharp lines of a lunatic's grin.

Chapter 4: Cry Havoc

"Back already? Heh..." The Captain breathed a tired sigh as he set down his coffee. "I heard yelling. I take it the BTD came in early" he continued, laughing quietly. "Always in a hurry, always rushing. Those people need to relax, take a break, get on a flight to Hawaii or something, eh Peterson?" He paused, reaching for his coffee again and grimacing when no answer came. "I take it you got a chance to talk with our sky martial? Get a look at what he's packing?" The Captain laughed again. "Some kind of custom? Anything interesting?"

"Just your standard, government issue forty-five, my fair Captain." A smile of black chrome flashed beside him, an unfamiliar voice in his ear-- hot coffee ran down his leg from the crumpled cup in his hand, shaking with shock and a steadily rising tide of fear.

"You... You're not Peterson." He said immediately, grasping for words as he turned slightly, trying to get a look at the newcomer.

"No, I'm afraid I'm not." Brock's grin widened incredibly, his pale blue tongue lashing eagerly within his mouth. "I am but one man on the grand stage of our world, and I, unlike this Peterson you speak of, must be in the palm of fortune herself to have found you utterly alone and unarmed!"

Looking away quickly, his lip quivering, the Captain's hand darted for the dark shape of a holster strapped to the wall of the cockpit beside him. Never before had he been so glad of the BTD's mandatory arms training program for commercial airline pilots, but then, he had never thought that he'd actually have to put that training to use. Instantly, Brock was in his face, long, lanky arm seizing the Captain's just short of the weapon. "I'd advise against that, Captain..." His chrome eyes flicked down to the other man's identification tag and he smiled, more of that ominous black steel. "Captain *Stevens*."

"Who--" Stevens swallowed nervously, recoiling in horror at Brock's appearance. "What the hell are you?"

"Oh, fair Captain, be not cruel." Brock leaned forward, his breath frigid and stale. "Am I not as human as thee? If you prick me do I not bleed? If you tickle me do I not laugh? If you poison me do I not die? If you wrong me," he paused dramatically, "shall I not revenge?"

"You're crazy." Their faces were only inches apart now. Brock's smile faded, his unhealthy lips slipping slowly back across his teeth.

"Perhaps, but though this may appear as little more than simple madness, there is yet method to it." He backed away slightly, drawing the pistol on the wall out of its holster in one fluid movement. "In truth, I want little more than the safety of the skies." He grinned again. "All I ask is that you do what you do best– fly, my fair Captain, fly, and let this mighty eagle soar to the very heights of the heavens as she was truly meant to!"

"Listen you freak, the BTD is going to be up here any minute! There's no way in hell I'm risking my career by going anywhere before they've got your skinny ass in handcuffs and off my flight." Baring his teeth suddenly, the Captain added "So why don't you put some pants on, Shakespeare, before they add indecent exposure to whatever other charges they've got on you."

"You'd do best to indulge me, fair Captain." Came Brock's ominous response. Before Stevens could do so much as flinch, the pistol was under his jaw, muzzle pressed in firmly against soft and quivering flesh. "For it is the very witching time of night, when churchyards yawn and hell itself breathes out contagion to this world." Brock was close again, closing the distance between them to mere centimeters, eyes alive with boiling insanity, sharp, flicking sadistic smiles playing across his face. "Now I could drink hot blood, and do such bitter business as the day would quake to look on."

"If you kill me, you'll still be stuck here." Stevens swallowed nervously again, his momentary burst of bravery utterly quashed. "And don't even think of trying to get Peterson to fly this thing, he'll never do it. He's smart, and he's man enough to stand up to freaks like you."

"Fortunately, I don't need either of you to fly this plane, I was simply trying to be charitable." Brock grinned again, shrugging casually. "But, I'm afraid the time for such trivial matters has come and gone. Goodbye, fair Captain– parting is, as they say, such sweet sorrow."

Fumbling for words quickly, the Captain struggled to say something, anything, but before he could manage more than the frightened edge of a hurried sound, the handgun fired, blasting a wet wedge of thick crimson across the ceiling. Grinning madly, Brock snagged the man's gore-soaked hat and set it gently on his own smooth, angular head like a macabre trophy, gently tracing the hole through the top with one thin finger.

Instantly the radio came alive with the crackle of a static-laced voice. "This is the BTD! You're surrounded! Drop your weapons and put your hands behind your head, now!"

Brock smiled gleefully as he yanked the radio off the wall, shifting both pistols to a single lanky hand. "Close pent-up guilts! Rive your concealing continents! Cry these dreadful summoners grace!" He howled excitedly, voice rich with sadistic joy and the highly-strung anxiety of the violently insane. "For I am a man more sinned against than sinning!"

Instantly his hands were on the controls, pistols resting on the panel as he ran through the last few unfinished preflight procedures and set the hydrogen systems into a pre-ignition cycle. For a brief moment, his hand rested lightly on the wide, gray plastic bars of the throttle, hesitating, lips quivering with concentration as he whispered, "once more into the breach, dear friends, once more."

There was another burst of static from the radio, drowned out as Brock jammed the throttle forward, engines flaring, roaring to life and scattering vehicles and personnel on the ground like frightened insects under a flame. Slowly, steadily, the liner began to move, wheels sluggishly turning. Brock's fingers darted across the panel, flicking switches and gently tapping gauges, his eyes preoccupied as he continued: "Now set the teeth and stretch the nostril wide," two more switches pressed, an absent glance spared toward the left wing. "Hold hard the breath!" Overhead, he thumbed another series of switches "and bend up every spirit to his full height!" He grinned, eyes finally focusing on a point somewhere ahead of him as the flaps and slats retracted. "On, on, you noblest English. Once more into the breach, once more!"

"This is your last warning!" Came the hurried yell. The plane was moving, moving slowly, but the BTD knew they had run out of time. "If you do not stop immediately we will be forced to fire!"

The radio was in Brock's hands again, his mouth twisted into an eager grin. Slowly, the plane turned and began taxiing toward the nearest runway. Already, other aircraft were making way for the liner, pulling onto side taxiways and mains in a desperate attempt to keep their payload of passengers safe from its barreling run across the tarmac.

"Tempt not a desperate man!" he shouted, cackling, pushing the aircraft onto a runway and quickly lining the nose up with the centerline. The plane was picking up speed quickly, thermoplastic tires screeching against the ancient asphalt, engines straining noisily. Overhead, a fragment of the pale moon shined through a crack in the clouds. "Cry Havoc! and let slip the dogs of war!" In the next moment, the liner's nose wheel was lifting, coming free of the ground and followed closely by the two rear gear. The radio crackled with something more, something thick with anger and frustration, but it was lost in the sound of the engines forcing the aircraft up into the dappled depths of the night sky.

Still grinning, Brock pressed the radio against the side of his face again. "Once I'm confident I've reached a steady cruising altitude, we can begin to discuss terms for the safe return of the passengers, no–! *my hostages!*"

Chapter 5: Poor Judgement Chain

With a flourish and the sound of the cockpit door slamming shut behind him, Brock appeared at the top of the aisle, a naked and gutted corpse hanging limply over one shoulder like a broken doll.

The grin plastered across Brock's face was sick, demented—he was dressed in the loose-fitting, disheveled and bloodstained uniform of the captain, looking like some horrific parody from some low budget slasher flick as he threw the captain's butchered body unceremoniously onto the deck and planted his boot firmly in the center of the dead man's chest. The passengers watched him in stark, silent horror, Cylea and the teenager exchanging worried looks, and Kyoung-Mi's face breaking into a full-on grin that looked about as out of place on her as it would have on the face of a glacier.

"Dear passengers, I'm afraid there's been a change of command!" Brock belted out suddenly. "I've relieved our fair Captain, rather permanently in fact, and have taken control of this aircraft in his place." He pursed his lips silently as he paused, carefully inspecting his nails. "I had originally hoped to postpone such drastic action until after we were airborne and well on our way to Hong Kong, but ah, such is the nature of things. His hand drifted back to his side and he sniffed absently.

"But! This is not the only change in plans I have had to endure, oh no!" He grinned at Kyoung-Mi as own her smile faded ever-so-slightly. "Now I have a mission, a new mission, one of great importance." His eyes skimmed slowly across the passengers. "So tell me, dearest friends, is there a miss Von Mitternacht on board?"

The whispers started immediately. A few frightened people shook their heads, and the sky martial allowed himself a small smile, all but ignoring the stewardess as she used a strip torn from her uniform to bind his hand. Brock grinned, brushing a red-tinged chunk of skull off his chest in a mockery of fastidiousness.

"It's a simple matter; I'm looking for a miss Cylea Von Mitternacht." He took two casual steps forward and Cylea swallowed nervously, looking away in an attempt to keep her face from betraying her. There was no way she was going to let this freak know who she was until she had a better idea of what was going on-- what did he want with her anyway? It seemed unlikely he'd taken control of an airliner owned by an internationally recognized Triad, perhaps the most powerful Triad in existence, just to claim the bounty on her head. If he had, he was a bigger fool than he looked. Between the BTD and the Golden Koi, he'd be lucky to escape with his life no matter where he decided to put the plane down.

"No one here carries such a name? Hmm." He chuckled briefly, eyes scanning the room. "Very well..." Casually, he drew one of the pistols out of a baggy pocket and in a single, seemingly careless movement, shot the person closest to him, spraying the nearby walls, seat, and passengers with crimson and bits of bone as he nonchalantly unloaded an entire clip into the man. The empty magazine ejected smoothly, smoking in the sudden, echoing silence. The corpse shivered once, fingers twitching, then slumped over and collapsed against its seat. Someone blubbered and shrieked, an infant somewhere half way down the aisle began to cry. Brock grinned again, wider this time, and pushed a fresh clip into the gun. "Delays have dangerous ends, miss Von Mitternacht! Shall I continue?"

"Nein." Slowly, deliberately, Cylea stood, eyes hard and icy. It took every ounce of restraint she could muster up to keep her nervousness under control. Brock practically beamed in response as she added: "I would have stood sooner if I'd– "

"Frailty, thy name is woman!" He cackled suddenly, cutting her off. The glare she shot him as she stepped into the aisle was harsh, venomous, and only made his grin stretch wider.

"You did not know this man!" He continued, gesturing briefly to the corpse. "You could have easily let me kill every passenger on board and not missed a soul, but instead you chose to stand up after I had dispatched only a single individual! So typically female! Sacrifice thyself so that others may live!"

"It has nothing to do with gender." Cylea said flatly. "I'm just not a coward."

"Ah, but in truth, does not conscience, in the end, make cowards of us all?" He countered, grinning again.

"*Conscience* is a word that cowards use, devised at first to keep the powerful in awe." She shot back calmly. For the first time in her entire life, her highschool electives seemed to be paying off. Brock's face lit up instantly.

"King Richard III, Act five, scene three!" He grinned widely. "Not perfect, but wonderful nonetheless! Few people can quote such a great master at will!"

"It seems even the devil is capable of reciting scripture for his purpose." She forced a grin, but it was more like a half-hearted baring of teeth than a smile. Her brain was running in circles— she needed every edge she could get against this freak, but there was no way she could keep quoting Shakespeare, not to this degree. Of the five English plays she had read in two years of literature, only three of those had been Shakespeare, and it wasn't easy to convert them back over to their native tongue after having only heard them in German. Not without losing something, some emphasis or linguistic nuance that didn't translate, or at least, that's how it felt.

"Ah! Ah!" He laughed, pointing at her accusingly. "But when comes the question, who is the greater evil, it seems the Bureau of Terran Defense labels the devil as you!"

So they were after her— it figured. With her luck, Brock had probably agreed to hand her over, or worse— kill her, for some kind of criminal amnesty. Of course, she'd escaped relatively unscathed from worse situations before, she just had to catch him when he was off guard— if she could somehow manage to close the distance between them quick enough, she might actually be able to put some of the moves that Hok had taught her to use, might be able to drop him without having to get her hands on a weapon first.

For the briefest moment, her eyes flicked nervously to Kyoung-Mi. There was her biggest challenge— the woman had the reflexes of a Class V cyborg, a full-body unit with enough illegal mods to make even the BTD's elite think twice before going toe-to-toe with her, especially considering that blade she carried hidden in her arm. Now that was a fancy piece of bioware.

"But, that is neither here nor there." Brock continued, breaking into her thoughts suddenly. "Your presence is required on the flight deck, m'lady. Someone important wishes to speak with you."

That caught her off guard. Someone wanted to talk to her? Perhaps this wasn't what she thought it was, perhaps Brock was working with the Golden Koi after all, trying to keep her safe from the BTD in his own twisted, sadistic way. It seemed improbable, but if there was even a chance... She forced another smile; she had to stall him, had to find out more.

"Tell me... m'lord," she stumbled over the word, trying to keep her language as true to Shakespearian English as possible. "Nay, entreat me...Who doth wish to speak with me?"

He waggled his finger at her, an amused half-smile playing across his face. "I'm afraid you'll have to work on your Middle English before you'll be able to impress me into revealing such secrets, no matter how momentary they may be, miss Von Mitternacht." He shrugged absently. "But it is no matter, let us just say that you come most carefully upon your hour."

She swallowed. That was it— she had to figure out what "hour" he was referring to. Her hour of triumph? Her hour of reckoning? Something else altogether? If she could just get him to give her more information, more of a hint... she wasn't about to risk attacking him if he was working for the Golden Koi. But, on the other hand, if he wasn't working for them, then that really only left two possibilities-- either he had made a deal with the BTD and the radio call was only meant to serve as a confirmation of her presence and overall condition, or he was working with someone else entirely, another crime syndicate or corporate entity that saw her as a valuable asset, a resource to be seized before the Golden Koi could get her back to their home turf. If that was the case, and whoever was pulling Brock's strings managed to succeed, it probably wouldn't prove to be the last time she'd end up changing hands-- it certainly wasn't the first.

The sound of a pistol cocking brought Cylea's attention back to him. One of Brock's weapons was pointed directly at her, and that same amused, half-smile flickered between irritation and a maddening, full-on grin.

"What did I say about delays, Miss Von Mitternacht?" She opened her mouth to reply, but he cut her off abruptly, his face twisting into a cruel, evil-looking grimace. "Now get moving before I bear thee to the edge of doom and force thee to suffer death with the hot and blessed sear of the lead thrown from mine own weapon!"

"Wait," she managed. It wasn't the first time she'd been held at gunpoint, but that didn't make it any easier. It wasn't as if anyone could actually get used to staring down the barrel of a loaded handgun, not without feeling at least a small twinge of fear. "Please... I'm sure it can't hurt to tell me who wants to talk to me."

"For someone with a sixty-million dollar bounty on her head, you certainly are naive!" He laughed. "It's a surprise, Miss Von Mitternacht! A secret! But, I'm sure you already know the answer to your persistent question. I wouldn't advise any rash courses of action, however!" His face turned suddenly serious. "The order stands as dead or alive, and if you're going to continue to test my patience, I may be forced to shoot you just to get things done!" His grin returned and he shrugged. "Corpses don't ask questions or stall for time, after all."

"They can't exactly speak to important people either." She shot back uneasily, struggling to harden her resolve. It was obvious now that he wasn't with the Golden Koi, or any other organization interested in sheltering her, for that matter, but she wasn't about to rush him, not with that gun pointed at her. "So you can stop with the idle threats, Brock."

There was only the barest hesitation before he fired, the round passing cleanly through her gut and ricocheting off the wall at the far end of the plane. Instantly, she paled, stumbling backwards, eyes wide with disbelief and fear as her fingers numbly crawled across her tanktop, carefully tracing the edges of the wound and the slowly moistening fabric around it. Brock's pistol stayed steady, still trained on her.

"I never make idle threats, Miss Von Mitternacht." He said darkly. His grin was terrible, a harsh grill of black steel that leered back at her like the teeth of some pestilent god. There was death in that grin, a dark promise that boiled up from the darkest depths of hell.

It wasn't long before the realization hit her full-force. She was going to die, finally, after coming so far, after all she had survived, she was going to die and there was no way around it, no alternatives, nowhere to run, no hope of rescue or escape. She swallowed, fear gripping her heart with icy talons– she was still so unready, so unprepared, it wasn't her time– not yet. There was no justice in such an abrupt, insensitive end, no justice for all those sacrifices, all that running– it just wasn't fair, not by any stretch of the imagination.

But it had all been in vain regardless. This was where it ended, this was where death would finally catch up to her, where it would finally claim her, and drag her down into the depths of whatever awaited her on the other side. It was the one thing she had dreaded most, the one thing she could not avoid, the one thing she had known she would have to face one day, but she had always held onto a vain hope that it wouldn't have come so soon, that death might have mercifully allowed her to slip through the cracks for another couple of decades, at the very least. Now, she guessed she hardly had the luxury of a couple of hours before she died, just enough time to be delivered into the hands of whoever Brock had made his deal with.

She shivered, and her eyes locked with his, vibrant blue searching his chromed gaze. She didn't want his cold, heartless eyes to be the last thing she saw. She wanted... she wanted... it didn't matter anymore. Death didn't give a damn what she wanted.

Chapter 6: Terminal Breakpoint

Cylea dropped to her knees, and a single salty tear broke from her eye to slide down and across her cheek on a thin film of liquid desperation.

Instantly, Brock was in her face, grinning cruelly as she gasped, lungs charged and frantic with the throes of shock. She was only dimly aware of the pain, of the feeling of air playing across the hole the round had torn through her gut. It was hard to focus on much more than the blatant confirmation of her own mortality, every breath painful and full of the cold scent of imminent death. If 'set vids were any guide, it wouldn't be long before the end came, bringing an unexpected close to a life still so new and full of potential, still so full of secrets and riddles begging to be uncovered, secrets and riddles that now would never be realized, never understood, never revealed. She'd die with her life still wrapped in mystery, unsure of something that so many people around her took for granted-- her very humanity.

"The end is near, Miss Von Mitternacht." Brock's demonic, dead blue tongue lashed against his teeth in sadistic ecstasy. She could feel his breath on her face, could taste the cold blasts of inhumanly clean air brushing up against her cheeks, the smell of the plastic sterility of his immaculately synthetic body pounding through her sinuses like the probing fingers of an eager doctor. She shivered uncontrollably, and Brock chuckled ominously in return, eyes glittering.

"Are you prepared for death?" His fingers stretched eagerly toward her, slipping almost gently between her own, intent on the wound. She tried to fight him, tried to stop him, struggled to brush his hands away, but every attempt she made was pushed aside and ignored, useless gestures sadly in vain. "Is your soul prepared?"

Before she could answer, he plunged his fingers into her ragged flesh, twisting and snaking them through the wound. With a harsh, gasping shudder, her eyes rolled wildly toward him, wide and terrified, mouth drifting open in a silent scream-- she could feel him inside of her, icy and rigid like frozen steel, pushing against sensitive viscera, forcing her innards roughly against each other and tracing the moist surfaces of her intestines with the sharp edges of his fingernails as he tried to lock eyes with her, matching her panicked gasping in a mockery that was more sexual than insolent.

"How does it feel to know that death is upon you? That your very life's blood is slipping slowly through your fingers?" Her eyes drifted downward in horrid fascination as his long, thin fingers drew back from the wound, slick with the murky red of her vital fluids. "Are you frightened, Cylea? Does death frighten you?"

"You-- You shot me." She stuttered suddenly, eyes meeting his, face still ashen as she slowly drew her own blood-tinged fingers away from her punctured abdomen.

"Indeed I did!" He responded quickly, pulling away from her so suddenly that she lurched, gasping and sputtering. "But, unfortunately, it is not fatal, at least, not just yet." He looked disappointed, but it didn't last– a wide grin stretched across his face as her eyes drifted to the carpet, his words still not registering completely. "If luck is with you, you won't go into toxic shock immediately," he shrugged, "and it is possible that you could last for days before the infection kills you." Smiling slyly, he pushed his stained fingers into his mouth, savoring the taste audibly. "But," he grinned, teeth tinged with red as he traced a finger across his thin, pale lips. Her eyes met his again, cold and wary over an ocean of anxious fear. "I would still count my blessings if I were you" instantly, the pistol was between them again, gently nudging against her jaw. "Because, if you can't make a point of cooperating with me, I can't guarantee you'll survive the next bullet I send on its merry way through your wretched little body."

Her eyes met his again, this time absent and unfocused with shock. On some level, she wanted to nod, to confirm that the last thing she wanted was to actually be shot again, that she would do almost anything to keep from being shot again, but no words would come. She stared blankly at him, mouth hanging open slightly, painfully pink lips quivering silently. His stare was wary, cold, unmoving, almost dead in its own frighteningly mechanical way.

"Now get up." He demanded levelly. "There are, as yet, still many events in the womb of time which wait to be delivered."

Slowly, silently, she stood, fighting against weak, shaky legs and the waves of pain and nausea that came in tandem, ragged flesh and weeping, oozing innards protesting every movement that forced them to shift from their sensitive positions or brought new air into the wound. Brock's eyes followed Cylea as she moved, his gaze staying firmly locked with hers. He smiled slightly and she looked away, trying not to think too much about the pistol pointed at her.

"Good." He gestured down the aisle with the pistol. "Now walk to the cockpit."

Her eyes flicked back to his, still quiet and considering beneath vibrant blue. There wasn't much else she could do– the wound was proof enough for her that Brock wasn't someone she really wanted to challenge or piss off. She spared Kyoung-Mi a quick glance, and the woman met her gaze with those same cold, jade-green eyes, so like Shang's that it hurt to think about it; class V or not, the woman seemed like an insurmountable obstacle now, Everest to an ant, and Brock's most effective guarantee that Cylea wouldn't try anything dangerous. But inside the cockpit, things would be different– there she would only have that pistol to contend with, though even that seemed like more than she could manage to handle before Kyoung-Mi got wind of what was going on and put her flimsy little insurrection down as easily as an entire army of vatgrowns might have in her place.

It was hard to stand, much less walk, which meant it would be even harder to run, but she managed a careful step forward anyway, testing herself. The feeling of everything rubbing uncomfortably against everything else was enough to distract her, forcing her to focus on each step individually to avoid collapsing into a heap on the floor. Just thinking about the fact that her innards were now exposed to a world of bacteria, viruses, lint, hair and dander from the thousands of passengers and god-only-knew how many pets that had traveled aboard the liner during its lifetime was enough to make her stomach curdle. She swallowed against the rising feeling, trying to harden her resolve, and pressed her hands flat against the wound, grimacing as the air continued to tease the ragged flesh around the exit hole at her back. Brock flicked the muzzle of his pistol toward the cockpit again, this time more emphatically than the last. "*Move.*"

She nodded quietly. All eyes were fixed on her as she took step after beleaguered step down the aisle, trudging slowly toward the door. Death still loomed in her thoughts, swathed in black and beckoning to her with skeletal fingers of bleached bone, but somewhere beyond that, somewhere in the very heart of the darkness that brewed within her, in the blackness so full of secrets and terrible potential ripe for a glorious and bloody birth, screaming with all the savagery of pure, unadulterated Id in a silent voice so vicious it would have shriveled even Brock, had he heard it, burned a tiny, angry fire. It was incredibly small, so minuscule and insignificant, yet so fierce, a flame that demanded retribution and promised another dose of that same sickly sweet power that had coursed through her veins on that day that seemed as if it had been so long ago, a part of another time, another life– the day that Smash had betrayed her, and payed the ultimate price for it.

Flailing with the shreds of her tattered resolve and courage, she forced her eyes forward, past Brock, past Kyoung-Mi, and to the cockpit door, with the captain's naked corpse sprawled out in front of it. Already, her mind was running through options, spinning across plans, and picking through the multitudes of "what-ifs" that plagued her hand-in-hand with the ever-present threat of death. In all likelihood, she was going to die even if she cooperated with Brock and his demands; in the end, it all came down to faith, her belief in her ability to overcome him and survive, her belief in her own tenacity and the almost vain hope that she might be able to unlock whatever power was within her now, when it mattered most. At the very least, she would struggle to meet death on her own terms, fighting until she could fight no more and was pulled into the abyss, kicking and screaming with teeth bared in some final act of defiance.

Brock and his Korean cyborg be damned-- this was her moment! One of her hands clenched into a fist at her side. This was the moment when she would finally stand, when she would not run, would not lie down, when she would fight back at long last. If she was going to die, it would not be with a whimper, but with a bang worthy of all the sacrifices that had been made to get her as close as she was to the end of all her running, the end of being held at gunpoint, of being hunted and pursued like an animal. This was it-- her hand closed around the handle of the cockpit door. Brock stood a few short paces behind her, the muzzle of his pistol still pointed at her. As soon as they were both inside, she'd show him just how wretched and frail she was, and with a little luck, she'd survive the attempt, leaving only Kyoung-Mi to be dealt with. All she needed was a little luck, just the tiniest dash to help her pull it all off. She licked her lips, trying not to think of just how ludicrous it sounded, and trying to ignore the protests of her wound.

But when it came right down to it, she told herself, there were no other options. She had to do this, had to do it for Bao and Hok and Jack, for Walt, Ying, and even Smash. Her mind was set, and there was no going back. This was her time, her moment, her stand, her own finest hour when she would force her way past her emotions, past the pain and the shock, past everything that held her back, everything that had made her hesitate, falter, or cry whenever fate threw her a cruel twist. This was the moment she was born for, the moment she would rise to the occasion and win through, or fall and be forgotten.

Her destiny awaited. Absently, she touched the key.

Chapter 7: Synthreversal

The instant the door closed, she hit him.

A blur of black boot leather caught Brock's spindly ankle and dropped him to the deck immediately. Another swift kick, this one twisting her innards into a painful knot that forced a rough grunt through clenched teeth, knocked the pistol from his grasp and sent the weapon clattering across the floor. He scarcely had a chance to shout before she went stumbling after it, gut throbbing and moistening with fresh blood. Something soft tore beneath bruised and punctured skin– vision blurred, numb fingers fumbling, reaching, straining dumbly for the handgun.

In the next instant, the weapon was in her hands. It came up fluidly, pointed directly at Brock as she slumped backwards, hunching toward the flight controls, teeth bared against the pain. The nauseating stab in her gut was growing stronger, finally awakening with all the wicked fury she would have expected from a bullet hole– it was hot, searing, all but blinding her as it reached its climax, painfully protesting any movement that might disturb the wound or the sensitive flesh beneath it. She blinked quickly, struggling to clear her vision and calm her uneasy, quivering hands, but the effect was less than negligible– even her resolve seemed weakened under the sudden burst of pain, but still she fought it, fought to block it out and move beyond it before Brock could take advantage of it.

She'd had very little experience firing guns before, much less handguns, but she was used to improvising– most of what she did know was gleaned from a few one-on-one sessions with her bartender friend Jack and some of the action or murder mystery films she had watched on Ying's broadband broadcast headset in the early mornings during her time at Chow Fun. One station or another was always playing some B or C-rated action thriller, another Hollywood production featuring big, beefy, neanderthal-like genehulks blowing up cars with rocket launchers or shotguns or something similar. When it came right down to it, there really didn't seem to be that much to firing a gun, or at least, not that much beyond the simple notion of "point and squeeze..."

Accuracy was important too, of course, but she felt like she could wing it, and with a little luck, Brock wouldn't even try to risk finding out how good of a shot she really was.

Brock rose slowly, pulling himself upward in a single, sinuous stretching movement, his face twisting into a wary, silent, and almost disgusted looking snarl. Cylea forced herself to relax, forced her heart to slow down, and set her jaw resolutely. She was the one with the gun, the one with the edge– what she needed now were demands, or maybe questions, something to convince him she meant business. The threat of death had to be as real as possible; he had to believe he was going to die if he didn't cooperate– she just hoped he was still human enough to be hurt by bullets.

"Oh happy dagger of mine own untimely demise!" He cackled, his expression slowly tightening into another sadistic grin. "Art thou not a fatal vision, or art thou merely a dagger of the mind, serving only to force me to do thy bidding!?"

"Shut up." She responded immediately.

"Or you'll what?" His grin intensified, suddenly excited. "Will you shoot me and claim your revenge for the wound I hath inflicted upon thy mortal coil? An eye for an eye? A bullet for a bullet?" Before she could answer, his features darkened suddenly. "What will you do if I am dead and no one is left to keep this great aluminum bird aloft? Eh!?" He spat, making a quick, vicious, sweeping gesture. "Make that thy question and go rot, foul wench."

"The co-pilot's just fine, Brock." She shot back, all but snarling. "I don't need you."

"Ah, and you think that my stunning wife will simply let you waltz in and claim him?" His eyes darted away for the briefest of moments. "She'd sooner die than see you walk away that easily."

"Then it's a good thing I can fly this thing too." She bit off, and instantly the hair stood up on the back of her neck in a chilling kind of worried regret. It was a desperate gamble, a bluff that could cost the lives of everyone onboard if Brock decided to call it. In truth, it was everything but an outright lie– the only experience she'd had flying anything came from two half-day lessons that Jack had urged her to take from a friend of his a year or so before, and even then it had been little more than a crash course in how to keep a flimsy little propeller-driven aircraft in the air.

She swallowed uneasily and instantly regretted the obviousness of the gesture. A car was a car and a plane was a plane, right? She just had to keep telling herself that the over-wing trainer rustbucket she'd flown before, a plane so old its original manufacturer had gone out of business, been forgotten, been revitalized and gone out of business again, handled just like the liner she was on. They were both old, one was just... bigger, with an extra engine, and a lot of really old-looking controls that probably should have been on display in a museum. Still, it was better than a direct neural feed with a password lock-out and a TSA-grade defense packet– even Brock would probably have had trouble with a setup like that.

Brock's face had gone cold, his grin fading slightly. He knew that his options were falling away and could feel fate closing in on him fast. His eyes flicked to the left, then to the right, casting about as nonchalantly as possible for answers, for some way to distract Cylea or disable her. The pistol felt heavy in the left pocket of his baggy uniform, almost begging him to use it. His hand twitched eagerly. Cylea's arms tensed.

"Now I want you to tell me exactly what's going on." She forced the words out, breaking the silence between them and attracting Brock's gaze. "I want names, organizations, everything you know. I want to know who wants me und why." He grinned slightly as she added: "No more Shakespeare und no more games, just the straight facts."

"Just the straight facts?" He asked innocently. "So then you truly are clueless, aren't you?"

Her hand quivered as she pushed the weapon forward threateningly. "I said no more games, Brock!" She bit off, shaking visibly. "Now answer the damn question."

"My my, you seem quite frightened." He grinned again. "You know, I'd bet a kingdom for a horse that you're bluffing about your prowess as a pilot." The grin softened in a mockery of concern as he added "Now, why don't you hand me that weapon before you hurt yourself with it."

"I swear, if you don't start answering my questions right now, I'll shoot you." She shifted, hands slick with sweat.

"I doubt it." Brock's face darkened again, taking on an ominous cast as he took a careful step toward her.

"Don't move, Brock." She warned, baring her teeth in sudden, violent desperation. "I'm done! Finished! Talk!"

"You won't shoot me." His voice was smooth as silk, so calm, so assured. "You need me, Cylea."

"The hell I do." She felt her bluff was wearing thin– soon she would have to make a decision. Soon, one of them would be dead.

"Then shoot me." He took another ominous step forward. "Show me that you mean what you say. I do not fear death."

She swallowed nervously again. It didn't matter how much of a freak he was, how sadistic he was, how much she would have liked to see him lying on the floor, dead. The last thing she wanted was to have to shoot him, to have more blood on her hands. For one brief moment, a cold calm settled over her, and in its wake she found herself desperately missing the days when she had been little more than a cute and relatively innocent little socialite living on the fringe of quasi-legality, a girl who didn't take abuse or threats, verbal or otherwise, yet never would have even dreamed of going so far as to kill anyone. It had been a time of blissful ignorance, a time when it seemed that no one would ever really have wanted to even kill her. Sure, there had been close calls, knife-fights that had left a few deep cuts requiring the delicate touch of a nanocosmetologist to erase the resulting scars, but the threat of death had always seemed far off– now it was ever present, inescapable. It wasn't right– the gun she held, the threats she was making to Brock. The whole mess was wrong, twisted. She shouldn't have to point a gun at someone, shouldn't have to threaten someone with death just to preserve those few scraps of the familiar and the normal that still clung tattered to the edges of her life– she shook her head, pushing the thoughts away roughly. In the here and now, it didn't matter, regrets didn't matter. She had to fight to survive, had to act fast to keep the edge she was already losing from slipping away entirely.

"I'm going to count to three." She managed, struggling to get a grip on her feelings. She licked her lips quickly, forcing herself to breathe levelly. Brock's lips stretched out into a strange parody of a smile.

"And if I tell you what you wish to hear, you'll graciously spare me a potent dose of death?" he laughed. "How do you know I do not wish to die? Would you enjoy being trapped in a body so hideously freakish and disturbing as mine?"

"One." She bit off, ignoring him. His grin widened, becoming a smug, amused smile as she continued. "Two." She shook her head, quietly adding "I'm serious Brock. Don't make me kill you."

"Bluffing does not become you, Cylea." His face brightened with sadistic intensity as he took another step forward. "Now give me the weapon before I take it from you and use it to do such things that would make you wish you had never been born female."

Cylea flinched as the echoing crack of the gunshot echoed through the cockpit, handgun bucking so much that she nearly dropped it. Brock's face slackened suddenly, but still he advanced, taking one short, shaky step forward, face already twisting into another sadistic grin. Three more times, she fired, each round passing cleanly through the sickly flesh of his chest, putting new, darker stains in the Captain's once-immaculate white shirt. Even after the last round had cleared the barrel, leaving the magazine hollow and empty in its wake, she continued to squeeze the trigger, every pull giving her only the echoing, hopeless clicks of a spent weapon's silent bark. Brock was close now, his features a rapidly changing mass of emotions, most of them dark and rich with foul intent that festered into something more wicked with every passing moment.

"Is this your promis'd end?" His lips curled back in a cruel snarl. Instantly, Cylea's back was against the controls, face paling as her resolve began to fall away like a cheap facade. "Or is it merely an image of that horror?"

In the next moment, he was in her face again, lanky and sickly form pressing against her. She sucked in a nervous, frightened breath as his mouth filled her eyes, black metal teeth and sharp blue tongue tinged with dark crimson, lips spattered with his own blood. He shivered as it welled up within him, slipping from the corners of his mouth in tiny streamers that stained his ashen flesh scarlet with their passing.

"Do you think bullets can kill me, miss Von Mitternacht?" He managed, shivering and choking on every word. Grinning ferally, he seized her chin with one thin hand and her eyes darted away, hands searching, twisting across the underside of the control panel behind her, desperately feeling for something, anything that she might be able to hit him with. Her throat tightened as he leaned in close, tongue stretching slowly toward her. Instantly, her hand brushed against something smooth, something cold and metal, something solid. Her fingers fumbled with a cheap metal clasp– then the thing was in her hand, its weight endlessly reassuring.

"I'm going to enjoy pulling you apart, ripping, savoring the taste–" she never gave him a chance to finish. With all the force she could muster in a single swing, she hit him, an arc of brilliant red darting in and colliding solidly with the side of his head. He shivered once with the sickening crunch of bone, convulsing and spitting, arms going taut and eyes darting wildly for an instant before he slackened suddenly and hit the deck like a limp rag.

Chapter 8: The Quickening

She hit Brock three more times with the thing, hit him until her arms burned and the wound in her gut throbbed with a pain so intense and so blinding that she dropped to her knees beside him with a shuddering whimper. Tears streamed down her cheeks unchecked as she let the thing fall to the floor beside her, eyes drifting across its dented form, across the canister of a fire extinguisher she had used to commit murder-- no! *to defend herself!* She'd had every right-- it rolled lopsidedly back across the carpeting and clanged noisily against the rudder pedals beneath a nearby control panel.

She must have bumped the controls at some point-- the plane was listing slowly forward, nose dipping slightly toward the sea, but it seemed unimportant, surreal, a thorn in some numb, insignificant part of her mind. before her, Brock lie bloody and comatose, one hand twitching spasmodically.

She closed her eyes against the rising, sickening sensation of guilt. She'd done it again-- she'd killed someone. Brock's face, crunched, beaten and broken, jaw hanging slack, dead eyes staring up at the ceiling, brought back memories of Smash, terrible memories that made her feel cold and brought a bad taste to her mouth. It was all so wrong, so twisted, so impersonal. Death seemed intent on following her wherever she went, its great scythe seeking her and always culling another in the process. Her eyes opened, just a crack, but it was enough. Her face was slick with tears and sweat, forehead tight and warm with stress and pain. For a brief moment, she wanted nothing more than to die, to lie down there on the deck next to Brock and let events unfold without her until the liner slipped beneath the waves in some grand aquatic fireball, leaving only bits of plastic and aluminum, the odd article of clothing, maybe a shoe or a ragged bit of flesh, floating on the surface in its wake.

It was the sound of the radio that finally forced Cylea back to reality, bringing her mind into a dull sort of focus with the telltale crackle of static. Her resolve reasserted itself with startling ease, that fire deep within her flaring suddenly, burning away all of her doubt, all of her fear, all of her remorse in one searing blast of revelation. Her eyes drifted open completely, so full of intent, so dark with terrible purpose. She still had reasons to live, still had a chance to survive, and no matter how wrong, twisted, or impersonal it seemed to admit it, she still had one more person to kill.

"This is NACC Interceptor control calling GKI air zero-five-three-tango, flight thirty-eight forty. Cut your engines to flight idle setting and establish straight and level flight if possible. We have two interceptors thirty-four seconds out and a recovery team is inbound, ETA five minutes. If you do not comply, we have been authorized to use force. Respond, over." As static crackled over the speakers, Cylea rose, eyes intent on the cabin door. She had five minutes, maybe less. Five minutes to save the Copilot from Kyoung mi, five short minutes to diffuse the situation and cut the impending hysteria to a manageable level– and even then, she still had to try to convince the Copilot to help her hide or escape before the BTD or the NACC had a chance to get aboard.

She bit her lip– it was going to be tricky. Even if they gave the Copilot permission to land the plane himself, the Bureau would be all over the runway the instant it touched down, looking for her– he was her only hope now, and with a little luck, there might be some kind of confusion, some kind of frenzied, panicked rushing that she could get lost in, a rapid decompression of frightened passengers streaming down the ramp and across the tarmac while the BTD struggled in vain to keep them contained and centralized so they could all be questioned later. She'd slipped out unnoticed during mass exoduses before, and she was sure she could do it again– still, it all came down to time, and time never seemed to be on her side. "GKI air zero-five-three-tango, heat scope shows you're in the cockpit. Please respond."

She stood, and the wound in her gut burned in protest, stabbing pain lancing through her innards with such ferocity that she shuddered. Fresh tears rimmed the edges of her eyes again, but she fought it, fought to force the pain away, force her eyes open, and force herself to ignore everything that nagged at her besides the solid, unwavering weight of her intent, her one primary, as-yet-unfulfilled goal. She let her eyes wander, vibrant blue drifting sporadically across the seats, the panel, the floor, the empty holster riveted to the wall, only half registering everything she saw. There had to be something, some kind of a weapon besides the dented fire extinguisher, something... she'd have to get creative– that's all there was to it. Maybe if she were lucky, she might even find a first aid kit or a box of bandages tucked somewhere out of the way– even something like a roll of duct tape would have been welcomed. Heck, any kind of emergency equipment would have been useful. When it came right down to it, the simple fact was that she needed every edge she could manage to get against Kyoung-Mi. Class V's never went down easy, and there was no reason to believe it wouldn't be the same with the Korean woman.

She dropped to her knees, desperately pulling plastic boxes and shrink-wrapped packages out from under the seats, yanking open wall-mounted cabinets and drawers, uncaring as their contents spilled out onto the floor, tiny glass bottles and fuses crunching beneath booted feet, nuts and bolts rolling toward the front of the aircraft. She had so little time, so little time to find something useful. She started ripping open packages, breaking the flimsy little black plastic clasps off orange boxes of emergency equipment, throwing whatever she couldn't immediately find a use for off to the side as she moved from box to box, package to package, sifting quickly through the debris on the floor. There just wasn't enough time, wasn't enough equipment to make much of a difference, to make a direct attack somehow less futile. She swallowed, knowing that in the end, there was no choice. She had to work with what little she had, had to make it work or die trying. Every second counted. Every second that passed one less between her and certain death.

She swallowed shakily. The clock was ticking.

Chapter 9: Awakening

In one smooth, swinging motion, the cockpit door slammed open.

As it swung to, it clanged noisily against the wall– Kyoung-Mi's eyes darted for the door like a pair of eager hunters, narrowing instantly. In the doorway, past more gutted corpses than she had remembered Brock leaving sprawled across stained carpet like grotesque lawn ornaments, Cylea pivoted fluidly, foot sliding back, gauze-wrapped midsection twisting, eyes a hard, deadly color of blue behind her unwavering, resolve-strengthened hands. Her knuckles were already tightening to white, fingers tense and firm against the grip of a stubby, neon-orange flare gun, each as hard as steel, taut as spun monowire cable.

She blinked, and time seemed to slow in the moment. At her back, the twisted shape of a small crowbar sat tucked into the stout leather belt she'd pulled off Brock's corpse– a backup weapon, something to keep the other woman's blade at bay if things got tight.

Kyoung-Mi's body tensed instantly, muscles suddenly rigid, as taut and deadly as a bowstring– her blade dropped out and extended to its full length, ominous beneath a face as hard as granite. Beside her, the Copilot paled, eyes growing distant with the expectation of death as they fixed on Cylea. Ten rows down from the front and past Kyoung-Mi, two men rose and stepped into the aisle, one cracking his knuckles expectantly.

Cylea took the new arrivals in stride– they were doubtlessly vatgrown, both corporate soldiers, probably a mid-grade batch of a Chinese strain, probably even engineered in Hong Kong, and dressed like all the other tourists she'd seen. Flamboyant Hawaiian shirts over beige shorts with flip-flop sandals, and only the dark, expensive sunglasses to set them apart from every other stereotypical tourist on the flight. There was no question– these were corporates, just another asset, a safety measure that had been placed on the flight to make certain she wouldn't get away.

It explained a lot– it was even almost expected. She doubted that, even if the BTD managed to catch her, she'd be in their custody for long. In all likelihood, these vatgrown guys were working for whoever had put up the sixty-million for her in the first place. She doubted anyone else had enough gall to tangle with the Golden Koi so directly.

There was a brief pause, just the barest moment of shared hesitation that passed between them before the snap of a knuckle tightening and the slightest curling of Kyoung-Mi's lip into the traces of a contemptuous snarl shattered the calm. In the next instant, the two vatgrowns were hurtling past the Korean woman, tearing down the narrow aisle toward Cylea with teeth bared and the murderous zeal of trained attack dogs glittering in their sunglassed eyes.

She didn't wait. Her finger tightened reflexively.

The weapon hardly bucked as the flare ripped from its squat barrel and screamed across the cabin to bury itself off-center in the first corporate's chest. Instantly, he was stumbling, mouth twisted in a wordless scream as he pivoted to the side, fighting against the cascade of sparks and fire shooting across his flesh. The second vatgrown pushed roughly past him, ripping across the carpet toward Cylea-- she hesitated for the barest fraction of a second, briefly considering her options. He was too close-- she couldn't reload before he hit her. The flaregun hit the deck and she shifted immediately into a defensive crouch.

The vatgrown came to a sudden, wary stop, watching her carefully though sunglassed eyes. Behind him, the other corporate grunted and shrieked, jerking and fumbling like a broken marionette as the flare burned its way across his flesh, melting skin and shirt alike, filling the cabin with a dark and acrid stench. Cylea's eyes locked with the second vatgrown soldier's, and the edge of his mouth twitched nervously. She blinked cautiously, secure in her stance, everything Hok had taught her flitting briefly through her mind. The forms, complex taolu, basic techniques and distracting gestures waited on the tense edges of her thoughts. She drew in a deep breath, and slowly stretched into a more useful stance, drawing back one leg as she extended the opposite arm, palm out, and curled the other into a tight and tense angle near her chest.

A forced calm began to settle over her as she used her resolve to temper her anger and gain control of her *qi*, her breathing, just as Hok had taught her. It was all practically second nature now, something she had practiced countless times to the point where it had become almost reflexive. Hok had called the stance *long stance*, and it had been one of the first stances he had taught her-- it was classic, intimidating, her favorite if only for the ease with which it was recognized by the average individual. Anyone who had ever seen a Kung-Fu flick recognized it-- heck, anyone who'd seen anything with a martial arts theme was likely to recognize it-- even some 'set commercials, and the occasional nanoprojection advert plastered to a wall or a hoverbus, or practically anything else anywhere else advertising could find a niche to occupy featured the stance or something similar to it, even if only a few people actually knew it by name. Dropping into the stance was usually enough for most people to realize that she was serious, that she knew what she was doing and was more than capable of defending herself.

The vatgrown set his jaw in a wary, unpleasant-looking grimace, inspecting her with careful eyes as one of Kyoung-Mi's brows rose in mild interest. Cylea's gaze stayed fixed, unwavering, as cold and deadly as the sea that rocketed by, somewhere far, yet not so far, beneath the soles of their feet.

There was a cry of pain as the first corporate finally hit the deck, slashing the tense, silent air wide open-- in the next instant, the second vatgrown was moving again, faster this time, hand outstretched and reaching, vicious and clawlike. Catching his wrist was a simple matter-- a fist darted in toward her, hard knuckles lightning fast, and came up hard against her arm, glancing off with a hasty outward block. Their eyes met for an instant in brief, sharp contact, stone cracking off ice-- before he could hit her again, she seized his free wrist, quickly twisted, and caught him firmly between the legs with a vicious kick that dropped him as instantly and as easily as a puppet suddenly severed from its master's strings.

Kyoung-Mi pivoted in the aisle and stepped forward, turning to face Cylea fully for the first time. The two vatgrown soldiers seemed pitiful between them, inconsequential, writhing and groaning on burnt and bloodwashed carpet. A dead calm fell between the two women as their eyes locked-- neither moved, neither blinked, neither stare wavering or giving way to the other. In the aisle, just a few feet from Kyoung-Mi, the cascade of sparks from the flare sputtered and died, leaving only an oily black smoke and the smell of charred flesh in its wake. Passengers turned white, watching apprehensively from their seats, all at once awestruck and frightened, frozen in a macabre mixture of curiosity and fear, totally helpless.

It was then that the little resolve-hardened flare, that tiny red pinprick of emotion that seemed to brew and fester in the darkest depths of Cylea's being suddenly pulsed. She could feel it boiling within her blood, that familiar survival instinct burning its way to the forefront of her thoughts, overriding everything that would normally contain it, would normally hold it back. It was incredibly easy to pull from now, to draw out-- already, her pupils were dilating incredibly, lips pulling back in a feral snarl, vision reddening as wordless anger and hatred welled up inside of her. It felt dark, even evil, but the allure of the power itself was incredible. For one glorious moment, nothing seemed to matter-- she was thrilled at her own awakening perfection, the angel of death in a mortal shell that suddenly seemed more like the body of the hunter than the hunted, the ultimate instrument of destruction and something that so transcended mankind in its divine elegance that no comparison could be drawn between the person she had been only a moment ago and the person she was now. For that one excruciatingly brief moment, she was something more, not quite a god, yet the very epitome of the perfect balance between life and death, an infant learning how to breathe for the first time. Confidence in her own superiority blossomed and washed over her like a boiling sea, all but drowning her humanity with a deluge of power and emotion that ebbed as the feeling dropped away suddenly, replaced by the cold, hard edge of something deeper, something, no– in essence, it was more of a somewhere, a spot on the edge of a wellspring of a whole new kind of power, something yet to be discovered, much less accessed. This thing, this place, was wholly different, an area within her being that seemed beyond normal modes of comprehension, as if it were the very threshold of reality itself.

As Kyoung-Mi stepped forward, Cylea's fingers twitched. Instantly, the crowbar was in her hands, with no memory of how it got there. The hair stood up on the back of her neck, but it seemed unimportant, a sensation she was acutely aware of that registered at the edges of her mind. There was power here, so much power lurking just beyond her fingertips, power she couldn't quite grasp. It was so close– painfully close. The cabin lights flickered. The floor creaked ominously beneath her feet. Kyoung-Mi's blade rose, flashed in the light, and then she was running down the aisle toward Cylea, her features an emotionless mask of unyielding stone.

The contact between them was jarring, a parry– specialized, vatgrown bone glancing hard against ancient stainless steel. The blade tip went slicing upwards though the air, less than an inch from her nose, so close to her eyes– a desperate strike with the crowbar darted in toward Kyoung-Mi, accented with a grunt of pain as Cylea twisted. Instantly, it was turned aside, deflected by the flat of the other woman's blade. Cylea's eyes narrowed slightly. Blood boiled and seethed in her veins. The cabin lights stuttered and flickered again.

"Hah!" Kyoung-Mi's voice rang out suddenly, ivory teeth bared as the blade arced in again, intent on Cylea. Another clang echoed through the cabin as the two weapons met in another parry, sparks flying. In the next moment, the Korean woman's arms went wide, blade swinging out, free hand reaching toward Cylea, coming in low under her taut arms. Throwing the crowbar up in the last minute as a desperate defense against the blade, Cylea tried to pivot and dodge the hand, eager and grasping as it came at her, but the other woman was faster, her grip stronger. Sharp nails dug into the flesh around Cylea's wound and she screamed reflexively, narrowly deflecting another deadly strike of the blade. Their eyes locked again, and a wild swing of Kyoung-Mi's weapon sliced cleanly through the corner of a seat mere inches from Cylea. Shifting quickly to the side, her fingers wrapped onto the wrist of Kyoung-Mi's vicious, unbladed hand, and her crowbar met another blow shakily.

The next slice came in from the side. As Cylea struggled to yank free of the other woman's grip, the crowbar came up in a sudden, reflexive movement, catching the blade at enough of an angle that it ripped the tool-turned-weapon out of her hand and sent it hurtling down the aisle, out of reach. Cylea's eyes widened, and the other woman's lips twisted into a cruel smile. The blade arced in, catching the light again in one deadly, downward sweep. The fire of resolve flickered and flared, twisting ominously.

It happened so suddenly that the resulting moment of hesitation seemed to stretch into eternity. As the blade came at her, she threw her arm up reflexively, the bone edge biting deep into her flesh. Their eyes met again as blood ran down Cylea's arm. The pain, the cracked bone, the bleeding flesh... all of it seemed distant. Kyoung-Mi's grip slackened, her eyes suddenly wider with an odd, aloof sort of fear, a mask over the twisting emotions that came with the realization– somehow, Cylea had stopped the blade using her bare arm, a razor-sharp blade kept to a perfect edge by nanites... it didn't seem possible. Their lips parted simultaneously. Kyoung-Mi managed a quiet, uneasy "How?"

"No." Came Cylea's immediate reply, so callous and commanding it shocked even her on some repressed, unimportant level. Strength came boiling up from within her, inhuman, deadly. her hand released Kyoung-Mi's wrist and easily knocked the entire arm aside, away from her wound, ignoring the blade still pressed hard against her arm. Their eyes stayed locked, the Korean woman all but paralyzed, lips quivering ever-so-slightly. There was no time left, no time to react. The blade stayed locked between them, still embedded in Cylea's arm.

In the next moment, Cylea's free hand was on the other woman's face, fingers digging, darting across skin and hair for some kind of grip, a place where she could exert pressure. Her scrabbling fingers gained purchase quickly, hand tightening, lips twisting into a sadistic grin as Kyoung-Mi's mouth came open in a wordless scream of pain. Betrayal, hate, fear, it all seemed irrelevant– as the bones in the Korean woman's face began to crack, skin splitting, skull caving in under the force of Cylea's inhuman grip, thoughts of Smash came unbidden to her mind. It was so similar, the blood, the painful gurgling, the restrained glee, the need to bring about swift justice in the form of a quick and painful death. Somehow it seemed wrong, even as the blade jerked spasmodically against her arm, driving her on, even as the hoarse, terrified shriek ripped from Kyoung-Mi's lungs, a panicked death-knell that echoed through the cabin as something popped and buckled beneath Cylea's grip. Bone crunched and splintered, shifting, tearing, slicing through soft tissues like needles and knives.

It couldn't be stopped, it wouldn't be stopped. Cylea no longer had any qualms, no longer had any doubts or a pension for mercy, not with this woman. Kyoung-Mi deserved this. It was as simple as that. Now she would never get the chance to hurt anyone again.

...and it felt so damn good.

Chapter 10: Silicon Lazarus

"Stop! Stop it!" Came the sudden shout. "What are you– are you trying to kill her!?"

In the next instant, the Copilot had a hand on Cylea's wrist, worried eyes searching her face for some kind of indication that she had heard him. The feeling of hot, steaming blood lay slick between her fingers, burning her skin, running across her palm, cooling ever-so-slightly as it slipped down her arm and stained her flesh in its slow journey to the edge of her tanktop. It seemed more important than any words, more special– she watched it run across her flesh with a macabre sort of awe, transfixed by its vibrant majesty, the essence of spilled life.

It was red, she noticed, the scarlet color of human hemoglobin and not the dark, synthetic circulatory fluid of a full body cyborg that she had expected to see. It was such a loss, in the end– Kyoung-Mi was organic, made sleek and dangerous through training and skill instead of replacements and software. Even her use of bioware seemed minimal– Kyoung-Mi had been something rare, she had been something special, truly *human.*

Cylea's eyes drifted across the edges of the other woman's face momentarily, watching as each sputtering convulsion played out across blood slick skin. Something popped sickeningly beneath Cylea's palm, and her gaze slid slowly away from the red-tinged flesh, meeting the Copilot's nervous stare with blank, unseeing eyes.

It was then that her grip relaxed ever-so-slightly, her concentration waning. For a brief moment, she wanted to strike him, wanted to knock him away while she finished with the Korean woman. She resisted in the pause, and it was in that moment that the true nature of what she had done, what she was doing, finally managed to sink in. Her fingers jerked away from Kyoung-Mi's face in a single startled, almost spasmodic movement.

The Copilot watched in silent shock as the Korean woman sucked in a broken breath and tried to stand on quivering, unsteady legs. For one moment, just the barest fraction of a second, she seemed to force the shreds of her indomitable willpower into her legs, tensing uncooperative muscles to firm attention, but it didn't hold. She collapsed in the next instant, burbling incoherently and twitching in the throes of death as she hit the floor face first.

"No!"

The frantic shout ripped through the air– a single word, slurred with violent emotion. It was a frightened, desperate sound, a moaning, hollow drawl accented by a hopeless, gasping breath so feral it made the skin crawl. The co-pilot's eyes flicked past Cylea, darting up the aisle toward the cockpit door in one sudden movement that she followed absently, more out of reflex than actual curiosity, and a tiny, hardly recognizable pulse of fear shot through her innards. The Co-pilot's face waxed to white, as pale and bloodless as dry bone.

In the doorway, Brock wavered on uncertain legs, his face drawn and pale, the side of his head and his torso oozing the dark synthetic blood common to full-body rebuilds. His chrome eyes were distant with pain and desperation, his dead blue tongue flat and comatose. A handgun rested in his unsteady hands, held half-heartedly with its muzzle pointed somewhere roughly between Cylea and the Co-Pilot.

"No." He repeated, eyes darting wildly, breath coming in ragged gasps. "No, no, no, no..." trailing off in an almost murderous, despondent series of gagging sobs, Brock's mouth worked until no more sound would come, lungs burning, harsh, synthetic tears running in unnaturally narrow, stingy trails down through his thin, sorrow-amplified wrinkles. Slowly, carefully, Cylea turned toward him, her mind still mostly locked in that distant place, that realm of the mind that existed apart from reality– no, what seemed like reality. She still wasn't completely sure where the line blurred, where the boundary truly lie.

Like an ebbing tide, the anger was already beginning to subside within her, all that hate replaced with a cold feeling of remorse as she stared at Brock, now a broken and desperate man because of her, because of what she had taken from him. Thoughts of Bao went arcing through her mind like crimson lightning, difficult to suppress, painful to acknowledge.

"Brock, I..." She trailed off as he looked up. Her mouth hung open for a moment– there were no words, no words that seemed to fit. She had meant to say something, but it was gone now. Slowly, she tried again. "I..."

"No!" Brock lashed out suddenly, his tone thick with burning hatred, a venomous strain of violent desperation shot with boiling madness. The pistol flicked up, shaky hands hardening against the grip of the weapon as he pushed it emphatically toward Cylea. "You– you–" he choked, all but screaming, "You heartless–! She was my love! My love! My– my sweet, vibrant flower! Oh, irreplaceable Kyoung-Mi!"

A tense silence hung in the air. The Co-Pilot licked his lips nervously. Cylea's eyes narrowed imperceptibly and almost of their own accord, her mind still hanging suspended somewhere between that inner darkness and the harsh world around her. One of her hands clenched at her side. Brock's lips peeled back hard against his teeth.

"And truly, naught but a single course of action remains to me now." He began ominously, voice quiet and strangely calm as the traces of a smile cracked across his face. "I want you to feel the agony and the sheer pressure of this hopelessness, Cylea, this hopelessness that I feel upon witnessing the death of my sweet–" His eyes widened with intensity, his voice a raw, rising croak as one of his spindly, skeletal hands fell away from the handgun's grip "I want you to see your last hope brutally extinguished before your very eyes like a feeble flame crushed in the hand of cold, unyielding hatred!"

Instantly the weapon bucked, once, twice, three times, belching fire as each round ripped across the cabin and punched through the Co-Pilot's chest. Cylea looked on in horror as he fell, eyes distant, crimson blossoms sprouting across fabric and flying in terrible spurts. His features twisted, then slackened instantly, relaxing, becoming resigned to death without even the barest traces of a fight slipping into his quiet eyes. Someone screamed, and the sound was like the echoing note of the last toll of bells at a funeral.

"Out, out, brief candle!" Brock shouted, forcing himself forward, each step driven by need, the raw hatred coupled with his burning desire for revenge. His face twisted with an insane fervor as round after round ripped through the Copilot's chest, but already his intensity was fading– that deep-set anger faltered, replaced by a deep, passionate sorrow that strangled his words in a desperate, choking sob, his chrome eyes wet and unmoving in their ashen sockets. "For the hour of the end draws nigh..."

The handgun clicked hollowly as the last round passed from the smoking barrel, leaving the breech empty and exposed. "And if I cannot live with my sweet, sweet Kyoung-Mi, then I shall choose the tender simplicity of death's embrace over the sour nectar of loneliness and failure, of torture and the disease of the heart that lingers in the wake of stolen love!" His spindly arm fell to his side, the weapon dropping unceremoniously from his fingers and hitting the deck with a hollow clunk. Cylea's eyes locked with his, the raw need to survive hanging between them, a stare of cold steel meeting the turbulent surface of some tropical ocean gone cold with an unnatural darkness, a darkness that ran deeper than any abyssal trench.

"But, if I am to die," he continued, breaking the stare. Instantly, his chrome eyes were flicking over the passengers, a tired smile stretching across his face as his arms unfurled, drawing out towards opposite sides of the aisle. "Then we all shall die! The great bosom of Neptune awaits us!" He laughed. "Yes! A seaman's grave!"

It took a moment for his words to sink in, just half a second, and then the passengers erupted into a panicked frenzy, fingers ripping into cushions, bags, clothing– someone struggled with a paper-thin silicon telephone, only to have it snatched away by an elderly woman raving about her grandchildren. In the rear, someone started sobbing loudly, almost shrieking with each gasping breath. A string of rosary beads rose above frantic heads like an omen, already being rolled between a pair of soft brown hands.

Brock's grin widened as chaos fell over the cabin like a thick sheet, and his chrome eyes swivelled to meet Cylea's again, as chilling as surgical steel under ice. One moment was all it took– her fists tightened, nails digging ruthlessly into her palms. Something wicked was stirring within her, something dark– it was so much easier to draw from now, to channel that raw emotion, all that hatred into something she could work with, something she could use to block out the throbbing pain of the wound and propel her forward in one last mad dash.

She was less than a foot from him when it happened, closing fast, fingers grasping eagerly, intent on grey, unhealthy flesh– in the moment, she was so consumed by raw, unbridled rage, building exponentially behind her eyes until she was blinded to all but her intent and never even saw the blow coming, only felt the impact of one of his spindly arms catching her across the face hard enough to send her spinning. A seat loomed into view suddenly, then someone's leg, the edge of a purse, and the hard floor, just a glimpse the instant before she hit it, eyes closing reflexively against a sharp pain that shot across her brow and arced through her nose like a driven nail. Fear and shock blossomed through her with electric purpose, pushing back the hatred, threatening to dispel every scrap of her resolve, threatening to turn her into a gibbering mass resigned to death, but she fought it– she choked back a sob, bared her teeth, tasted blood. Raw, nameless emotion burned within her, so cold, yet hot enough that sweat broke across her body.

Her vision was red now, boiling, her forehead burning with all the fury of a fever. The wound in her gut protested violently, nerves flaring up like unlit matches on a bonfire and burning through the numbing rage with an excited fervor. The pain that came with the blood was hot, blazing, the flow already wetting the bandage after something broke open or... it was... something important... something with a lot of... she winced, bared her teeth again. Something with a lot of blood flowing through it had broken open or popped... she was losing blood fast... too fast. No time to think. *Act.*

"Fall and cease!" Brock snarled. Cylea struggled to push herself up, tried to recapture some of that lost strength, but hardly managed to lift her battered body much more than an inch before the pain forced her back down, lips quivering. She grasped desperately at the retreating shape of her resolve, her strength, her hatred, her anger, trying to recapture the rage, the edge of that murderous red haze as it retreated cruelly to the edges of her vision. "For he who dares damnation only summons it sooner, and I do sincerely wish for you to experience this pain for as long as heaven hath a mind to stretch it, knowing that you will die no matter how you might struggle." He bent down next to her as a bloody mist came across her ragged breath, coating her lips. "Consider it divine justice, miss Von Mitternacht, and I, merely the instrument of God's own will."

"Save it, you freak." She managed, eyes swivelling up to meet his. Within her, everything was becoming numb again, cauterized by the return of her hatred, driven out of hiding by her surging resolve. If she was going to die, it would be on her terms, as much as she could manage, and she'd take Brock with her if she had to use her last breath to do it.

"Temper, temper!" Brock's smug grin came back too soon. Her eyes narrowed. "With such a fiery soul, Hell may be a welcome change for you from this dull and dreary world." He laughed, and her lips peeled back in a silent snarl, ivory teeth streaked with crimson. "I'm certain you'll give the devil his due–" In the next instant her hand was on his throat, fingers digging, thumb pressing mercilessly into his airway. He choked audibly, unable to breathe, eyes widening. Traces of amusement played about at the edges of her expression, eyes flickering with their own measure of insanity.

"Not before I give you yours." Cylea's fingers tightened. She was on her side now, one arm cradled against the wet gauze wrapped around her gut. Their eyes locked immediately, Brock's hands fumbling to get a grip on her arm. Hollow pops signaled his body's secondary respirators coming online, tiny filtered breathing holes designed as a failsafe against anything that might constrict the body's flow of oxygen, and his eyes bulged again with the sudden return of breath.

Her grip was strong, but as fresh air shot into his lungs, Brock's strength came back full force, and in one swift movement, he pushed her away. She bit off a shrieking gurgle as she flipped over onto her chest, arm twisting and thrown in hard against her wound. Red fogged her eyes again, thick and sudden as she squeezed them shut, squeezed down and against it all, struggling to block out the world around her.

"Nice try," Brock croaked, his voice raspy, "and though I may welcome the well-earned sleep of death shortly, I plan to live long enough to see you suffer until the very moment the reaper comes to claim you."

She blinked, trying to clear the wet, groggy blur from her eyes. Everything was hazy, foggy– the floor seemed to shift of its own accord, like a living carpet in a psychedelic hallway. She coughed, and blood shot past her tortured lips, staining the carpet. Again, she felt her resolve slipping, and again she fought to keep her scrabblehold on the side of that wickedly sheer cliff face. Her body screamed in protest of every movement, every breath, urging her to stop, to give up and lie down. The plane was tilting further and further toward the ocean, further and further toward the abyss. Brock had killed the only two people truly qualified to fly the liner, besides perhaps, himself. She swallowed against a knot of torture and welling blood. Death seemed inevitable.

Then something slid down the aisle toward her, slipping slowly along the carpet until it came to rest next to her, its metal surface cold against the side of her hand. For a moment, she forced her eyes open to their fullest, trying to clear her vision, trying to get a look at the thing, already half knowing that it was a dash of hope, a tiny ray, a chance. Behind her, Brock dropped back to his haunches, chuckling softly.

"Perhaps dying on your belly like a filthy maggot is too easy." He said absently, smiling past his own blood-stained and broken features. "The torture! The suffering! It must be amplified!" He made a resolute fist and shot half a grin at her back. "For if Hell truly awaits us, I should prove that I have earned my passage by doing something the devil himself would look down upon with a sort of fatherly pride."

Cylea's vision cleared a little in that instant– just enough. her heart hardened, the shreds of her resolve flaring for one last desperate effort, one final attempt to cut him down before the end cut off all hope, all chance of survival. Her hand stretched toward the thing, toward the crowbar, fingers shakily closing over the cold metal. Brock's grin tilted to cover half his face at an odd, wry angle as he finished "I should indulge myself, do something to your bodily form that would make even the most hardened sadist cringe, something I can inflict upon thy broken soul and languish on in these our final moments."

When he reached for her, she tensed. For an instant the pain flared, only to be dismissed entirely in the next, burned away once again by a darker flow, something that came shooting through her like crude oil blasting into a furnace, powering her resolve and pushing her anger back to the surface, back where it could be drawn from, where it could be harnessed.

In one sudden, yet oddly fluid movement, Cylea flipped over and away from him, baring her teeth in an expression so feral that he recoiled from her reflexively. In the next instant, she was on her knees and pushing to her feet, howling with all the insane rage of a berserker as she swung the crowbar in wild arcs, narrowly missing him with each hastily-aimed swing.

He threw up his hands instantly, stumbling backwards, trying to get away from Cylea's raging advance. Every swing came closer and closer to striking him, each so close and so quick that it utterly destroyed any concentration, any chance for thought to form, leaving only the most basic instinct in its wake-- the need to flee, to retreat from the blows that threatened to connect on every pass. He bit back a desperate noise as his eyes locked with Cylea's, finding only fire there, a rage that brewed within like dark clouds over a turbulent sea and expressed itself in violent, blood-burning shrieks that ripped from her mouth with every swing of the tool-turned-weapon. Blinded by rage, she was no longer in control of her body, no longer aware of her actions-- and they both knew it.

In the next instant, they were in the cockpit, Brock coming up hard against the panel. His eyes scarcely had time to widen before the crowbar took him hard across the face, impacting with enough force that the resounding crunch echoed through the flight deck. There was a flash of shattered chrome accented by thick, dark blood, spilling across the panel in generous rivers. Twice more, she hit him, screaming with each delivered blow-- there was fear in his eyes, but it only fueled her rage, only drove her on. For her, he had become the embodiment of everything she hated, everything that had gone wrong and everyone that had tried to kill her since the night she had run across Brent in the Eye of Ra. All that registered now was the hate, the pain, the fury, how much she wanted this whole nightmare to end.

He screamed as she lifted the crowbar over her head and, in one solid movement, drove it mercilessly through the center of his chest, pinning him to the control panel in a shower of sparks and arcing electricity. Her hands came away and something flared between them, something that flared green as it burned hot trails across his ashen skin and sent fractures through the panel and into the walls and windshield of the cockpit. Inside the aircraft's bulky control panel, somewhere beneath the hard surface, the displays, the buttons and the yokes, a cacophony of hollow pops and sizzles erupted, sounding the knell of Brock's death, hot black plastic scorching pale skin.

Chapter 11: Faith-Leap Catalyst

Cylea shuddered as her hand slid off the crowbar, lifting to touch her sweaty forehead with shaky fingers. An apprehensive swallow slipped past a trembling exhale, eyes flicking.

It was done.

Her fingertips slipped slowly across and down the curved end of the tool-turned-weapon in silent awe. The crowbar had pierced Brock's chest as effortlessly as a rivet through old leather, the long end buried to the head in sickly flesh and firmly locked into a mass of frothing, slowly carbonizing ooze the color of rotting death. Sputtering and slumping off to the side, she stumbled and braced her arms against the smoldering panel, sucking in breath after ragged breath, fighting off the icy sweat and the visceral, almost reflexive urge to vomit. One bitter fact kept roaring through her mind, kicking and screaming in an endless cycle.

She'd killed again.

The rage that had built itself like a temple in her soul subsided and dissolved as instantly as a mirage dismissed by a careless gesture, replaced by a growing sense of shock and fear that clawed at her, taking advantage of every weak spot opening in the tatters of her fading resolve, but it was the pain that returned the quickest, sharp hot lances driving through her gut, arm and face with enough intensity that she had to bare her teeth just to keep it at bay. Her innards felt raw, bruised, beaten into submission and then beaten again for good measure-- it was all she could do to keep from collapsing against the smoking controls next to Brock, to give up entirely, uncaring as to where the plane went or how many more people died.

Dark smoke hung heavy in the cockpit, thick with the acrid smell of burning plastic and scorched flesh. In the cabin, the passengers' frantic and chaotic panicking had died down to a low rumble, a simmer of random shouting interspersed with sobbing and loud, desperate praying in English and Chinese.

Absently, her gaze drifted to the radio. There was still no word from the NACC. Either they had stopped transmitting, or impaling Brock on the controls had fried the radios– it figured, the only thing in the cockpit that still seemed to be working were the overhead lights. A quick glance outside proved that, at the very least, they hadn't given up on her; on either side of the cockpit, drone interceptors kept pace with the jet, both razor-thin and bleach-white with long, slender wings that sloped outward from bulbous, dome-shaped sensor arrays. They hung ominously in the night sky like two skeletal vultures, just far enough away to be seen, yet cloaked in shadow as they watched her with red-glowing, camera lens eyes. She met the stare of one of the interceptors for only a moment and then looked away. Someone was on the other end of that camera, watching her, working in concert with the recovery team that was already on its way, probably strapped down and checking its gear in the belly of another BTD interceptor, a bigger one, loaded to the hilt with as much firepower as manpower.

She swallowed nervously. The crew was dead, Brock and Kyoung-Mi were dead– only the bulk of the passengers were still alive, and she doubted that there was much, if anything, that could convince them to stop panicking long enough to so much as glance at her, much less help keep her out of BTD hands. She bared her teeth again, this time in a sardonic grin– it was such a novel thought. As if there were anything a handful of passengers could have even done anyway.

Her eyes drifted across the control panel again. The electronics in the cockpit were completely shot. Even if she had been able to fly the thing, her limited experience aside, there wasn't much she could have done with a bunch of toasted displays and a bank of inoperative controls, besides scream or maybe pray, and bang her head against them in frustration during whatever short passage of time she still had left to live.

Slowly, warily, like a child facing an angry parent, she let her eyes drift upward to the approaching sea, perched below the nose of the aircraft at a harsh angle, and suddenly doubted the recovery team would even risk coming aboard now– as soon as the NACC realized the cockpit's controls were toast, that the plane was going to nosedive into the ocean before they could get anyone with any expertise aboard with a large enough safety margin to push the plane back into straight and level flight again, they'd switch to plan "B", which was, more often than not, little more than simply passing the proverbial buck off on another agency entirely. The Civil Corps would probably end up withdrawing discretely, leaving the mess for lower ranking emergency personnel, meaning the North American district reserve kids unlucky enough to be devoting their two days in exchange for a minimal salary and a college scholarship that would hardly cover the first month's books and beer tab.

Her eyes returned to her hands, pressed hard against the panel. If the NACC wasn't going to make the effort to save the doomed liner, then it was up to her, and that thought twisted her stomach into a hopeless knot that felt impossible to untie. If there was a way, then she would find it... she had to. No one else aboard was more qualified, or more sane, at least, at the moment, and no one would be busting down the door to save them. She swallowed nervously, fighting to recapture some of that resolve, to bring it to the surface and mold it into a tool she could use to lever herself up and into action. Her eyes were already rising back to the panel, looking for something, anything that might indicate an emergency or a backup system, *anything*. She had to work fast. No time to waste. *Dammit. There has to be something!*

"Is he dead?"

Startled, Cylea whirled around. The dark-haired girl with the full-motion band shirt that had been seated next to her stood in the cockpit doorway, eyes as calm as death as they lighted on Brock's chest and drifted emotionlessly over the head of the crowbar.

It took Cylea a moment to respond. She swallowed. "Ja."

"Good." the girl's eyes flicked up to meet Cylea's and a small smile touched her lips. "I'm glad you killed him."

The harsh beginnings of fresh tears broke and burned in Cylea's eyes and she turned away from the girl, turned back to the smoking console and swallowed again in sudden, irrepressible desperation. She tried to say something, tried to force some response she wouldn't regret, but managed little more than a single, gasping laugh in response-- the words sounded so heartless coming from the girl, so basic and cold, a statement that seemed to carry the vague traces of a vengeful sort of satisfaction. Wetness clung to the edges of Cylea's vision, but she fought it, squeezing her eyes tight against the tears. She sniffed, quickly ran a hand across her eyes, and turned her gaze back toward the sea.

"Are we going to die?" Came the girl's almost timid response.

"Nein." Cylea turned immediately back to the girl, shaking her head resolutely, forcing a brave face. "Not if I can help it."

"But... the controls..." the girl stepped forward, eyes suddenly intense. "They're all broken."

"I know." Cylea tried to meet the girl's stare, but faltered, her eyes slowly drifting to her hands, her thoughts in turmoil. She was so young, so...

"Why are you wearing a key for a necklace?" The girl asked suddenly. The question took Cylea by surprise and she hesitated, gently running a thumb across its cold, brass surface, across the word engraved in the metal. *Gramercy*.

"I--" She forced her eyes to meet the girl's again. "A friend gave it to me."

"What does it go to?" The question was as direct and sudden as the last.

Cylea swallowed as a cold spot formed in the pit of her stomach. She hadn't given it much thought, hadn't had the time to give it enough thought. To her, it had simply been a key, a memento or a hint of some kind or another, something symbolic... the writing on the envelope her Silent Savior had given her flashed through her mind. *Forest of Denial.*

"Do you think it's the key to something important?" The girl pushed forward, eyes unwavering. "Maybe something your friend wanted you to open?"

The cold spot in the bottom of her stomach turned suddenly icy, numbing her senses. Her eyes flicked up to meet the girl's emotionless gaze and were immediately snared, locked into a silent stare. In her hand, the key almost seemed to pulse, just once, like the last beat of a dying heart.

"Are you going to use it?" The girl asked abruptly. "I bet it opens something really cool."

Cylea swallowed again. Something wasn't right– the air felt different, the girl seemed too direct, too artificial. Her eyes drifted to her hand as it came slowly open, the key resting in the center of her palm, light glinting off the word as it echoed through her mind again. *Gramercy.*

"I– I don't know–" She tried, only to be cut off by the girl

"It's time to stop being afraid of the dark, Cylea." She stated forcefully. Another shiver shot along Cylea's spine as the girl finished. She looked up slowly, meeting those cold, dead eyes again, and swallowed uneasily.

Her mouth opened, painfully pink lips quivering in hesitation for the barest moment. "Who are you?"

"A friend of your father." Traces of a grin shot across the girl's face, then promptly vanished, as electric and momentary as wild lightning. "Someone who wants to see you finally stretch your wings and fly." Cylea's eyes hardened slightly as the girl stepped forward, stopping a few scant paces from her. "You know what you are capable of, inside. You know you're something more, *that you're capable of something more.*"

"What am I?" It came out suddenly, so direct and demanding, blurted and unhampered by even the slightest trace of fear or restraint.

"You'll never find out if we die here." The girl assured with another brief, flickering smile.

Cylea swallowed nervously, tried to speak, shook her head, then met the girl's eyes again, desperation already softening her gaze.

"But... I can't... how?" She looked away. "I mean, the controls are shot, und I've never flown something this big... or this complex before."

"It's inside you, Cylea." The girl said, her tone level and oddly reassuring. "You already know all you need to."

Cylea's eyes flicked back to the key, back to the silver kanji resting against it, the eye of Ra emblazoned on her bloodstained tanktop, and the bloody gauze wrapped across her abdomen. Everything felt cold, empty— a sweaty, disease-wracked sense of lightheadedness was fighting for purchase in her body, fighting to sap the last of her strength from her, to weaken every muscle to a point of unmitigated surrender. Everything hurt and nothing seemed untouched by the day's events, from her first bout of exercise early that morning, the gunfight at chow fun, the mad sprinting through those underground tunnels and her tussle with Brent, everything that the two agents had done to her until her Silent Savior had dispatched them like a couple of frightened animals, and every new scratch, ache, wound and dull pain she had picked up from Kyoung-Mi and Brock to this, she felt as though she'd plunged headfirst into hell and only now reached the threshold, somehow still alive despite all odds. Now there was only this last hurdle to be overcome, this last leap of faith before the end. It had to be the end... she doubted she could last much longer, doubted she could keep on going without suddenly collapsing from exhaustion. Her eyes met the girl's one last time, and she squeezed the key emphatically, turning back toward the console.

This was it. There were no other choices.

Her hands quivered as her fingers struggled to gain purchase on the curved head of the crowbar. Hard, carbonized synth-hemoglobin had formed a large, glossy scab around the tool-turned-weapon, leaving only the barest edges for her to work with. She worked quickly, fingers getting under the edges, each barely finding a place to grip— Brock's skin felt clammy and rigid where the scab hadn't touched it, inhumanly slick and smooth. She tried not to look at his face, that stricken visage frozen in a scream of terror with his black teeth and chrome eyes exposed, his tongue curled up against the back of his throat, twisted into a dead mass of blue flesh.

Pulling the crowbar out of his chest proved to be more difficult than driving it in had been, a testament to the power that lay dormant in her body, a power which seemed all but inaccessible until she let her rage override her every sense of humanity— and then it surged like ocean tide through an open floodgate. Those dark waters, so full of potential, so wild and angry, surged behind a wall somewhere deep in her psyche, waiting to be released, waiting to roar through her body in a torrent of destruction that seemed consistent only in that it always lead to someone's death.

Her arms tensed, fingers wedging under steel, digging into scab and flesh. She yelled, teeth flashing white in the poor light as the crowbar came free in a single, desperate yank— the shaft slid out of the panel and corpse alike with a sputter of electricity and a metallic clang accented by the sickening sound of blood-slick flesh and bone sliding across cold, hard steel. Instantly, she dropped it, letting the crowbar fall to the floor as Brock's body slipped unceremoniously off the panel like a limp doll, leaving a fractured stretch of smoking electronics in its wake.

There was a pause, a moment of silence. Cylea's grimy, blood-stained hands flexed in hesitation. A single bead of sweat traced a quick line across her cheek.

"Do it." The girl urged suddenly, her voice a hurried whisper tinged with traces of an odd, anxious sort of excitement. "You know *exactly* what you are capable of."

Cylea looked up one last time, eyes searching the darkness. The wicked crests stirring across the tense skin of the ocean were rushing at them so fast, getting so close that every writhing wave loomed in the night like the scale of some grand watery nightmare, filling the cockpit with its abyssal darkness. She was out of options, out of time. Cold and resigned, a tired, forced calm settled across her shoulders, restraining a tide of harsh, rash emotions that wanted to rise with the increasing strain of descent rattling and screeching around her. Pupils dilated as she drew a quick breath, shivering, *hesitating*. Urged on by the girl and a handful of burning feelings she could not explain nor deny, she did the only thing that seemed to be left, a vain, half-remembered suggestion that fought for dominance in her mind, boiling suddenly to the surface from a miasma somewhere deep within her, a dark and hidden pit that seemed out of place in her memories, like a portal into the darkness of someone else's mind.

In that moment, there was no room for thought. Her fingers flexed once, then darted for the panel, slamming into the smoldering stretch of exposed electronics with a single, solid motion.

Chapter 12: A Wing and a Prayer

For the briefest of moments, there was calm.

It wasn't an ordinary calm– it was steady, a death-like calm that seemed to envelope the world in a sheet of smooth grey light, a calm that almost seemed to exist somewhere outside of time, fading to a single point and then slowly drifting away, replaced by the blackness of a stark void. For a moment, everything was dark and silent, an endless stretch of oblivion that she hung suspended in like some forgotten marionette. At her neck, the key pulsed once with a soft blue-green light, then flared brightly, the word carved across its face a stark black at the heart of the already fading glow. *Gramercy.*

Without thinking and somehow seeing herself from some other angle, she manipulated her fingers with all the dexterity of an infant, trying to reach for the key and then immediately recoiling at the touch. It wasn't painful, not cold or hot, but dark, far darker than the void she hung suspended in. But even that wasn't quite right– it was if the key were not a key at all, but rather a gateway, a portal that lead to or rather held onto the very apex of some strange sense of darkness, a door to the secrets that stirred within her, awaiting release, hoping for another chance to wrestle control from her grasp. She had the key– she was on her way; fears retreated from the light as she let herself sink into the feeling, let herself become one with of the darkness. Somewhere, somewhere else, far away, in another century or another dimension, perhaps, she screamed. Her hands clasped desperately at the key as the sound ripped from her throat, a pan-dimensional cry of pain that echoed through everything and nothing in one deafening blast of sound.

That was when everything changed.

Reality inverted suddenly, darkness flared and became the light, and slowly, steadily, she became aware of the plane in a way totally unlike anything she'd ever experienced before. It was as if she were the plane, as if the frail flesh in the cockpit that she knew as her own, fingers blistered and burning in the smoking plastic ruins of the panel, were merely the brain and the liner itself her body. The air rushed by around her, yet time seemed to have slowed, letting her feel each and every molecule as it slipped over the wings and into nothingness, slipped over *her wings*, and spiraled off like waterfalls in the turbulent wake. Her hydrogen engines burned at just a notch above half power, her aluminum skin straining with the pressure of her airspeed and steady descent. In the darkness below her, the sea stretched out like a huge blue sheet, so close, yet so far.

And there was something else, as well, something darker. Another layer waited beneath it all, another floodgate hidden by the twisting darkness within her, buried somewhere just beyond her reach. It was brimming with power, glowing in the murky depths of everything she had only just begun to embrace, had only even scratched the surface of. This new layer was something so rich, so full of potential, that the merest prying glimpse brought with it an intense, almost surreal burst of pain– she wasn't ready, and the ferocity of the overload that seized her nerves and lit them up with a vicious fire was enough to warn her off. It took all of her effort just to concentrate enough to stay focused, to stay as one with the plane, but on some level, she still felt detached, apart, like there was more to be done, more that could be done. In the cockpit, she bared her teeth, smooth ivory tight against glaring pink. If she let the plane crash, if she let it carry her and the girl and its frightened payload of passengers to a watery grave, she'd never find out just what it was that lurked within her, what potential remained to be unlocked. The power beckoned, and immediately, she answered its call.

With a blast that scorched the ancient engine housings, sending a streamer of fire shooting into the night sky with a hazy crack of burning turbine shrapnel and oily smoke, she forced the plane up. Safety limiters burst into flame, melting and flying apart as the frame creaked violently in protest, fuselage rippling, wings vibrating with the force of the wind roaring against them while the nose steadily drifted upward, slowing the descent ever-so-slightly. The ocean was still so close, and getting closer and closer with every passing second. The plane screamed with the strain and she screamed with it, its fuselage, her fuselage, splitting, quivering skin tweaking and bending, rivets shearing and ripping loose, edges of decals flapping in the merciless wind.

Working with what little she knew from flying that barely airworthy, single-engine rustbucket so long ago as the plane steadily approached a level pitch attitude, she forced the flaps down to their limits, dropped the landing gear, and coerced her aluminum body sideways into a slip, little more than a few hundred feet above the water. Ahead, the sprawling shoreline of Venice Beach spread out across the horizon, a jungle of lights reflecting off shining metal and glass, still more than a dozen miles out. She was too close to the surface of the ocean, losing altitude too fast– She had to slow down!

Traveling at a speed that would turn the liner into a crumpled ball of aluminum and plastic if it so much as grazed the water, she forced her mind deeper, wading through the darkness, that hidden potential never wavering from the edges of her fingertips, never becoming more accessible, merely teasing her. She struggled with the plane's design, struggled with its systems as they traced their way through her mind, schematics and pathways as seen by flowing electrons and the memories of aging metal– there had to be a way to slow it down more! There had to be!

Instantly, she was aware of the wings, acutely aware of every square micron of pressure exerting itself on the aluminum, of the wind darting across the surface at an incredible speed. There was something very different, something she could use– That was it!

As the engines detonated, ripping free of their housings in twin balls of oily flame, something snapped in the wings and both ailerons dropped simultaneously, locked in place by the force of her will alone. Working quickly, she neutralized the rudder, yanking her way out of the slip, and threw her last edge into the mix, forcing the slats along the leading edges of the wings to extend fully, and pushing the nose upward suddenly. Again the plane screamed, and again she screamed with it– she felt every moment and movement intimately as it pitched upward only momentarily, frame bending and twisting as the tension on the fuselage reached a critical point and splintered with all the ferocity of a thin bone locked tight in a vise. The doors blasted open and every emergency system came alive instantly, dropping oxygen masks, inflating ramps, and triggering a harsh, bleating alarm that cut into her concentration like a white-hot knife. At her wingtips, the two interceptors wavered and broke away, chirping off brief, encoded transmissions stating that the GKI liner was going down and effectively notifying the coastguard that whatever was left of the passengers would need to be picked up, if anything, much less anyone, managed to survive the crash in enough pieces to make a difference.

The ocean was close now, so close. Time slowed, the air over her wings– the plane's wings– god, it didn't matter anymore, they were both going to die. The plane was locked in a stall, dropping like a rock, tilted up only slightly, a hundred or so feet above the surface of the sea. In the cockpit, she bit her lip, bit it so hard it bled, and as the icy waves of the Pacific came up to greet her, ready to welcome her into their wide, saltwater embrace, she screamed– but this time, she screamed alone, and the raw, ripping, animal sound of her vocal cords straining and howling with all the fear and anguish built in her struggle against death followed her into the sudden, painful darkness.

The plane hit in that instant, skipping off the waves, extended gear crumpling beneath the fuselage like cheap paper, forcing the nose back toward the water so rapidly that the little part of her inside the cockpit, that beat-up little fuse of flesh and bone that struggled to guide her larger, aluminum body to safety, careened off the panel like a limp rag and bounced across a solid wall, severing her connection to everything else the instant before she lost consciousness.

The last words she heard in the surging darkness were the girl's, breathed on a ragged gasp of pride and wonder in the final moments before the world collapsed in on itself: "There! See! Cirrus knew! He knew! Like an angel... or a valkyrie! Even when the others doubted–" The words ended abruptly, cutoff by a sickening crunch and the icy sensation of water blasting into the cockpit.

Chapter 13: Pacific Dawn Deliverance

What happened next came in jagged fragments.

Discolored chunks of reality like cruel dreams stirred somewhere between the world of waking and the unconscious realms of her mind. Disjointed blurs of sound, shades, and sensation forced their way into her groggy synapses, hitting her in sporadic bursts of consciousness with all the intensity of a runaway freight train.

The pain flared red through the darkness. She remembered shivering, sputtering in the icy eternity of blurred blue sea, paddling for something to hang on to-- hair and fabric clung like a wall of mud, plastered against her body and sucking the warmth from her flesh. Choking, labored breaths and bloody, blurry vision stirred-- something metal sank nearby, a pale hand reached, reached for her-- boiling water tinged with red, and the screams that howled on into the night. A single frightened, desperate eye sank into the waves, staring-- and then the darkness swooped in and took her.

Somewhere, somehow, her raw fingers caught the low edge of a slow-moving automated barge, a slab of fiberglass and cheap alloy loaded down with so much rusty junk and rotting garbage that it hung low in the water, its bed only a few short inches from the waves. Minutes seemed to stretch into hours, and hours into days, every shivering, half-conscious moment a long, dark, frigid abyss that seemed poised somewhere on the edge of dawn, until the fog moved in and drowned her world in a deep sheet of dull grey haze.

It hadn't happened suddenly, but the steady change from black to grey-white had still taken her by surprise. Between blinks, or perhaps, between fading, dreary moments of consciousness, the mists had enveloped her and the tug, getting so thick that the leading edge of the barge was totally obscured, sheared down to little more than a narrow line of black heaped with the twisted leavings of a civilization that seemed like a bad and distant memory, some part of a life that wasn't hers, couldn't be hers, a life she would only be too happy to forget.

At some point, the water calmed, steadily changing from the careless, unpredictable surging of the ocean to the steady backward flow of a river or a canal, but the barge pushed on, moving against the current without wavering, Cylea trailing like a broken streamer in its wake.

More comatose darkness shrouded her memories-- she held onto the edge of the barge with white knuckles, fingers twisted into a dead, frozen grip as solid and unmoving as stone. Her moments of unconsciousness were shallow and restless, filled with cold, shapeless terrors that jolted her into the grey area between sleep and waking and left her stranded in that placid layer of nothingness, a place apart from and yet connected to both the conscious and unconscious worlds. She was dimly aware of the water, of the barge and its steady advance against the current of the steadily narrowing channel, and felt the sun touch her skin as the fog burned away, replaced by clear sky and the gentle whisper of a soft breeze.

Her feet brushed against something hard and abrasive, something sunken in the muddy bottom of the channel, and she slipped, her startled hands quivering, reaching desperately for the edge of the barge as she disappeared beneath the waves. Flailing and gasping for breath with each panicked swallow of cold, polluted water, her eyes fluttered in an attempt at forcing focus, but it was too little and too late. Slowly, the barge slipped away from her slow-grasping fingers and her waning strength betrayed her, darkness threatening to close in on her again. Her eyes slid shut instinctively as the water slipped over her head, and she managed little more than a single, desperate grab for something, anything, her hand shaking and weak, clasping blindly at air until it followed the rest of her beneath the filth-choked waves.

But somehow, it didn't end there. Vaguely she was aware of struggling again, of cold water stifling every attempt to breathe until she finally managed to break through, gasping as she emerged from the waves and into a gritty world of tainted air and muddy sand. There was a blur of light, then oily sludge, a half-remembered whisper from somewhere she'd seen in a dream, or perhaps, in a memory. Her hands tightened around the squishy, foul smelling silt desperately, each grimy granule sliding wet through her fingers and leaving a fist of hard-packed rot in its wake as she dragged herself from the lapping edges of the water and planted her face wearily in the wet slick of tainted mud. She pushed out a shivering, tired exhale. *Land.*

Where she'd managed to come ashore was impossible to tell, a thought that came and was dismissed almost immediately. All that seemed to matter was the terrible taste in her mouth and the cold, festering feeling that clung to every muscle and organ in her battered body. The feeling stuck with her, so cold and virulent, even as she retched and screamed, emptying her stomach onto the shore and crying out in a desperate, sputtering howl that dissolved into bouts of violent heaving and ended with a gurgling gasp of surrender. For one brief moment, she was still, propped up on her hands and knees, fighting the urge to heave again, then her eyes suddenly rolled back into her head and she collapsed into the mud, immediately sucked into the blissful void of unconsciousness with one last labored, choking breath.

When she finally came to, it was only briefly.

The world was a haze of swirling grays and harsh, wet colors now. She was dimly aware of a dull, rocking sensation, of heavy fabric against her cold, clammy skin, and the smell of mothballs, or perhaps new plastic. She coughed and sputtered wetly, sucking in a ragged breath as she tried to hang onto the blurry shreds of her consciousness, wrestling with the oddly familiar, oddly comforting smell that teased her senses. With a shiver, she tried to curl up into a ball, to recapture some of the lost body heat she knew had to be there, somewhere, but the angle at which she hung, suspended between two thick bars of fabric as rigid as steel, made it impossible to do much more than shift uneasily. She blinked again, but her eyes refused to cooperate, refused to focus or clear the blurriness that held the world, making the silhouette above her seem distant and strange.

Slowly, weakly, like an infant stretching its muscles for the first time, she reached toward the shape, and instantly the motion around her slowed and shifted. Something wrapped around her hand, something cold and skeletal, yet tender and well-meaning. Sounds hung on her lips, sounds that her mind couldn't manage to form into words. The shape leaned in, becoming pale and drawn as it neared her eyes, the face of a man cloaked in the dark halo of a black, wide-brim hat. She blinked again, and he smiled, or at least, he seemed to try– his thin, bloodless lips peeled back over hard chrome teeth with all the innocence of a child, but the grin that cracked there was like the leer of a sick mannikin twisting on forgotten strings. She sputtered a weak laugh, tried to smile, and squeezed his hand gently. Somehow, she'd expected him to show up. Somehow she'd known he'd come to pull her from the jaws of death once more.

She opened her mouth to say something, to ask a question or make an attempt at wit, but it came out garbled, or perhaps it was simply forgotten the moment she'd spoken it. He only chuckled in response, that same deep, unnatural sounding laugh that served as his response to everything– or so it seemed.

A small smile drifted across her face as the darkness came for her again, but this time, it was welcome, a restful sleep at the end of a long journey. She'd cut her way headfirst through hell and left a harsh trail behind her in a painful blur of color and sound that was already fading into the dark obscurity of a memory she was only too happy to forget, and somehow, at the end of it all, she'd ended up here, in the arms of her Silent Savior, once again finding herself clinging to his rigid, comforting embrace.

Absently, she tried to touch his face, to trace one of the blue lines beneath the skin of his cheek, but her fingers faltered, her vision blurring again the instant before sleep took her. Her tongue swelled in her mouth, and in the darkness, she felt her arm fall comatose to her side.

Chapter 14: Restoration of Form

The instant her eyes snapped open, she screamed.

Throwing off scratchy wool blankets soaked with sweat, she reached for the ceiling, fingers twisting, back arching, eyes blurry and out of focus, every pain receptor in her weakened body flaring for one excruciating instant. There was a flurry of activity somewhere in the darkness, a crash of paper, a worried shout. She heard her name, but didn't recognize the voice. A hand reached for her, followed closely by the cuff of a black suit, and caught her wrist. She screamed louder, still not fully conscious, still reeling from some terror more imagined than real, even as the worried, comforting words reaching her ears hardened, becoming frightened barks almost ordering her to calm down.

Then the face came into view, a face she'd almost forgotten, a face she could have gone her entire life without ever seeing again.

"Gott im Himmel! Dai?" She breathed, her chest tightening as a cold sensation played along the edges of her frazzled nerves. His jet-black eyes stared back at her, crouched beneath dark, furrowed brows and a smooth, polished scalp, all as hard and unforgiving as they had been the first time she'd met him, when he'd been under Ou Shi Bing's thumb, a cleaner for his triad with a quartet of assassins at his back, ready to kill her the instant the word was given.

She tried to say something more, but no words would come. It seemed impossible– one minute she'd been in the arms of her Silent Savior, only to wake up the next with a dangerous criminal staring her in the face. She choked back a whimper and Dai grimaced, the thin crop of stubble on his chin twitching in irritation.

"Mein gott– Bitte töten Sie mich nicht!" It all came out at once on a hurried breath, sputtered so suddenly it was practically reflexive. Dai held up his hands in immediate resignation.

"In case you have forgotten, I am Chinese, not German." There was a brief, almost awkward silence. "You still know how to speak English, yes?"

She swallowed uneasily. "Ja."

Dai cocked his head to the side "*Ja* as in yes, or *Ja* as in I have no fucking clue what you have just said?"

She tried to keep the disgust from showing "Where am I?"

"Good, English! Now we are getting somewhere!" He let go of her wrist. "Though it would not have hurt if the first two words out of your mouth had been 'thank you'."

"Is 'go to hell' close enough?" She asked, forcing heat into her voice.

He muttered something unsavory sounding in Chinese, then fixed her with a brutal stare and waggled a finger at her. "I don't care what Shang says about you, you are still just an insolent *gwailo*!"

"Shang?" She caught her breath, considering his words for a brief moment. "Is she alive?"

He nodded once, firmly, then looked away, unable to keep a stern face under her wide-eyed and desperate gaze. She sat up quickly, and immediately regretted it, head reeling with the effort "Where is–"

"Do not push yourself!" Instantly, he was beside her, concern showing in his eyes. It was strange, seeing a hard-faced brute like Dai acting so gentle, his rough hands carefully urging her to lie back down. She swallowed and collapsed back lightly, head coming to rest against a cold, sweat-soaked pillow.

He sighed and sat on the bed beside her, eyes absently drifting across the wall. "Do not worry about Shang. She is a full-body rebuild, and a Representative of the Golden Koi Triad– it would take a nuclear weapon to kill that woman."

"Und the others?" Cylea asked, her voice flat from the effort she put into keeping the worry out of her tone. She doubted they had, but she had to ask, vainly hoping that he might tell her that Bao or Ying or Hok had managed to make it out alive, but she quickly quashed those thoughts– they were just too painful. It was likely Shang was the only one, the only survivor from that brutal attack on a family that had practically become her own, a family that had taken her in and defended her to the very end, had loved her and sacrificed themselves so that she might live to see another day. She sniffed and looked away, gently scooping a tear from the edge of her eye with a fingernail.

"I do not know for certain." Dai said at last. "But I am sure that some of them, at least, did survive." He turned, meeting her moist, heavy-hearted gaze. "Hok was a tough man with a tough family. I doubt any one of them died that day."

"I hope you're right." She closed her eyes against the building tears, chastising herself inside for showing weakness. "I really do."

He reached out and took her hand, squeezing it gently. "As do I."

Their eyes locked for a long moment. To Cylea, it seemed utterly strange, yet no less comforting, witnessing this side of Dai's personality, a side she never would have believed existed had she not seen it. He squeezed her hand again, lightly this time, and turned back to the walls.

Slowly, she let her eyes drift past him to take in her surroundings. It was a narrow, boxy building, a single rectangular room that was unlit but for a single ancient desk lamp and the dull shafts of yellow light that stabbed in from the cracks around the door at the opposite end, past stacks of yellowing paper and an equally old, plastic, rotating desk fan that hung from the rafters by a stout piece of white nylon cord, its flat base twisting uselessly from right to left and back again. The walls themselves were patchwork, an amalgam of boards and corrugated aluminum sheets nailed, riveted, and bolted together around the doorframe and the edges of two sluggishly-spinning industrial-sized fans set over dark, upward-sloping vents. At one point, someone had taken a coat of lime green paint to the whole mess, but most of it had peeled or rotted off long ago. Even the ceiling, half sheet rock and half exposed bracing, showed wide patches of white texturing where the green had given way to the original coloring of the building.

"Where are we?" She asked, genuinely curious. She wanted to sit up and get a better look at the room, but the instant she so much as shifted, her body rebelled with a blast of dizzying pain.

"One of the Golden Koi's safe houses." He glanced back at her. "We are still in Los Angeles, if you were wondering."

"I figured." She managed, then sighed. "So how'd you find me?"

"Shang told me exactly where you were." He shrugged. "Do not ask me how she knew– the way you were stretched out under that bridge, I thought for certain that you were already dead."

"Thanks for not giving up on me." It didn't come out quite the way she had meant it to– there was no feeling in the statement, it actually sounded almost sarcastic. Dai's eyes drifted to his hands.

"It is not like I had a choice in the matter." He stated absently. "We are both part of the same Triad now. Shang thinks that you are very important, and she believes that this is the simplest way for my honor debt to be satisfied." He shrugged again. "So I am supposed to watch over you until you reach Hong Kong."

Hong Kong. The name brought a cold feeling to the pit of her stomach, reminded her of that ill fated GKI air flight. It all seemed like a bad dream, a nightmare meant to be forgotten. Cautiously, she lifted the blankets, all wool and the same rustic color of green as the walls, and stared down at her body, afraid of what she might find horribly mutilated or gone.

Instantly the blankets came back down, wrapped tighter this time. "Why am I naked?"

"Because your clothes were soaked and ripped." His eyes stayed fixed ahead, never wavering, his voice flat and emotionless. "I still do not have fresh clothes for you as yet." He glanced at her. "But Shang has assured me that one of her go-to men will bring some today, along with all the identification materials you probably lost on the plane and a few other things."

She swallowed. "Und the bandages?"

"Yes, I did those." He sighed, looking away again. "You had some pretty serious injuries, all swollen and infected." He glanced at her again. "It is not like I got off on patching up your wounds or giving you antibiotic nanoinjections, it is just my job to keep you alive."

She looked away, lifting the arm that Kyoung-Mi's blade had sliced into, eyes drifting absently across the smooth, white dermal patch hiding the wound. "I... I'm sorry." She glanced at him. "Thank you."

Dai shrugged. "Whatever. You do not trust me. I understand." He turned to her again and smiled weakly. "It is okay. You will be out of here before very much longer." His eyes returned to the wall as he stood, then stretched and turned to face her again. "I will make some calls tonight. If everything goes as planned, we should have you on a flight to Hong Kong by tomorrow afternoon."

"But, isn't that a bad idea, I mean, after what happened..." She swallowed nervously.

"Do not worry, now that we know the extent of what we are dealing with here, we will use every precaution to guarantee your safety. You will probably be flown out 'penthouse' on an airline owned by a wealthy Mediterranean banking firm or an Australian shopping mall mogul."

She smiled, and this time it was genuine, forming of its own accord. For the first time in what seemed like ages, an eternity comprised of mere hours, things finally seemed to be looking up. With a little luck, things would only get better– it was something she could cling to, hoping against hope that whatever tatters of her luck still remained after all the close shaves she'd been through would hold long enough for her to get to Hong Kong safely. It all seemed so direct, so easy.

But then what was it Shang had said? *Nothing important is ever easy.*

Chapter 15: Simple Things

"I hope you like Mexican." Dai plopped down in a rickety aluminum, fold-out chair next to the bed and dropped something in a white plastic bag beside Cylea, something her half-asleep senses identified as food, something he'd picked up during one of her shorter lapses in consciousness.

Absently, she turned her bleary, sleep-fogged eyes to the other end of the room. It was night now-- only darkness came through the cracks between the door and its ancient frame, leaving little more than the dull, yellow light cast off by the desk lamp. Some of her strength had come back during the day, or at least, she'd recovered enough of it to sit up without the pain or the sudden dizziness. Now all she needed were some clothes so she wouldn't have to constantly keep the blankets pinned to her chest with a modest arm.

She blinked tiredly and gave the bag an absent glance. Dai was already peeling the aluminum foil off a thick burrito, exposing the soft, white tortilla with hard, work-tanned hands. The smell was welcoming, warm and spicy with the kind of organic, sense-teasing something that made her mouth water, that thickness and texture of smell that labeled it as real food, not something squirted out of a tube and run through a nanochef processing unit like practically everything else you could pick up for a few bucks was. Briefly, she thought of Smash, and his tales of a time before nanomolecularly reprocessed foods had existed, a time when a couple dollars would buy you a genuine, flame-broiled hunk of beef slathered in ketchup, mustard, and a dozen other things, held tight between two pieces of bread and wrapped in a piece of real paper.

The thought brought a smile to her lips. It all seemed so primitive, but then, there was nothing wrong with simple and natural, at least in moderation. For her, though, the past was more of a curiosity, something that always seemed just a little too barbaric to spend too much effort thinking about.

"What, no Chinese?" She asked, managing a grin as she reached into the bag and pulled out a foil-wrapped meal of her own. Another glance into the bag revealed only two cheap memory plastic forks sealed in shrinkwrap and a few thin napkins manufactured from reprocessed materials, essentially recycled bits of anything and everything broken down by nanomolecular machines and reconstituted into an approximation of paper that seemed to have more in common with threadbare fabric than anything else. *Oh well*, she thought– it couldn't all be retro. Era-themed restaurants had laid claim to that particular niche long before the invention of recycled beef-in-a-tube.

"Chinese?" Dai laughed sardonically as Cylea carefully unwrapped her burrito. "Didn't you get enough of that living with Hok and his family?"

"Nope." She bit into the burrito quickly, too quickly, and tried not to think about Bao or any of the others, using the food to give her mouth something to do before the smile could fade from her lips. Somehow, it didn't seem to taste as good as she had imagined it would.

"Hmm." He commented, oblivious to her discomfort. "Well, I am not a big fan of it myself, especially the way it is made over here."

"Is it really that different?" She asked, genuinely curious, eager to think about something besides the past.

"It all depends on where you go." He gestured absently. "Some of it is close, but most of it has been so Americanized that it is like a bad joke."

"I believe it." An amused smile crawled across her face. "But, you know, food is food, und it's all good when you're hungry, right?"

"Right." He nodded once, firmly. "So tell me, how is your burrito?"

"Great," She smiled, chewing in the pause. "But I don't think I'm going to be able to eat it all, though." She gave the burrito a calculating, almost wary look. "It's kind of big."

"Really?" Dai couldn't help but smile. "The way you heal, it seemed that you would be eager to eat all the food you could get your hands on."

"What do you mean?" She blinked, smile giving way to amusement tinged by mild confusion. Absently, she glanced at her bandaged arm. "Oh, you mean the effect of the nanoregenerative booster I got a few years ago..."

"No, it is something more than that." He paused, chewing in between sentences. "When I brought you here three days ago, there were some wounds I doubted you would ever fully recover from." He shrugged. "I even doubted that you would live." He took a bite, then gestured at her. "Now, most of your injuries have healed, and with very little scarring– none in some cases."

The look she gave him was blank, disbelieving. He gestured vaguely. "Go ahead, check for yourself."

Slowly, she turned back to her arm, eyes hovering over the bandage for a moment before she laid back, using gravity to preserve her modesty and free up her other hand, then carefully set the burrito on the blanket between her breasts.

She hesitated for only a moment, then licked her lips and gently peeled up the edge of the dermal patch. Beneath the white gauze, sticky with a thin layer of mucous-like nanoregenerative goo that glittered silver, the gash where Kyoung-Mi's blade had sliced into her arm and bit to the bone had almost knitted closed, leaving only a thin split in the pale skin that was oddly pink around the edges.

Slowly, carefully, she smoothed the bandage back over the wound. It made her wonder how much the bullet wound had healed, but she wasn't about to throw off the blankets and check, not with Dai in the same room.

"Odd, isn't it?" He asked.

"I always figured it was the injection." Cylea said absently, letting her eyes drift across the ceiling, the smell of the burrito teasing her senses. "But then, I've never had injuries this serious before. Not even the few times I got slashed in knife fights."

"Knife fights?" His eyebrows rose in genuine interest.

She laughed and turned her gaze toward him. "It only happened one or two times, und it wasn't like I did it for fun or anything." She let her eyes slip back to the ceiling, chuckling quietly. "It was all in self defense, y'know?"

Dai nodded understandingly and took another bite out of his burrito. There was a brief pause, and then she pushed herself back into a sitting position, holding the blanket against her bare chest as she bit into her burrito again. In the silence, her thoughts drifted back to the pallid man, her Silent Savior.

"Dai," She began, attracting his gaze. "When you found me, you didn't happen to see a man..." She trailed off as he looked at her. "You know, nearby? Guy with a coat... uh... big hat?" She gestured vaguely, miming the wide brim of the hat her Silent Savior had worn both times she had seen him.

"No." He stated plainly. "You know, now that I think about it, I did not see anyone around. It was very quiet. Why?"

She swallowed a bite of her burrito, then tried a relatively nonchalant shrug. "No reason. Just curious."

"Is he a friend of yours?" Dai asked; the response wasn't quite immediate, but his casualness seemed almost as forced as hers.

"Not sure." She paused, chewing, and cocked her head absently, letting her eyes play across the ceiling. "I mean, I think so. He's saved my life twice, but I've got no idea why, und I've never been able to get anything more than a laugh out of him."

"Hmmm." This time, his response seemed completely genuine. "Sounds like a guardian angel... or something." He arched an eyebrow at her as she turned back to him, meeting his gaze. "I would count your blessings and thank whatever god you believe in that someone out there cares enough to watch out for you."

"Ja..." She trailed off, looking away again. "Still would have been nice to have had his help on the plane though."

Dai's response was immediate. "What happened out there, anyway?"

"What didn't happen?" she scoffed. "Some crazy guy with a full-body refit probably as expensive as Shang's decided to hijack the plane with his girlfriend und got all trigger happy when he found out there was someone on board worth sixty million dollars."

"Sounds rough" he commented blandly, his interest fading exponentially. He had probably been hoping for something more in-depth, something more entertaining than the brief explanation she'd shot at him in a manner that was all but hostile. Absently, he gestured in her direction. "Is that how you got those wounds?"

"Ja, everything but the arm was his handiwork" She sighed, meeting his gaze again. "His girlfriend, on the other hand, was totally organic, except for some kind of vat-grown bone blade mounted in her arm that she tried to fillet me with." Her eyes drifted to her arm as she continued, her tone taking on a tired, almost absent quality. "It was pretty sharp... I'm still kind of amazed it didn't slice clean through." She shrugged and met his gaze again. "I guess I'm made of sterner stuff than I thought I was."

"It might explain why there is such a large bounty on your head." Dai offered. Cylea nodded absently, breathing a sigh. They both knew that it was exactly why, or rather, one of the reasons why. There were plenty of things about her that were abnormal, things that seemed intent on forcing her to question the validity of her own humanity. She opened her mouth to say something, but the sound of a phone bleating in a crisp, clean fashion cut her off.

Shifting the burrito between his hands, Dai reached into a pocket and pulled out a small, glossy black cell phone, the standard thin, flip-open model that had been around for more than a century and a half, despite enough functional improvements in every aspect to make it worthy of a name as radically different from the label of its ancestors as it was. Nevertheless, when it came right down to it, they still fell into the same collective category of their predecessors. A phone was a phone, and in another two centuries, it would still be a phone.

"Dai." He stated immediately. There was a pause, just a brief moment before he mumbled a quick, simple response in Chinese, then closed the phone and stood.

"What is it?" Cylea asked, curiosity plain on her face.

Dai smiled. "We have a delivery."

Chapter 16: Degrees of Acceptable Risk

Cylea flicked open the package Shang had sent for her and promptly rummaged through it.

Made of durable, clear plastic, it had more in common with an oversized envelope than almost anything else. Inside was a second, smaller package, almost identical to the one she'd been given before her mad dash through the tunnel beneath Chow Fun, and filled with the same paperwork, but with a corporate credit chip instead of a cash card, wedged against a shrink-wrapped parcel of smooth and pressed clothing that had probably come fresh from a vending machine somewhere in downtown. It was a typical set, a rough, starched-white, long sleeve shirt with matching pants and underwear clearly cut for what was considered to be the average female form. She couldn't help but laugh– it was all so puritan, and baggy in a way that transcended casual, making everything but the shirt and pants virtually unwearable –and it wasn't like she was small, per se. With a population that had become increasingly more sedentary through the last two centuries, the North American average had simply never managed to get away from its stereotypical bodily width, especially among the consumers of cheap vend-clothing. Oh sure, beauty could be bought, but it wasn't cheap, and quiet, slogan-smothered social groups were an ever present force against the rampant use of cosmetic alteration, nano or otherwise, working hard to instill the average individual with an odd sort of pride over anything that might be seen as a physical defect, no matter how small. Small signs touting blatant mantras like "fat and proud" or "Mutation is Adaptation" always cropped up alongside colorful nanoprojection ads filled with flowers and Japanese swimsuit models towering over catchphrases like "don't be fat a day longer than you have to" and a hundred others that were considerably more blatant and even vulgar– it was the way of things, the new face of North American Culture, as two-sided and capital driven as any politician.

Cylea had hardly managed to pull on the pants and shirt, leaving everything else in the package, when Dai scoffed suddenly, interrupting her thoughts. Still pulling everything into place, she turned to him and he shot her a wry grin. "Someone is very interested in you."

She managed a quick and decidedly sardonic laugh. "Ja? Tell me something I don't know."

"Okay, try this." He tapped a finger against the note in his hands. "The recovery team that was called in to pick up what was left of the flight you were aboard found no survivors, but someone placed an anonymous call to the BTD about you, apparently providing proof that you were still alive and had escaped." He set the paper down on his lap and laughed quietly. "With support from a dozen anonymous firms and corporations, all probably the puppets of a single larger company, they have managed to effectively secure every airport and seaport in the Los Angeles area, and have already installed nano-sized cameras on every route out of the area, all with the intent of finding you."

She swallowed against a hard knot that was steadily rising in her throat. "Damn"

"My thoughts exactly." He nodded absently. "According to the reports of Shang's field agents, it is a very smooth, very unobtrusive operation complete with a total media blackout. To the untrained eye, it may seem like very little more than a slightly heightened presence of security personnel, but it has got all ten of the local triads nervous." A crease formed across the middle of the paper as it bent between his absently tightening fingers. looking past it to a spot on the wall, his eyes seemed to become distant, withdrawn.

"Shang is very concerned, more so than I have ever seen her." He blinked absently, then looked back to Cylea. "They have also begun a process of staking out and raiding Triad safe houses at random throughout Los Angeles, and not only those used by the Golden Koi." His eyes drifted back to the paper. "The Shui Quan, the Kao Chi, and even the Industrial Sun have reported being hit." He paused for a moment, swallowing uneasily, then added: "There is, of course, more." His eyes flicked to hers "Whoever it is that is after you, they have been very *thorough*."

Cylea looked away immediately. It still didn't make sense. First the bounty, and now this. How much worse would it have to get before the Golden Koi would surrender her to preserve itself, or before she would have to turn herself in to spare them and the lives of anyone else who might get hurt in the crossfire? Already it seemed like a viable alternative. Not a pleasant one, but an alternative to be considered nonetheless.

"What are we going to do?" She asked absently.

He breathed a long, tired sigh, then pulled a perforated tab off the corner of the paper and gave it a slight, upward push. Instantly, the note flared, leaving only a faint powder of thin, white ash to sink to the floor in its wake. "Nothing tonight. Tomorrow we will relocate to another safe house. Shang has one picked out for us already that she and her closest aides seem to think is the safest choice." He shrugged. "From there, I am not sure." He met her gaze again. "It might be a while before we can get you to Hong Kong."

"How long?" Her eyes were unfocused with absent thought, fixed on some distant point.

"However long it takes Shang to find a safe way through." He shrugged again, "After what happened aboard that airliner, I doubt she will be taking any more chances unless they are absolutely necessary for your survival."

Cylea swallowed again. Shang's stance seemed to be one of waiting until everything blew over, until the tight fist wrapped around their collective throats got tired of squeezing and relaxed. In any ordinary circumstance, it might have been the smartest and easiest course of action, but Cylea doubted it would do much more than hasten the eventual surrender, bring that final move that would put Golden Koi guns at her back again that much closer. The moment of that cruel fist's grip becoming too tight to bear could be just around the corner.

"Do not worry, Shang is a smart woman. I doubt it will take long." Dai grinned, but Cylea could only meet his gaze with a blank expression, fighting against the reflexive urge to pale at the thought that Dai's words were probably more true for an eventual betrayal than her ultimate salvation. "You will be in Hong Kong before you know it."

"I hope so." She managed. The smile he gave her was friendly and soft, a gesture meant to be reassuring, but she turned away anyway, her heart cold with worry. She wanted to believe Hok's words, wanted to believe that the Golden Koi would protect her no matter the cost, but it was a foolish notion to cling to– everyone had a price, and everyone's honor could be bought or bargained for. It was just a matter of finding the right amount and the right currency to deal in. Money wasn't the only way to grease the wheels that led to capitulation and cooperation.

"You will be fine!" His smile became a wide, happy grin as he reached over and gently patted her hand. "I promise." She forced a smile and he continued. "But for now, you should get some more rest. We will be leaving early tomorrow, and I need you to be able to walk on your own two feet."

She nodded silently as he stood and started for the desk lamp. It wouldn't be easy to sleep, knowing that the morning could bring a whole new set of orders for Dai, orders that could put her in the maw of the beast that hunted her. As she laid back, she forced down the fear struggling to rise within her and drew in a long, deep breath.

Knowing it would come was half the battle. For now, she'd just have to bide her time, and hope she was prepared when the time finally came.

If ever it did.

Chapter 17: The Vise Tightens

Cylea was only half awake when she felt Dai's hand on her shoulder, urging her out of the comforting darkness of sleep.

Her eyes drifted open, bleary and fogged with fatigue– somehow, it was still dark, or at least, the sun hadn't managed to penetrate to the little one-room hideout yet and Dai hadn't bothered to turn on the desk lamp. She groaned, pulling in a deep breath of frigid air, and forced herself upright, already missing the rough warmth as it dissipated into the darkness, no longer trapped against her sleeping form by blankets and sheets.

"What time is it?" She asked, her mind still groggy and slow.

Dai grinned at her from somewhere nearby in the darkness. "Time to go."

Cylea groaned again, then slipped a leg off the edge of the bed and fumbled for the plastic package Shang had sent for her. Ten more minutes of friendly goading from Dai put her stumbling sleepily through the door and grumbling quietly in German as she followed him from a narrow path between two buildings and toward a nondescript, older model hoversedan parked lazily a foot or so from a nearby wall. Small bits of litter stirred near its suspensors, swept around beneath the silent and unmoving vehicle, toyed with by the weak artificial gravity generated during its parking cycle. As soon as she was inside, Dai handed her a rough wool blanket and told her to keep her head down. She was only too happy to oblige him.

Quickened by bouts of shallow sleep, the ride passed in a blur of half-heard sounds and half-felt stops for lights and signs. Someone honked once, but whether it was at Dai or another car, she couldn't tell. It didn't seem to matter as much as letting sleep take her back, letting it pull her back into its unfathomable depths.

When the hoversedan pulled to a stop halfway down an alley, she drifted partly awake again, but before she could recapture that fleeting void of unconsciousness, Dai's hand was on her shoulder, once more urging her back into the waking world.

"I will be right back." He stated, forcing a smile to keep concern from threading its way through his expression. "Stay here and watch for anything out of the ordinary, warn me if you can." Her bleary eyes locked with his, contrastingly clear and alert as he added, "but try to stay low. We do not want to risk anyone seeing you."

Somehow, the traces of a smile found her face as she stretched, back rubbing against the seat and arms coming up against the doors. "Expecting trouble?"

"With you in the car?" He grinned. "Always."

She shot him a wry grin of her own, then propped herself up on her elbows as he stepped out into the alley.

In all, it was relatively nondescript, just another narrow stretch of pavecrete between the ugly backsides of buildings somewhere deep in the metropolitan jungle of Los Angeles. Her eyes drifted across a rusty dumpster, a few scattered bags of trash left to rot against the walls, and the bent, rusty frame of a bicycle propped up on cinder blocks halfway down to the next road. Nothing out of the ordinary. She blinked tiredly, then let her eyes drift to Dai, making his way slowly across the path toward a lone door set into the wall less than fifteen feet from the hoversedan on the left side of the alley. In a way, it was almost reminiscent of the alleyway outside the warehouse where she had first met Dai, the alleyway where Ou and several other Triads had fallen in the ensuing shootout with a rabid mob of heavily-armed law enforcement officers. The thought sent a chill down her spine, but she shook it off quickly, forcing her mind back to the present. This was a different alley, and this time, her survival was inextricably linked to Dai's. If something caught him off guard because she hadn't been paying attention, she could never forgive herself. Not after all the Golden Koi had done for her, much less all that they were still willing to do to keep her safe.

Dai's eyes darted uneasily down the alleyway, just a quick check to the left and right before he nonchalantly fished a thin plastic card out of a pocket on his suit. His hand hesitated over the door's reader for the briefest moment, then stilled with resolve. The instant the card descended and just before it touched the reader, the familiar click of a handgun cocking echoed across the walls of the alley.

Dai froze.

"Don't move." The voice was strong, laced with the barest hint of a midwestern accent. "I want you to put your hands behind your head and get down on the ground like the dog you are, Triad boy."

Dumbstruck, she could only watch, her mind locked with fear, shock, and the fog of thoughts still hampered by sleep's pervasive touch. Dai swallowed uneasily, then slowly complied, the card still held between his index and middle fingers. The stringy, lanky shape of a tall, almost anorexic looking man rose from the opposite side of the dumpster, one bony hand wrapped around the grip of a dark, large caliber handgun and the other making a quick pass through his short and wavy, greasy black hair. "So where's the girl?"

Dai was on his knees when the man reached him, stopping just out of arm's reach. His lips pursed quickly in frustration-- he knew he had been beat, but shook his head and met the other man's gaze solidly nonetheless.

"I have no idea what you're talking about." It came out so clean and so flawlessly that it could have been a simple statement of fact-- it was a trained response, good enough to fool all but the most sensitive of lie detectors.

The other man nodded silently, then paused, chewing the inside of his lip for the briefest of agitated moments. In the next instant, he shouted and lashed out, his handgun catching Dai across the face hard enough that it sent him reeling. "Liar!"

Before the Triad could respond, the other man hit him again, and this time drew blood. Crimson shot across pavecrete on a line of spittle, a thin mist coloring Dai's lips in its wake. A slight dribble leaked from his nose, dragging its own thin trail of scarlet across his skin with it.

Lifting his head with visible effort, the Triad met the other man's gaze again almost immediately, his anger visible only in his eyes, shades of a dark glitter. She knew that look-- last time she'd seen it, Dai had been prepared to shoot her, and would have in a heartbeat, if Ou Shi Bing had given him a reason to.

Managing a smile that was more frustrated than sadistic, the other man stared back at Dai, silently watching the Triad before his eyes suddenly flicked from one end of the alley to the other, then lighted on the car. Reflexively, Cylea dropped an inch further, trying to get out of sight as quickly as possible, but it was too late. He'd seen her.

"Motherf..." He mumbled, shaking his head, then turning back to Dai with a wry half-grin on his face. "Shoulda guessed. She's in the car, isn't she?"

The look Dai gave him was harsh, hatred mixing with mock disappointment in a glare that only made the other man's smile widen. "Smart man."

"Shut it." The other shot back, then lashed out with one foot and caught Dai firmly in the shoulder hard enough to knock him onto his side. Dai's hand flailed for the pavecrete, gained purchase, and before the other man could do so much as flinch, the Triad was on his feet, crimson tracing a quick line across his cheek as his fist went straight for the other man's jaw. The pistol came up instantly, reflexively, its fearsome muzzle pushing forward ahead of fiercely bared teeth. Two shots echoed in the alleyway, flashes leaving the stench of burnt gunpowder in the air as both rounds passed harmlessly past Dai and buried themselves into the nearest wall. One fluid slash of the hand, and the weapon went flying out of the other man's grasp, clattering across pavecrete and slipping under the dumpster the instant before Dai's hand darted back and leveled out, ready to deal what Cylea recognized immediately as a killing blow.

What happened next seemed almost unbelievable, almost surreal; one instant Dai was drawing back his arm for a fatal strike, one hand wrapped tight in the fabric of the other man's shirt, and the next, they were both reeling, the other's eyes incredibly wide as he collapsed against the Triad and screamed, his fingers flailing hopelessly in the air and the sound echoing across the walls, so intense and so feral that it made Cylea's hackles rise instantly. There was blood in the air-- wide streaks of crimson splashed across both men and a single scarlet drop caught dark fabric, running its own serpentine course through narrow folds until it splattered against pavecrete amid bloodwashed limbs twisting and convulsing sickeningly in the smog-dim light. The other man was sputtering something incoherent, reaching blindly into the air and gasping as he shook, fighting for air that wouldn't come. Cylea drew a quick breath as Dai stepped back, hand reaching reflexively for his own pistol, but the other man's back stole her glance and held her eye-- ragged and bleeding around a gaping wound of shredded flesh, his shoulders twitched above a field of butchered meat where something had punched through the center of his torso and left only carnage in its wake, something vicious and no-nonsense, something wide bore.

Dai's mouth opened, but before he could get off a word, something hit the ground a few feet from him, cracking the pavecrete with its impact. It was massive and dark, the thick and wide shape of an inhumanly large man, a giant swathed in depthless, midnight black.

Thick boots of smooth leather the color of polished jet scuffed against pavecrete, as dark and imposing as the thick, midnight fabric of his long, wide-collared coat with its broad, angular plates of black steel set at angles across his shoulders and forearms to the perfectly chiseled slide of his fearsome, grotesquely large handgun, something with a bore that looked wide enough to put holes in tanks or puncture the walls of a fortified building. It was sleek for its size, a glossy-black monster nearly two-feet long that was broken only by a polished chrome breech and the thick, jointed ammo feed that jutted from the base of the weapon on one end and slipped into the flesh of his pale arm on the other.

His thin, bloodless lips peeled back in a harsh grin, revealing teeth like polished chrome pegs beneath his high, sharp, almost German nose and the black, perfectly circular lenses of a pair of silver-framed sunglasses that shaded his eyes under the wide brim of his rigid, black hat. For one terrible moment of uneasy silence, he met Dai's gaze, that same grin twisting lines through his pallid, waxen skin, milky and translucent over a weblike network of thick, blue veins and sunken cheeks. He was twice Dai's size, if not larger, but as he rose, uncoiling like a giant serpent intent on its prey, it was abundantly clear that he possessed an inhuman sort of grace and strength. Paralyzed, the Triad could only watch as the newcomer stretched to his full height-- the mass of writhing cables, leads, tubes, and wires that snaked through the depths of his coat protruded past the rectangular bulges of a black, thickly armored vest set with thin silver chains that caught the light eerily, glowing an almost ethereal color of grey-white over patches of ashen skin that stirred unpleasantly in the depths of his coat. The muffled sound of interlocking armor plates clicking against each other echoed through the alleyway, suddenly drowned out by an inhuman laugh that somehow seemed more chilling than his dark and gothic appearance. He was the very essence of death incarnate, a modern retelling of the grim reaper himself, with even the old scythe abandoned in favor of a gun too large for any human to hold. It was impossible not to recognize him-- Cylea pulled in a wary, expectant breath. The pallid man, her Silent Savior, had arrived.

Shaking off his fear in one hasty, reflexive movement, Dai's weapon flicked up and hastily darted for the pallid man's face, but the action was too slow, too predictable. Instantly, one of the newcomer's thin, skeletal hands was on the Triad, clutching at his throat and yanking him up off his feet. One of the pallid man's boots scuffed against the pavecrete as he pivoted, carrying Dai all the way to the nearest wall in one solid movement with enough force behind it that the surface cracked on impact, belching a thin cloud of dust across his shoulders. Before Dai could manage much more than a choking gasp, the muzzle of the pallid man's gargantuan handgun snapped up and pressed in hard against his chest, pinning him to the wall with one skeletal finger held taut over the trigger. The Triad sputtered, struggling for the barest instant before his limbs went slack in resignation, but the pallid man simply grinned, his sadistic, amused chuckle echoing through the alleyway.

"Stop!" Cylea shouted, scrambling frantically out of the hoversedan. Instantly, the eyes of both men were on her, Dai's attempts at covering the panic and fear filling his gaze a perfect contrast to the dark, impassive lenses of the pallid man's sunglasses.

"No! Cylea!" Dai choked, mouth working soundlessly as the pallid man turned back to him and tightened his grip, crushing the Triad's throat. Fighting against the grip, Dai pried at the pallid man's fingers with weak gurgling sputters, managing to croak one more hoarse word before the fist tightened enough to silence him utterly. "Run!"

"Leave him alone!" The words ripped from her throat. It was a frightened, desperate scream, set loose and lancing through the air, intense and brutal. She wasn't about to let her Silent Savior kill her one chance at freedom-- without

Dai, there was nowhere to go, nowhere safe. It wasn't like she even knew where she was, and it would have been suicide to wander around, trying to find some familiar landmark or business that might give her an idea of where she was and how to get back... if she'd even had a place somewhere in Los Angeles to go back to.

The pallid man spared her a blank, almost innocent glance. There was no feeling in his eyes, no emotion, just the silent blankness of an inspection that seemed as basic and impartial as the glance of an infant– and yet his eyes were so heartless, so *cold*.

His eyes stayed locked with hers even as the barest twitch of acknowledgment crossed his features. He understood, or seemed to. The pause dragged on. Armored plates creaked expectantly under dark fabric. Cylea breathed a silently grateful exhale.

Then, in one smooth, unrestrained movement, the pallid man's finger came down hard on the trigger.

Two rounds pumped through Dai's chest and passed into the wall of the building with a pair of thunderous cracks– fractured pavecrete and rivulets of thick blood that ran against gravity shot up and across the alleyway, carried on the silence that followed like the ringing pounding deafly in Cylea's ears. She screamed, paled instantly.

It seemed impossible, unreal. Her mouth dropped open, lips quivering as she collapsed to her knees with little more than a noise of startled disbelief that was half grunt, half whimper. A cold sense of finality slowly settled over her, dropping across her shoulders and paralyzing her soul. Her eyes darted to Dai first, then slowed, slipping to meet the pallid man's gaze again, seeking an answer, seeking anything that might bring some cryptic reasoning to light or provide some way out of this situation, a situation that was looking more and more hopeless with every passing moment.

"Why?" She croaked, looking away as the pallid man released his grip on the Triad's convulsing corpse and let it slide unceremoniously down the fractured wall to the blood-stained pavecrete below. His boots echoed through the alley as he stepped slowly toward her, making his way between both bodies with long, deliberate strides. "You bastard... He– he..."

The pallid man dropped down onto one knee with the sound of a boot scuffing against pavecrete, and carefully inspected her in the silence. She looked up past harsh tears and met his eyes again, but the look in his own eyes was impassive, uncaring, his face that same blank mask swathed in folds and hard lines of black fabric.

Gently, he reached out and touched her shoulder. It was such a tender gesture, something gentle and meant to be comforting, yet it was so uncharacteristic of his brutal, sadistic nature– it was almost as if he were two entirely different people wrapped up in the same body, one violent and one kind, a cybernetic Jekyll and Hyde. Baring her teeth, she forced the thoughts aside and made an indignant, almost feral noise, slamming against his chest in a half-hearted lunge that did nothing to move him. He was as hard and unyielding as a brick wall, and her tears ran across the black fabric of his thick vest unimpeded, flowing freely with a harsh sort of desperation, a current fueled by all the pain she had been forced to hold back for so long.

"Zum donnerwetter! It's not fair" she screamed, sputtering as her hands clutched desperately for something to hang onto within his thick coat, fingers grinding against the coarse surface of his vest. Gently, carefully, his arms encircled her, holding her. Part of her wanted to hurt him, to dig her fingers into his flesh and hit him, but part of her was also grateful for the support. She sniffed loudly and buried her face in his chest, unable to do much more than wallow in the harsh emotions that boiled within her, fighting to come to the surface, refusing to be silenced. "Your such an *arschloche*." She burbled, getting only a soft, amused laugh in response.

Her hands found purchase on his chest. "Can't you say something for a change?" She asked, pushing away slightly to look up at him through moist eyes. The world beyond his coat seemed suddenly unimportant, inconsequential, a sour backdrop of color she was only to happy to forget about. "At least tell me your name so I know what to call you, you stupid bastard."

There was a long moment of silence. Heavy lines of concentration formed across his forehead and his brows furrowed, working and knitting above his shaded eyes. Chrome teeth flashed in the light as he opened his mouth, but no words came, just the edge of a sound, as deep, rich and strange as his laughter. "Gih..."

"Don't hurt yourself." She sniffed, gently wiping her eyes and smiling wryly despite herself. He watched her for only a moment more, then closed his mouth, a thin smile slipping across his face. "Gih, huh? That's not your name is it?" A chuckle and the slight shaking of his head was his only response. Slowly, carefully, he opened his mouth again.

"Gih...ins..." His tongue hovered between sounds, uncertain and held silent in the pause. "L... lee... Gih...n...s...ley" He paused again and pulled in a deep breath. "Gin.. sley."

"Ginsley?" She managed a laugh and he smiled back in response, the expression so basic and pure, utterly childlike, if it hadn't been stretched almost mockingly across a face that seemed like death's own visage plastered on a steel frame. "It doesn't really seem like it fits you very well. Is it a project name or something?"

His lips parted, but before he could respond, before he could even manage a gesture to answer her question, the bleating sound of approaching sirens reached their ears, drowning out the little noises in the alleyway-- the jangle of chains, the soft sound of fabric against fabric, and the amused, almost expectant chuckle that slipped from Ginsley's mouth as his bloodless lips peeled back in anticipation, shattering that soft, innocent expression in favor of a sadistic baring of chrome teeth.

"What--" She began, but already the pallid man was rising, suddenly aloof, and grinning like a madman drunk on blood. She caught his hand, but it didn't stop him-- his mind was already somewhere else, focused entirely on whatever twisted eruption of carnage he was planning, whatever visions of death were already spinning through his mind.

In the next moment, the first patrol car slid in behind Dai's hoversedan and all but blocked the entrance to the alleyway, lights flicking across the walls, siren blasting with deafening intensity. Instantly, one of Ginsley's skeletal hands was on Cylea, yanking her to her feet and pushing her behind him in a single smooth move, effectively putting himself between her and the phalanx of officers scrambling from a handful of patrol cars already lining up around the entrance to the alleyway with a cacophony of shouts and the clicks of disabled safeties.

Stumbling backwards, reeling from the noise, the sudden movement, and the panic that spiked dangerously within her, she came up against a wall as the massive weapon her Silent Savior carried bucked, belching fire. Three successive echoing blasts ripped into the cavalcade of squad cars and armed officers-- past the edge of his thick coat, she caught a glimpse of fragmented steel and plastic ripping through the air like flak, burning and falling across pavecrete and plasticore like cataclysmic rain. Bullets flew by, whizzing past and ricocheting off pavecrete as someone screamed and the steady thunk-thunk of rounds lodging themselves in Ginsley's armored body reached her, mixing with the sound of his insane laughter echoing across the walls. It was all too much-- already he was charging toward them, his handgun now longer and leaner, spraying half-size rounds without much discretion as to what he hit. Her ears ached, her mind ached, and the urge to flee was overwhelming. There was nowhere to go, but it was suicide to stay and see whether or not the pallid man would survive or go down in a blaze of glory like some easily forgotten hero. She swallowed-- there was only one course of action left.

She turned and ran. She ran, and she didn't look back.

Chapter 18: Metric Network Jazz

The sound of gunfire echoed all around her.

Reality blossomed into a hurricane of lead, a cacophony of fire so fierce and chaotic that she panicked instantly, her mind crazed with fear. At any moment, she expected a round to take her, to punch through her flesh and drop her to the pavecrete, bleeding and yelping like an injured animal.

Ground rushed by beneath bare feet. She pounded down the alleyway and slipped across a street, narrowly avoiding a speeding hoversedan that honked noisily as she passed. Her mind kept slipping back to Dai, to Hok, to the last time she'd had to run from the law to survive. The drawn, pallid face of her Silent Savior shot through her mind, followed closely by broken images of their first encounter, of Aiko's face the moment she'd collapsed, half her torso ground into hamburger, of Brent's back as he sprinted through the mud with Ginsley half a pace behind him, grinning and cackling like a madman. She blinked against the remaining tears caught and stirred by the air rushing by and steeled her heart– in all likelihood, they were dead, all of them, Brent, Aiko, Hok, Ying, Bao, and all the rest, all dispatched as reflexively and heartlessly as Dai had been. At one time in her life, she had actually entertained the idea that fate had a sense of humor, that it dealt out good and bad in a just fashion according to a system of karma or something like it, but now she knew that it was simply cruel, a sadist that teased her with good, trustworthy people and visions of a safe future, only to burn it all away in a single, violent bloodbath that left her running again, running until she could run no more, only to find death staring her in the face again at the end of every run.

The wound in her gut spiked with pain, interrupting her thoughts. It was still tender, still soft, viciously throbbing with every hurried step, every jolt that went shooting through it. She hadn't had the chance yet to see exactly how much of it had healed, but knew that it was not enough to put herself through this kind of strain, not yet. She bit her lip, breathed a quick prayer and an equally quick curse, hoping against hope that nothing would break or rupture. Internal bleeding was the last thing she needed.

Sprinting around a corner into a side alleyway a few blocks down from where her Silent Savior was still swapping rounds with a team of officers, reality froze in a sudden, unpleasant sensation of cold fear. Instantly, her feet slid to a stop beneath her and thought stuttered on the edge of a word. In the alley before her, another team of officers dressed in the dark blue uniforms of local law enforcement leveled their weapons at her-- the collective sound of a handful of pistols and shotguns cocking was enough to force her to swallow in sudden, almost panicked apprehension and take an uneasy step backwards. One of the officers, a man with dark eyes and a hawkish nose, stepped forward suddenly, forcing the muzzle of a formidable looking shotgun at her with all the kindness and consideration of a psychotic drill sergeant.

"Hands in the air! Right now!" He barked. She hesitated, and the cop practically screamed at her. "Do it!"

Instantly, her hands were up. One quick gesture with his weapon, and two officers holstered their handguns and stepped forward, one holding a pair of handcuffs. The dark-eyed officer chewed absently, watching her, hands firm and steady on his weapon.

"Ah, that won't be necessary."

The officers approaching her hesitated. The voice had cut through the air so cleanly, so unexpectedly, that even Cylea had looked up in surprise. Beyond the line of officers, a tall, well-dressed man flanked by two hulking bodyguards approached from a glossy black hoverlimo that sat idling at the end of the alley. He smiled benignly back, tugged gently at his tie.

"And just who the hell are you?" The dark-eyed officer wheeled on him, shotgun dropping almost casually to his side. All eyes flicked nervously from the officer to the well-dressed newcomer, no one certain of what to do next. The suit labeled the newcomer and his bodyguards as important, wealthy-- likely corporate, the kind of people who were more than capable of having you killed for a careless word or glance.

"Special Agent Castillo." The newcomer responded with a gentle smile and a flash of his badge. His accent was decidedly British, rich with a tone that was commanding, yet soft and cultured, the iron fist in a velvet glove and the voice of nobility trained to be both polite and firm, clean and direct, still young and charismatic, but tempered by uncommon patience and experience, the kind of man who made a good leader, the kind of man you were taught to trust. "Sorry boys, but I'm afraid that this is now officially government business."

The dark-eyed officer hesitated for only a moment, looked to the two officers halfway between himself and Cylea, and spat.

"Well, you heard the man." Instantly, the two officers nodded at their superior, then cast wary glances at Cylea before taking a few steps back toward their brethren. Castillo moved effortlessly through the line of officers, a knife through silk, his two bodyguards shouldering their way forward a few scant paces from him.

"I don't care who you are, but if you touch me, I swear to god I'll rip your arms off." Cylea growled, letting her hands drift back down to her sides. It didn't matter if he was government or corporate, Castillo radiated power and influence in an almost permeable fashion, something made all the more obvious by the little touches on his suit and his short, dark, nanocosmetically perfect hair style, shades of a dozen popular twentieth century actors. He was the kind of man she could see coming after her, the man or the liaison to the man that was willing to put up sixty million dollars to see her dragged in before him, dead or alive.

"My, my, such ferocity, such spirit!" He grinned, making a playful fist and shaking it. "Still, I must admit that I'd hate to have any of my limbs replaced just yet."

"You sure you don't want her handcuffed, Agent?" The dark-eyed officer cast a wary glance at Cylea.

"Quite sure." Castillo took a step toward her, his smile softening again. "She's not going to hurt me."

"Want a bet?" She arched an eyebrow at him and crossed her arms menacingly.

"Agent..." The dark-eyed officer shifted uneasily.

"Don't worry," the Agent took another step toward her. "I know exactly what I'm doing."

Cylea's eyes flicked from him to the two bodyguards and then back again. It was a long shot, but a well-aimed strike could injure the Agent and buy her enough time to run away– that is, if the line of officers behind him didn't instantly pelt her with mace-gel and rubber rounds the moment she so much as moved. Her eyes locked with Castillo's as he stepped toward her again, putting himself within striking distance. She licked her lips. It was now or never.

In one fluid move, her hand darted for his face, palm outward– a fatal strike would buy her the most time, leave one less person to chase after her. It seemed so simple, aimed so perfect, that her eyes widened and time seemed to stop as Castillo stepped deftly to the side, easily dodging the blow. Her mouth opened slightly– the ease and speed with which he had evaded the strike threw her off guard, leaving her stumbling and exposed.

Instantly, he seized her arm in one white-gloved hand and swung it back behind her, pinning her with a degree of finesse that seemed almost inhuman. It was a simple grip, yet modified subtly and held with such precision that any techniques Hok had taught her to break from it were useless, a point driven home by the stabbing pain that shot through her arm as his fingers tapped a handful of points across her skin and sent her nerves into a hot and panicked frenzy. As soon as she stopped struggling, he gently held up a hand to keep the two bulky suits that flanked him from moving in on her, their fists clenching in nervous agitation.

"Listen to me." He whispered, voice firm yet civil, with an edge that spoke of subtly veiled promises of savage cruelty and the experience to execute them flawlessly. "There are only two ways out of this situation. One is with me, and the other is with them." Her gaze swivelled toward him, and out of the corner of her eyes she saw his steel-grey stare, as hard and unyielding as her own icy blue glare. "Honestly, who do you trust more? The men with the guns, or the men with the suits?"

She pursed her lips in irritation. It wasn't easy admitting that she had been beaten, even if it might only be a temporary setback before she could manage to get free again. The choice was obvious– suits meant status, money, power, and sometimes even a softer touch. With a little luck, she would finally get the answers to all those burning questions, or even merely some of them. She wouldn't get anything from rotting in a cell until someone came to get her, besides perhaps a new series of injuries, and she was still too raw from her last run-in with violence to even consider that an option. Castillo's expression never wavered, that same hard, yet still strangely charismatic and oddly comforting look slowly melting away her desperate rage until she finally sighed and looked away.

A soft smile spread across his lips at her silent surrender as his grip on her arm relaxed steadily. "Good. I had a feeling you'd come 'round to reason." The look she shot him as she turned to face him was more of a glance than a glare, but the residual fury only made him smile wider.

"Come, there are a number of things I have been waiting for some time to discuss with you." He grinned, holding one white-gloved hand out in the direction of the hoverlimo. "Miss Cylea Von Mitternacht."

Chapter 19: Metric Network Jazz, 2nd Movement

"Who the hell are you?" She demanded. Outside the Hoverlimo, Los Angeles rolled by impassively. "Und don't give me that 'Special Agent' crap. I can tell from the suits that you're not government, you're part of something bigger, probably corporate."

"Nothing so philistine, I assure you." He grinned, snapping his fingers at the suited brute sitting next to him, his eyes never leaving Cylea's. Instantly, there was a beige folder in his hands, and his expression brightened slightly. "Thank you, James."

The brute managed a firm, shallow nod as the folder was easily handed off to Cylea. Castillo settled back in his seat and steepled his fingers in front of his lips, watching her with those steel grey eyes, so old and full of wisdom for someone that still looked so young.

"What is this?" She asked carefully, eyes flicking from the folder to meet his steady, unwavering gaze.

Castillo gestured lazily. "Go ahead, open it, it won't bite you."

Her eyes stayed locked with his for only a moment, carefully inspecting him, searching for something nameless that might betray any less-than-honorable intent, then shifted away and slipped silently back to the folder. Her thumb traced the edge warily, then slipped beneath, flicking it open in one smooth motion. As her eyes fell across the page within, a hard knot formed in her stomach, a cold strain of discomfort that shot through her heart at the sight of what was paperclipped to the first page. The cover dropped quickly back into place.

"What the hell is going on?" She all but shouted, shooting him a fierce glare. Castillo only grinned, the brutes on either side of him staying motionless, their faces as hard and unmoving as tempered steel. "Why is there a picture of a mutilated corpse in here!?"

"It's not just any picture," Castillo commented, his smile softening with amusement. "It's a silicon video capture-- same size, just as glossy, and yet capable of cycling through several dozen shots of the same crime scene to provide the optimum level of efficiency for space used. Very useful, and relatively inexpensive."

"Like I give a damn." She shot back, eyes as hard as her tone. "I asked you why it was in there."

"Because, quite frankly, I wanted to see how you would react." He shrugged absently. "Because it's one of the many things that we have brought you here to discuss." Gesturing vaguely to the folder, he shifted in his seat. "Don't you recognize the body?"

She met his gaze for a long moment, then curiosity got the better of her, and she looked down, fingers hesitating on the edge of the folder. An amused, half smile pulled at the edges of Castillo's lips. Carefully, she flicked it open again.

Two frames flicked by on the video capture before she recognized the body– it was difficult at first, considering the entire face had been turned into a pulpy mess of ragged flesh, but ultimately it was the lower body, the chair that was more life-support equipment than seat that betrayed the corpse's identity. She swallowed against tears– the name came unbidden to her lips, whispered in a tone that spoke of wounds she'd rather have forgotten about. "Smash."

"Good." Castillo grinned. "Now the next one."

Morbid curiosity drove her on. The next video capture was of a bloated body with a ragged hole in its chest, stretched unceremoniously out on the edge of a dock. "Brock."

"Mm." Castillo nodded as she flipped the page again.

"Kyoung-Mi," she shook her head and flipped to the last page, a series of still frames from when she'd gone sprinting blindly across a street and had been hit by a luxury hoversedan, a dusty gold Mersaroise Gullwing that had been utterly totaled by the accident. Pursing her lips, she closed the folder and looked up.

"So, you figured out that I'm not human." She shrugged, struggling to force wit over her failing fiery resolve. "Join the club."

Castillo chuckled quietly. "What you are is so far beyond human that it denies any conventional classification." He leaned forward. "These reports, these captures... they're proof of that, especially this– " He reached out and flipped open the folder again, going directly to Kyoung-Mi's page as Cylea looked on, unsure of how to react, and still locked in the grip of her own macabre sense of interest. The silicon video capture flicked silently between pictures– his finger slid across the page, and traced a line half-way down the length of the sheet. "Subject shows extensive damage to cranium consistent with high pressure and high temperatures. Cause unknown." His eyes met hers again. "The pressure damage is consistent across all your victims, so we can safely attribute it to your abnormal physical strength in times of danger, but the heat? The fact that you literally baked her brain into a soup, why that's--"

"Stop." She said levelly, forcing away the emotions with a cold wall of resolve. "Just tell me what you want with me."

"Only the same things that you want," Castillo grinned and leaned back in his seat again. "Answers."

"Well, I'm sorry, but I don't have any." She looked away, letting her gaze drift across store fronts that blurred by outside the windows. "That much should be obvious."

"Only because you have not yet been presented with the *means* to obtain them, I think." He paused and she met his gaze. His eyes were serious now, his tone honest and pure. "My people can provide that. We ask only that you allow us to help you."

Cylea watched him blankly for a long moment. "Und all you want in exchange is answers? I don't believe it."

"I can see how it would be difficult to trust an offer like that." He grinned again. "So I'll be perfectly candid with you. We don't simply want the answers, we want your loyalty, and we're willing to do almost anything to get it."

"Then you'll have to take it up with the Golden Koi Triad." She looked away again. "I don't think they're going to let me go that easily." She met his gaze again. "Is there some place in particular that you're taking me, or can you let me out at the next block?"

"Don't you think it would be wiser to let us help you?" His grin faded to a shadow of a smile. "My people have resources the likes of which I doubt you've seen or imagined before."

"Nein, because frankly, I don't trust you." She began, eyes already hardening with indignant resolve.

"And yet you'd place your trust instead in the hands of an international crime syndicate operating out of one of the largest festering sores of chaos and lawlessness on the face of the planet?" He shook his head, his smile all but gone now. "Your reasoning boggles the mind."

She chewed her lip for a moment. He definitely had a point, but there was no reason as yet to trust him, to blindly follow this handout without any thought given for the Triad that had helped her escape a situation that might otherwise have been hopeless-- and then there was the other side of that same tarnished coin-- by even speaking with Castillo, she might be putting herself in danger, an untrustworthy asset that someone as direct and no-nonsense as Shang might suddenly decide is too unreliable to let live. The choice between a prize, or a tool, however they saw her, that might slip from the Triad's grasp at any moment, no matter how critical, and the firm reassurance of a sixty-million dollar payoff was an easy one to make. She breathed a tense sigh and brushed aside the thoughts roughly; she couldn't let fear and impulse guide her actions, not when her life hung in the balance.

"Ja, whatever." She forced a tone of casual coolness that seemed almost icy, almost too aloof and distant. Handing back the folder, she gestured vaguely toward the side of the road. "You know, you can drop me off anywhere along here."

"Please, at least let us take you somewhere safe." Castillo's face instantly took on a worried cast. "Anywhere you'd like, just name the place." He all but pleaded. "Consider it an act of goodwill on my part, in case you change your mind about us. There are many things we can teach you, things that make the arts of the Triads seem juvenile at best."

"I'm sure." She managed, her tone degenerating into something absent and uncaring as her eyes darted back to the road blurring by outside the window. "Look, if you want to drop me off somewhere safe, find the nearest Triad safehouse or affiliate or whatever und let me out there. I can't think of anywhere else that's safer than that."

Castillo grimaced. "I'd rather not deliver you into the hands of a group as dangerous and unpredictable as that." She opened her mouth to say something, but he cut her off. "Regardless of the experiences you may have had, you cannot deny the fact that the Triads are criminals, and therefore unpredictable and inherently dangerous. If they were anything else, any tamer, they would never have survived for as long as they have."

Cylea set her jaw resolutely. "Ja? Then where? Can you think of any place safer?" This time, it was her turn to cut him off as he tried to say something. "Und not some place with connections to whoever it is you work for."

"How about the club your friend Jack works at? The Eye of Ra?" He asked, gesturing toward the front of the car. "It's just a few blocks up, if I remember correctly."

She swallowed uneasily. Thinking about Jack brought back a whole new wave of emotions. When she'd left to board that flight for Hong Kong, they'd agreed to meet again, but it seemed almost too soon, too many visits too close together. She couldn't bear the thought of Jack getting hurt because of the bounty on her head, and she didn't want him getting involved any more than he had already been. Inside, something fierce burned, telling her that the only way to protect him was to stay away, to put as much distance between them as possible until things cooled down at least to the point where even globe-spanning organizations like the Golden Koi could operate without having to step lightly every time they so much as twitched. Thinking about it brought back memories of Bao, painful little thoughts and the heavy regrets that came with knowing what Hok and his family had done for her, came with knowing that something as simple as her presence had ultimately destroyed the little harmony they had fostered together as a family beneath the roof of Chow Fun.

Castillo watched her absently, his eyes fixed and yet distant, ambivalent. In a way, it almost seemed like he could see into her mind, like he could read her thoughts and was merely lost in the jumble of emotions that festered and brewed and mixed like some tepid stew within her tired brain. She looked away suddenly, and he breathed a sigh, shifting ever-so-slightly in his seat.

"If you'd rather, I'm sure we can arrange some other–"

"Nein." She cut him off, eyes flicking immediately back to fix on his. "The club will be fine."

He nodded, and she looked away again, swallowing against the knot forming in her throat. She wouldn't stay long, just long enough for Jack to call in some of his contacts and find a new place for her to stay, and then she'd be gone again. She needed a place where she could think, a place where she wouldn't have to worry about people like Shang or Castillo popping in, a hole she could crawl into where no one would find her until she was ready to come back out into the light again.

It was a long shot, but if such a place existed, Jack would know exactly where it was.

Chapter 20: Dirty Pavecrete Blues

As the hoverlimo pulled up to the curb, Cylea shifted and immediately reached for the door. Instantly, Castillo's hand was on her wrist, catching her just short of the handle.

"Please, consider my offer, will you?" He gave her a soft, charming smile. "You can't keep running to the Triads or to your friend Jack. Eventually, one or the other is going to fall under pressure from outside forces and hand you over to the highest bidder." His smile faded slightly under her wary glare. "Don't tell yourself it won't happen, we both know that it will. It's only a matter of time."

She paused, uncertainty boiling past her resolve. A long moment passed before she swallowed, then finally managed a quiet "How will I find you?" His words had struck a chord with her, and the last thing she wanted was to burn any bridges that might ultimately mean the difference between survival and death in the perhaps not-so-distant future.

"Don't worry." The man's smile came back full force. "I have eyes and ears everywhere. Simply call my name, and we'll come for you."

"Sounds too easy." Her eyes narrowed ever-so-slightly. "Who do you work for, anyway?"

"I act on behalf of only the finest mankind has to offer." He grinned. "Perhaps next time we meet, I'll tell you all about us."

"If there is a next time." She managed a wry smile. "It's going to take more than just sugary promises und displays of wealth to get me to join anything."

"Name it, and it's yours." He immediately responded, that charming grin still stretched across his face, his tone soft, cordial, and yet ripe with seriousness and honesty. He obviously meant what he said, and the concept of a single individual having that much power at his fingertips was enough to make her head spin.

"Keep trying, Castillo." It took her a moment, but she forced a spunky grin. "Don't worry, if I need you, I'll let you know."

"That's all I ask." He let go of her wrist.

"Ja, well, don't expect to hear from me anytime soon." She shot back as she opened the door, stepping out onto the smooth surface of pavecrete sidewalk. Cool air brushed across her skin, and she pulled in a deep breath before continuing. "I plan to be in Hong Kong as soon as possible."

"That's a shame." Castillo began, traces of concern threading themselves through his otherwise impartial expression as he watched her with those steely grey eyes. "Someone of your *uniqueness* deserves better company than criminals, backstabbers, and thieves."

She paused for a moment, her eyes searching his face. Part of her urged her to trust him, to cut her losses and run away with Castillo before things got any worse, if ever they did, but a larger portion of her psyche insisted on remaining distant, still suspect of this new offer. It seemed too good to be true, and it was only too easy to remember that such things generally were just that.

Forcing a smile, she nodded silently, and Castillo returned the gesture, his own smile coming back full force. It was impossible not to admit that he was handsome, even charming, but then perhaps that was part of the allure, and yet thinking about it brought a twinge of pain to her heart. It had only been a few scant days since she had lost Bao, and yet it seemed as if an eternity were stretched out behind her like a tattered and bloodstained rug, a stretch of time she wished she could forget, and yet was secretly glad that it had stayed with her. What had Dai said? That he doubted any of Hok's family had died that day? Perhaps some twist of fate or luck would put her in Bao's arms again soon, letting her bury her face in his chest, breathing in his musky, orange-peel smell and crying desperate tears of relief as he held her, perhaps doing something romantic and sweet like kissing...

Suddenly she was aware of the pause, aware of the fact that the smile had fallen from her face and that she was standing there staring into Castillo's eyes. He offered a soft smile, and she struggled to return it, then turned away, wiping the building moistness of hot, determined tears from her eyes. She missed Bao, and it was impossible to deny it, but breaking down in front of someone as determined and persuasive as Castillo wasn't an option. She sniffed, and he seemed to take the hint; he only hesitated a moment before the door came closed, sealing him and his vatgrown escorts off from the outside world, from her. A wall of gloss-black metal and glass stared blankly back at her.

And then the Hoverlimo was gone, leaving her alone on the corner as it roared to life again and pushed off down the street, disappearing into the dull grey depths of Los Angeles with the gentle, purring hum of expensive, well maintained suspensors. Overhead, scattered clouds the color of dull, tarnished silver stirred restlessly with silent, almost ominous potential, slipping smoothly across a slate-blue sky crisscrossed with the fading white lines of contrails.

The street itself was quiet, empty. Only a few hoversedans lined the edges of the plasticore roadway, each cold and dark, floating silently in the gentle stirrings of their parking cycles. One glance to the right showed more of the same, just empty strips of grey pavecrete and the long black lines of a road detailed with the perfectly sculpted lines of nanoregenerative bioluminescent paint that had served as a guide for countless cars, hover or otherwise, since the day they had been laid down across that smooth, dark surface.

Her eyes flicked away again, wandering absently down the road, tracing the lines of a phantom hoverlimo that existed only in memory, a hoverlimo that part of her wished she had never stepped out of. She closed her eyes and took another deep breath. She had to have faith, had to have confidence that she was making the right decision. If she'd been religious, she told herself, she might have taken a moment to pray, or sing, or cross herself, or whatever it was that religious people did in times of self doubt. It had never been something she'd given much thought to.

Touching the key at her neck, she opened her eyes and turned to face the looming, golden shape of the club, its huge white neon eye, so stylistically Egyptian, staring down at her from its perch between the two massive, gently sloping pillars that framed the equally large shape of a door the color of screaming scarlet, that shade of bright, glossy red that typically graced fast cars or the lips of prostitutes and seemed out of place on the door of a nightclub that was mostly stucco spray painted with a cheap, peeling gold.

She stood there for a long moment, eyes drifting across the face of the club, taking in the details as her mind spun off into the realm of memory of its own accord. The world around her faded to the grey pastel of silent reverie, bringing back the loud nights of her past and casting the specters of long forgotten friends, associates, even some of the club's other regulars she'd only known by name across the dull metallic luster of the walls.

The first shadow to come into focus was Jimmy Daybach, his neon-blue fedora complete with that orange-glowing bioluminescent feather that stuck out of his hat and bobbed slightly as he nodded to her. He leaned against the wall, propped at an angle with one thin elbow, absently spinning an ancient coin –something he'd called a Morgan Dollar– through his bony brown fingers, acknowledging her silently and paying her as much, or rather, as little attention as he ever did. He had always been there, rooted to that same spot like some permanent part of the club that vanished in the daylight hours, only to reappear again the next night, like a holographic vampire, a man of the dark streets who seemed to have an odd affinity for the Eye of Ra, or perhaps he merely used it as a place to conduct his business. It wouldn't have been surprising, most of the club's regulars worked the night crowds in one way or another– the music was just a beat to keep the mind alert and alive, ready to seize any opportunity to make a buck.

Fading into the background, Jimmy gave way to the bulky shapes of the Latori brothers, twins with bodies that surged with thick knots of vatgrown muscle, not the expensive strains that the Chinese spun out of genevats and passed off on the open market for hundreds of thousands of dollars, but the cheap, domestic-grown kind that didn't have much more than cosmetic value. They came to the club nearly every night, always dressed in their modern replicas of the leather vests originally worn by the Hell's Angels themselves, identical down to the threadbare patches for hard liquor and bands so old they were remembered only by historians and in the cover songs of eccentric musicians. One or the other always found a chance to brag about the vests being genuine leather, or some new ear to fill with tales of drunken whorehouse raids on rumbling choppers, but she'd known better; she'd seen the same vests on sale at Swinzels, the shop downtown that specialized in vatgrown hide clothing, and read the same tales plastered to the walls of The Saxon, the run-down dive biker bar on the corner of Crenshaw and West Imperial.

She sneered unconsciously to herself. Neither of the Latori brothers had been happy when she'd called them on it, especially in front of the two women they'd had their arms wrapped around on that particular night, even if they were just a pair of nearly identical, emaciated orphans of the street, so high on neuro-nans that they were all but unconscious. It wasn't uncommon to see their kind in the club– life was hard on the streets, and nanohallucinogens were a cheap and easy way to take the pain away. Later that same week, the older twin –and only so by a good seven and a half seconds, or so he claimed– had ended up caught in the bowels of the legal system, on trial for eighteen counts of murder, all street orphans, all women abused by the dark underworld of society until they were all but dead inside, women just waiting to run into someone like one of the Latori brothers, someone who could release them from a world that didn't want them, didn't need them. Someone who could take the pain away once and for all.

After the sentencing, things had gone sour between her and the younger Latori twin– not that things had ever been anything better than grudging tolerance, but now the silences that lingered between them were thick with open hostility. One thing led to another, rumors started about sex, dirty, raunchy, hate-filled sex, and then he'd said something, something off color she couldn't remember, something that had cracked her self control and let the rage of every wrong she'd ever suffered pour through. She clearly remembered hitting him, the sound of bone shattering beneath her fist, and the shocked reaction of the scuzzy, green-eyed street orphan at his side as blood and teeth shot through the air. It was a mess. She hadn't seen all the damage, but she'd heard that it had taken extensive reconstructive surgery to fix, and he'd never said another word to or about her again, good or otherwise. From then on, he had actually been afraid of her, and remembering that made her uneasy, reminded her she wasn't truly human, couldn't be... *could she?*

She breathed a sigh, and her mind's eye shifted back to the doorway, to the big shape of Syle, the club's bouncer, a man built wide and thick like the son of a freight train, with every stretch of lightly tanned skin, from his arms to his scalp, shaved and polished to a shine that was reminiscent of smooth plastic, except where the black lines of intricate old-fashioned tattoos wound their way across his flesh, making him all that much more intimidating. She'd never exchanged more than a few words with him, a nod of greeting the few times she'd come in after the music had begun, perhaps a sentence or two here or there, but nothing really beyond that. But then, he was a naturally quiet kind of man, shy, or so Jack speculated, though Cylea had her doubts, especially considering his formidable appearance, and the fact that he was one of the few staff members who only stuck around the club when he was paid to. Where he went in his off time was a mystery even to Vinnie knew everybody-- It was Vinnie's club, after all.

So many times before, she'd walked through those doors, past Syle, past the crowds that haunted her memories, and into the smooth, wide-open dance floor beyond, immersing herself in the pulsing throng of sweaty dancers that shimmered liquid in the hazy metallic dust of airborne nanohallucinogens, surging against one another like the excited waves of a turbulent silver sea. The hypnotic beat was easy to get lost in, those mind-bending riffs of techno-jazz mated with death-metal muzak, the twisted, ear-shattering wails of a high-frequency distortion piano, a chorus of screaming, synthesized double-electric, reverse reverberation violins, and a bass beat that made the blood boil like nothing else to produce the flaming bastard child of music that was Zatvam. The sound reverberated across the smooth, grey walls of the club, bouncing and hammering the ears with relentless intensity as it played off the effects of the airborne narcotics in ways so strangely akin to sexual ecstacy and hypnotic euphoria that any attempts to put the sensations into words seemed hollow and oddly inadequate. It was human need distilled, youth and desperation squeezed from the pores of society by a world swollen and thick with the maggots of the past, a world whose children were trying to forget reality's every facet and lose themselves in emotion, in sound, in the basic pleasures of the body that denied the mind any control, any voice to stop or slow the actions and desires of the flesh.

Her lips drifted open, and she could almost taste the sweat, almost hear the music. A passing hoversedan shattered the reverie, and then the sensations were gone, lost on the cruel breezes of a tired civilization. Her feet were on the pavecrete again, and those days of becoming one with the desperate crowds of the night slipped back into the shadowy depths of memory, a part of her life that had come and gone. It was a younger Cylea that had danced for hours at a time, returning to her apartment in the dark-grey hours before dawn to wash the shimmering slickness from her tired limbs before she collapsed into bed, too tired to cover herself, too tired to sleep, too tired to do anything but lay there, naked and wet, staring up at the broken ceiling fan that spun sluggishly above her, wobbling and creaking with every turn of its rusty metal blades. It was a younger Cylea, and yet it was the same Cylea, that short stretch of time between her life before and her life now packed with an eternity of experiences that had ultimately changed her, jaded her, left her wishing for those days so full of that innocent simplicity she might never manage to recapture again.

She blinked, and a tide of harsh reality swept away the memories and the regrets, the wishes and the dreams, leaving her cold and empty, a shell of the woman she once was and yet so much more. The shadows of her past were numerous and rich with sensations that were easy to get lost in, but the murky, uncertain darkness of the future seemed to carry a weight all its own, pulling her back to the ground, back to the cold, hard pavecrete of reality before she could float off on the phlogiston of a past she'd lost to the cruel talons of fate and someone else's greed.

Breathing a sigh, she took one cautious step forward. Part of her urged restraint– of all the places she might go to seek refuge, the Eye of Ra was the most predictable. She doubted that Jack had been left alone– it had only been a few days since she'd last seen him, but images of the bartender being questioned or brutally interrogated by ruthless, suited vatgrowns already shifted through her mind, torturing her with the knowledge that she was to blame, that she was the core reason these corporates and government types were willing to do some of the things they had done in their attempts to capture or kill her.

She swallowed uneasily. With any luck, he hadn't been replaced– Jack was the best at what he did, and Vinnie would only have brought on a new bartender if things had gotten really out of hand, with feds and suits scaring away all but the club's most hardened regulars, or if Jack had disappeared utterly, spirited away in the silent, grey hours of the morning, never to be heard from again, or perhaps to wash up on some distant shore, a beaten and bloated, unidenifiable corpse that would be scanned, photographed, dissected, and fed into an industrial nanoreprocessor, atomically recycled into materials that would eventually become hoversedan parts or soda bottles or vend clothing or any number of other things that the world consumed *en masse*. Only the information recorded would remain, a series of stills like those that Castillo had shown her, paperclipped to an unmarked file likely catalogued under something as simple and callous as "White Male, Age 35-50"

The urge to restrain herself, to stay away from the club was quickly fading–she needed to see Jack, to know that he was all right. Deep inside, she was desperate for refuge, for sanctuary, for any kind of sanctuary, real or illusory, and the feeling was growing, flaring, building within her and urging her to run, to push through those red doors and sprint into Jack's strong embrace, to leave the cold, empty streets behind and pull every last ounce of safety and solace out of fate's cruel grasp until there was none left to fight for. She needed this, needed Jack, needed an excuse to forget the world around her, to forget about the bounty and the heartless masses that stirred in the shadows that she had once called home, waiting for the misstep that would set them on her like starved wolves

She swallowed again, closed her eyes, and breathed a shaky sigh, stilling her heart as best she could and pushing her fears roughly aside. Half a dozen paces put her at the door, curled fist hovering over smooth scarlet, hesitating for the briefest moment before coming down hard and delivering four clean, purposeful knocks that echoed through the empty, cavernous interior of the club like a hammer driving coffin nails.

For a moment, there was only the maddening silence, that quiet pause that tightened every muscle in her chest until she could scarcely breathe, and then the release ended it all– quickly, sweetly. Her heart jumped into her throat, suddenly tight as Jack's voice, so stereotypically Australian outback in every manner and nuance, came muffled through the door, so familiar, so simple, and yet something her very soul had ached to hear.

"Club's closed. Come back at four, yeah?"

Chapter 21: The Heart Beneath the Steel

"Jack!"

It came out suddenly, a harsh, hoarse, frightened yelp that ripped through the air with all the desperate, feral intensity of an animal's last bid for life. An instant later, just the scant passing of a tense moment, and the locks in the door withdrew. He reached for her, and she threw herself into his arms, pulling herself up as close to his warmth, as close to that familiar smell of leather and musk as she could manage. They stood there like that for a long moment, clinging to one another in the open doorway of the Eye of Ra like long separated siblings or friends that had gone beyond the trappings of romance long before, though the feelings were still there, feelings that ran deep, hidden away in the darkest corners of their souls where they could be ignored, all but forgotten.

Jack drew a shaky breath. It took him a moment, but with a quiet, ironic chuckle, he choked out a handful of heart-wrenching words that brought a layer of moisture to her eyes, a haze of wetness that was mirrored in the bartender's own gaze.

"They said you were dead, they... they said that you hijacked that bird and flew it straight into the drink, killed everyone in an instant." Cylea's eyes searched Jack's, moist blue desperately darting across that slick gray gaze, so like wet steel, the color of primer on a rainy day. "Some o' them reporters said they hadn't found your body in the wreckage yet, that you might be alive, but it just seemed like too long of a shot. All that ocean, all that money being offered for your head." He broke down, sniffing as a wide, crocodile tear rolled down his careworn cheek. She opened her mouth to say something, but he buried his face in her shoulder, drawing in one long, shaky breath. "I- I wanted to believe, but..." He trailed off, his voice muffled. "By jingoes, I'm so glad you're alive! Nobody should have to have so many run-ins with death at your age, least of all you..." He shuddered, blinking against the tears and the cheap fabric of her shirt as she squeezed him gently, feeling tears of her own pulling free and tracing thin lines across her face.

"I missed you, Jack." Her voice was oddly stable. Hot emotion had leaked through the layers she'd built up against it over time, but the effect it had on her tone was minimal, infusing every word with a cracking sadness. Somehow, the words seemed inadequate– it was such a basic phrase that she couldn't help but laugh quietly at herself, at the sheer inexpressability of the emotions that boiled within her –relief, love, longing, needing, hope, hopelessness– it all seemed like a single incomprehensible jumble, a concept drawn up in pastel that surged within her heart and within the stark confines of her mind, begging for release, slowly leaking out on hot, salty tears.

She tried to continue, but he gently shushed her, then looked away as she pecked his wet cheek with a soft, loving kiss. In the next moment, there was a metal hand between them, the fingers of the club's Ja-Serve droid, affectionately renamed Sheila by the bartender, gently urging them into the club, away from the eyes of anyone who might be watching, waiting for the moment to heartlessly end their little reunion with a shout or the violent, offensive bark of a weapon.

They broke apart then, only in form, hands still as close and connected as their souls. Their eyes met, worry and fear slowly giving way to relief and the tender kind of caring that came with two raw hearts beating together, that loving understanding that she had shared with so few people, a soul touching warmth that bound her to Jack in the same way it had bound her to Bao. Not love, but something deeper, an emotion, a connection for which there was no word, only sensations, only feelings, only those tender looks and touches that transcended the stark limitations of language and left a mark on the psyche that could never be forgotten, never be erased.

The three slipped silently into the club and let the door come closed behind them, shutting away the outside world as Sheila chirped her own perky, excited sentiments that Cylea was alive, and gently pulled at the edges of her french maid outfit with chrome fingers that seemed unusually shaky and nervous for a machine.

*   *   *

In a dark, rusty hovervan sitting lopsidedly on suspensors badly in need of maintenance, a single blinking red light came to life, flaring in the quiet darkness and casting a soft, scarlet glow across the hard face of a vatgrown corporate soldier dressed in a pristine black suit of perfectly cut silk.

He cast a quick, almost anxious glance in the direction of the Eye of Ra. It was still several blocks away and obscured by the stucco and glass bulk of a dirty, off-white storefront besides, but part of his mind saw it. In the dark recesses of that part of his brain that was no longer human, but rather machine, a static-laced camera feed supplied the visual, projecting those golden pillars and that scarlet door across the lens of his inner eye, followed by a stream of neon codes that his mind translated instantaneously. They were command codes, the identifier sequence for another vatgrown soldier, one of his many brothers. In one smooth motion, his finger flicked to his ear and pressed hard against the subdermal transceiver imbedded in his flesh there.

"Gabriel." He began, the name slipping from his tongue like rich silk. "Talk to me."

"Michael reports a sighting of the target at point lima with Dundee and the Tin Can." Came the quick reply. "All three are inside now. No sign of the GK boys or Captain Hook." There was a pause, a moment of brief and cautious hesitation between his words that spoke of apprehension, a quality, or perhaps a defect, that was rare in expensive strains like those that he had been grown from. Vatgrowns were supposed to be fearless, merciless, swift and deadly. Hesitation, caution, and fear were traits that, if determined during the initial stages of clone maturation, usually resulted in the termination of the individual, and in rare cases, the entire batch. how Gabriel had managed to survive was a mystery– still, he was a competent soldier, and his loss would have only weakened the team. Perhaps that was why he had been spared. "Should we proceed with action S-22?"

"No." It was sudden, direct, final. "The big man has given the bureau authority on this one. Notify the Agent immediately and support him with Uriel, Selaphiel, and Raphael, but leave Michael and Remiel in recon positions in case things start to get dicey."

"Roger that." Static bit into Gabriel's response. "Should I bring in team Hashmillam to secure the exits?"

The man in the van cracked his knuckles expectantly.

"No, keep them on standby as support for the Agent." He grinned. "And make sure to save me a spot up front. I want to see how this one plays out."

Chapter 22: Unstable Elements

The club's door burst open with the ear-shattering crack of a lock exploding through wood paneling. In the next instant there were four Vatgrowns in the gaping doorway, all higher-end models, all men that looked cut from the same mold, each seemingly a subtle variant on a central theme.

They were tall and lean, lightly tanned skin stretched across a gymnast's frame-- every one of them had the same style of closely cropped hair, as dark and chic as the suits they wore or the sunglasses that hid their dark eyes, every one of them as imposing and deadly as the next. Together they were like a pack of staggered stone pillars swathed in black, obelisks of almost biblical portent, every one of them envisioning himself as a reflection of the very angel of death.

For a half-second, the air was tense, chilled to a standstill by shock and a paralyzing strain of fear. In the next moment, Sheila screamed, shattering the forced calm, and then Cylea was on her feet, knocking over a barstool as Jack reached for the familiar shape of the handgun tucked into his belt behind his back.

Instantly, all three of the vatgrowns had weapons drawn, hard hands gripping snub-nosed automatic rifles that clacked in an almost excited, yet decidedly mechanical tone, the sound rich with a note of finality even as it was lost on an echo that bounced across the walls of the club. One of them, the one furthest back from the Bartender and Cylea, cracked a harsh grin.

"Don't even think about it, Mister Hutchinson." Came the immediate, ominous warning. None of the Vatgrowns had spoken-- the tall shape of a man stepped slowly into the club, shadows and dust parting to reveal another suit, this one cut almost as perfectly as those worn by the vatgrown soldiers, but of fabric half a shade lighter that was mostly hidden beneath the folds of a long, dark trenchcoat. A thick and equally chic pair of sunglasses came away from his face, revealing a pair of eerie, neon-green eyes centered over his strong nose and sharp, amused smile. She knew that face-- she'd seen it too many times before to ever forget it, and the realization forced a hard spot into the pit of her stomach. "Because if I see you reaching for that weapon again, I'll blow your head off, and that's the long-and-short of it. As a Special Agent of the Federal Bureau of Investigation, I've got enough experience to make that kind of threat and actually carry through with it."

"Brent." The name sounded more like a curse as it slipped from Cylea's lips than the vilest of words might have in its place. Ironically, or perhaps not so ironically, he smiled.

"Well, if it isn't my favorite little German girl." His smile widened slightly as his eyes shifted to meet hers. "Surprised to see me?" A handful of casual steps put him next to the bar and, glancing once at Jack, he leaned against it lightly, propping himself up with an elbow. "Your friend may have left me for dead but, unfortunately for you, I don't give up that easily."

"Obviously." She managed, tempering the venom in her tone with a degree of forced civility. Brent seemed completely and totally oblivious to it, still grinning at her like a salesman trying to pawn off some cheap nanoreprocessed hunk of plastic garbage with the word "wonder" or "super" in its name.

"Speaking of your friend, he wouldn't happen to be around, would he?" The Agent's grin slipped to one side of his face as he absently cast his gaze around the club. "I still owe him a good old-fashioned ass-kicking for what he did to Aiko," his eyes flicked back to Cylea, seriousness fighting for purchase under a now tight smile. "And, of course, for what he did to me."

"Must not have been too bad." Cylea chuckled sardonically. "You can still walk."

"Yeah, thanks to *prosthetics*." The word sounded so basic when he said it, so firm and unquestionable, yet so rich with loathing, a bitter word bit off by a man who felt the cold hand of the machine had finally begun to stifle the innate organic independence his body had once enjoyed, an independence that had been snatched away the moment his knees had been blasted into hamburger by some of Ginsley's lighter ordinance. "Nanoagents cut the swelling to almost nothing," he gestured vaguely, "but my partner, well, that's a different story. She's in much worse shape." He swallowed against a knot rising in his throat and looked away, his eyes suddenly moist and unusually dark. "For her, it was touch and go. Most of her torso was..." He shook his head.

"I... I'm sorry." Cylea managed. Nothing else seemed appropriate to say– Reflexively, Brent's neon eyes flicked up to meet her gaze, and he all but sneered.

"Yeah right, I'm sure you're absolutely guilt-ridden." The statement came out in a tone that was everything short of a snarl. The harsh, curled edges of his lips relaxed back into a half-hearted attempt at a smile as he made a tired, dismissive gesture and laughed cynically. "Whatever. We both know you're in league with that freak." Emotion fought beneath his features, boiling to the surface despite his attempts to maintain a calm, reserved facade– he was losing control, and the battle within him seemed almost tangible.

There was the barest pause, just a moment when it seemed as if control had perhaps won out, then he suddenly bared his teeth in a desperate act of defiance and stabbed a shaky, accusing finger at her. "You know, it really should be you in that tank, not Aiko." He bit the words off, his voice picking up a notch in intensity. "Better yet, you should be dead." Shaking his head again and pursing his lips angrily, he added in a growling, threatening tone: "Honestly, I have half a mind to kill you right here. The only thing stopping me from putting a bullet between your eyes right now, right in front of your Aussie wannabe friend and this stupid servedroid that thinks it's a Japanese schoolgirl or something is the fact that I want to kill your freak-friend first, and something tells me he won't come out to play if you're dead."

"And you're supposed to be with the bloody FBI." Jack spoke up suddenly, scoffing. "Whatever happened to due process?"

"Due process is dead." Brent's eyes met the bartender's "If I kill all three of you, and I will eventually, I'll be able to make up any story I want, and the best part is that these vatgrown boys will back me." He nodded toward the four thugs in the doorway. "Ain't that right Azrael?"

"As always, sir." The vatgrown furthest back responded, his voice calm and strong, the voice of a man used to taking orders and obeying them without question.

"That's a good boy." Brent smiled, his eyes never leaving Jack's. "See, that's what I like about these guys they grow in genevats; unlike ordinary people, these mass-produced clones actually know their place."

Jack opened his mouth to respond, but Brent promptly cut him off.

"You know what, that hat makes you look like a prick." In one smooth motion, Brent reached out and plucked the bartender's brown, felt, outback-style hat off the man's head and pushed it snugly onto his own. A wide grin spread across his face, and those neon green eyes flicked to Cylea again, rich with condescending amusement, begging her to say something, anything that he could turn around and chastise her for. Clenched fists shook angrily at her sides.

"What?" He chuckled. "Don't I look sexy? I mean, the color of the hat really goes well with my eyes, don't you think?"

"No." Jack broke in, his tone level, direct. Instantly, all eyes flicked to him, but his gaze stayed fixed on Brent. "It makes you look like a bloody kiwi."

There was only a moment of hesitation, an instant of emotion waging a fierce battle against the Agent's control, sinking its harsh talons through the semblance of smooth calmness he'd been trying to foster and grow, ripping and rending until his rage could leak through, and then he was on the bar, crouched down like some kind of animal, eyes burning with a feral rage as he pushed his handgun in Jack's face, finger tense against the trigger.

"I didn't ask for *your* opinion." The Agent bared his teeth again, almost growling. "You know, I really don't need you. You're not much more than dead weight as far as I'm concerned." An amused cast came over his features. "I want a reason. Give me one really good reason why I shouldn't kill you right here, right now."

"What the hell is wrong with you, Brent?" Cylea shouted. Wasting only a moment, the Agent reluctantly tore his eyes away from the bartender's to meet her intense gaze. "Is it just suddenly okay for you to go postal now that Aiko isn't here to hold onto your freaking leash? You're a federal agent, aren't you?" She paused, and in the break, that dark flame within her breast flared, begging for her to seize it and smite Brent with whatever strength she could muster before he threatened to shoot anyone else. "Fucking act like one."

It wasn't much, but it was enough to take some of the heat out of his eyes. Jack relaxed ever-so-slightly as the weapon was slipped back into the folds of Brent's coat, but his gaze stayed hard and wary, the untrusting stare of a man expecting death to rear its ugly head at any given moment.

"You certainly are uppity all of a sudden." Brent slipped back off the bar and forced a casual smile, though rage still burned in the neon depths of his eyes. Some of the control had come back, but it was obvious that his restraint was thin, his patience nearly consumed by his anger and the burning need for revenge. "You on your period or--"

"You want a shot at the guy in the dark coat, Brent?" She cut him off suddenly, all but snarling as she drew some of that dark fire forward, siphoning off some of that insidious potential and bringing it into the light to fuel her confidence and burn away her fears and doubts in a bright flare that left the dim, cool greyness within her exposed. It was all so close, surging and begging for release, so close she could touch it, so close she could feel the power burning out of control somewhere deep within her being, ready to roar through the floodgates of her mind and rush through her body. What it was capable of, what it wanted to do, she was unsure of, but it begged for release and fought against her control like a rabid and starved animal chained outside a butcher shop, crazed and hungry for the only thing that would satiate it-- the raw bleeding meat of wild carnage.

Her hackles rose and Brent hesitated visibly, almost taking a step backwards. Somehow he seemed to sense it, seemed to be able to pick up on the thing brewing within her, and it made him uneasy. Some part of her took a sick joy in knowing that, but it was a small part-- she had to fight to concentrate and keep the beast within her from ripping open its fragile cage. Sweat beaded on her forehead, and a smug, eager smile slipped across her face as she continued.

"Do you really think facing him is anything less than suicide?" The smile continued to spread, becoming a near mirror of that same sharp, wicked grin that she'd seen on Ginsley's face so many times before. That same wicked laugh seemed close, almost like a reflex aching to be satisfied, and the thought scared her-- part of her mind seemed as insane and eager to satiate its desire for bloodshed as her Silent Savior always seemed to be, slowly spreading its influence through her mind like the insidious tentacles of some deadly poison.

"Go home, Brent." She chuckled, and it was Ginsley's voice that echoed within her head, or rather it was Ginsley's voice that she heard, that same undercurrent carried on her words and laughter that she'd heard in his. Brent bristled visibly, more in fear than anger, but every hair on his body seemed to stand on end at once. "Go home und take your corporate fuckheads with you before you all end up regretting that you ever even picked up a weapon in the first place."

The pause was brief, cold; in the ensuing silence, while Brent seemed to be wavering beneath her icy gaze, unsure of what to do, the vatgrown furthest back grimaced and stepped forward, every tap of his expensive shoes hard and precise, the very sound of authority and power.

"Agent Revna, we cannot–"

"Shut it, Azrael." Brent spat, "If you honestly believe I might let this little girl talk me into leaving here without that man's head, or at least a good-sized chunk of his corpse, then you're a bigger fool than she is." He drew his pistol and pointed it directly at Cylea, thumb easily pulling back the hammer. "Stop whatever it is you're doing. I don't like it."

"Does it make you nervous?" She asked, still grinning maniacally despite the fact that Brent had put a gun in her face. She was staring death in the face again, and some dark, sadistic part of her seemed almost giddy about it.

"Doesn't matter." He bit off, baring his teeth again. "Stop doing it now." He swung the handgun smoothly toward the bartender. "Remember, I don't need him or the Ja-serve, so I suggest you listen to me, unless you want to see what they look like as corpses."

Cylea sneered; the darkness within her was boiling now, frothing, threatening to spill over at any moment and break through her control in a desperate explosion of burning hate. Something twitched spasmodically within her chest, one last bastion of restraint crying out for her to back down before she did something she might ultimately regret.

"Last warning." Brent said, eyes locked with Cylea's. "You've got three seconds."

A cold spot shot through the flame within her, and the wicked grin that had spread almost unchecked across her features slackened slightly. Fighting for control, she seized that sense of calm restraint immediately, clinging to it, struggling to reign in the feelings, to conquer the rage and the darkness within her before it was too late. Brent's voice was level and direct. "One."

Breathing deeply, she shot a glance at Jack. He blinked, trying to maintain his own facade of cool, assured bravado, but the threat of death was wearing it down, wearing it so thin that it seemed as if he might crack at any moment. It was sobering, seeing the bartender on the verge of panic and tears– it was something wholly new that Cylea wished she would never have had to witness, something that disturbed her deeply. It was all too much all at once for him, and the change in his demeanor was almost too much for her to bear without breaking into tears herself.

"Two." Brent cocked his head to the side. "This is not a game, Cylea. I hope you realize that I'm not fucking around here. I really am ready to kill him."

"Brent." She managed, turning back to him and taking a deep, relaxing breath. "It's done."

He watched her carefully for a long moment, seemingly inspecting her, searching her eyes for some kind of proof, and in the next instant, his arms relaxed slightly, his finger no longer tense against the trigger. The muscles in her shoulders unknotted subtly, slowly, and she glanced at Jack again.

The gunshot rang out cleanly, as cleanly as the round came punching through her left shoulder. In the next instant, Brent was on her, carrying Cylea to the ground while the Vatgrowns kept Jack and Sheila pinned in place with the threat of being perforated by a quartet of high-velocity automatic rifles. Her mouth came open in a silent scream as the wind was knocked from her lungs, Brent's eyes filling her vision. The pistol came up hard against her head, muzzle pressing ruthlessly into her temple.

"Stupid bitch." He snarled. "I can't wait to see the look on your face when I kill that freak. I'll cut off whatever's left of his skinny little head and drop it in your lap before I kill you. It'll be something you can take back to hell with you when you go."

"Fuck you." She spat back. "You haven't got a prayer."

"You've got way too much faith in your friend." He whispered back, hesitating only a moment before he lashed out viciously with the butt of his handgun, hitting her squarely. She hardly had time to sputter– darkness came instantly.

Chapter 23: Behind Inhuman Eyes

It was a little after four when the band arrived.

Strapped to a cheap office chair in the club's bunker-like aquatic room with enough monowire and atomically-hardening nanoelastic cable to keep her from doing much more than breathing without getting blisters or severing a limb, Cylea's only means of discerning the level of activity on the floor above came from the little sounds that echoed across the walls whenever one of the vatgrowns came pushing through the door to check on her or to confer with Brent. The Agent had been unhappy when she'd woken, and his mood had only deteriorated from there. Ginsley hadn't shown himself yet, every sensor and alarm had stayed silent, untripped, and every vatgrown eye within three blocks had reported in regularly, offering nothing more than the occasional homeless man or woman and the usual packs of skinny bicyclists that pushed sporadically through the streets on a sort of mass aluminum exodus that only ended once they reached the dirty little nooks and crannies that housed whatever struggling, ethnically-oriented businesses they had managed to find work at, from Panderias and Italian delis to liquor stores and Chinese pharmacies.

If Ginsley knew what was going on, and she suspected that he probably did, then he was simply waiting, but for what, she couldn't tell. With a little luck, he'd manage to catch Brent and the vatgrowns by surprise and leave the Agent with something a little more substantial than just two false knees to remind him that her Silent Savior was more than he could handle. The agent needed something that would instill some fear, something to foster a healthy sort of respect that just might keep him away from her for good, if only for fear of crossing paths with Ginsley again. Not that there wouldn't be others, but Brent was different somehow, a creature all his own, a man with an almost wolfish demeanor and those odd, neon-green eyes, among a dozen other things, idiosyncrasies and mannerisms that put his very humanity in question, perhaps as much as her own. It was a fact that left her feeling oddly connected to him, wondering if he even knew what he was, and if so, did he know something that might shed some light on some of her own mysteries, perhaps answer some of the questions that burned within her about the very nature of her being?

She looked up and locked eyes with him. He sat quietly in another cheap office chair directly across from her, his hand still wrapped around the grip of the handgun he had used to knock her out twice now, the pistol she had seen flashing out of his coat nearly every time they'd crossed paths since that first time, when he'd met her in the very same club and tried to snare her for selling a copy of Ivan Wajahowski's 'Evil Empire'. It wasn't much, just a disc imprinted with a piece of political commentary that had been banned globally, along with a hundred or so other books during the commercial accords of 2060, when Ted Solomon had singlehandedly seized the reins of commerce and wrangled every corporate bigshot with half a brain cell and a fistful of dollars into a swollen agreement that bordered on a global monopoly on nearly anything that they could slap a price tag on.

Even when she looked away again, Brent's eyes never left hers, never wavered. They stayed locked on her, fixed perfectly in place, like those of a cat just waiting for its prey to step into paw's reach. The likelihood that she could escape, even left unguarded, was almost laughable. One wrong twitch and the monowire would slice into her skin like a hot knife through butter, and the Agent would probably just let her bleed, smiling as death came for her yet again, its cold, skeletal fingers itching to claim the soul it had fought so hard to seize for so long now. Of course, it didn't help any that she'd been beat absolutely to hell, to say the least, during the process of the past few days, her body wracked by so much abuse that she hardly felt the pain anymore, just a dull, throbbing sensation that drilled at her mind, burying her awareness and control beneath a heap of fatigue and numb, uncomfortable warmth.

She shook her head, more to keep herself awake than to dispel whatever thoughts of getting answers from the Agent might have been percolating through her mind. If Brent knew anything, it was a sure bet that he wouldn't tell her. As far as he was concerned, she was just a bounty, an organic check waiting to be cashed in behind the back of the very government he worked for, conspiring with an organization that was merely a body of that government, a sick and dying, almost vestigial agency, to shuffle sixty million dollars into a handful of private bank accounts, each deposit disguised as a donation, which was merely a kinder word to use than something more appropriate, such as "bribe" or "payoff", as well as an easy way to secure himself a hefty chunk of the cash for an early retirement besides.

She sighed, forcing her wandering mind back. Part of her was worried, worried that Brent might get tired of waiting for her Silent Savior and start making threats, or worse, start shooting people, Jack and the Ja-serve or otherwise. With the amount of airborne nanohallucinogens floating through the club at the highest points of activity, it wouldn't be hard for Brent and the vatgrowns to go on a shooting spree and manage to get away with it by claiming that each and every casualty was little more than an unfortunate circumstance of a botched narcotics raid.

An uneasy swallow forced the knot in her throat a little lower. She had to have faith, had to trust that she had made the right decision in turning herself over without a fight, in giving total control of the situation over to Brent in a desperate gamble that, if she were lucky, would save not only the bartender and the Ja-serve, but keep Brent from popping up unexpectedly again. She couldn't help but laugh sardonically to herself at the arrogance of her own thoughts-- she might have had the chance to end it, she might have been able to lose control and single-handedly put down Brent and his quartet of vatgrowns, but it had been a fleeting moment, one that wasn't likely to return.

And yet, there was still a tiny part of her that worried for the Agent. Regardless of what he had done to her, regardless of how he saw her, how he treated her, he was still human, or perhaps only something close to it, but close enough that she couldn't help but see him as such, and no matter how hard the trials time forced her to overcome might make her, no matter how jaded and direct she might become, so far from that carefree and all-but-innocent girl that used to dance and use every ounce of her charm to get her way and soften the edges of harsh reality, she still had an innate sense of compassion, the basic belief that at the core of everyone's being lay goodness, something pure and untouched by the rigors and darker moments of life. In a way, she almost wished Ginsley might choose to stay away, that Brent might perhaps come to his senses or even turn coat unexpectedly, becoming a new savior, a secret, suited savior like Castillo and not merely a vindictive opportunist *arsheloch* intent on indulging his cheapest, most basic emotions at the expense of others and in the name of the justice system he had pledged himself to.

It was thoughts of him holding a gun to her head, thoughts of him urging his partner Aiko to take advantage of the bounty on her head and that harsh gleam in his toxic green eyes when he looked at her that made her jaw harden suddenly, making every moment of sympathy she had felt for him into a bittersweet evil. His eyes were so full of pain, so full of rage and a handful of other emotions that boiled fitfully in their verdant depths, poisoning him slowly, steadily, rotting him from the core outward as it all mingled with his greed and something darker, an older pain that he carried with him as obviously as if it were painted on the breast pocket of his smooth, dark suit.

The sound of the band warming up with a few broken fragments of popular Zatvam riffs echoed across the smooth cement walls as one of the corporate suits stepped crisply into the room and came to stop a scant few paces from the Agent, his face as cold and emotionless as the face of a statue, as if his very features had been chiseled from a chunk of hard, unmoving stone.

"Remiel has made contact with Captain Hook." he stated plainly, only the slightest touch of unease in his voice. "The target is moving fast through point Québec and point Romeo for a northeasterly entry into point Lima. He's running in stealth mode, looks like Total-Optic Camouflage, and should be arriving within a few minutes at his current speed."

"At last," Brent stood, "I was wondering when the big man himself would show. He certainly took his sweet time." he shrugged. "Whatever. Tell Pan his dinner is on its way."

The vatgrown nodded once, curtly, then turned on his heel and left, departing as stiffly and formally as a well-disciplined officer might have in the days before the word soldier had become associated with corporate-financed clones that had more in common with assassins and thugs than generals and those who actually fought on the side of freedom. Everything Smash had taught her about the twentieth century made the comparison almost comical, if it hadn't been so utterly depressing to really consider.

"You haven't met Peter yet, have you?" An amused, half grin popped across Brent's face as Cylea's eyes flicked up and met his. "He's really something. Pretty much a masterpiece. They put a lot of work into him, and it really shows in how he fights."

"If Captain Hook is who I think it is, you better start saying your prayers while you still have a chance." Cylea shot back immediately, ignoring him. "Because once he gets here, all hell is going to break loose, und you'll have a front seat to your own personal version of the apocalypse as the whole fucking world burns und falls in around you."

"How very poetic." He laughed wryly. "Can I quote it before I send you and that pale-skinned freak back to hell?"

"He's going to rip right through those vatgrown fuckheads und leave you begging for mercy on those new knees of yours." She continued, laughing. "Four suits und you?" She shook her head quickly. "You've got about a snowball's chance in hell."

"Maybe, but then, that's why we brought Peter along with us. After all, someone of your friend's prowess needs more to entertain him than just a handful of lost boys." A harsh, sadistic smile crawled across his face, something so full of dark intent that it reminded her immediately of something Brock might have done, and she shivered uncontrollably. "That is, if your guardian angel is even capable of standing up to our pride and joy." He laughed. "And if I remember the story correctly, it was Peter Pan who was the victor in the end, not Captain Hook."

"You know your fairytales. I'm so proud." Cylea bit off harshly, but her mind was elsewhere. This was something she hadn't counted on, something that worried her. After seeing Ginsley in action twice, she was certain that he could handle Brent and probably all of the vatgrowns as well, but this Peter was a new variable she hadn't considered, something that just might dash her plans against the rocks like so many fragile eggshells and leave her floundering in a dangerous ocean of uncertainty, caught on the vicious barbs of a steel hook reeling her steadily toward oblivion and the eager hands of death.

Brent's harsh, leering grin filled her eyes, so full of confidence, so assured that it cast a shadow of doubt across her heart, shaking her resolve and leaving her questioning her faith in her Silent Savior. She swallowed uneasily again–death might be a welcome release from the pain and abuse she'd suffered, but she wanted to survive, wanted to cheat death and find herself on the favorable side of the hand of fate again, even if only just once more. Only the future and perhaps God, if ever there was one, truly knew whether she would scrape by again or see her guardian angel fall in a blaze of hollow glory before she finally met her end at the hands of a man as inhuman as herself.

Only time would tell, and all she could do was wait.

Chapter 24: Burning Nocturne

It began so quickly, so fluidly.

A shimmer of light rippled across the scarlet surface of the door. A Vatgrown pushed a pair of smooth, dark shades in hard against his eyes with a gloved thumb, the long, polished shape of a sleek black assault rifle lifting from within the folds of his dark suit. Silver nanohallucinogens caught the light smoothly, flinging rays of green, red and blue through the club, rays that rapidly traced their way across hard, chiseled faces, sweat-slicked bodies and pallid skin alike. Through the blaring music, there was silence– the hectic, electric quiet before the worst of storms, that period of preparation when weapons were drawn, lips pursed anxiously, eyes darting from shadow to shadow. A thin smile stretched across a waxen pale face, drawing up at the corners to reveal a sharp grin the color of harsh chrome.

Gunfire erupted suddenly, a cascade of thunder and flame that shattered the hypnotic sounds of the band, hacking through the musical nuances with all the finesse of a blunt and rusty knife. There was no pause, no brief instant of tranquility between the hurried silence and the moment that the Eye of Ra erupted into chaos– it all happened so suddenly, flowing together as panicked dancers and junkies stopped mid-step and scattered, hurtling for the door, bouncing off one another as rounds went tearing and hissing through the air, each chased by flashes of light and echoing cracks that drowned out the already disintegrating music with their harsh staccato barks.

Someone screamed, a Vatgrown shouted something that was lost in the chaos, and the solid thunk of rounds burying themselves in flesh and armor alike filled the air, accented by the sound of hot, ricocheting lead bouncing and splintering through the silvery haze like so much ragged shrapnel. The thick, wide brim of a dark hat shimmered into the fog of chromatic dust, a hard black line over drawn, ashen cheeks and that sharp, silver smile of a madman. One gnarled, pale hand twisted across the grip of an impossibly huge firearm, something he wielded like a pistol that belched flame and lead with all the ferocity and power of a cannon, and his thick, dark boots squealed against the smooth floor, every blast buffeting him with enough recoil to crumple any ordinary man.

But he was no ordinary man. He was Ginsley, and his every move was blunt grace, smooth power dealt with careless precision.

Two vatgrowns went down instantly, one air-rending round catching the first in the shoulder and sending him spinning off into the crowd, little more than a pair of legs supporting a grisly pillar of frantic, bloody meat while the second merely splattered against the wall, one arm twitching spasmodically as he drew two final, desperate breaths through the tatters of shattered lungs. A third vatgrown shouted, running toward Ginsley, wildly squeezing off rounds as the pallid man's sadistic smile loomed in the dark surface of his sunglasses and that monstrous weapon swung toward the clone, chains jangling, breech smoking and hot, eager to loose another round and deal death with swift, definitive justice yet again.

Pale blue eyes shifted with a twisted sense of excitement. The weapon bucked, and suddenly the vatgrown's rush was cut short, leaving him stumbling, finger twitching and faltering on the trigger of his assault rifle, a ragged depression between his shoulders where his head had once been. Crimson traced its way through the creases of his suit as he tripped over himself and collapsed onto the floor with a spasmodic burble. All around the two, innocents surged by, running panicked for the door, trampling the weak beneath their frantic, collective feet.

And then, suddenly, there was a fourth vatgrown in the calmness between streaming lines of frantic humanity. Hair disheveled, one button ripped from his suit, and a maddening grin to match Ginsley's stretched at an odd angle across his face– he looked almost human, almost original, something more real and unique than the mass produced clone that he was. Fluidly, he threw his assault rifle to the floor, and shed his suit coat with a flourish, letting it fall in a heap of smooth dark silk.

"I am Azrael" He said, voice eager and anxious, fingers sliding quickly down the smooth, hairless lengths of both arms to seize a pair of grooved rings jutting from his elbows. In one fluid, seemingly effortless movement, he flung his arms wide, ripping open the soft skin of his underarms as he drew out two long lengths of wire so thin they were only visible where they caught the light, and seemed to slice the very fabric of reality where they passed, shimmering with deadly promise.

Crimson shot through the air as Azrael wove a deadly web in the silver haze, then whipped the wire so that, for a moment, it took on a shape vaguely reminiscent of the silver-black edges of a pair of massive wings, the air between their borders shimmering suddenly with the excited shrapnel of fragmenting nanohallucinogens and a thin, scarlet mist of his own blood. His eyes burned with a dark, unearthly fire as he bowed elegantly, a web of monowire descending behind his back, the skin lashed with a network of harsh, bleeding lines. He grinned sadistically, then added: "I am the angel of death."

Ginsley's grin stretched wide as he chuckled, just two quick, eager bursts of sound that echoed through the club, carried on air that was already starting to dull for the sudden lack of nanohallucinogens being pumped through the ventilation system. His waxen, skeletal fingers twitched anxiously against the sleek dark steel of his weapon, itching and excited while Azrael watched silently, silver-black wire drawn taut between his hands, wet scarlet running down his arms to patter quietly against the floor.

The squeak of a thick boot against smooth floor abruptly shattered the moment. As Ginsley swung his weapon toward Azrael, the vatgrown slipped lithely to the side, flicking a finger toward the pallid man, wire and ring rolling smoothly across skin and fabric to lash out and kiss the man's ashen cheek just hard enough to slice a line of bleeding royal blue across his waxen skin. As the monowire fell away, catching the light, Ginsley's grin widened-- so few men seemed capable of making him bleed, but this vatgrown clone had done it so quickly and effortlessly, a single fluid movement that was likely little more than a taste of what he was truly capable of. A sadistic laugh echoed from behind Ginsley's sharp chrome teeth, an excited sound filled with a sick sort of glee that seemed almost inhuman, almost demonic. Angel of death indeed-- the prospect of facing his own demise was enough to get the pallid man's heart beating, throbbing fast against the walls of his armored chest.

Veins pulsed across sickly ashen skin, a thick web of rich blue lines over hard knots of surging muscle. Black steel rose with a burst of echoing laughter as Ginsley's pale blue eyes widened imperceptibly, pupils pushing back color and replacing it with an ominous darkness. Azrael's fingers wove the wires quickly, smoothly, nimbly, rings spinning and shifting across skin as lines of silver-black shot through the air. Time seemed to slow, reality to blur-- it was fast, calculated, every move met and countered in an incredible dance of barking gunfire and deadly wire, but neither man could avoid every strike. Rich scarlet and deep azure mingled on the floor, blood flowing freely from a thousand tiny wounds, a collection of grazes and nicks that wept openly, leaving that amalgam of hemoglobin spread and slicked across smooth grey like the pallet of some mad artist, every step and pivot stamping a sticky mixture of the two thick fluids into the center of a grisly canvas framed with corpses.

Sliding to the left, Azrael's grin widened a trace, the shock of a round passing a scant few inches from his face leaving a moment of deaf ringing in its wake. Wires crossed, keening as they burned across one another, and Ginsley shifted half a step backwards, tracking a slow-moving coil of wire as it darted toward him. It was all so perfectly calculated— in the next instant, Azrael pulled, fingers flexing, yanking wires apart with every ounce of strength he could muster as he swung his arms wide.

Instantly, Ginsley's weapon pivoted to the left, dragging his arm with it. The move caught him off guard, and even as he struggled to recover, twisting nimbly, the wires bit into smooth metal, gaining purchase for the briefest instant before they slipped and sliced cleanly through, carving out thick, angular chunks of steel as easily as a larger wire might have cut through soft cheese or clay.

As the pieces fell away, clattering against the ground amid the trampled and smeared leavings of the frantic and grisly dance of deadly grace that had slowed to a virtual stand still nearly as suddenly as it had begun, Ginsley's eyes locked with Azrael's, the smile gone from his waxen features and replaced by a blank, flat expression more like the silent gaze of death than the wicked skull-like grin he usually wore. His finger twitched anxiously against the lifeless trigger, jerking spasmodically like the fingers of an addict trying to squeeze one last trace of a dose out of an empty syringe, that painful block of desperate need growing in his mind, surging through his limbs, tightening his veins. It was useless— Azrael's monowire had sliced through every component that kept the weapon functioning, leaving nothing more than a ragged stump of black steel in his pale hand, something almost worthless as a weapon, except perhaps as a short club. Not that it would slow Ginsley down any— the prospect of bludgeoning the wire-wielding vatgrown to death with a broken gun held the promise of a unique sort of sadistic satisfaction that the pallid man was eager to experience. He flexed the muscles on his free hand as the smile cracked across his face again. He'd have to be faster, craftier— it was time to end the dance, and there were a thousand wonderful ways to do that, each as bloody and ultimately satisfying as the next.

Azrael chuckled as Ginsley shifted in his stance, right foot sliding back across the floor. In one fluid movement, he raised the stump of his pistol and pointed it directly at the Vatgrown, squeezing the trigger as his mind screamed into overdrive, plotting, preparing, analyzing. His lips pursed, and a single word slipped from his mouth, so full of purpose and intent.

"Bang."

The pause was deafening. Azrael blinked, Ginsley's smile widened.

"Wha–" Azrael chuckled again, wires going slack. "Is this, is this some kind of joke? Bang? You've got to be–" Ginsley struck like lightning, slipping in between loops of relaxed monowire with the same flawless, graceful precision and plunging his free hand solidly into the vatgrown's gut. Surging pallid fingers cut through flesh and organs, sheared through soft tissue and seized bone, snapping and twisting until his eager digits punched through to the other side, dragging ragged shards of bone and a perforated length of intestine with them. Azrael's dark eyes met Ginsley's pale blue in one silent instant of shared understanding, one tool of mankind to another, and for the first time in his life, the vatgrown felt fear– that sharp chrome grin, the very visage of death, sent icy daggers of sheer terror screaming into his frantic heart. The very thing that he had embodied for so long had finally caught up with him. Death was at long last ready to receive him and take him back into the dark bosom of oblivion.

"Hey you." The voice came from behind, thick and deep with all the flourish and elegance of a stack of bricks hitting a pavecrete sidewalk. Ginsley's smile slackened visibly. Somehow, he'd failed to pick up on the newcomer, and that made him uneasy; everyone else in the Eye of Ra, living or dead, put off some kind of emissions, gas, heat, noise, electromagnetics, something–whoever this was, he seemed capable of blocking or masking anything that might reveal his presence. "Why not pick on someone your own size?"

Synthleather creaked, boots squeaked against the floor. Ginsley pivoted, yanking his hand out of Azrael's near-lifeless body as he swung around, eyes darting toward the voice the instant before he was sent reeling, four massive steel knuckles connecting with all the force of four hopped-up jackhammers. The impact would have killed any normal man, but it only threw Ginsley off balance, leaving him stumbling and flailing for a half second before another hand seized his collar and hurled him effortlessly toward the nearest wall. It was a show of strength that the pallid man had never experienced firsthand before, and his simple mind reveled at the sheer power exerted in every action that had been taken against him, laughing silently the instant before the world exploded around him in a shower of pavecrete and shattered steel.

Chapter 25: Burning Nocturne, 2nd Movement

The sound of the impact was deafening.

With a gritty rattle and the sharp jangling of chains, the room exploded in a shower of dust and ragged chunks of falling pavecrete, a death-knell note of steel and stone that ended with a choking gasp and a quick burst of insanely amused laughter.

The crunch and squeak of a booted foot pivoting from the heel echoed through the club as the last bit of debris fell crumbling to the floor. Ginsley's eyes were alive with silent intensity, sharp chrome grin beaming unpleasantly at the man standing opposite him, beyond the pavecrete chunks and Azrael's still twitching corpse, fingers still spasmodically jerking the limp lengths of monowire that sprawled across the floor like the strings of some forgotten marionette.

The man was a monolith, a perfectly chiseled obelisk of black marble and gunmetal, every rippling line of high-yield nanofibrous muscle smooth and bristling with thousands of tiny pins, each a combination growth-enhancement unit and neural-electrical stimulator, the kind of equipment that cost hundreds of dollars per pin, and boosted genevat muscle efficiency to astronomical levels. It didn't matter that the man looked like the large cousin of a angry, silver-striped pincushion— when every cooling system precision-threaded into the structure of his body came online, the amount of sheer power at his disposal was enough to make even Hercules sit up and take notice.

Cracking his steel-belted knuckles once, a beaming white grin unfolded across his midnight face, splitting lips the color of radial treads beneath a thick band of steel that stretched across his eyes and encompassed his ears with a dark, narrow channel of high-end optics long enough to indicate a visual range almost twice that of an ordinary human, with no blind spots and no perceptible loss of detail or color at the peripherals, and more functions than most military-grade headgear or contacts came with. With cutting edge optics like that hardwired directly into a brain that was, at best, genetically engineered for optimum efficiency and, at worst, was more techware than organic, it was likely that the man could see anything and everything *all the time*, including a dozen or more other things that the human eye could never be capable of perceiving, like sound or electromagnetic waves at extreme ends of the spectrum.

"Enjoying the show?" Brent laughed, gesturing excitedly toward Ginsley and the pincushion newcomer. He'd disabled just enough of the restraints to drag Cylea up the stairs, one hand tight in her hair, the other flailing as he talked, and one finger resting half-relaxed over the trigger of his handgun. "His project name is the Police Extraordinary Threats Elimination and Response unit, but they shortened that to PETER."

Cylea's mind was elsewhere. Her eyes shot toward Ginsley as Brent blathered on excitedly about every cutting edge nuance of Peter's design, his voice full of that same arrogant confidence that she'd heard in the aquatic room, only more so, more haughty, more self-righteous.

Normally, the details might actually have been interesting, but right now it was little more than half-heard technobabble that drifted into one ear and out the other. Right now, Ginsley was spreadeagle in a crater of shattered pavecrete with a mangled and useless handgun hanging limply from his arm. Right now, her fate hung on how well the pallid man could fare against Brent's pride and joy, and the outcome was questionable at best.

She bit her lip and repressed a desperate curse. Her guardian angel had to survive! He had to! She wanted to run to him, to yank him out of the wall and stand by his side, the two of them facing Peter together, an unstoppable duo of inhuman skill and strength, coiled and angry, ready to smash both Brent and his pet into the ground before disappearing off into the depths of the city and leaving the club behind, a dead ruin.

But her bonds were still tight and sharp, making even breathing a dangerous task. If she could actually manage to wriggle out of Brent's grip, she'd probably end up on the ground with a dozen deep lacerations, if not something more serious. Even moving against her monowire bindings was worse than falling naked into a bed of concertina wire-- the latter certainly would have hurt alot less.

The sound of amused, ominous chuckling derailed her train of thought instantly. There was a flicker of movement, then dust and fractured pavecrete stirred at the edges of the crater, knocked loose by fingers jerking spasmodically to life. For one brief moment, Cylea held her breath. Brent grunted.

What happened next seemed almost reflexive. Just as the pallid man's arms lifted, coat-sleeves sliding back, hands moving to grip ragged pavecrete and push his enormous body upright, Peter's hands darted for his back, almost too fast to follow, giant fingers jerking loose a length of dark hose and something cylindrical fitted with a wide-bore nozzle, like the last foot or two of a pressure washer. In the next instant, it was down, level with Ginsley, Peter's eager fingers hesitating only slightly before they jammed hard against a pair of dark, rubbery levers.

Cylea screamed as Brent's pride and joy shot her Silent Savior in the chest with a burning stream of petrochemicals that blossomed and filled the crater almost instantly, bathing pallid flesh and pavecrete alike in flame, quickly swallowing Ginsley's leering grin with a brilliant flash of hungry orange fire. A burning, waxen hand reached weakly out of the inferno, only to be viciously kicked aside and sprayed with another burst of pressurized flame.

There was a pop, a screech of something liquid boiling to a pregnant and angry bursting, a flailing of burning limbs and smoking fabric– Peter's grin was sickening to look at, so confident and gleeful, a study of sadism in sharp ivory. But then, the agent was no better– slipping a cigarette into the corner of a hideously triumphant smile that had crawled across his face, Brent laughed quietly to himself, enjoying every spitting pop, every hot gurgling squeal, and pausing in contented reflection, the very image of a general standing at the edge of the field of victory, lording over the corpses of foes and the refuse of battle with that same, smug, unchanging grin that had graced the faces of countless western warlords before him, men like Napoleon, *men like Hitler*.

"Welmmh." He managed, the sound muffled as he pressed his lips against the filter and lit the stick, pausing only long enough to shake the flame off the old-fashioned match and take a long, leisurely drag off the cigarette. "That's that, I suppose." He gestured to the flames with a wry smile, the cloud of fire fed by sputtering bursts of burning fuel as Peter struggled to coax every last drop out of the high-pressure nozzle. "Unless you're up for a well-done cut of barbequed freak, that is."

Cylea rounded on him immediately, shooting him a harsh, hard glare rich with raw hatred. Tears streamed down her face, twin rivers running across her cheeks to the point of her chin. Anger boiled up within her, fierce and venomous, tongue suddenly eager, ready to lash out, ready to give Brent a piece of her mind so bitter and nasty that he'd never forget it. With Ginsley out of the picture, it wasn't likely she'd get another chance– She'd be lucky to live through the next hour.

She opened her mouth, then hesitated. Brent's eyes had flicked back to the fire, slightly wider, some unidentifiable emotion flickering across neon green as he absently chewed the end of his cigarette. He made to whisper something, but she was already looking away, following his gaze back to the burning stretch of pavecrete.

Two waxen hands slipped through the flames and parted the flickering tongues of fire easily, almost biblically so. Steam rose in thick streamers from Ginsley's pale, clammy skin as he put one smoking boot down on the floor, taking a single, steady, purposeful step that put him beyond the blaze, scarlet and orange ripples of flame slipping in waves off the dark, bullet-riddled fabric of his coat, cascading across his arms and back and licking at every inch of his pallid flesh, skin shimmering and pocked-marked, sliver of a chrome grin catching the light eerily, blue veins surging vibrantly. A few spots of dark fabric burned weakly, tiny, stubborn flames that clung to him briefly before winking out, one by one. Peter mumbled something electronic that sounded like a curse. Cylea smiled. Brent frowned, and exhaled a long streamer of shaky, uncertain smoke.

With a hiss of cold steam, the leads between Ginsley's arm and the remains of his handgun shot loose, snaking excitedly through the air for a moment before being sucked fluidly back into his rapidly cooling flesh. The weapon hung in his limp grip for just an instant, then seemed to peel itself loose, slowly disconnecting from his pale palm until it dropped off completely, a piece of grotesque steel fruit falling from the pallid limb of an ominous tree to clatter against the unnaturally unyielding pavecrete floor.

Flexing his fingers eagerly, that madman's grin bloomed across his pale face again, returning full force, a stretch of sharp chrome pegs set between pallid and drawn lips like the blades of a dozen well-polished knives. He shivered, and something hissed within his coat, piston-shaped bulges that rose out of his back with quick hisses, pushing the fabric outward in four cylindrical towers of black that whirred angrily, spitting and smoking as a faint blue light eked its way out of the dark depths of his coat and grew brighter with each passing moment, even as the sharp smell of hot electronics and burning ozone sliced through the air, instantly smothering the competing smells of self-sterilizing nanohallucinogens and the sweaty odors that the dancers had left in their wake. All at once, he was alive with arcing, electric blue lines of crackling energy, hot, burning azure shooting down the lengths of his arms, pale skin blistering and boiling at every point of contact, coat smoking as rich blue veins pulsed brightly, rising out against his flesh with eager, anxious promise. Twin fists, skin as pale and luminescent as the moon, tightened and unfurled again and again, tiny arcs of electric blue playing across talon-like fingers, shooting through his nails, crawling up his arms, burning the ragged edges of bullet holes into smooth, hard rings. When he laughed, it was a terrible sound, a resounding chuckle that went beyond madness, something that came from the deepest, darkest depths of a disturbed and rotting soul, something diseased and infested, expanding against the walls of the jar into which it had been mercilessly squeezed, squishing itself into every crack and crevice until there was no more left to grow into, until only that awful pressure that came with the endless swelling remained, making a sound like a laugh that might have come from someplace worse than the bottom of the deepest pit in hell.

For a moment, no one moved. Peter seemed paralyzed, watching Ginsley through that dark trench of cutting edge optics. Cylea shifted uneasily, her face blank. Brent was the first to recover.

"What are you waiting for, you piece of electronic shit?" The Agent spun to face Peter, suddenly shouting as he stabbed his finger at the pallid man. "Tear that crazy bastard a new asshole!"

A quick nod and a quiet cracking of knuckles was all the Agent got in response. Peter's muscles, massive and inhumanly bulky, stirred anxiously, flexing and twitching, pins catching the light. Ginsley's grin widened, his face the embodiment of insanity, and he laughed again, that same soul-poisoning laugh. Brent sneered. "Put that fucker out of his misery."

It wasn't clear who struck first; two blurs of color, one black on white and one white on black, shot toward one another, hands outstretched and reaching, the air alive with a flurry of arcing blue light and polished steel as they collided, seemingly in midair, and spun off from one another just as rapidly, dust and smoke rising, mingling into a dull grey haze around them the instant they slid to a stop, facing each other, mere inches apart.

When it started again, the clash of steel and flesh was deafening. Every move was met and parried perfectly, every stroke flawlessly delivered and turned aside just as easily. It was a dance of grace and precision unlike anything Cylea had ever seen, a veritable kata of thrusting fists, grasping fingers, and driving elbows that seemed almost too perfect, almost rehearsed.

As they shot and pivoted across the bloodstained floor, twisting and reaching, one thing became immediately clear– Ginsley had only been playing with Azrael, a cat taunting a mouse until the moment of the final killing stroke that had ended it all, leaving the vatgrown splayed out on the floor, wires laying side-by-side with his spilled and broken entrails. Peter was more than twice the man Azrael had been, more than twice as fast, twice as deadly, with more than twice the techware wired into his hulking body, but Ginsley kept up with him easily, perhaps playing with him as he had with the Vatgrown, never revealing his full strength, his full potential. Even as Peter picked up speed, sweat beaded and slick across hard, smooth skin, striking with surgical precision, Ginsley matched his every move, that maddening laughter echoing, broken only by the sound of skin, steel, and rustling fabric.

Then something happened. It happened so fast that no one, save perhaps Ginsley himself, realized that the blurred battle had come to a sudden and complete stop until a moment later, and by then, Peter was already howling.

Waxen hands gripped Peter's biceps, fingers curling, digging impatiently into flesh as the pins in the other man's skin dug into Ginsley's palms with equal fervor. Blue blood shot through bulging veins with such force that they seemed almost ready to pop, every capillary bright and luminous, a spiderweb network of rich lines that etched their way through his skin, tinging every inch of pale flesh an uncomfortable shade of azure. Lightning, the same electric blue as Ginsley's blood, crackled through the air between them, dancing off black fabric and burning into dark flesh, playing across the forest of pins, arcing through his neck, his chest, and across every inch of steel that was bolted or grafted into his body.

A look of sheer horror spread across Brent's face as Peter's skin surged spasmodically under Ginsley's talon-like hands, burning and flexing, blood boiling out from around the arcing pins-- it was spreading, muscles jerking insanely in strong cords that shot into his chest and neck, flesh tightening and hardening, winding itself into harsh, powerful knots. Peter's scream picked up in intensity, sharp and gurgling, tire-tread lips pulling back hard against perfect, ivory teeth, mind struggling to block out the excruciating pain of having his body torn apart by the vicious contractions of his own muscles. Cylea's mouth drifted open, her face slack, stunned and blank. A single thought pierced through the shock, penetrating to the back of her mind like the point of a sharp, silver needle. *If he... if Ginsley is my brother, if he really is... then what am I?* She looked at her hands. *What am I capable of?*

In the next instant, the grotesque moment came to a sudden end. As Peter's scream reached a deafening climax, dark skin surging violently, ripping and bursting, flaying itself loose in excited ribbons of sparking carnage and spurting scarlet, Ginsley lifted him and hurled him into the nearest wall, ending the grisly scene in a shower of pale grey pavecrete dust. Brent's cigarette slipped from the corner of his mouth, hit the bloodstained floor, burning end first, and bounced once, rolling to a stop next to a pair of synthetic crocodile skin boots. He hardly had time to notice the loss before the cold muzzle of a handgun pressed in hard against the side of his head.

"It's over. You've lost. Let her go." Jack said, eyes never wavering. Brent sneered back, but as Ginsley's pale blue eyes swivelled toward him, eager and soulless, traces of that madman's smile still playing at the edges of his face, he hesitated and swallowed uneasily.

"You're not going to get away with this." The Agent shot back, quickly working Cylea's bonds free. He hated doing it, but with the bartender holding him at gunpoint and tiny lines of electric blue still arcing ominously across Ginsley's pallid, steaming hands, anything else would have been suicide. "You can't outrun the government. Sooner or later, you're going to fuck up, someone in the BTD or the FBI is gonna get lucky and put a bullet through--"

"Y'know something? You talk too bloody much." Jack cut him off, cocking the pistol immediately. "Now hurry up before I put you down and set the kid loose myself, yeah?"

"Yeah." Brent managed, snapping the last atomically-hardening nanoelastic cable loose with enough force that it bit into Cylea's wrists the instant before it went slack, not hard enough to draw blood, but just hard enough to bruise. The instant his hands withdrew, she whirled on him, whipping around and planting her fist firmly in his face. He reeled from the impact, but caught himself quickly, hands darting for his shattered and bleeding nose.

"Ah, God," He snorted, struggling to breathe through his mouth. "Fucking... You fucking hit me, you--!"

"Ah, bite ya bum, ya twit." Jack laughed, cutting the Agent off as he pushed his handgun into his belt. "That's the least you deserve, and you know it."

"Payback's a bitch, isn't it?" Cylea added, shooting him a feisty grin before turning back to the Bartender and winking.

Brent made to reply, but Jack promptly cut him off. "Well, as great as it'd be to stay and chat with a feddie drongo like yourself, we've got places to be." He clapped the Agent hard on the back, grinning widely as the other man simply shuddered, bloody hands cupped over his nose. "Sheila'll take care of ya, yeah?" He looked up. "Hey! Sheila! Where'd you get to now?"

Almost instantly, the Ja-serve popped out from behind the bar, french maid outfit still in excellent shape, chrome limbs still smooth and polished.

"Ah!" He grinned, gesturing her over. "Come on, I got a job for ya."

Curious, she shuffled over to Jack, her face a mix of the plastic approximations of a whole host of conflicting emotions. Brent's neon green eyes flicked up and met hers, just for an instant, and then she looked away, forcing a cheery smile as she turned to face Jack fully.

"What can I do for you?" She piped, eyes never flicking to Jack's hands as he carefully drew the pistol back out of his belt.

"Simple. Here." He pushed the weapon into the Ja-Serve's hands, lifted her arms to bring the weapon level with Brent's head, and guided her finger gently to the trigger. "If he moves, I want you to shoot him."

"But Jack!" Sheila protested immediately. "That conflicts with--"

"Emergency override." Jack cut her off. "Consider it a security function, yeah? If this banana bender escapes, two people die, maybe more. If you shoot him," he grinned at the Agent, "only one does."

"The needs of the many outweigh the needs of the few." She droned, then smiled again, cocking the weapon suddenly. "Yes sir, Mister Jack sir!"

"That's a good girl." He patted Sheila gently on one of her chrome shoulders and let his eyes flick to Cylea. "Good thing they build these japo-bots so well, eh?"

She nodded once, turning back to Ginsley as she opened her mouth to say something, but it flickered and died on the edge of her tongue as her eyes searched the empty darkness for a trace of her Silent Savior, even a flicker of light that might betray the use of optic camouflage, but there was nothing there but dimness and shattered pavecrete. Every fragment, every leftover, every trace, save the blue stains smeared across the floor, had simply evaporated, almost as if he had never been there.

Chapter 26: Synthleather Sunrise

Cylea glanced back over her shoulder, just once, quickly.

The darkness swirled behind her, that red light, a moist, dead eye swallowed by swirling seawater, looming out of oblivion– pale, bloated arms reaching for her. The words echoed in her mind over and over again. *Child of Cirrus.*

She shivered, screamed, stumbled– it kept getting closer, kept reaching, slick, fat fingers so near, the air around them thick and cold as they loomed into her vision, impossibly huge. Her eyes flicked back to the endless darkness ahead of her, and then suddenly everything came to a painful, grinding halt. Time seemed to pause, every swirl in the blackness, either real or imagined, stalled in place. It lasted for only a moment, and then a figure stepped out of the abyss, parting reality like thin sheets of some exotic fabric.

Paralyzed and hanging in the void, Cylea watched as the figure approached, slowly coming into focus, slowly resolving into something full of the hard lines and gentle curves of living flesh– She swallowed nervously, eyes meeting those of a teenage girl with dark hair that was slightly longer than shoulder-length, flaring out at odd angles just past the collar of her shirt. She was unremarkable, just a typical, lanky, high school-age girl, but it was the shirt that held Cylea's attention– so familiar, so impossibly familiar. The five musicians that made up the Screaming Scarlet Dundlemen danced across the shimmering stage emblazoned into the fabric, moving to the repetitive beat of a thirty second soundbite, just a chunk of the song "Sweden." The girl spoke suddenly, her mouth unmoving, lips pale and drawn, skin turning translucent, almost ghostly, revealing thin cords of rotting muscle and bleached bone beneath.

Time to stop being afraid of the dark Cylea... stretch your wings... you already know all you need to.

She raised her hand, one ghastly finger pointing to the key nestled between Cylea's breasts, and then it ended, a brilliant flash of light burning away the void with a deafening crack that left only the afterimage of a pair of massive, white-feathered wings in its wake.

Cold shot into her blurry reality. There was no warning– suddenly everything was whirling, flashes of light and dark cascading through unfocused vision like a snowglobe seen through a kaleidoscope. None of it made any sense– it was all too sudden, too strange. Her mind grappled with the basics, unsure of where she was, who she was, what was going on.

Before she could recover, she was shoved forward, something dark and leather seizing her collar and dragging her out of the soft warmth, forcing her to stand on legs that refused to cooperate. Everything was cold and grey, hard and featureless. A face came into view– female, fair-skinned with high cheekbones, eyes hidden by a pair of expensive, titanium-frame adjustables that had blue, vaguely circular lenses. Wild, spiky, sandy blond hair framed her face, slight traces of a smile playing across her lips as they formed words, perfect words with that generic west-coast intonation.

"Yeah, it's her." The woman turned away just as quickly, suddenly talking to someone else. "Get the capture team over here stat." A muffled "Yes Ma'am" was the only reply.

Cylea's mind chose that moment to come alive again, memories and sudden awareness shooting through her foggy brain in an instantaneous current of raw light and sound, painting a world around her that went beyond the borders of the other woman's face, a world that included other people, other things– Jack, several riot-gear equipped officers, and the Bartender's yellow, brick-like hovertruck hung on at the edges of awareness.

After the confrontation between Ginsley and Peter, after they had left Sheila pointing a gun at Brent, Jack had driven all the way out to Santa Monica and parked his hovertruck in an alleyway just a few short blocks from Venice Beach, doing what he could with her injuries and making quick, half-formed plans about where to run to next until Cylea fell into a restless sleep. They'd driven past Hok's restaurant before then, and the moment stuck in her mind with grim tenacity– neither had spoken, both simply taking in the gutted two-story building wrapped tight in yellow and red tape, its cheery sign hanging loosely over the doorway, a darkened cuneiform proclaiming "Chow Fun" in a boxy and dismal fashion that seemed about as Chinese as refried beans or banana pancakes.

Then the woman was smiling at Cylea again, gently slipping off her adjustables to fix the younger woman with a cool, steely-grey gaze– the gesture was simple and smooth, jerking Cylea's mind back to the present in a sharp snap of cold reality. She shivered, and the hand on her shoulder tightened warily.

Sky blue eyes drifted curiously, halfheartedly across the newcomer, a handful of absent, random glances gathering fragments that fell together to form a whole, a complete picture of a typical hardass cop, a fed, a government mudstick, someone that probably worked for the FBI or the BTD and had the look of someone who shuffled paperwork or spent long hours at the range in her off-time.

The woman was tall, thin, Japanese– her beige uniform hung open, revealing a white, collared, button-up shirt set with a burgundy necktie and a glossy white, custom, forty-one long-slide automatic holstered at her side, its smooth finish broken only by the equally smooth, red design of the rising sun of old Japan. Her boots had been polished until they shone, dark mirrors of black leather as bright as the brass bar over her left breast that labeled her as "K. Kagami," Special Agent of the BTD. Cylea's eyes flicked away, lighting on a squad of heavily armed officers dressed in riot gear that were pounding across the industrial plasticore toward her, hands full of stunsticks and shockwebs– it all registered, every fact and nuance, but none of it seemed to matter, none of it seemed to stick. It was all too surreal, too familiar. Somehow, her mind simply *refused* to believe that the end had come.

Squealing thermoplastic wheels and a haze of black smoke caught her attention. Just beyond Kagami and the squad of officers, a black sedan slid sideways across the plasticore roadway and came to a screeching stop, tires smoking, glossy black paint thick with glare except where patches of flat color and streaks of dust absorbed the light like the scar tissue of some ancient warrior.

The door came open immediately, light dancing crazily off its pitted and dented surface– a strong hand gripped the worn, steel edge of the door, pushing and flexing as the sharp corner of a black trenchcoat cut into the cold, grey light like an omen.

"Special Agent Revna." Kagami looked up, giving the car a disdainful glance before she let her gaze flick to meet Brent's neon-green eyes, traces of amusement already playing across her face. "Nice wheels."

"Yeah" Brent managed. Impatience was clear in his voice as he closed the door behind him in a single, solid push, free hand drifting reflexively to the bandage across his nose. "I was in a hurry." A comment brewed at the back of his mind, something Aiko might have spat back about the FBI not wasting funds on new hoversedans like the BTD did, but it didn't come together– it just didn't sound the same as it would have coming from his partner's sharp and venomous tongue.

"What happened to your nose?" Kagami turned to face him fully, smile creasing smugly. "Did Aiko finally snap and pop you one?"

Brent gave her a withering stare, never once glancing at Cylea. "Can we keep this professional, Special Agent Kagami?"

"Of course." Kagami let her eyes drift quickly across the vehicle again, nodding. Everything about her was calm, cool, and aware, all perfect, calculated grace-- Brent's uneasy preoccupation was a perfect contrast, something sick, nervous, and just as permeable. "Where is your charming partner, by the way?"

"Aiko?" He asked, then immediately added: "She's indisposed." The brush-off was direct, painfully obvious. Kagami frowned-- Brent's mind was somewhere else entirely, eyes already firmly fastened on Cylea. It was clear what he wanted, why he hadn't wasted any time getting there, and Kagami didn't have the patience to beat around the bush-- She opened her mouth to speak, her features already taking on a suspicious cast, but Brent cut her off before she could get a word in. "Good, you've got her. I'll be taking her from here."

Kagami scoffed immediately.

"No, you won't." The female Agent shifted in her stance, folding her arms in a gesture of resolute defiance. "You shouldn't even be here. We both know that."

"With all due respect, Special Agent Kagami," Brent began, "this is an internal matter of district security, not an international crisis." He made a quick, sweeping gesture. "The BTD has no jurisdiction here--"

"The BTD got jurisdiction the moment it was discovered that Miss Von Mitternacht was being inducted into an international crime syndicate." Kagami shot back. "The incident aboard Flight thirty-eight forty alone is more than enough to cement the BTD's claim here. We both know that this is well within the jurisdiction of *my bureau*." She unfolded her arms, making an all-encompassing gesture. "Why do we keep having these run-ins? I haven't seen a single member of the district police or the NACC during the entire pursuit. I just see their reports, and yet you keep turning up." A smile spread across Kagami's face, half knowing, half suspicious. "Do you have some kind of personal interest in this case, Agent Revna?"

"You listen to me, Kagami." Brent's eyes narrowed, anger tinging his tone. "I don't care what you think or what you want! I have a direct order from Assistant Director Anderson right here that states--!"

The sharp crack of a rifle report shattered the animosity hanging between them in a single, swift strike. In the next moment, Brent and Kagami were on the ground, weapons drawn, squatting, darting for cover behind Jack's massive hovertruck. One of the officers in riot gear clutched at his transparent faceplate, crimson spurting between the rubbery treads of darkly-gloved fingers as he fell, hitting the pavecrete with a hollow, plastic crunch and a gurgling, half-muffled grunt.

Someone started firing then, wildly squeezing off rounds into the pitted pavecrete and gaping windows of surrounding buildings. Another crack sounded, and another officer stumbled through the street, collapsing unceremoniously against the blacktop, a ragged, scarlet-stained hole in the center of his chest.

Jack took that as his cue, not wasting any time– in the next instant, he was past the Agents, pushing Brent into Kagami hard enough that they both went sprawling into the side of the hovertruck, a tangle of fighting limbs and pressed fabric. Cylea hardly had time to shift before the bartender hauled her to her feet, all but dragging her out of there even as a third shot rang out, punching a fearsome hole through the hood of the hovertruck a few scant inches from Brent's head. Brent reached for her, Kagami pivoted, and then they were gone, obscured by a wall of garish, glossy yellow, Jack's feet echoing across the ground.

Chapter 27: Retro-Blitzkrieg Market

Instantly, they were in the street.

There was no-where to run, no close cover to zone in on and gun for. Jack glanced across the street, eyes darting quickly across two parked, sport-model hoversedans and the stretch of empty road beyond them. An elderly man pushing a cart out of a decrepit-looking supermarket caught his eye-- it was nothing special, but it was a shot, the kind of place with windows that hadn't been replaced in centuries, just washed until the bars bolted to the inside were almost obscured by the scuffmarks of a thousand or more vigorous once-overs, the kind of place with the cheap, lightbox signs, wax-paper sale posters, and a name like "Raj's One Stop" or "Habib's Grocery."

Before Cylea could protest, she was scooped up by one of Jack's bulky arms, carried as he went barreling toward Hassan's Market at full speed. Behind them, Kagami bolted upright, half hidden by Jack's hovertruck as she gestured quickly, her handgun's glossy white finish flashing in the light while she barked commands, urging the riot-gear equipped officers to action. Brent was already gone, ducking immediately out of sight.

The doors of the Market came sliding open slowly, too slowly. With one hard shoulder, Jack rammed into them, throwing them open in a burst of angry pneumatic hissing and plexiglass banging excitedly against iron. Shouting chased them inside, stray rounds already punching through windows, ricocheting off steel, passing into the off-white walls with red and grey puffs of dust from brick and mortar.

A handful of people stopped dead in their tracks the instant Jack appeared-- a young mother folded herself against her shopping cart, shielding an excited baby with her body as two teenagers bickering over a few loose cash cards looked up, eyes wide. An elderly woman clutched her purse tight against her chest, someone darted behind a line of shelving, and a checker, likely no more than fifteen, ducked behind the register with a frantic yelp. A chocolate flavored NanoBoost energy bar slipped from a frightened hand, bouncing off the ancient linoleum with a quiet thump and a flash of brown plastic.

Booted feet echoed across pavecrete sidewalk– there was only a moment of hesitation before everyone scattered, diving and sprinting for shelves and registers like frightened cockroaches as the officers decked out in full riot-gear fanned out in the doorway of the market and unslung their assault rifles in fluid, practiced movements. The commander's voice rung out clearly, seasoned and strong. "Fire!"

Instantly the rifles were blazing, bullets whizzing through the air, biting into tin, puncturing plastic, shattering glass. A ripping, bloodcurdling scream of raw terror shot through the noise, forcing itself between the rapid cracks of hot lead ripping from dark, smoking barrels.

Rows of cans rushed past as Jack hunched down and hurtled through a narrow aisle, blues, reds, and silvers blurring into a rapidly-changing patchwork tapestry of painted tin and synth-paper labeling. A jar of atomically reconstituted tomato paste exploded in front of them, and then she was on the ground, Jack shielding her with his massive chest as thick crimson blasted across her vision, cheap aluminum shelving shuddering audibly with another spray of screaming, fragmenting rounds. Something else popped nearby, a tall bottle of something carbonated that burst open in a flurry of ragged plastic and shot a wild cascade of dark fizz into the air.

There was only the briefest moment of hesitation before she was hauled to her feet again, yanked across the pitted and peeling linoleum toward a pair of massive, swinging double doors at the back of the market. A volley of rounds ripped past them, peppering a line of plastic-packaged meats, spraying chunky crimson and cheap white nanofoam into the air with hot, explosive pops.

Jack wasted no time. In the next instant, he was ramming through the doors, rushing through the dark and greasy stockroom and darting around boxes of produce as more bullets whizzed through the air around them, hot lead popping through watermelon and genevat citrus hybrids, frosting the inside of cheap Bolivian crates with creamed banana, boring through lettuce and celery with hollow cracks and snaps. Someone was shrieking hysterically, a young woman hunched down somewhere in the darkness– Cylea caught a glimpse of a terrified face, the edge of a garish blue apron, auburn hair. Jack's eyes stayed fixed forward, intent on another door, the last door between them and freedom.

Pivoting smoothly, Jack hardly slowed as one of his thick boots connected with the door in a savage kick that blasted the cheap aluminum thing cleanly off its hinges, flinging it across a stretch of cracked pavecrete to bounce against the opposite wall of a narrow alley. In the next moment, Cylea was outside, all but shoved out of the darkness and into the harsh light as Jack yanked a handgun out of his belt. It was an oddly familiar piece– somehow, he'd managed to lift it off Brent in the confusion. She hesitated, even as he shifted, already drawing a bead on something still in the market.

"GO!" The bartender shouted at her suddenly, gesturing wildly down the alley. She turned on him quickly, feet scraping against the gritty dust as she made to face him fully, her mouth opening, ready to offer protest. The look in Jack's eyes melted her resolve immediately, making it clear exactly what he expected her to do, that there would be no going back, no bargaining, no compromises. Not this time. "GO NOW!"

She bit her lip and turned fluidly away, doing the one thing she'd promised herself too many times now that she'd never do again. It was too simple, too easy, too much like surrender for her own tastes.

She turned, and she ran.

Again.

Chapter 28: Weavings of the Neon Prophet

The sound of gunfire chased Cylea down the alley and across the street, chased her even as she ran, until suddenly she realized that she couldn't hear it anymore, but whether it had ceased or simply been drowned out by the sounds of traffic and the ever-present buzzing hum of the city was unclear. She was perfectly happy leaving it a mystery– the last thing on her mind was backtracking to find out if the people after her were done gutting another business in the name of justice.

Sirens echoed in the distance. A black and white hoversedan darted past the entrance to the alley, lights flashing as she flung herself reflexively into a stack of trashbags. Someone shouted, another voice further off answered, and an old, noisy bicycle went whizzing by, the rider quietly singing some pop song in half-hearted Korean.

She waited a moment before shifting, listening for any sound of pursuit, eyes searching for the telltale red or blue of cop lights, then pushed her way back out of the stack, brushing grit and dirt off the starchy white surface of the vend clothing. On either side of the alley, cars slipped by sporadically– there was no sign of Kagami, no sign of Brent, and no sign of the officers they'd had with them, but then, there was no sign of Jack either. She bit her lip. Part of her was ready to run back and save him, though she had to keep reminding herself that there wasn't much she could have done– facing off against a pack of BTD men decked out in full riot gear with assault rifles and itchy trigger fingers was insane, especially unarmed. Even with Brent's handgun, she doubted Jack had survived. She doubted he'd lasted very long at all.

That was when it hit her– she was alone again, alone in the depths of Los Angeles, a wanted woman with no cash, no cards, no identification, and no weapons. She swallowed nervously as sweat broke across her skin, hand desperately aching for the familiar grip of a switchblade. It would have been a small comfort, but a welcome one nonetheless.

She didn't stick around for long– there wasn't much else to do but stay on the move, hoping that chance or fate might put her in the hands of Shang and the Golden Koi Triads before the law caught up to her, or something far worse descended on her, carrying her off like a mouse trapped in the claws of a mighty owl. She'd have to stick to the shadows, stay out of sight, away from people and surveillance equipment. It wouldn't be easy, and it certainly didn't seem likely, but she had to do it. She had no choice. When the sirens started up again, she picked the opposite direction and ran.

Two blocks further from the market put her in a maze of smooth pavecrete, a sort of gently sloping, communal parking lot with high walls and an abundance of luscious crawling greenery that seemed too rich to be anything but a single strain of engineered hybrid, something cooked up in one of those floating botanical labs fifty miles off the coast of Japan because they were harder to contain than crabgrass and bamboo combined. Until the meat market went totally vatgrown, a lot of farmers had been up in arms about it because it spread like wildfire, and their livestock wouldn't touch it. A few organic, free-range farmers still had trouble with its insidious nature, but you rarely heard much more than a quick, two sentence blurb about those anymore, if even that much. Too much money involved in urban renewal and green-party projects made it more the problem of the farmer than of the multinational conglomerates that had designed the thing. Besides, there were chemicals that would kill it, or at least, mostly. Sure, it was an expensive weedkiller, but what alternatives did farmers have? The only other thing capable of killing off the hardier strains of hybrid greenery was nuclear waste, and that was slightly harder on the land. Lesser of two evils, the corporates said, and that was enough to convince the cash-fattened shreds of the EPA to back off when an ounce of the stuff leaked into the water supply and killed several thousand people overnight, somewhere off in the boondocks of what had once been Ohio. Cylea shook her head. At least the greenery here was well contained, trapped on all sides by impenetrable pavecrete. Good thing it only spread by root.

The maze slipped by quick, feet pounding against smooth grey pavecrete. At the end, another strip of industrial plasticore roadway separated her from another maze, this one larger, a paved lot littered with some kind of cheap, rusty storage buildings, the kind that were little more than a flimsy frame and a couple of large sheets of corrugated aluminum. Not wasting any time, she darted across the street and disappeared in among them, narrowly avoiding the steady gaze of a district security camera swinging in to inspect license plates and record the faces of anyone that might be trying to jaywalk.

Shooting straight for the rear of the lot, she glanced once back over her shoulder, checking for signs of pursuit and finding none. In the next instant, she rounded the rusty corner of a metal shed and froze, eyes fixing immediately on the last thing she'd expected to come across, the last thing she'd wanted to come across– someone else.

At first he didn't seem to notice her, standing alone with his back to her near a burnt-out oil drum and a ratty old tent stuffed and bulging with yellowed newsprint and discarded silicon magazines. He worked feverishly with a neon-fusion etcher, carving a massive web of neon green runes and symbols into the side of an ancient concrete building, something huge and thick like a gigantic bunker, organizing everything along a spiral path set with hundreds of smaller lines that worked their way in and out of the pattern at seemingly random intervals, weaving a grid-like tapestry of neon over six feet across and just as high.

That was when she noticed it. Far above him, centered on the side of the bunker, a giant neon "2" pulsed with a dying blue light. It didn't seem to have any real significance until he turned around, beaming madly at her– the moment she recognized him.

He looked old, not in the way that comes with real age, but in the way that comes from life on the street, comes in doses with used needles, long, cold, lonely nights, and run-ins with insanity– he had the look of a beggar, but also of someone who had once been *someone*, a corporate ramrod who didn't make the grade or pissed off the boss one too many times on the wrong day. He still wore the suit he'd been wearing when she'd first seen him drawing runes on the sidewalk with chalk, something perfectly cut and probably of french manufacture– an expensive suit, if it hadn't been falling apart, tattered and threadbare with hundreds of greasy stains spotting the once-black fabric. He sniffed absently, rubbing his fat, red nose, and wiping a loose crumb of something out of his bushy, scraggly beard as she caught her breath. "No way."

"Told you! Told you!" He brightened suddenly, laughing excitedly and managing a quick, stumbling jig that seemed almost drunkenly cartoonish before jabbing the hot end of the neon-fusion etcher in her direction. "Not the last time, either! Two, two, two, two, two..." He trailed off, words quickly degenerating into uncontrollable laughter. She opened her mouth to say something, but before the words could come, he was speaking again.

"You saw him, didn't you?" The old man cackled, and the sound lapsed into an unpleasantly wet cough. "Shakes– Shakes–" He stood stiffly at attention suddenly, a mockery of formality in his shabby clothing. "This is your Captain speaking!" He slipped into laughing again, then turned and jammed the etcher into the grid, slicing through an oddly curved section of runes a few lines in from the outer rim. Instantly, he dropped the etcher, shocked at his own mistake, and slipped one grubby finger into his mouth in innocent amazement.

Cylea's eyes darted across the grid, mind doing flips, trying to make sense of the runes and symbols, the lines, anything. It all seemed to have some form of order to it, like a carefully plotted map of... something– what it was a map of was still a mystery.

The man grunted unpleasantly and scooped up the etcher. As he rose, her gaze shot back to him, just in time to see his expression change radically, suddenly angry as he belted out another nonsensical line that grated as much on her ears as it did on her mind. "Dear sister! Dear sister! And after you did that to his face! Hah!" He made a quick, harsh, sweeping gesture with one hand. "Pitiful, pitiful. Poor, poor little Gideon."

Cylea shook her head in confusion. Everything he said seemed odd, like disjointed fragments of some prophesy that she was blindly slogging through–part of her wanted to believe it, but she couldn't help having her doubts. He was crazy, but it took a leap of faith to believe that was all there was to his ramblings, as much of a leap as it took to believe that there was something more, something almost prophetic. Her eyes became distant and absent with thought, slipping back to the bright green lines of the grid as he rambled on, cackling and grinning as often as he shouted and screamed.

"The burning lotus is almost upon us!" He squealed excitedly, attracting her attention again as he jumped and clapped his hands together like a tired parody of a schoolgirl on a caffeine high. "From all angles, they come," he continued, grinning broadly and making a wide, all-encompassing gesture. "But victory is in the hands of the experiment!" He clenched one fist tightly. "And the illusionist lingers to the bitter end, challenged and driven into the ground by fountain sword and electric green!" His speech degenerated into crazy laughter again. "And the club doesn't believe in death!" Instantly his face was serious again, and he pointed the etcher at something invisible on the ground, shooting the pavecrete a venomous look. "Yeah, well I do. Bang." The crazy laughter came again. "Ah... magic tattoos."

She shook her head in utter confusion. "I don't get it. I'm trying to understand, but I..." She shrugged and trailed off as he fixed her with an excited look, gaze darting to her chest, eyes sparkling eagerly. "I... What–?"

Before she could finish, he closed the distance between them and seized the key hanging from the string around her neck. She opened her mouth to say something, but he looked up suddenly, blasting her with rank and fetid breath as he grinned again and laughed in quiet excitement. "Poetic, isn't it? Face white? The Id wasn't meant to be starved, after all!" he cackled again. "And where to find it?" A high pitched squeal replaced the laughter. "So Cirrus! So Cirrus! So very Cirrus!" In the next instant, he spun away, letting the key fall back to her chest before putting his back to her and screaming at a rusty dumpster perched on a line of pavecrete across the street. "CIRRUS! If only she knew! Twisted, you twisted son of a ..." the rest was lost in angry grumbling, his words unintelligible but for "Twentieth Century" and "Obsession."

Cylea stepped forward. "Cirrus? What are you talking about?"

His shoulders sagged suddenly, arms dropping to his sides carelessly enough that the etcher burnt a hole in his suit pants. In the next instant, he whirled on her, already smiling in pleasant amusement as he plainly stated: "Your father."

Cylea blinked, stunned for a moment before she mumbled, "My father?" He nodded, and she nearly paled, taking another step toward him. "What about my father? Is he still alive?" It was hard to resist the urge to reach out and shake the old man. "Where is he!?"

"CIRRUS!" The man hissed suddenly, one gnarled, skeletal finger shooting toward a window on the top floor of a four-story building across the street from the corner where they stood. Her eyes followed his accusing jab, and stopped on the shadowy shape of another man, a tall, imposing silhouette standing on the other side of the glass, watching them. Blinds fell across the window instantly.

For one brief moment, Cylea and the crazy man locked eyes. A silent air of intent passed between them, and then she was gone, sprinting toward the building's only door as he watched in mild amusement.

The door came open easily, or rather, fell easily under the force that Cylea exerted without thinking, every action the product of sheer reflex. Ramming the thing hard enough with one shoulder that it was ripped cleanly off the doorframe and went flying into the staircase beyond, she sprinted past it, clearing the dusty, wooden planks three steps at a time as she all but flew toward the fourth floor, careening through the rusty door that hung half-open there and coming to a skidding halt on the decrepit floor.

"Father!" She cried, but the room was empty-- only one window was blocked by the ancient, dusty blinds, no trace of her father, no trace of anyone. For a long moment, she stood there stunned, taking it all in, unable to move. She opened her mouth, tried to speak, but the only sound that would come was a hollow wheeze.

It was too much. It had all seemed so close, answers and safety and a thousand other nameless things, but fate had cruelly snatched it all away again, leaving her with nothing but the painful shadows of her past. *Cirrus. Father?*

She couldn't stand anymore. The weight was too much.

She sunk to her knees and cried.

Chapter 29: Dust and Destiny

She knelt there for a long moment, crying, not knowing why, not understanding– it just came. She needed the release, needed something, needed information, needed answers, needed her father. She fought back the urge to scream, fought back the urge to punch something, struggling with every unsavory emotion that bubbled up from the darkness within her, but still– it just wasn't enough. In the next instant, she was on her feet again, baring her teeth at the window where the silhouette had stood, her fists clenching, her hate brimming. The world had fucked her over one too many times, and this time it had left her wanting to kill something. *Anything.*

"Irritating, isn't it?" The sound caught her off guard, lessening her rage even as she whirled toward the doorway, coming face to face with the calm, regal features of Castillo, his hair and suit as smooth and perfect as they had been the day before. He carefully inspected his fingernails before letting his gaze drift up to meet hers. "Or are you afraid?"

"You *fuck*!" She screamed, feeling every hair on her body stand up on end simultaneously, suddenly charged and alive with electric intensity. "What the hell is going on!? Spill it Castillo!"

"What is there to spill?" He brushed casually at his suit, all but ignoring her as she bristled. "Your father isn't here, Cylea."

She opened her mouth to rip off another harsh retort, but he looked up, eyes meeting hers again, this time so full of intensity that his stare froze her tongue instantly. "Demands are so unbecoming of a woman such as yourself. Come with me and we can help you find your father. At the very least, you owe yourself that much."

"I don't need your help," she shot back, "What I need are answers, so start talking."

"And if I refuse?"

For a moment, Cylea's grip on her hate loosened, then a flicker of unrestrained rage shot across her face, and in the next instant, she had Castillo's collar bound tight in her fist, her fierce gaze boring into those calm, soft grey eyes. The two vatgrowns on either side of him tensed, leather and silk creaking against itself as their hands darted immediately for their handguns, both waiting for the sign from Castillo that Cylea had gone too far, that they could do what they did best as genetically engineered thugs and put her down for good. They tensed, but the signal never came.

"Listen to me, you pompous prick, my father is dead! He's been dead for years." Cylea bit off. "Someone out there named Cirrus is calling himself my father und I think you know more about it than you're letting on, so you better tell me before I start coming up with some creative ways to make you regret not saying something sooner."

"My, my" the traces of a smile slipped across Castillo's face. "You know, this kind of anger is really only amusing for so long." The smile faded ever-so-slightly. "Do keep in mind that I do not take kindly to threats, and neither do they." He flicked his head in the direction of the vatgrowns. "So, if you want to keep your skin intact, I would advise you to *back off*." He bit off the last two words in a show of failing restraint-- the change in his demeanor shocked Cylea just enough to loosen her grip on his collar reflexively.

It was just enough-- Castillo's smile widened a trace the instant before he ripped free of her grasp, his almost inhuman reflexes immediately putting him several paces back from her. Panicking, she reached for him, hand grasping for his collar again, trying to gain purchase. In one fluid movement he caught her wrist and yanked smoothly upward, sending her spinning to the ground with startling ease.

The impact was perfectly calculated-- she hit the dusty floor just hard enough to knock the breath from her lungs, and yet not hard enough to cause any real injury. While she lay there, gasping, eyes wide, mind spinning, Castillo took a smooth step forward and carefully inspected his fingernails again, as if the whole thing had been little more than a simple exercise.

"Wha--" she panted, struggling for breath. Castillo's eyes flicked to her, so cold and disinterested, the kind of look he might have given an insect if it had happened to cross his path. Slowly, smoothly, he knelt next to her, leaning in close, lips parting to whisper something in her ear.

"This doesn't have to be hard, Cylea. You can end this." He paused, every word perfect, so dynamic, so dramatic. "Come with me, Cylea. We can teach you how to become so much more than you are now. We can help you answer all those burning questions that keep you awake at night. We can give you everything that you desire." Her eyes flicked to him, and he sat back on his haunches, offering her his hand. "Come with me, Cylea, and I promise you won't regret it."

"What choice... do I have?" She managed, ignoring his gesture.

"Only the streets, the cold world that stretches beyond this sad, dusty little building." He shook his head. "There's nothing there for you, Cylea. Not even the Golden Koi can offer you what we can." He smiled gently. "Please. Let us help you."

She eyed his hand carefully. He was persistent, but his words rang true. She knew that he was right, that he'd been right from the beginning, and if she had just set her pride aside that first time... She closed her eyes against a rising tide of painful thoughts. There were so many terrible things that had happened since the last time she'd crossed paths with Castillo, so many things that might have been avoided, so much death. Tears fought to break from her eyes again, but she forced them back, biting the inside of her mouth in defiance. It hurt to think that she'd ultimately been responsible for whatever had happened to Jack– in all likelihood, he was dead, and probably Sheila too. Two more friends that had willingly sacrificed themselves to keep her alive.

Drawing in a deep breath, she nodded and took Castillo's hand. In the next instant, she was on her feet, Castillo smiling brightly even as he silently directed one of the bodyguards out of the room with a quick series of one-handed sign-gestures. The vatgrown had hardly been gone a moment when the steady, thobbing hum of a helicopter approached, beating against the building as it touched lightly down on the rooftop above them.

"So... anything I want, huh?" She managed a smile, blinking away the tears.

"Anything." He assured, grinning.

"Sir." A third vatgrown bodyguard slipped through the doorway, sunglasses catching a quick line of glare as his gaze flicked from Castillo to Cylea and back. "Lotus seven is ready."

"Excellent." Castillo squeezed Cylea's hand gently. "Well, shall we?"

Chapter 30: Saltwater Salvation

Lotus seven was a modest little chopper, a black and chrome number that was more plastic than aluminum, with a distinct lack of hard, angular edges. The pilot and Castillo exchanged a quick series of silent gestures through the curved glass of the cockpit and the side door came open, swinging back along tracks to reveal a hard floor of grip-textured steel and a series of fold-down seats set with five-point harnesses. Inside, two men were already seated and waiting, one of them a suited vatgrown, the other a grizzled old veteran decked out in baggy olive-drab, gnarled hands gripping the smooth camouflage stock of a formidable looking, high-caliber rifle. He looked up at Castillo, then nodded once, letting his eyes drift to Cylea. An unlit and mangled, hand-rolled cigarette twitched at the edge of his mouth.

Castillo went first, offering his hand to help her up into the chopper– smiling gently, she ignored the gesture and climbed in past him, taking a seat between the veteran and the far wall. Let him think what he wanted– he may have caught her, even earned a little bit of her trust and respect, but he was still corporate as far as she was concerned, a suit through and through. Castillo glanced at her, mild curiosity playing across his features, but she ignored it, belting in quickly while he watched. He seemed to take the hint– a moment later, he was seated across from her, securing his own harness, the veteran watching the entire exchange with quiet, detached amusement.

A nearly imperceptible change in the sound of the rotors signaled their departure, and a moment later, they were in the air, darting off over Santa Monica and headed west, away from the hazy glare of the morning sun. Castillo leaned forward in his seat, watching the cockpit while the vatgrown beside him conferred quietly with someone through an implanted transceiver that was probably tied into the chopper's comm network. Cylea glanced at the veteran, but his eyes were closed, the cigarette hanging limply at the edge of his lip, a tiny, whiskey-colored head of stringy tobacco poking out from the end of the crumpled white jacket.

He looked seasoned and weathered, as old and tired as the cigarette. He was probably in his late fifties, with the kind of rough, rugged look that came from spending several decades in the rough climates of the far north, a victim to harsh glare and the biting cold– the pair of antique, multi-spectrum goggles pushed halfway up his forehead seemed capable of attesting to that sort of lifestyle, as flaked and worn as they were.

He looked up under her scrutiny and smiled, a surprisingly gentle smile that she couldn't help but return. Slowly, carefully, he plucked the cigarette from his lips and slipped it back behind his ear.

"'Name's Mac." He smiled again. She shook his offered hand, already grinning. "You're Cylea, right?"

"Right." She affirmed. It was to be expected– the way Castillo had been chasing her, it wouldn't have been a surprise if the entire organization he worked for knew who she was, what she looked like, what she'd spent the last five years of her life doing, and probably a dozen other odd things on the side. It didn't really bother her– she'd gotten used to getting it from corporate types and criminals with high-power connections. Heck, anyone who knew what they were doing knew who she was before she ever even met them– only amateurs went into deals without picking up fed-grade intel from their hacker contacts beforehand.

"Mac provided the little diversion that got you out of the BTD's grasp this morning." Castillo broke in, the grizzled veteran nodding silently as the other continued. "We tried to track you and your friend Jack after the shootout at the market, but our orbital units lost you until you stopped moving long enough for us to locate you again." She opened her mouth to say something, but Castillo frowned slightly, adding. "I'm sorry. We still don't have any details on your bartender friend as yet."

Cylea looked away and closed her eyes. "Figures."

"If it's any consolation," Castillo tried, "the BTD still has him listed as missing."

Cylea shook her head. It was still too soon for the BTD records to have anything relevant or useful on the situation. Still, entertaining fantasies of Jack emerging from Hassan's Market victorious, despite how badly he'd been outnumbered, brought the traces of a smile back to her face. Jack was good with a pistol, but she doubted he was that good. Castillo caught the change in her features and tried to reassure her with another gentle smile.

"Sir," The vatgrown interjected suddenly, "Lotus three and twelve have radioed in, the motorcade's ETA is fifteen minutes, and the *Alekzandr* is standing by for departure." He smiled slightly as Castillo met his gaze. "Captain Angeletti has already obtained priority clearance, says we can leave the moment you give the word."

"Excellent." Castillo nodded once at the vatgrown, then cast a glance toward Cylea again, but her attention had already drifted elsewhere, eyes watching the city slipping by beneath them, a tapestry of glass and steel bound together by thick lines of black plasticore and grey pavecrete. His harness came loose easily, and a moment later, he was crouched on the deck, flipping back the lid of a squat orange plastic crate mounted beside the seat. The noise attracted a glance from Cylea, but by the time she'd torn her eyes away from the sprawling pavecrete jungle below, he was already standing, the lid coming closed with a satisfying sigh and a quiet click.

"Here," He pivoted, pushing a neatly folded bundle of dark fabric into her hands. "You'll need this. It gets cold where we're going, and I doubt that vend clothing will be enough to keep you warm."

"What?" She asked, but Castillo had already turned away, striking up a conversation with the pilot that came back to Cylea as little more than half-heard words, quick gestures, and simple, understanding nods. Her eyes flicked back to the bundle.

It unfolded easily, opening to reveal a long trenchcoat of thick, dark fabric–it looked like something made for weathering strong winters in the northern reaches of the European District, the kind of thing that might come in handy in Moscow or maybe somewhere in Norway. Her eyes flicked back to Mac. "Where are we going?"

Mac opened his mouth to say something, but closed it again as Castillo approached, a wide grin already spreading across his face. "Come up to the cockpit, there's something you should see." She smiled back and nodded once, quickly working the harness loose and slipping on the trenchcoat as she came up to stand beside him, peering past the pilot and out through the glass. At first she didn't see it, just saw the city, the coastline, and the sludge that slowly became the endless blue of the ocean stretching on beyond it, but as Castillo pointed, her eyes immediately picked out the details of a ship, floating at the edge of civilization, a buoyant building with the girth of a massive skyscraper laid out longways across the water. A pack of black helicopters perched across its back, taking up nearly the entire space but for a single glowing halo that marked the one unoccupied roost.

"Is that..." She trailed off. "No, no way."

"The *Alekzandr* is top of the line, a vessel designed to rival the most expansive and luxurious cruiseline ships, capable of quickly traversing the widest oceans and fitted with the latest in nautical electronics. Everything is updated and replaced on a bi-yearly basis at our own drydock facility in the South American district's Panama province." He smiled at her. "Right down to the gambling machines."

Cylea gaped. The boat was immense, a monster of glass, chrome, and glossy bright colors washed across a brilliant white hull that stretched fifteen stories from the surface of the sea to the sky above. Only the hulking backswept cylinder of the ship's massive smokestack stood higher, towering over the ship's highest deck, a stretch of high-carbon nanofiber plates woven together and treated to look like genuine wood around the edges, while the center was reinforced and sprayed with a layer of gritty high-traction plasticore. It was the kind of stuff that was strong enough to stand up to the abuse of countless landing and departing helicopters while still staying soft enough to cushion and support the feet, putting a spring in the step of practically every technician, vatgrown, and suit that wandered across its dark surface.

As the chopper descended, she shook her head, marveling at the vessel's incredible length– the thing stretched out along nearly a quarter of a mile of polluted coastline, pumping black smoke into the air as the sludge stirred and boiled around it, a halo of frothy black and green set with hundreds of tiny pieces of garbage. Tires and planks bobbed on the waves, mingling with other trash, soda cans, antifreeze jugs and silicon magazines. Some of it was old– grungy pieces of god-only-knew-what that had been shifting between the shoreline and the depths of the pacific for close to a century, or in some cases, perhaps longer.

Touchdown was soft, a slight bump, and then the rotors slowed suddenly, spinning down as the pilot unbuckled his harness and popped sideways out of the cabin, followed shortly by Mac and the vatgrown. Cylea stalled for a moment, still awestuck, but a quick glance exchanged with Castillo got her moving again. A moment later and she was on the deck, Castillo trailing a few paces behind her.

It was then, standing there on the soft, textured plasticore, that the true immensity of the ship hit home, the realization that thousands of tons of iron and dense carbon stood swaying gently beneath her, perched impossibly on the surface of the ocean. She turned, holding the trenchcoat tight against herself with both arms as the blast from the helicopter's rotors and the natural current of the wind whipped past her, whistling through her hair and throwing the coat's tail out behind her dramatically. She fixed Castillo with a gaze that was serious, yet open and receptive, ready to accept whatever it was that he might tell her. It was obvious there was power here– everything about Castillo, every manner, form, and nuance with which he delivered his words, whether they be a simple command or a lengthy explanation and the sleek, unusually high-end vatgrowns that trailed him, radiated affluence and status. The limo, the helicopter, the boat– every bit of it seemed to fit perfectly. This was a man elevated high above the average corporate exec, this was a man who, while likely not number one on whatever totem pole he had chosen to integrate himself into, seemed to have an incredible amount of power at his disposal. Oh sure, it probably wasn't even close to something that someone like Ted Solomon or a handful of other multi-trillionaires who pulled the strings behind thousands of smaller corporate entities might have pulled off in an attempt to impress her, to win her trust and her respect, but it certainly seemed close.

Castillo met her gaze for a moment, then looked away, a smile touching his lips again, so knowing and amused, as if he could read her thoughts, as if he knew exactly what she was thinking.

She swallowed uneasily, putting stray thoughts aside. There were more important things to focus on than his smile, no matter how knowing or charming it might be.

"I want to know who you are." She said levelly. "I want to know who you work for. Tell me everything."

Castillo nodded once. "Follow me."

Chapter 31: Creme and Country

"The organization which I directly represent is very old." Castillo began, only stopping to quietly thank one of the hulking bodyguards as two cups of tea were handed off. Cylea nodded her thanks, but set the steaming drink gently on the smooth grey surface of the table between them without giving it another thought.

Ten minutes earlier, they had been on the highest deck of the *Alekzandr*, but Castillo had been insistent that her questions wait until they were in more comfortable surroundings, as he put it. A pair of vatgrown bodyguards had then led them down into the bowels of the ship and then moved on to other duties, leaving them sitting on cushy velvet seats in a little alcove on the second level, close to the water. Tucked away next to a huge circular window at the far end of the ship's expansive lobby with only a table between them, they were finally alone, or so it seemed– there was no sign of the vatgrowns, except when they were called upon to deliver whatever refreshments Castillo asked for, but that didn't mean she and Castillo weren't being watched. Cylea knew better– when a suit was involved, you were never truly alone.

Castillo smiled gently at her and took a sip of his tea. "Would you care for a canape? Perhaps caviar?" She shook her head silently and his smile widened. "Have you ever tried caviar? It's really quite exquisite."

"I'm sure." She managed, that serious, careful, considering gaze still holding his eyes. "Maybe I'll try it some time." She crossed her legs anxiously. "You were saying..."

"Ah, yes." He nodded quickly, setting down his own tea. "The organization I represent is so old, in fact, that one of our most elderly and esteemed members can actually recall a time when the RAF of the United Kingdom–" He gestured quickly as he elaborated. "The Royal Air Force," He paused a moment, "Erm... the United Kingdom is the old name for the British Isles, something from before the unification" He reached for his tea again. "Regardless, he remembers a time when the RAF were actively engaging the German Luftwaffe during the Battle of Britain."

Cylea blinked once in calm disbelief, opened her mouth and hesitated on the edge of a thought. "You're not talking about something that happened during World War two, are you?" Her eyes darted away uncertainly, then locked with his again. "I mean, that was... that was over two hundred years ago, wasn't it?"

"Approximately two hundred and twenty years ago." He smiled congenially.

"But..." She laughed, shaking her head. "That's... you're telling me you work for someone almost three hundred years old?"

Castillo chuckled. "Work for? Heavens no!" He shot her a quick grin. "Sir Reed is merely an *esteemed Noble* of the Order– and, he's not so old as you might think." Castillo shrugged absently. "In a few months we'll be celebrating his two hundred and thirty-fourth birthday."

Cylea stared at him for a long moment before answering, considering her response carefully– it seemed almost impossible that someone could live to be so old, and the thought intrigued her, but it was something else entirely that had caught her interest and held it like a sluggish fly in the thick web of a quick and dangerous spider.

"Order?" She asked. Castillo nodded once, silently. "What Order?"

Setting his tea back down, Castillo grinned and leaned back into his seat with a satisfied sigh. "*The* Order." He spread his arms in a wide gesture. "We call ourselves the Immortals, those who live in Eternity."

"You must be pretty good at keeping hidden." She arched an eyebrow at him. "I've never even heard of your people before."

Castillo grinned. "Not surprising, actually." Sitting up and reaching for his tea again, he continued quickly. "The public isn't typically aware of us– individual members of the *Order* are generally hand-picked to take the praise for the things that we do to improve the well-being of our countrymen," he took a sip and gestured vaguely. "The reworking of the London Underground system into something actually tolerable, for instance."

"How do you deal with the media?" She glanced briefly at her own tea, still steaming on the table between them. "I mean, I'm sure someone out there is smart enough to connect the dots und find out what's going on, especially when you've got people as old as... Sir Reed?" Castillo nodded firmly, and she continued "Especially when you've got people as old as Sir Reed in your ranks."

"We actually have a sort of agreement with the media." He set the cup down lightly. "Every major news agency that does business in the Isles has a member of the Order within their infrastructure to assure that nothing is ever aired that might even hint at our existence." He gestured vaguely again. "We have other measures in place to deter the smaller agencies and private individuals out to make a name for themselves."

"Bounties?" She asked carefully.

"Rarely." His response was quick, level. "With a little delicate manipulation, we have made most such threats to our security simply give up of their own volition." He chuckled. "After all, who would believe a cocky young reporter claiming that a secret society of ageless and affluent British citizens were operating out of the bowels of the British Museum, the British Library at Saint Pancras, and a dozen other historic locations throughout the Isles, including the infamous Rosslyn Castle, most of them packed to the brim with tourists on any given day– and when so little proof exists!" A wide grin spread across his features. "Imagine the response if such a reporter actually tried to implicate the Queen!" He laughed. "He'd be carted off to the loony bin, and the best part of it is– he'd still be correct!"

Cylea swallowed carefully.

"Exactly." He grinned again. "We've worked very hard to become *untouchable*."

"So what do you want with me?" She asked. "The truth this time."

"My dear, what you don't seem to understand is that I've told you nothing but the truth thus far–" He picked up the tea again, sipped, gestured vaguely. "You're an extraordinary woman, and we're an extraordinary organization." He smiled benignly. "The perfect match."

"Und that's it? Just looking for an 'extraordinary' girl to pull into your flock?" She scoffed. "There's got to be more to it than that."

"As I told you before," He gently set the tea down again. "We're as interested in finding out exactly what you are and where you came from as you are." An amused and oddly charming smile slipped across his face. "Of course, I'd be lying if I said we weren't hoping to find something along the way that might make the Order more... *extraordinary* itself."

"So you're looking to see what makes me tick?" She asked, voice picking up a note of hostility. "I hope this doesn't involve cutting me open or injecting me with anything."

Castillo backed off immediately, instantly submissive. "Oh, no, no no. This is your search, Cylea, we're merely here to provide whatever assistance you may need to find your answers." He shrugged. "Think of it as a research grant," He gestured quickly, "We work together, your brains, our brawn," he smiled again, "shared profits."

"Hmm." She paused for a moment, studying his face. "Und no catch, right?"

"Unless you consider our protection a catch." He grinned.

"Well, I..." She trailed off, then shrugged, laughing as she stood, then stretching. "Jeez, I have no idea where to start! I guess I need some time to think."

"I can have one of the Derivatives show you to your stateroom, if you wish." Castillo quickly offered.

"Sure, ja." She said absently; Castillo raised his finger as she turned away, gesturing to some hidden piece of surveillance equipment. "Wait." She rounded on him, curiosity playing across his face. "Derivatives?"

"The vatgrown bodyguards." He gestured as one appeared, coming to a stop next to the table. "They're our own special mix– there is nothing quite like them in the world, and we're always working to improve them." He smiled up at the Derivative. "Orin, please, tell us about yourself."

"Yes sir," the Derivative shifted in his stance. "I am a thirty-four epsilon batch product, version six point oh two of vat twelve's standard lineup, factory designation 00R511N, field designation 'Orin.'"

"They're very well behaved," Castillo added, grinning again. "We've only had one go rogue, and we solved that problem by promoting him and securing him citizenship." He studied the Derivative's face. "What do you think of that, Orin?"

"You are speaking of unit Cain?" Castillo nodded, and the Vatgrown grimaced. "Cain is weak. Power has given him an easy lifestyle and made him *weak*." Orin shook his head. "He serves only as an example of freethinking leading to failure and corruption. He should have been shot the moment he began to go rogue."

"Careful Orin," Castillo grinned again, "That's a superior you're talking about."

"Sorry sir." The Derivative's face became blank again instantly. "I am willing to be punished for my transgression."

"That's not necessary." Castillo's grin widened as he continued. "But you are a good boy for suggesting it." He glanced at Cylea, who arched an eyebrow back at him. "Why don't you show Miss Von Mitternacht to her stateroom, get her anything she needs."

Orin nodded immediately, then turned to face her, offering his arm. "Miss?"

She shot Castillo a wry smile before turning back to the Derivative. "Sure."

Chapter 32: Mission of Mercy

By the third day, Castillo had stopped calling.

It was a waste of time, he had decided. Cylea never answered, and the camera in the hallway outside her stateroom hadn't recorded anyone going in or out, except the *Alekzandr*'s chief physician and Humberto, the svelt little cabana boy that brought whatever food and drinks Cylea ordered through room service, and even they had been ignored a few times.

With his status, it was easy to obtain a duplicate room key. If she wouldn't answer the phone, he'd have to speak with her in person, and the only way to do that, it seemed, was to enter unannounced and face her directly. It was rude, but desperate times required desperate measures, or so he told himself. Even knowing that, even with the resolve he had built up with reserved, tempered frustration, layer by layer until it had driven him to take an action he considered to be both drastic and uncivilized, his hand still hesitated before smoothly pushing the keycard into the reader on her stateroom door. He had to do this– if it wasn't done, she would end up staying in that room for the entire journey, locked away from conversation, from opportunity, and a thousand other wonderful things that the *Alekzandr* had to offer.

The door came open smoothly. Cylea's eyes flicked up and met his in the reflection on the glass door between her and the balcony outside–beyond, deep blue ocean rolled by, sharp, frothy white peaks stained with the orange and scarlets of sunset and cresting each restless wave to the dark line of the horizon, where the coming night was still dominated by the brilliant bloody rays of a dying day. Castillo took one step into the room and Cylea's eyes flicked away from him, turning to focus on some distant point outside.

"Ah, sorry to come in unannounced." He began, carefully picking his way between stacks of dishes left over from a dozen meals and twice as many drinks. Cylea sat alone on the room's only bed with her back to him– beside her, a fashion model winked seductively at him from the cover of a silicon magazine. "But... ah... you weren't answering my calls, so I..." He trailed off. "I hope I'm not intruding too terribly much."

"It doesn't matter." She managed, eyes unmoving. "I knew you'd show up eventually. It is your boat after all."

Castillo chuckled. "Am I really that easy to predict? I've always prided myself on my spontaneity."

"You've got money und power," Cylea turned to face him, "Sorry, but you're a suit, und you act like one."

"Don't be so quick to judge." He shot her a well-meaning smile. "Not all men with money are the same, nor do they all have the same principles."

"I'll have to see it to believe it." she turned away again.

"Ah, yes well, as entertaining as it might be to debate with you about the mannerisms of the wealthy, it is not the reason I came." he paused, taking a deep breath. "I know it's important for you to carefully consider how you're going to approach this dilemma of discovering exactly what you are, but you don't honestly plan to spend the entire cruise locked up in here do you?" He grinned. "After all, all work and no play makes... well, you know the rest, I'm sure."

"Ja." She shot him a tired glance. "I don't know, maybe I'll just stay here und sleep until we get wherever it is we're going." She shook her head. "I... haven't really decided. Where are we going, anyway?"

"England." He responded immediately. "London, actually. Through Panama."

"Mm." She managed.

"You really should get out a little while we're at sea."

"Why?" she asked absently, letting her eyes drift back to the view of the ocean as it rolled past the balcony like the surface of some endless river stretching off into foggy eternity. "There's a great view of the sea here, room service brings everything I need, und the 'set has more service channels than I ever imagined existed." She gestured to the stylish chrome broadband broadcast headset resting on a nearby folding table, the light playing oddly across the 'set's blue-teal eye-teasing edges, throwing colored isometric shapes against the room's creamy orange walls. "I still haven't had a chance to flick through them all yet. I made it through the news, the evangelism, the porn, the porn-evangelism–"

"Well, the *Alekzandr* has more to offer than just BBH channels," Castillo cut her off hastily, forcing another grin as she glanced back up at him. "You should get out and explore the vessel, hmm? Try to meet some people, catch one of the shows."

"I've still got that bounty on my head, Castillo." She sighed. "No offense to your people, but I'm just not interested in taking any chance on getting my head blown off, no matter how small that chance may be."

Castillo grimaced and Cylea looked away again.

"I know it must seem like I'm being paranoid, but..." she trailed off, sighing again in the pause. "You know, I just need some time alone... A lot's happened, I've got a lot on my mind."

"Very well," Castillo stood and sighed loudly, too loudly, pushing his hands into his suit coat pockets. "I guess I'll have to find someone else to attend the concert with, then."

"Ja, guess so" she managed, her thoughts already somewhere else. "Have fun."

He paused for a moment, slightly stunned at the ease with which she had dismissed him, then shifted in his stance and cocked a harsh, questioning eyebrow at her. "You aren't even going to ask who it is that is performing tonight, are you?"

"Nein." She said absently, shrugging as she turned back to him again. "Enjoy the show, you can tell me all about it when we get to London."

Castillo all but sputtered. "Cylea, you have no idea what you would be missing if I simply let you stay cooped up here in this room!" He tried. "I promise that it will be worth whatever risk might be involved. Just..."

"So what if I miss someone dancing around on a stage singing about heartbreak or how much they love someone else." She shook her head and scoffed. "No thanks, Castillo. I've gotten a big enough dose of emotional crap in the past week to last me for my entire life, und then some."

"What if that someone dancing around on stage was the most esteemed Miss Arizona Alhambra?" he asked suddenly.

Now it was her turn to cock an eyebrow at him. "You're joking right?"

Castillo shook his head in silent denial, and Cylea looked away. It had always been one of her dreams, a distant and seemingly unattainable one, yet a dream she'd hoped to fulfill nonetheless, to see the Neoclassic Electrorock goddess perform live, even if only over a Neuroline feed; to be faced with a chance to see that now put an anxious knot in her throat and made her suddenly self-conscious of the cheap vend clothing the Immortals had provided her with.

Her eyes shot back to Castillo's. "You're telling me that Arizona Alhambra is onboard this ship, und that she's going to be putting on a *live* performance tonight?"

Castillo's hand flicked casually out of his pocket, nonchalantly displaying two old-style paper tickets with the words "Arizona Alhambra, special showing" and "front row" stamped in goldleaf across their pale, textured surfaces. Cylea hesitated on the edge of a dry swallow.

A wide, knowing smile spread across Castillo's face. "The show starts in one hour. I'll send one of the Derivatives down with something fancy for you to wear, and then I'll be back in forty-five minutes to pick you up."

She swallowed anxiously, breathing an excited "okay" before getting hurriedly to her feet and running a single, trembling hand through her hair.

Castillo's smile cracked into a full-on grin and a similar, excited expression shot across Cylea's face, ivory teeth shining in the light. it seemed almost unreal, almost too good to be true, as if it were some dream that might spiral down into some nightmarish twist at any moment, sending her careening into the claws of the hulking, boulbous shapes that hunted her through the labyrinthine tunnels of her darker dreams. But then, it was all still so real– carefully, hesitating only slightly at first, she reached out and touched him, her fingers brushing lightly against the soft fabric of his suit.

Castillo's grin widened again, and he caught her hand gently before it could fall back to her side.

"This is real." He beamed. "This is not a dream, and I can promise you that it's only going to get better from here. Let the Immortals take care of you, and even your wildest dreams may come to pass."

"Thank you, Castillo." She breathed.

"Alan," he gently squeezed her hand. "Please, call me Alan."

Chapter 33: Walpurgisnacht

At first, there was nothing but blackness, the weak, quiet chatter of an audience cloaked in darkness adding to the suspenseful ambiance-- Arizona Alhambra's performances were few and far between, and to say that the woman had earned her title as Queen of Neuroline was an understatement at the very least. In the music industry, she was nothing short of a legend, her performances the work of divinity, every nuance and move that of a goddess. No one else was as good, no one even came close, and every member of the audience knew it.

A thin silver line was faintly visible in the darkness, the slightly curved edge of an unlit stage sitting at the bottom of five levels of wraparound tiers utterly packed with seated fans. A pack of hulking, ominous shapes traded whispers in the pit beneath the stage, barely visible in the darkness but for the occasional shifting of black on black. Cylea grinned at Castillo, hardly able to contain her excitement. Someone a dozen seats to the left was already singing quietly.

As the tempo for Arizona's hit song, "Fire Away" began to echo through the auditorium, the crowd shot up out of their seats, standing seemingly as one, an ocean of immaculate suits and glittering dresses cheering and clapping, faces suddenly lit up as a narrow edge of cold light the color of frozen steel sliced through the depthless abyss. In the next instant, it flickered, splitting into a thousand oscillating rays that pulsed wildly and formed a rich, erratic halo centered around a single bright point of burning green chrome.

The point flashed once, then darkened, collapsing to a faded spot of blue-black that stirred and grew amidst the frenzied lights-- in the next moment, it slipped up between them, a tapered bar of washed-out, vaguely pink shadow that quickly resolved itself into a more defined shape, a silhouette that took on color and feature as it stepped elegantly through a shimmering sheet of silver light. Liquid chrome washed over shadow, revealing a seductive smile as it played across luscious lips the color of glossy wet red cherries.

One simple, fluid gesture of one heavily-gloved hand, and a wave of neon green washed across the stage, shooting a streamer of eager electric foam up the sides of her knee-length high-heel boots, liquid light bright against black leather. A toss of her head sent shimmers of silver-cerulean spiraling through her wild, red-brown hair, twisting sensuously past her dark eyes and playing across the textured brass of her moon-shaped earrings. A smooth, tantalizingly shallow pivot of the hips sent burning tendrils of electric orange threading their way across her short, blindingly teal skirt before they divided, some etching lines down the unnaturally smooth skin of her legs, while others shot northward into the tight red leather of her smooth, sleeveless, low cut top and across bare arms to disappear into the black fabric of her gloves, dozens of chrome contact points flashing excitedly, putting on their own lightshow of refracted colors.

She snapped her fingers and the sound was deafening, a shockwave that kicked the heart into gear and whipped the audience into a frenzy– She flashed them all a smile, and then instantly her hands were alive with a flurry of color, darting left and right to summon the framework of an instrument drawn up in three-dimensional lines of glowing aquamarine. The instant her fingers glanced off one another, completing the design, it exploded into a shower of brilliant, color-changing sparks that fell away to reveal a neon pink electric guitar, a simple, almost stereotypical six string design that hung from a shimmering strap of liquid silver with hot lines of glowing electric teal playing excitedly along the edges. Another toss of her wild hair, and she threw her arms wide, pure white light dancing off the contacts of her gloves as she screamed in ecstasy, instantly summoning a pair of muscular dancers that materialized from tiny whirlwinds of hot white sparks spinning apart in the darkness behind her. The crowd went insane, and she winked at the writing mass of amped and screaming bodies pulsing in the darkness. Without saying a word, she'd instantly turned hundreds of polite, reserved corporates into animals, shocking all those dead hearts back to life with an infusion of fresh, boiling blood and a mild dose of genetically engineered pheromones carried on a wave of sound, a flash of light, and a series of sexy gestures.

Arizona Alhambra was the embodiment of Neoclassic Electrorock in every way, a woman with the voice, the grace, the style, the mind, and the body of a Goddess. There wasn't a man alive that didn't want her or a woman that didn't want to be her. She was everything, the ultimate, the one, and she knew it. It was obvious in the way she smiled, in the way her lips curved just right, or those stunning teeth caught the light, the way she swung her hips, and the way she sang. Peerless, that's how the critics described her. Perfect.

The subdermal microphone came alive as she took a half step forward, planting one boot hard on the dark floor of the stage, the sound echoing, orange flame etching across the floor from the point of impact, chasing away the darkness with seething streamers of rich color.

"You ready?" She asked– the response was immediate, a resounding, collective "Yeah!"

"Boys?"

"Yeah!" Came the immediate response, distinctively male.

"Girls?"

"Yeah!" Cylea screamed, voice lost in the sound of a hundred or more other women echoing her sentiment.

Arizona grinned again and leaned in close, face suddenly serious. "Yeah?" She paused. "Let's skin this cat."

Her fingers fell across the chords as she took a step back. The first note shot through the auditorium and hit the cheering audience like the shockwave of a jetfighter breaking the sound barrier, forcing some back into their seats while others simply grinned, shaken by the passing wavefront. The brilliant ivory grin that shot across Arizona's face flickered and dropped away as she hammered out the notes, matching the tempo perfectly, lances of lime-green laser tracing erratically across the stage and carving upward through the darkness. She opened her mouth, and suddenly the audience was awestruck, paralyzed by a sudden overload of chemicals, light, and sound.

How 'bout some latex

Or some leather

Burning rubber

And stormy weather

A hidden place

In the hills

Have some fun

We've got our thrills

No time to cuddle

Or coochie-coo

You've got a thousand hornets coming after you!

She swung the guitar up and out in a sudden movement, sliding one foot backward fluidly, fingers dancing across the strings with electric precision as the dancers crossed behind her, bathed in light the color of beveled gold that quickly gave way to a cascade of shimmering, hot blue waves. Lips curved– the next lines came hot and fast, accented by deep bass, held together by phantom synth.

'And it's frantic

Electric

I know what I like

It's shocking
And sexy
An adrenaline high

'Cause it's quick,
I'm eager,
Potent and spry
It's hot
And wet
Getting mud in your eyes

The transition was almost instantaneous, every line flowing into the next. Arizona was a mile away and wholly there all at once, absorbed by the music. Rich ribbons of neon scarlet carved through the air, hot tracers following in their wake.

'Cause I'm ridin',
I am ridin'
'Cause I'm ridin',
I am ridin'

She swung into the next transition just as perfectly as the last, synth picking up, irradiating the riff with hot electric notes that burned behind the guitar, a machine caught in a raging inferno, blasting apart, detonating with Hollywood ferocity.

And I've got mud on my 'bars
And mud on my wheels,
Rubber spinnin' through muddy hills
Then I slide into town
And boys start grinnin'
So I whip out my gun and say—

The guitar was suddenly gone, obliterated in a quick flash of silver to be replaced by a stylish forty-five revolver. An eager, triumphant smile shot across her face as the lights came to a sudden stop, bathing the stage in bright crimson. She bit off a quick laugh, shattering the moment.

Fire Away.

The heavy lines of a disembodied bass roared through the auditorium. The lights flashed green, then blue, the dancers mimicking her every move before suddenly dropping into a crouch and cartwheeling past each other to drop into another crouch. She swung her finger out toward the crowd in a slow arc, light following the movement, illuminating faces one by one as she sang, the revolver gone as quickly as it had come.

Fire awaaaaaaaaaay,

Fire Away.

Fire awaaaaaaaaaay,

"Yeah!" She shouted. "*Fire away!*"

There was a blinding flash of blue flame, and then she was striking the chords of that pink guitar again, hammering on the fretboard and spinning off into a windmilling motion as she shifted in her stance. Letting the guitar drop to her waist, she swung the neck out toward the crowd again, fingers moving too fast to track, then slowing again. Squealing electric notes shot through the darkness, harsh distortion bending the senses, killing thought, drawing everyone into the moment. A shrill whistle shot through the guitar solo, earning someone in the crowd a quick nod and a wink that came and went so fluidly that they almost seemed part of the whole performance, something almost reflexive despite its inherent perfection. The cheering picked up, Arizona soaking up every bit of it. After a moment, the notes slowed again and she let another grin shoot across her face, shifting in her stance and swinging the neck of the guitar around as her fingers knocked the final few marks of the solo from the strings, lips parting eagerly.

Got no time for hover

Or headset rides

Mud and rubber

Is what I like

My hidden place

In the hills

A crotch-rocket

And rainy chills

So much power

Between my thighs

I'll sail my dirt-bike through your sky!

She shifted again, guitar blasting, shrieking. A quick jerk of the head, and the dancers went into a spin behind her, bathed in a flash of chromatic sparks that shot into the darkness like a cloud of angry iridescent fireflies, blinding in their brilliance the instant before they fell again, burning out to cold embers of sapphire blue.

'Cause it's frantic

Electric

I know what I like

It's shocking

And sexy

An adrenaline high

'And it's quick,
I'm eager,
Potent and spry
It's hot
And wet
Getting mud in your eyes

Sweeping rays of blazing purple ate hot lines through the thick darkness, trailing incandescence in their wake as she slipped through the transition perfectly, fingers as intensely alive as her eyes. Everything seemed to be building, picking up speed as it rushed toward an eventual climax, a welcome release that urged the crowd on, a body of like minds screaming for their collective mental orgasm.

Yeah, it's frantic
Electric
I know what I like
It's shocking
And sexy
An adrenaline high

It's quick,
I'm eager,
Potent and spry
It's hot
And wet
Getting mud in your eyes

And I've got it on my 'bars
And I got it on my wheels,
That rubber spinnin' through muddy hills
    Then I slide into town
    And boys start grinnin'
    So I whip out my gun and say.
Fire Away.

The crowd echoed her, screaming the two words with insane need, the voices of hundreds of restrained lunatics held inches away from the light of freedom. The air was hot, thick, rich with sweat and chemicals, the heat of passionate, unearthly sex distilled and atomized, blasted out of the ceiling, absorbed into every pore, inhaled with every breath. The beat only drove them on, pulse quickening, eyes widening, sweat breaking across every inch of skin, every body adding its own mix of chemicals to the fray, a fierce pheromone cocktail that was kept cycling through the auditorium by a silent and highly efficient ventilation system.

Fire awaaaaaaaaaay,

Fire Away.

Fire awaaaaaaaaaay,

"Yeah!" She screamed again, jumping, throwing a finger up in the air. There was no revolver this time, just her and the pink guitar screaming together, pummeling the senses as she ripped through the notes, moving seductively, dancers darting impossibly fast.

Fire awaaaaaaaaaay!

Fire away!

Instantly she was on her knees, skidding to the edge of the stage as she tore the final few shrieking notes from her guitar, the dancers behind her exploding into a cascade of blinding blue sparks and a flash of neon green fire that shot past her and into the audience, startling some as it flickered and fell away in a thin shower of sparkling silver dust. The silence that followed in its wake was shocking, oppressive. Airborne nanoagents instantly neutralized the chemicals in the air, leaving a sense of emptiness that everyone seemed to feel, a sense of release, a sense of finality. Someone on a tier further up screamed. "*You fucking rock!*"

Arizona caught it and flashed that killer grin into the sea of suddenly clapping and cheering fans, managing a sultry sounding "I know" that was lost on a rising tide of applause. A moment later, and she was on her feet again, fingers hovering over the chords. An expectant hush fell over the crowd immediately, almost too fast, suddenly serious, like addicts offered a hit for a moment of silence. She grinned again, and gave them exactly what they needed, guitar thundering even as they exploded into cheering again. A quick series of notes brought her to the lyrics, hundreds of voices screaming every word even as she did.

Rock isn't dead

And it ain't never gonna die!

We've got an eternity

So shut up and jam.

"Sir, we have a situation."

The voice cut through the moment and the squealing guitar like a knife, instantly drawing Cylea's attention to a single Derivative who stood in the aisle, nodding apologies to both her and Castillo.

Alan nodded once, firmly, then disappeared into the darkness, following the vatgrown bodyguard. Cylea watched them for a moment before her eyes darted back, following Arizona's movements as she busted a blazing riff of gritty notes across the strings of her guitar.

"Miss Von Mitternacht?" The gently smiling face of a Japanese man slipped into view beside her– Slowly, reluctantly, she tore her eyes from the scene again and met his benign gaze, taking in the finely made suit of dark silk and the brilliant silver dragon that stretched the length of his sleeve. "Could I have a moment of your time? Your very safety may be at stake."

Chapter 34: Honor and Choice

Cylea was still grinning when they reached the leisure deck, an open stretch of long pools and sturdy aluminum furniture that lay open to the night. All of the helicopters had long since taken flight, the gritty plasticore landing pads broken down and rolled away for future use, leaving the pools, the bars, and the buffet tables exposed. Brilliant white lights feebly pushed away the darkness that pressed in from the endless sea like a thick black pudding. Long, dark shadows stretched across textured and synthetic hardwood like eager hands.

Arizona Alhambra's words still echoed through her mind as she walked. The thrill, the light, the sound– the reverberations from "Rock isn't dead," chased her through the ship, that amazing voice pumped through the shipwide intercom direct from the performance, echoing quietly along the walls of the elevator and blasting into the night from a trio of massive speakers mounted around the centralmost pool. It wasn't the same as being there, as basking in the tangible, radiating aura that seemed to wash out from the woman as she moved across the stage, darting out from her feet to consume the audience with every screaming note that was ripped from her thundering guitar– not by a long shot, but the sound was still her, and the memory of seeing her live made even the experience of just listening all that much better.

The Japanese man that led Cylea was gentle and yet efficient, his silence as clean and fitting as the suit he wore. Everything about him was strikingly immaculate and oddly simple, even practical, right down to every line of silver stitched into the black fabric of his sleeve– and he was aware to an unusual degree. The instant that Cylea glanced at him, he met her gaze, almost as if he had known the precise moment that her eyes would begin to move before even she did, but his smile was a soft and constant crease across an otherwise hard face, never wavering, never changing, his features like the carefully sculpted visage of some long forgotten shogun. He almost seemed like some representative of all the culture and history that had come before him, centuries of Japanese pride distilled into his perfect, clean-cut appearance, and yet everything about him was unmistakably westernized, like an overseas businessman who loved Japan, and yet had found some odd solace in conforming to the North American ideal.

His feet were silent on the textured tile of the deck as he led her to a poolside bar, nodding once to the bartender. The distinct lack of Derivatives was odd, as was the fact that, aside from the bartender and a trio of suits laughing over drinks a few tables away, she and the Japanese man were alone. It didn't help to ease her suspicions when she realized that she was the only person in sight who *wasn't* Japanese, but then, there was still a lot about the Immortals she didn't know-- maybe they had some contract with a Japanese company, an investor or a security agency that provided protection for the cruise ship aside from that already provided by the Derivatives Castillo seemed to be so proud of. Speculations replaced the songs rumbling through her head, but her thoughts came to an abrupt halt as the Japanese man carefully offered her a chair and pushed a little ceramic cup of warm liquid into her hands.

"Here, a drink."

Her eyes flicked first to the cup, then back to him, one eyebrow arching warily. "That bad, huh?"

"Of course not." He grinned, gesturing at the seat. "But, your whole life may be about to change, so in a sense, a drink is warranted. Here, sit."

She glanced at the cup again, then gently set it on the counter, taking the proffered seat, her eyes never leaving his dark gaze. "Und you are?" She gestured vaguely, and he grinned in response.

"Of course." He made a quick, shallow bow. "Please, you may call me Yamazaki."

A moment later, and he was seated beside her, the bartender offering him a cup of the same liquid. Cylea eyed hers warily, then let her eyes drift back to meet his again. "What is it?"

"Sake." He replied immediately, taking a quick sip before setting his own back on the counter. "Japanese rice wine. Very good."

"Very good," She echoed, then glanced at the cup again, considering. It was warm alcohol, which wasn't a new concept to her, but it wasn't something she'd ever had a taste for. But then, she'd never tried sake-- someone like Yamazaki probably knew exactly what he was talking about, knew it was better warm than cold, and the air was cooling steadily as the night deepened around them...

Ah, what the hell, she thought, and scooped up the cup, glancing once into its steaming depths before taking a quick sip. She grimaced reflexively-- it tasted oddly wheat-like, something close to the earthiness of bread. It wasn't a bad flavor, just... different, not what she had expected something like rice wine to taste like.

"I should tell you that I am not a member of the Immortals." Yamazaki began, setting his cup down on the bar, his face hardening, suddenly becoming a blank mask utterly devoid of emotion. Cylea looked up slowly, blankly, her mind half on the sake, half on him.

"Right." She nodded once, eyes on his as she took another sip. "You're a business man– A corporate suit in with Castillo und his people, right?" She shrugged, "I take it some kind of joint business venture thing is going on." She gestured vaguely again. "Something involving me, ja?

"Not quite." He grinned thinly, baring teeth. "Those that I work for... how shall I put it? We tend to find ourselves, ah... *in competition* with the Immortals." Cylea raised an eyebrow at him and he added. "It is a friendly competition, of course."

"How friendly?" She asked, setting the cup down. The bartender immediately topped the drink off, steam rising off dark sake, but Cylea ignored it, keeping her eyes fixed on Yamazaki.

"Friendly enough." He brushed the question aside with another benign smile. "Blood is rarely spilled between us."

"Who are you with?" She asked pointedly, unwilling to let him beat around the bush.

Yamazaki smiled. "Let us sidestep such blunt questions for now. Tell me, do you consider yourself to be an honorable woman?"

She arched an eyebrow warily, considering the question for a moment, half wondering why he'd asked it, and then simply shrugged, nodding quickly. "Ja." She reached for her sake.

"Then..." Yamazaki gestured vaguely, putting on an almost casual air. It was odd seeing the regal stiffness dissipate from his face and shoulders so quickly. "Your leaving of the Golden Koi was merely..." He trailed off.

"I haven't left the Golden Koi," She responded quickly, putting an edge in her voice. "I was in a pinch und Castillo's people pulled me out. I'm just under the protection of the Immortals right now." She narrowed her eyes at him. "Why, are you a Triad rep? Someone working with Shang?"

"No, my people rarely do business with the syndicates that come out of Hong Kong." He said, distaste tainting his tone. "The practices of most *Gaijin* organizations are too barbaric for our tastes."

Cylea paused for a moment, blinking. The foreign word had caught her off guard, more for the fact that she actually recognized it from somewhere, some broken fragment of memory, than for any other reason. Then realization came suddenly, and her breathing stalled momentarily— the name came to her lips with a quiet, macabre sort of reverence. "*Yakuza.*"

"Smart girl." Yamazaki grinned widely, picking up his sake cup and raising it slightly in a shallow imitation of a toast. Sweat broke across her forehead.

Everyone who operated beneath the radar of the law in any real capacity knew about the Yakuza. They were clean, direct, stealthy, and peerless in their efficiency. Looking back, she was almost surprised she hadn't noticed it immediately-- Yamazaki was Yakuza in every way, and painfully so, as sharp and deadly as the edge of an Emperor's katana. In lower circles, they were legend, the unseen hand that reached in and grabbed whatever it wanted whenever it wished-- people were known to disappear in the blink of an eye, corporations to go utterly bankrupt overnight, entire syndicates to collapse in on themselves and spontaneously combust, all at the hands of the Yakuza. And it wasn't just happenstance or a simple scapegoat either-- the Yakuza left their mark on everything they did, making it undeniably clear who was responsible, and erased anyone who tried to copycat their work or frame them for crimes they might consider minor or in anyway dishonorable. In a way, they were even more influential than the Immortals-- the Yakuza actually had a reputation, a name that actually inspired fear.

Cylea repressed a shiver. Yamazaki grinned again. She forced the issue: "What do you want?"

"What everyone else seems to want." He took a sip. "You and your loyalty."

"Why?" She asked, already knowing the answer, refusing to believe it.

"Because you are something special." He smiled benignly again. "The things you have done have given almost every corporate big wig and crime boss in the world an insatiable hard-on for you."

"How pleasant." She looked away, then took another sip of sake, trying to drown the bad taste rising across her palate.

"So--" He began again, after the pause, setting down his sake and leaning in toward her. The glance she gave him was distrust and mild disgust twisted together into something just short of a grimace. "What do you say to a chance to trade in the protection of the exorbitantly rich for that of an organization with the prestige of the Yakuza? No one would dare touch you in Tokyo."

"That's probably true, Hiro, but I think we both know what she's going to say."

Yamazaki and Cylea turned immediately, eyes fixing simultaneously on Castillo as he stepped out of the shadows, harsh white light making the hand wrapped around the grip of a handgun held loosely at his side a shade of pale just short of a death-like pallor. The sound of a shotgun action cycling echoed behind them, the clink of a shell bouncing against the floor-- the Bartender had pulled an ominous looking weapon from the shadows behind the bar and stood pointing the muzzle directly at Castillo, his stern features unwavering even as two Derivatives moved in behind him, pistols drawn, fingers taut against cold steel triggers.

"Alan Castillo, Spade of Alekzandr's great Triumvirate, right?" Yamazaki grinned. "And it seems you already know who I am."

"Hiro Yamazaki, one of the Yakuza's finest Sweepers." Castillo's eyes flicked to the bartender, the man's face blank, shotgun never wavering. "And the man behind you is Takeshi Nomura, if I'm not mistaken, the same man who trained you."

Yamazaki's grin widened. "Indeed. So the Immortals are still a force to be reckoned with after all." He shifted in his seat, reaching for his sake, his eyes still fixed solidly on Castillo. "Tell me, how is Mason? Last time we met, she ruined one of my best suits with buckshot. It is a good thing I always wear a vest."

"Sara is both alive and well, but then, you already knew that." Castillo made a quick, dismissive gesture with his free hand, the pistol never leaving his side. "Shall we cut the idle chatter and get down to business?"

"Of course" A benign smile slipped across Yamazaki's face as he leaned back on the barstool, putting his elbows up on the bar. Castillo's eyes flicked to Takeshi, meeting the old man's cold, expressionless gaze, and the solid, undeniable finality of his shotgun before slipping back to Yamazaki. The younger sweeper shifted and grinned mockingly. "Let us negotiate terms for our release then."

"I've been watching you since you came aboard last night, Hiro, and you've managed to stay out of the way for the most part, though the Yakuza can expect a bill for the Derivative that was killed this morning." Castillo began. The smile on Yamazaki's face shifted to one side and became wry as Alan added, "So as long as you cause no more trouble, you may stay and enjoy the luxuries of the *Alekzandr* as my personal guest, along with the others." He gestured absently at the Bartender and the three men sitting at the lone table.

"And no harm will come to us?" Hiro asked quickly, an amused smile playing across his lips.

"None." Castillo affirmed just as quickly. He slipped the handgun into a pocket beneath the breast of his suit coat as if to illustrate, then spread his hands in a benevolent gesture. "You have my word on that."

"The word of an honorable man is a rare commodity in these times." Hiro gestured with a single finger, and Takeshi's shotgun fell away, dropping fluidly back to his side, though his eyes stayed fixed on Castillo's face and his features stayed hard, refusing to soften even slightly. "And while the hospitality of your organization is both rich and tempting, I am sorry to say that we will in fact be leaving tonight." He shot Cylea a careful, expectant grin. "Unless, that is, you would like some more time to consider my offer."

Cylea glanced at Castillo, then back to Yamazaki. She had no intention of going with the Yakuza, but the thought of making Castillo uneasy by asking the man to stay a little longer held some appeal for her– putting an organization like the Immortals on uncertain footing might present more opportunities and a better deal for her in the end. But then, Castillo had done so much for her, saved her, gotten her front row seats to an Arizona Alhambra concert... She swallowed uneasily.

"I..." She began, then breathed a quiet sigh. "Nein. I've made my decision. I'm staying here." She reached out and took Castillo's hand, shooting Yamazaki a meaningful look. "I'm staying under the protection of Alan und the Immortals."

"Then, there is something I'd like you to have, Cylea, should you change your mind in the near or distant future." He grinned, then nodded once and reached into his suit coat. Instantly the Derivatives tensed, and the look Castillo shot him was pure wariness, but Yamazaki held up a hand in a submissive gesture and casually removed what he had been reaching for, the small folded square of a cotton handkerchief. "Something to remember me by that may serve you well between now and then."

Yamazaki smiled gently at the Immortals, then turned his gaze back to Cylea. in one smooth, deliberate motion, he laid the handkerchief on his open palm, then lifted his hand and offered it to her. Castillo's face softened with the gesture, and the Derivatives relaxed visibly. Cylea's eyes flicked from the small white square to the benign smile that hung across the Yakuza sweeper's face.

"Go on, take it." He urged, his smile widening slightly. "It won't bite, I promise."

Icy blue eyes fixed on him for the briefest moment before she reached out, fingers moving toward the handkerchief. All at once, there was a stirring in his sleeve, but before she could give it much thought, something the color of polished silver shot out over his wrist and across his palm.

The collective clicks of hammers drawing back on Derivative handguns was deafening. She tried to pull away, but before she could manage it, he pressed the spinning, silver thing into her palm along with the handkerchief and smiled.

"Hiro?" Castillo's hand was hovering dangerously close to his weapon. The Derivatives' pistols never wavered, still trained on the Yakuza sweeper, ready to fill him full of bullets with inhuman accuracy as soon as the word was given. "What are you doing?"

"It's okay." Cylea managed. The little silver object rested elegantly on the handkerchief in her palm, the beautiful, perfectly machined shape of a small and easily concealable handgun gleaming at her in the deck light. Yamazaki was grinning again.

The Derivatives relaxed again, and Alan's hand flexed anxiously before it slid away from the handgun at his side. The relief in the air was almost permeable, and Yamazaki almost seemed to be feeding off it, casting a fleeting, amused glance at Takeshi that didn't go unnoticed by Cylea. It was all a game between Alan and Hiro, the Yakuza sweeper knowing all the moves to get the best of his opponent and keep the other man on his toes. He'd probably learned them all from Takeshi, but those were games for men of money and influence. A tiny smile slipped across her lips. She still had a card up her sleeve that would restore the balance in the game.

"Thank you, *Hiro*." She all but cooed, closing the distance between them. "It's so... lovely, und it makes me feel *so* much safer." He opened his mouth to say something, but she silenced him with a quick finger and planted a firm kiss on his cheek. "Thank you so, so much."

Now it was Castillo's turn to grin. Yamazaki swallowed as she pulled away and shared a secret wink with Alan, slipping the handgun into the folds of her dress. The Yakuza had come aboard in an attempt to show up the Immortals in any way possible, Hiro and Alan playing the part of old rivals immersed in the familiar game of politics and honor between international organizations, but the Yakuza hadn't counted on her awareness of the game. In the end, it was good for both her and the Immortals– the Yakuza would have more respect for her and the Order from that point forward, and Cylea had a feeling that she hadn't seen the last of Yamazaki. If the Yakuza decided to approach her again or make an offer that might involve her or Alan, they'd send Hiro to do the negotiations, and that was just fine. He was a familiar face, a trusted face, and trust was the only thing that really mattered in the game between the Immortals and the Yakuza.

Chapter 35: End to Dreaming

Sleep was an elusive specter that night. Quick, frantic fragments of half-remembered dreams pushed through the oppressive darkness of her stateroom as she tossed and turned, burying her face into the sweat soaked sheets that twisted around her arms and twined through her legs. They were soft, smooth, comforting, smelling vaguely clean, vaguely like the jasmine-scented odor of her own sterilized sweat. Brief images flickered through her mind, flashes of smiling faces and gentle gestures– Castillo, Yamazaki, Shang, Smash, little splintered pieces of her life where the timelines of their lives had intersected with hers, each and every little chunk ripped directly from memory and seeded cruelly into her subconscious mind along with a hundred other accompanying visions of death and carnage, most of it imagined, some of it real. They all ended the same, bloody handprints streaking white plaster walls, a mangled, nearly unrecognizable corpse at her feet, her own crimson-stained hands leering into view, raw and broken, dripping with gore.

And then, out of the darkness, Brock's gaunt gray face came at her, a brutal, bone-gnashing sound somewhere between laugh and scream ripping across his neon-blue tongue and over the midnight-chrome rim of his demonic teeth, piercing the thin, numbing membrane of sleep like a plasmatic round and burning mercilessly into the meaty depths of her brain.

When she awoke, she was sitting upright, eyes wide, mouth dry, chest heaving crazily in the throes of near hyperventilation. In some remote corner of her mind, somewhere near the back of her skull, Brock's noise was still a low, mechanical buzz that was already fading, leaving her all alone in the suddenly cavernous-seeming stateroom.

She checked her hands reflexively, then breathed a quiet sigh of relief as her eyes traveled across smooth, pale flesh wet with cold, clear beads of sweat instead of the rich, sticky scarlet of someone else's blood. Her heart thrummed in her chest like a frightened bird beating its wings against a bony cage, and somewhere beneath and between her breasts, deep in the core of her vital organs, the beginnings of a frustrated heat burned and twisted, an ache offset by the cold, cool weight of the strange key.

She pushed a shaky hand through damp hair and closed her eyes. Sleep was a lost cause, she decided. Her eyes opened, then drifted absently to the clock mounted beside the bed. Four twenty three, and she'd already seen enough corpses mangled by her own hand to last her for the rest of her life. A wry, quiet chuckle escaped her lips, her hand dropping limply into her lap. Even without the carnage plaguing her dreams, she'd already seen more than her fair share of corpses and killed more people than she'd ever wanted to.

Pushing aside the damp mass of sodden sheets, Cylea carefully slipped off the bed and cracked the door to the balcony outside. Cool, sea-salted air rushed in, the breeze rifling through her hair and drying the sweat on her shoulders with its gentle caresses. She stood there for a long while afterward, eyes closed, reveling in the refreshing, almost cleansing feeling of being so close to the sea in the softly dark hours before the first rays of dawn poked golden above the distant horizon, then wedged a loose towel into the jamb to keep the door from closing and settled back down heavily onto the bed.

She glanced idly at the twisted white mounds of sweat-knotted bedding and sighed quietly. Sleep was still out of the question– even if she hadn't had the startled awareness borne of waking suddenly from a restless and nightmare-plagued attempt at capturing a few winks, the memories of what she had dreamed, still vivid but softening steadily around the edges, were enough to keep her from slipping back into slumber. She didn't trust her subconscious– she knew that even if she managed to drop off again, the dreams would resurface and play through her unconscious mind like some unstoppable slasher film, darting across her eyelids and forcing her back into the hated role of killer yet again.

Looking up, her eyes caught the refraction of soft light playing off the side of the broadband broadcast headset and the little chrome plug lying on the counter next to it. Castillo had been kind enough to pick up a copy of Arizona Alhambra's concert on a BBH datastick after the show, and its smooth metallic shell emblazoned with the neon-pink undulations of the Neoclassic Electrorock Goddess' artful signature beckoned to her silently. It wasn't as good as seeing her live, heck, it wasn't even as good as seeing her on Neuroline, but it was still Arizona, and Cylea was only too happy to sink into the music and the movement of the performance.

Slipping the headset on and plugging the datastick into the BBH's console deck, she laid back on the soft mattress and kicked off the knotted sheets, letting them fall into a loose heap on the floor at the foot of her bed. As the darkness filled her eyes and gave way to the familiar light show and pulse-pounding audio, she stretched out and yawned, arms coming to rest folded across each other behind her head.

As the recording pushed on and the first song reached its climax, she remembered mouthing the words, only slightly at first, then steadily more so, lipsynching with Arizona. Not long after, she was singing quietly, her voice projecting the words in the gentle whispers of an almost reverent sing-along that never climbed in volume. At some point she must have fallen asleep-- the dreams that came were welcome ones, visions that were soft and faded, the color of old denim and overcast summer skies. She saw Arizona there, that perfect white smile, that rich red-brown hair, wild and free in a breeze that smelled like the gentle brown moistness of the first rain on the stretching grasslands of a country road mingling with the gentle salty coolness of the sea. A serpentine line of pitted black asphalt meandered beneath her feet, wandering aimlessly across fields of dead grass and past rusty and forgotten lines of barbed wire fence as she followed it, the steady, hornet-like drone of a dirt bike echoing from some distant and mud-crusted hill.

The lyrics came to her out of nowhere: "I wanna run... I wanna run to the ocean sun..." something about sweat breaking across golden skin and pushing a blue-eyed boy down in the tall grass, kissing, wet, passionate kisses, hands caressing damp skin, rain and sweat, rain and sweat. Shuddering sighs.

She recognized the lyrics-- they came from somewhere, slipping through Arizona's luscious red lips and converting themselves into images that drifted lazily across the tireless lens of her inner eye. Somewhere, somehow, she smiled, and Arizona seemed to smile back.

When she woke, she stared blearily into flat darkness. It took her a moment to orient herself and discover that the blackness filling her eyes was merely the BBH's dead screen. The headset had automatically switched itself off at some point during the night, leaving her dreaming mind to weave sleepy pastel tapestries of faded blue jeans and Arizona Alhambra's voice in the wake of her performance. But now all that was gone, pleasant memory dulling and fading the way dreams often did.

The next few days passed her by like a blur of smooth light. No more unexpected visitors showed up on the *Alekzandr*, and no more Derivatives turned up missing or dead. The Yakuza had been the only group brazen enough to try to contact her, or at least, the only ones that had managed to get past the Immortals and outwit them just enough to get to her. Silently, she wondered how many other interlopers had been picked off and quietly disposed of in the night, representatives and mercenaries aboard only long enough to become corpses riddled with rounds from silenced pistols and to be pitched ignobly over the railing into the impassive, churning depths of the dark and bottomless sea.

It was cold when Cylea awoke to the brilliant, gothic spires and shimmering glass facades of London, the sky slate grey and thick with moisture from the sea and tainted dew off the brackish waters of the Thames. The scent of ancient salts and sea men hung heavy in the air, mixing with the thicker smells of spoiled fish and pollution left in the wake of long-forgotten forms of industry. It was a shivering stew of thick and unpleasant air, like a gust from the bowels of a moldy tomb, steaming up from the dark and dead edges of the city in the faint traces of a lazy fog.

London wasn't what she had expected it to be. It wasn't the same city she had remembered from watching old vids, and yet in some strange way, it was; it had all the dark and murky charm of that old city, still as ancient and still rotting as gracefully into the ground, a corpse of age-darkened brick and stone with the cheery lights of Piccadilly glowing ghostlike in the distance, competitive neon adverts for the products of Western district megacorporations and Eastern district zaibatsus futilely trying to beat back the fog. But the difference was still there, still keen. The corpse was filled with the stirrings of new life, its rotting sprawl steadily being devoured from within by the towers and fortresses of a much younger generation. The process of renewal was spreading, snaking sharp tendrils of chrome and polished glass through once gutted and dead sectors of the city and following the motorways out toward other cities and into the countryside like a cancer spreading along an artery. It was a plague of steel and nano-processed aluminum that reached out beyond the borders of corpulent London and stretched along toward sweeter meats like Oxford and Reading and an equally virulent and threatening scourge of carbon-fiber plastic and glare-ridden glass that worked its way toward the invitingly urban depths of Northampton and Brighton.

She blinked and sighed-- behind every facet of the renewal was the silent hand of the Immortals, every carefully orchestrated move part of a larger technological renovation of the British Isles that was merely made to look like simple progress run rampant. Castillo had explained that while development and growth were paramount, the Immortals were still working to preserve some of the charm of that old and forgotten London, and here and there she could see what he had meant. Ancient mansions, centuries old, stood shoulder to shoulder with gyroscopically stabilized skyscrapers that had been built in the last ten years, and little lanes of dark cobblestone snaked through the city, intersecting crowded blocks of silver and sheen, each little stone boulevard a little vein of familiar rot preserved amongst the purity of chrome and glass that came with a generation straining toward the silver-lined future that Castillo and his people had laid out for it.

In a way, the rot reminded her of Los Angeles. Sure, it wasn't the same, but both cities seemed to have so much about them that was dead and rotting. Part of London's charm, however, was that its rot was older, silent, more noble, and ever-present. Los Angeles rotted with all the grace of a box of old dynamite, growing steadily more dangerous year by year, just waiting for the careless bump that would set it off in a display of fireworks and destruction that wouldn't leave much else left in its wake, just more rot. You could feel the tension in the air, the anger like crackling electricity jumping from person to person along the sidewalks and the streets-- Jack had said once that New York was the same way, only colder. In New York, most people were just as likely to shoot you as they were to look at you in passing, and even that was almost a common, accepted practice. He said it was like a steam valve, and with instantly disposable nano-replicated three-shot handgun vendors on every other street corner, there wasn't much that could be done about it. The government just provided a subscriber service that kept track of hot zones and tried to promote the formation of safety corridors, but even that was only marginally effective. In the end, most people simply shrugged and silently prayed that it didn't spread beyond the big apple.

But it did, off and on, ebbing and flowing according to some unspoken schedule, or perhaps merely randomly-- researchers claimed they were still looking into that. PCMP they called it, Population Critical Mass Phenomenon. Like a bunch of rats, society grew until, cramped for space, people started to kill each other off, and it only got worse from there. One of the bigger BBH news stations had done a quick blurb on it a few years back, interviewing doctors with ridiculously long names like "Oswannadocski" and "Packhaddameyer" and showing grainy, jumpy clips of the riots in Chicago, Detroit and Austin and the explosive anti-government demonstrations in Melbourne that had turned into a chaotic inferno of hatred and destruction until the OCC had gone in and wiped out a third of the local population. That had been a real mess, and the news had been all over it, playing it up from every political angle imaginable. Even five years later it was considered newsworthy material; survivors of the "Melbourne Crisis" or "Aussie Holocaust" were still being interviewed in popular silicon magazines, and waving angry prosthetic limbs on late night BBH shows.

Cylea sighed again and extinguished that line of thought. Too depressing. The boat was slowing. Damp London stretched on into foggy eternity beyond the docks.

Her eyes drifted downward. The Derivatives were already stirring on the deck below her balcony, shuffling baggage quickly back and forth, black suits stark and crisp against the soft brown of the false wood beneath them, each a black pillar of silk fading steadily into a gentle sheet of fog as they hurried toward opposite ends of the ship.

Breakfast came almost immediately, the usual heaping tray of food that was like a fusion of European and North American tastes on steroids, and none of it with the familiar blandness or oddly sterile taste of the lab-grown or nanoreprocessed crap that passed for food on the streets. It was all there: eggs, ham, a half-dozen real sausages, buttered toast dripping in real marmalade, pancakes, mushrooms, sliced tomato, parsley, four kinds of melon, the works and then some. The only difference was that this time the meal was delivered by a typically emotionless, yet courteous Derivative instead of the sleek little cabana boy she'd gotten used to seeing. Humberto, according to the Derivative, was "taking it easy" along with the rest of the non-Derivative staff in the stainless steel labyrinth of kitchens and staff rooms that were below decks.

"It is standard procedure, Miss Von Mitternacht. Nothing to be alarmed about." He explained. "Just a security precaution." The smile he cracked was a sad and unpracticed parody. "There are, after all, many very important persons aboard this vessel currently preparing to debark."

After little more than an hour the activity on the deck below the balcony had died down– Cylea had decimated the breakfast in a frenzy of excited anxiety and a ferocious hunger that the Immortal's life of plenty had awakened. She was eating better on the *Alekzandr* than she had ever managed to before, even when she had been working at Chow Fun back home in Los Angeles...

She sighed again– another depressing line of thought quickly brushed aside and mercifully extinguished. She didn't want to forget Chow Fun or Hok or Bao or any of the others she had come to love in her time there, and yet, in a way, she did. She wanted to bury the memories and the pain and start over, she wanted to forget about them utterly, erase that cluster of data from the hard drive of her mind completely and leave a pleasantly numb blank spot in its wake.

But that would mean forgetting all of the amazing things that Ming and Shen could do with a wok full of nanoreprocessed vegetables and in-vitro pork, or about Ying, Hok's fiery young daughter who had been nothing short of a violent would-be revolutionary with all the grace of a molotov cocktail smashing through a suburban windshield. They had been her friends, the family she had never had, and Bao... She closed her eyes and swallowed uneasily. It hurt, but she was tired of crying. She'd find out who was responsible for all of it someday, and then...

A firm, echoing knock brought her back to the *Alekzandr* and her stateroom. Slipping the little silver pistol Yamazaki had given her into a pocket, she moved to answer the door and found Castillo standing on the other side, flanked by Mac and a pair of Derivatives with his suit coat slung casually over one shoulder like some British version of a Mafioso. Ten minutes later, she was out the door and walking beside him down the hall, dressed in a pair of faded denim jeans a shade lighter than her eyes and a black tank top with the two Derivatives and the grizzled old sniper following a pace behind.

From there they took a midship elevator to the first deck and met the motorcade at the dock, boarding the same black hoverlimo that had carried them through the streets of Los Angeles. Derivatives were everywhere– some were suited, others disguised as ordinary civilian security personnel or dockworkers dressed in obnoxiously orange plastic. Every visible roof was alive with the telltale shimmering of quickly moving packs of the Immortals' own people cloaked with optical camouflage and the faint green stains on the fabric of reality that betrayed the presence of heavy machinery disguised by phase units. Expensive stuff, she noted.

Coming up from the dock in the sleek limousine, they were immediately waved past an innocent-looking checkpoint by a grizzled and scarred Derivative with a bright yellow poncho clinging to the damp curves of his silk suit. Several other similar hoverlimos and a score of identical glossy black hoversedans followed suit, each coming to a stop long enough for the Derivative at the checkpoint to receive confirmation from the nanocode scanner imbedded in his palm that each driver was, in fact, who and what he was supposed to be. Castillo watched from the darkly tinted back window until the last Hoversedan had cleared the checkpoint and the flimsy nanocarbon guard folded back down into place behind it, sealing off the dock and all access, except by air, to the hulking white bulk of the *Alekzandr* perched on the waters of the Thames beyond it.

"That doesn't happen very often." He stated absently. "Normally at least one of our drivers gets replaced with a specialized vatgrown from some other organization when we travel overseas."

"The drivers?" Cylea asked. "Why the drivers?"

"Because people tend to say things in the privacy of soundproof vehicles that they wouldn't ordinarily expect to leave the confines of that vehicle, things that they don't want leaked to rivals or even *friendly competitors*." He made a generous gesture. "Besides, who would ever suspect someone as low in the scheme of things as a driver to be replaced? Security personnel and research assistants are so much more productive as informers."

Beyond the dock, London unfolded around them with picturesque elegance as they slipped into the city's murky depths, dark and iridescent puddles shivering beneath gently humming suspensors and cobblestone avenues creaking wetly with the passage of each vehicle. Castillo smiled casually at the passing cityscape, Mac ordered a pair of bourbons from the little nanobar built into the limousine, and the two Derivatives sat opposite their three human charges like a couple of rigid black pillars, eyes slowly scanning the windows from behind identical pairs of dark and impenetrable lenses. The grizzled old sniper silently offered Cylea one of the bourbons, ice crackling in the rich, amber-brown liquid, but she declined and he shrugged, downing the first and then lazily nursing the second as the limo made its way through the contrasting tangle of old stone and polished metal toward its destination somewhere near the northern end of the city.

"Ah, here it is." Castillo sat up suddenly, gesturing toward a spot where a dark lane of fine gravel diverged from the cobblestones and disappeared into a verdant grotto of bramble and delicate greenery wet with glistening drops of morning dew and drizzle. The entrance was an archway of large, fleshy leaves and gnarled vines that swallowed the motorcade whole, closing in on each vehicle like the walls of a cave to form the perfectly curved roof and straight sides of a carefully sculpted passage. Dim, green-tinged light filled the hoverlimo, and Mac drained the last of his second bourbon with only a brusk, wet exhale and a quick brush of the back of his hand across his lips to mark its passage. Castillo grimaced slightly. The Derivatives hardly wavered in their endless visual scanning.

The motorcade plunged headfirst into the lush tunnel, the dark lane snaking serpentine and bordered by walls like those of some twisted and otherworldly hedge labyrinth moving inexorably toward some unknowable destiny that waited in the darkness somewhere beyond that last obscuring turn. It was almost oppressive, the way the walls drew in around them, filling every window with an endless quilt of leaves that filtered the cloud-dimmed light into something glowing, ethereal, and green.

Then, almost as suddenly as the tunnel's verdant depths had consumed them and sent them sliding smoothly down its leafy esophagus, the lane rounded its last corner and straightened, the corridor opening to brilliant yellow light that burned away the green and painted everything beyond the last lush fringe of sculpted foliage with a washed out shade of pale. The dark gravel lane seemed to disappear into blinding eternity beyond the tunnel, bordered by short, perfectly manicured hedges as it cut its way past something else perched at the exit, something tall, gleaming and metallic. Another checkpoint.

As the sleek black hoversedan leading the motorcade pulled into the checkpoint, six immaculately suited Derivatives armed with snub-nosed assault rifles descended upon it immediately, each disengaging weapon safeties and laying a restraining hand on the car's hood before its suspensors could manage a complete stop. A seventh Derivative emerged from the shimmering cloak of optical camouflage and detached from the wall of the tunnel, closing the distance between himself and the sedan's driver instantly. Assault rifles were leveled menacingly. A swarm of Derivatives slipped out of the foliage further down, taut bodies and impassive faces fixed firmly on the motorcade, fingers resting uncomfortably close to the triggers of their weapons. The two Derivatives in the hoverlimo had stopped scanning. The mangled cigarette danced absently on Mac's lip.

Then, all at once, the motorcade was waved through as a whole, disgorged from the sculpted tunnel as optical camouflage came online again and the swarm of Derivatives melted back into the leafy walls, nothing more than faint shadows among the green dimness. Only the seventh remained to watch the last hoversedan clear the tunnel before he too shimmered back into the shadows, shouldering his rifle casually as he faded past the stark steel walls of the checkpoint.

Beyond the tunnel, the world opened up again to the gull grey undersides of high clouds and a massive courtyard that unfolded beyond the hedges that bordered the little gravel lane, dwarfing the motorcade. Directly before them, and dead center in the middle of the grounds, sat the estate itself.

The estate was immense, a mammoth mansion of dark and gothic masonry that stretched skyward with sharp towers of black brick and a collection of harsh angles that manifested themselves in a host of wide stretches of midnight tiled roof and narrow, sky-piercing spires. Ominous stone brows overhanging elegant and darkly regal windows beat down on the motorcade from several dozen different perches among the stonework, glaringly perceptive and yet mercifully closed at the same time, each a dead eye lidded with a flowing, dusky purple curtain. The outline of a lotus in cold lavender lines of neon tracery crawled across the face of the building, mounted just above the wide double doors that served as the only visible entrance and a pair of unarmed Derivatives that stood at silent attention beside it.

Hoversedans and limousines alike came to whispering stops on the gravel beneath the looming presence of the estate, only half encompassing the wide, marble bowl of a towering fountain resting at the base of the manor. It was an incredible piece of sculpture, a macabre masterpiece depicting two giant marble warriors locked in a brutal, eternal struggle, wide blades clutched in hard-knuckled hands and plunging deep into each others' breasts to pierce stony hearts and leave the clear water of their lifeblood spilling down the flashing steel of their swords in endless runnels, forever mingling with welling tears that never ceased, streaking across frozen cheeks in cold rivulets.

Cylea couldn't help but gape at the scene carved so stunningly in stone as Derivatives began opening doors and the motorcade steadily disgorged its payload of passengers. Castillo's hand was on her arm, carefully leading her out into the light. Fine gravel crunched underfoot.

Immaculate black suits were everywhere, and beyond them, beyond the hulking black masonry of the mansion and the sleek shapes of the motorcade crouched against the ring of dark gravel looping around the fountain, the rest of the courtyard stretched to the edge of a distant curve swallowed by a wall of thick and bushy foliage. Long, seamless stretches of stone the color of desert sand formed a perfect circle around the estate, immense in size, broken only by wide tracts of vibrant emerald greenery and long, rolling swathes of rich, luscious-looking flowers, every delicate blossom one of a thousand impossible colors and all flowing seamlessly into one another like the threads of some massive floral tapestry. Everywhere, perfect spheres, elegant benches, and small fountains depicting classical figures like cherubs, Venuses, and Davids cut from some pure, luminescent white stone sat in regal repose, each a fragment of some vision of serenity that seemed otherworldly, as if gold-paved streets might suddenly spring up among them and the voices of some angelic choir might suddenly cry out joyously, filling the air with divine song while rays of pure white light poured from the heavens above, piercing clouds and driving away the last traces of gloom and shadow.

"Gott im Himmel..." She managed. "It's incredible."

Castillo touched her shoulder gently and she blinked reflexively, eyes caught on every incandescent detail. It wasn't just incredible, it was beyond incredible– this massive courtyard like something from some celestial vision stretching out from the immense and brooding shape of the mansion with the two marble giants eternally slaying one another atop the impressive fountain at its feet. There were no words to describe it, no words that could do the scene the justice it deserved. She swallowed weakly.

"Come," Castillo urged softly. "Alekzandr awaits."

Chapter 36: Himmel & Hölle

If the courtyard outside the estate had been a vision of heaven, then the interior of the mansion was, in its own right, a vision of hell, or perhaps of some soft and noble side of purgatory.

But it was not like hell in the classic sense-- there was no brimstone, no wailing of tortured souls, no raging infernos or bottomless pits filled with gnawed and splintered human bone. The mansion was more like the luxuriant quarters enjoyed by the elite among demons or perhaps hell's own political prison, where souls of the most elegantly and artfully sadistic sort were kept locked away in expansive, book-laden rooms with silk buttoned handcuffs and three course meals complete with filet mignon or lobster bisque and long, fluted glasses filled to brimming with vintage wine-- not the kind of place that Hell's more common riff raff would ever lay eyes upon.

The mansion's entryway was enormous, a slab of seamless black marble polished until it shone like some dark and depthless scrying mirror from which visions of fate and finality might begin to twist and stir at any moment, rising to hold the eyes and grip the heart in icy, unyielding talons. Beyond the entryway, the black marble stretched on into a hundred darkened alcoves and archways, disappearing under cover of luxuriant carpet the color of rich scarlet and soft furniture of creamy crimson leather and silk. Every chair, bench, loveseat and table crouching along the black stone walls or sprouting from the carpet like mushrooms from a pureed corpse seemed taken from some silk upholstered den of wealthy vampires and gore-fattened succubi, dark and otherworldly in all their curvy, black and crimson opulence.

The far end of the entryway was dominated by a massive staircase that was all sharp and polished angles of flat black steel, save for the thick ivory banisters sliding down the dark metal curves like lines of thick cream, shiny and tainted with yellow, the color of ancient and bleached bone. Dark and gothic tracery, all sharp angles and hard, supporting lines with gently curving arches and elegantly pronounced crosses worked its way up beneath the banisters and into the strong frame of the railing on the overlooking balcony, as flat and expressionless as the eyes of a Derivative. Another neon lavender lotus blossom stared down from the wall at the apex of the stairs.

Amidst it all, a tall man in a perfectly cut suit moved wraithlike toward Castillo and Cylea, a pillar of pure white light that effortlessly parted the sea of black silk suits surging through the entryway in a fashion that was almost biblical to behold. Gliding along the dark floor with practiced grace, his polished white wingtips whispering against the marble, he was given a wide berth by human and Derivative alike, a god in his own right. Castillo stopped, the barest traces of a smile touching his lips. Cylea looked up at him uncertainly. "Alekzandr?"

"No." He managed, voice quiet. "Another member of the Triumvirate, like myself."

Cylea gave the man a second glance. He was pale and lithe, yet had all the curves and flushes of a man in the peak of health. Dark blue eyes the color of cobalt bored back at her from a pinched face with hard, sharp, platinum eyebrows and the soft traces of wrinkles that fit his scowl more evenly than his smile. Long locks of platinum hair, pulled back tight against his scalp, fed into a perfectly sculpted ponytail that stretched to the base of his spine, unbraided and yet still as obedient and smooth as a silk cord. In a way, he was oddly handsome, but his charm was ethereal and strangely regal, like that of a creature from another world.

"Castillo." His voice was as smooth as a leather glove and cruelly casual in the same fashion, with an air to it that seemed both posh and regal, and his smile was sharp, a shining slash of machine-perfect ivory, the best mouth job money could buy. "Welcome back."

"Ah, Exeter. Thank you." Alan offered the other man a brief smile, then tried to move past him. "Excuse us, but–"

"And I see we have a guest." Exeter cut him off and sidestepped to block them, eyeing Cylea carefully. "I think that perhaps introductions are in order."

Castillo's eyes met Exeter's solidly, unwavering, gaze as hard as steel. In the uneasy pause, Cylea extended her hand to Exeter and gave him the most charming smile she could muster, but he merely arched one harsh eyebrow back, unwilling to shake her offered hand and looking at her as if she were little more than some disgusting piece of street trash that had ambled into the mansion of its own volition. His gaze was intense, and so contrary to his tone that she couldn't help but swallow under the cruel scrutiny and look away.

"Let's not play these games now, Exeter." Castillo's voice sliced through the intimidating silence like hot monowire. "If you'll excuse us, we have an urgent meeting with Alekzandr and–"

"Castillo, wait..." Exeter cut him off again, promptly stepping up to block their path a second time, dark blue eyes solidly meeting Castillo's steely grey. The look that Castillo shot him was dark and full of warning.

"Alan." Exeter smiled again, this time softly and genuinely, gently squeezing the other man's shoulders with both hands in a gesture that was decidedly friendly. "Tell me, are you sure that this is wise?"

"Yes." Castillo's response was immediate, solid.

"Ah, but Alan," Exeter's smile faded slightly, his hands coming away and slipping into a generous gesture immediately. "Surely you haven't forgotten our ways..." He glanced once at Cylea, restraining his grimace to just a few bare traces. "She is not one of us, she is..." He wrinkled his nose distastefully at Castillo. "Unclean."

"She's already been aboard the Alekzandr, Exeter. She has bathed regularly in our showers, has been given new and properly sterilized clothing, has lived among us and has seen our ways first hand for over a week." Castillo said, his voice unusually defensive and hard "It's not as if we dragged her in off the streets of Soho just now."

"It does not matter." Exeter waved dismissively. "I can still smell the sour, salty reek of the sea and the thickness of directionless American hatred on her from here." He wrinkled his nose again, this time much more emphatically. "Even you know that a ritual cleansing is a must before anyone, *even a member of the great Triumvirate*," he said meaningfully, "may pass over the Bridge and through Heaven's Gate to Alekzandr's realm."

"There is sterilizing equipment installed throughout the entire length of the Bridge, Exeter." Castillo's tone was bland, direct. "We both know that the cleansing is little more than a useless tradition, something old to be remembered but not necessarily observed or practiced... much like *death*." He said pointedly, then shifted in his stance, making a casual gesture that dispelled the uneasy air clinging between them. "Come now, we're still too young to indulge contempt or stodginess!" The grin that spread across his face was wide, toothy. Exeter merely folded his arms in response.

"Leniency!" Castillo reminded, tone friendly and encouraging. "You must bend like a reed in the wind–"

"I am being *quite* lenient, *Alan*, and you know it." Exeter's tone had gone flat. "Very few people from outside the Order are ever allowed the privilege of setting foot within the grounds, much less the honor of what you're asking, and never without first submitting to the ritual cleansing."

"This is not just some whimsical request." Castillo shot back immediately. "Alekzandr specifically requested for her to be brought before him–"

"Four in the last five decades, Alan." Exeter stated suddenly, voice stern and loud as he held up his fingers to illustrate. "Only four people from outside the Order have met with the Ageless in the last five decades, and only six since he retired."

"Don't think that I haven't kept count, Exeter." Castillo responded just as suddenly, matching the other man in the harshness of his tone. "This one," He gripped Cylea's shoulder, and the gesture was a perfect contrast to his voice, still as gentle and controlled as if he'd done it to comfort her. "This one is special."

"Aren't they all." Exeter sneered, and it was a disturbing thing.

"I really do not have time for your games," came the immediate, dismissive response. "Alekzandr has been waiting patiently for us to arrive. Alekzandr wants to see her *now*, and I don't intend to keep him waiting any longer than is *absolutely* necessary."

"Something amiss, boys?"

The anger sparking between Exeter and Castillo shattered instantly, disintegrating into a clean mist of meaningless fragments that gave way to the gentle clicking of plated bootheels on marble. All eyes turned to the newcomer as she slipped fluidly in among them, brilliant and stunning, incredible smile flashing.

"Miss Sara Mason," Castillo said almost reverently. "Third and final member of the Great Triumvirate."

Cylea swallowed nervously. Where Exeter and Castillo were stark opposites, one man's black silk suit a perfect contrast to the other man's white, Mason was vibrant and alive with color. Everything she wore, from the thick, rich and lapis-blue fabric of her brilliant vest and her soft, billowing pants to the shining silver links of a thin chain that slipped down between the voluptuous curves of her breasts, perfectly accented by the vest in such a way that it brought a pang of jealousy welling up from somewhere deep within Cylea's own chest, was cut to perfection, Neuroline celebrity perfect. Her hair was silky and bold in its fiery elegance, spilling down her shoulders like waves of burning copper, elegant and perfect in every curve as it fell sensuously past the twin points of the incredible, piercing shade of violet in her gently almond-shaped eyes. Cylea couldn't help but swallow again– Mason was the only woman she'd ever seen whose beauty was so perfectly engineered that it was actually, on some level, comparable to Arizona Alhambra's.

Exeter was the first to strike. "Everyone who seeks an audience with the Ageless must first submit to the ritual cleansing, correct?"

"Correct." Mason's tone was cool, levelheaded. She turned a gently curious eye on Castillo and Cylea, then smiled gently. "Why, has there been a breach of protocol?"

"Not yet." Exeter said coldly, folding his arms and turning back to Castillo.

Alan arched a harsh eyebrow at the other man. "I'm tired of rituals." He made a weak gesture. "The sterilizers on the bridge are more than capable of picking up any stray dirt or bacteria--"

"That's not the point!" Exeter shouted back suddenly, startling several passing men in darkly elegant suits. Eyes wide, Castillo made to reply harshly to the other man's outburst, but Mason raised a hand and both fell reluctantly silent, Alan stifling a frustrated huff.

"The cleansing is more than just a physical ordeal, Alan, you know that." She gave him another gentle smile. "Most of it is energetic in nature," gesturing openly, she continued, "the world is full of all kinds of dirty energy, and we must purge ourselves of it before we can be allowed to cross through Heaven's Gate-- it is our duty as keyholders," she made an all encompassing gesture, glancing at scowling Exeter and coldly impassive Castillo each in turn "to assure that the energetic fabric of Alekzandr's realm stays as pure as possible, until the day."

"Until the day, amen." Exeter whispered, bowing shallowly.

"You know I've never bought into any of that." Castillo managed a wry half-smile, getting only a self-righteous scowl from Exeter and another soft smile from Mason. "The whole idea that our energetic fields pollute or rub off on others..."

"Even after seeing psionically active people like our mutual friend, mister Steven Welles, in action on numerous occasions? Even after seeing him lay seals in the foyer of this very mansion? Even after perfecting your own *Tempeflictus* as an art of *Adflictus*?" She laughed. "And even after seeing the work of our cute little friend here, feeling the spirit that burns within her." She smiled softly at Cylea and gently stroked her cheek. It had the unpleasant effect of making Cylea feel like a child caught in the middle of an adult's conversation, but the soft gesture brought a smile to her lips anyway. "Very impressive, by the way, what you did aboard the airliner."

"In time, all spiritual and superstitious phenomena are laid bare and worked into observable rules by science." Castillo shrugged, bringing Mason's attention away from Cylea again. "The assumptions of ritual and religion can't hold a candle to fact."

"You're so old-fashioned." Mason laughed and gave him a goodnatured smile, "pitting science against faith." She raised a lithe finger, still smiling.

"They prove and supplement one another unquestionably, if you know where to look."

"I'm not arguing that there isn't something more, Sara. We all know of *energy* and the ways in which it can be worked, but I firmly believe that all the ritual we garb it in is simply extraneous." He grinned, and Exeter's face twisted into a dark knot. "When I meet God in one of Aerin's rituals," he added, "Or Alekzandr walks on water, I'll come out of the stone age of reason and join you two in the realm of enlightenment. You can show me where to look then."

Exeter scoffed, opening his mouth to bite off a vicious remark, but Mason cut him off.

"At least there is hope then," She teased. "In the meantime, however, would you at least indulge us? I think you can agree that the ritual cleansing is neither long nor unpleasant." Her violet eyes flicked to Cylea, then met Castillo's again as her tone grew gentler and she added: "besides, I'm sure our guest is tired from her long journey and from having to adjust to such a radically different time zone." She smiled at Cylea again, the kind of smile that sweet aunts reserved for indecisive children. "I'm sure it would prove to be both a relaxing and enriching experience for you."

Alan sighed. He knew when he was beaten. Mason had a way with words, and could sway the heart gently, a stark contrast to Exeter's way of forcing his opinion with sword and fire, shouting and scowling like a shrewd mother when those he considered below him would not listen or obey. The argument was pointless anyway– he'd already wasted a fair amount of time arguing with Exeter, and the familiar walls of his own chambers were calling to him...

"What do you think?" Castillo turned to Cylea and gave her a smile that was both kind and gentle. She blinked in response– it seemed like a matter that was beyond her, and yet Castillo expected her to decide the next course of action? She glanced at the other two members of the Triumvirate, Exeter's crossed arms and scowl lessening ever-so-slightly, giving way to a mixture of curiosity and interest and Mason's gentle smile beaming softly at her from between flaming copper curls. She swallowed; the last thing she wanted to do was cause trouble, and the argument was already two against one...

"Ok." She nodded at Mason, forcing meekness into her voice. Best to kiss ass around angry people with this kind of power. "I'll go through with the ritual. I'm sorry for any trouble I've caused."

"It's not you that's causing trouble, it's Castillo." Exeter fixed the other man with a harsh stare. "It's not the first time he's tried something utterly unorthodox and uncalled for like this."

"Ah, you mean like the time I commandeered Lotus twelve and personally dealt with the last noble brave enough to embezzle money from the Order?" Castillo laughed. "Or perhaps like the time that– "

"Yes, like that." Exeter sneered again, changing the subject abruptly. "Regardless, I'll inform Alekzandr of my decision to divert you from your task while you undergo the cleansing yourself." His smile was sickeningly sweet. "I'm sure he will understand the reason for the inevitable delay."

"I'm sure." Castillo echoed, an air of mutual contempt passing between them. Both men knew *exactly* what Exeter was going to tell Alekzandr.

"I'll alert the House Derivatives." Mason breathed a tired sigh, then added: "I wish you boys wouldn't fight so much."

Chapter 37: The Elegance of Vatgrown Angels

The House Derivatives were quick, efficient. Three of them came out of the shadows the instant Mason called for them, luminous white skin and flowing silk clothing a perfect contrast to the rough, stark appearances of the Derivatives Cylea was used to seeing. A quick, silent gesture from Sara, and they were leading Cylea away, smiling soft, gentle smiles and caressing her with the silky palms of their lithe little hands.

At first they seemed female, but on closer inspection, Cylea noticed something different about them– their bodies were thin and waif-like, their glowingly pale skin stretched tight over long, spindly arms like milky silk over rods of brittle balsa. Every curve of their bodies was sleek, hard and masculine, yet strangely feminine in smoothness and placement– shallow curves that could have been indications of breasts rose from strong chests over hips too wide to be male and yet too narrow to be female. Strong shoulders, gently curving jawlines and rich eyelashes added to their androgynous appearance, and their eyes were strange, a soft shade of color somewhere between pink and purple made strong and rich beneath short, swept-back hair like layered sheets of platinum moonlight. And their smell– a tantalizing, seductive scent somewhere between lavender and rose water that was both subtle and rich.

"What are you?" She asked, then winced reflexively. It sounded so basic, so crudely primitive, like the words of a confused child, but the House Derivatives didn't pause or seem to take offense– they only chuckled in response, smiles brightening playfully as they moved gracefully over carpeted floors, leading her along luxuriant hallways with high, vaulted ceilings and lines of vintage Victorian windows that looked out on vibrant gardens and idyllic flowerbeds. Twice she thought she saw the House Derivatives mouthing single, simple syllables to one another, but there was no sound, nothing but the laughing to indicate they even had voices or any sense of language. She waited a while before she tried again: "Are you all... I mean, are you..." She stumbled over the words, uncertain of how to phrase her question. "You're all women, right?"

One of the three squeezed her hand gently and she looked down, getting an almost sultry look in response. Its voice was shocking, a soft, melodious, almost purring sound with the consistency and sweet fluidity of rich velvet. "We are whatever it pleases the mistress for us to be." More laughing.

"Right." Cylea managed, ignoring the barrage of laughter that came immediately after. Ask a stupid question, get a stupid answer, she guessed. *Or a vague one, at least.*

The rest of the walk passed in silence, the House Derivatives chuckling in quick, impish little bursts as they flitted faerie-like around her, hands running softly across her arms and the exposed skin of her midriff. Their touch wasn't unpleasant– they were likely engineered to thrill the skin with little more than a simple caress, but it wasn't something she was used to. In a sense, she almost felt like she could grow to enjoy it if she were around it long enough, if it became an ordinary, expected part of her day, but in the present, she still couldn't quite manage to bring herself to feel anything other than uncomfortable when they touched her.

"These will be your chambers." One of the House Derivatives said suddenly, gently bringing her to a stop and pushing open a massive wooden door that led off the hallway into the plush depths of the room beyond. The door itself was incredibly thick, a beautiful piece of wood marbled with rich reds and browns and cut with elegant spirals, twists and spindles– like everything else in the mansion, it spoke of wealth and luxuriant taste, a door that had probably cost thousands, cut and milled the old fashioned way, from a *real* tree. She peered into the room cautiously, taking in every decadent line, every wave and silken nuance, eyes moving across the gentle fusion of modern and timeless tastes, canopy bed and jacuzzi, elegant crystal chandelier and BBH identical to the 'set back in her stateroom on the *Alekzandr*. Everything was done up in rich chocolate-and-creme colors, making the room look like something out of a confectioner's wet dream. Behind her, one of the House Derivatives chuckled, almost as if he... or was it she... had picked up on Cylea's thoughts. "Well, go on in!"

One glance back, and she took a careful step into the room. The carpet was soft underfoot, almost too soft, like walking on cushions. Another step put her past the threshold of the door, and she drew in a deep breath, senses tingling with the scent of freshly-cut citrus mingling through an odor of roses and lilac.

There was movement at the far end of the room, a brush of iridescent scarlet behind a creamy wave of chocolate silk– She was four steps in when the door swung closed behind her with an impish laugh.

"Don't worry about them." Came the gentle chuckle. She'd half glanced behind her when the voice came brushing through the perfumed air, out of place in the elegant decadence. It was rich, full, strong, but with all the rough jadedness she might expect from the madam of a street cyber-brothel in Chinatown. She couldn't help but shiver at the thought.

"Oh...uh... Ja, okay." Cylea managed, eyes flicking across the room. A pair of pale, lithe hands with strong, visible tendons and lacquered nails that flashed blue-silver in the light pushed aside a curtain of mocha silk, working easily and with a practiced grace that seemed inhuman, almost seraphic, as if the hands belonged to a leader among angels who had taken up residence in this little slice of earthly heaven, the time-strengthened hands of an Archangel.

It smiled benignly as it worked, or rather, as he worked, because while he was clearly a House Derivative like the others and appeared just as androgynous as they did, he was somehow different. He seemed more masculine, as if his curves were tighter and leaner, his muscles larger and more toned, and he seemed to have more of a presence, a stronger presence than any of the others. Watching him move and stretch, she almost expected grand wings of white light and sleek feathers to push aside the sheets of fiery silk draped across his glowing skin and burst from his back, offering a single intimidating and yet divinely regal flap before settling back into place as if they had always been there.

"My name is Aerin." He said plainly, offering another smile as he brushed aside a loose rivulet of hair the color of iridescent scarlet that played across his shoulder like a tiny cascade of moonlit wine. "What would it please you to be called?"

"C-Cylea." She stumbled. Her brain felt like it was on overload– the design and luxurious elegance of the Alekzandr had been incredible, but it paled in comparison to everything she'd seen since she'd arrived at the estate. It was almost too much to take in, and the sheer amount of wealth poured into everything that the eye might happen to even drift across was staggering, as if the entire mansion were paved and dripping with diamonds and liquid gold. Even the House Derivatives were beyond belief– Aerin was incredible, a sleek god among his lesser bretheren.

"Just Cylea." She forced her mind back to the present and tried a smile, but it didn't stick. "I've been called 'Miss Von Mitternacht' enough times in the last week that I'm starting to feel like some kind of celebrity..." She punctuated her words with a nervous laugh. Inside, she was already chastising herself. Everyone seemed to know your name when you were suddenly worth sixty million dollars– It might actually have been funny if it wasn't so damn unnerving.

Aerin nodded absently, hardly paying her any mind as he went about opening every curtain and drape, moving with an odd, almost regal sort of elegance, feet whispering across the floor. Silk undulated sensuously across skin like shimmering liquid fire as he moved, collecting in golden folds of burnished and burning sheets of crimson that flickered across arms and shoulders with an otherworldly radiance, adding to his enigmatic, celestial mystique.

Again she was struck with an image of angelic wings. Aerin had the kind of presence that was substantial, filling, grounded, real, and at the same time oddly ethereal, almost as if the very fabric of the universe, every planet and star nestled in the cosmos, might bow to his will in an instant. He had an air about him somewhere between divine seraphim and seasoned madam, like the Michael or Gabriel of a royally esteemed harem-- if heaven had a brothel, Aerin would have been its master or madam without question.

"Well, *just Cylea.*" He turned to her, and she met his gaze, eyes stunning, unyielding, fierce violet flame captured by orbs of moist, clear white. Tendons flexed eagerly across his wrists, and the regal lines of age etching themselves across his long face stretched to accommodate a wider smile.

"Welcome to Eternity." He gave the slightest of nods. "Now strip down."

Chapter 38: Of Silk and Silicon

"Eternity?" Cylea blinked, stifled a startled cough. *Strip?*

"That's what the estate is called." Aerin's smile widened, taking on an amused cast. "We Live in Eternity, or just 'Eternity' if you prefer the shorter label." He paused while Cylea lapsed into silent thought, then added: "It's a metaphor. Now, strip."

Cylea's eyes flicked up and caught his, lingering on the line of a wary stare. "Why?"

"Because that is the first, and likely most important part of any form of cleansing, ritual or otherwise." He paused, smile spreading, nearly breaking into a full-on grin as he chided: "I assume you've taken at least one bath before."

She fought it, but a smile spread steadily across her face in response, blossoming out until it matched Aerin's. His violet eyes flickered playfully.

"Only since I've been around Castillo." She joked. "Before that it was just kind of touch und go, once every other year or so." She made a quick gesture, gave him an ironic laugh. "I am *unclean* after all, y'know, not one of *you*..."

"Ah, so you've met Exeter then, I take it." Aerin chuckled back. "Charming fellow, isn't he?"

"Oh, ja." Cylea rolled her eyes and laughed. "So what's the story on him anyway? He acts like he has a hoversedan wedged up his nose or something. I mean, I don't know anything about tradition or your rituals or whatever, but the way he went off on Castillo..." She trailed off, still grinning. "There's got to be something juicy between them."

Aerin's laugh was quick and musical, the lilting notes of a pipe organ caught on fleeting woodwinds. "Exeter can be rather stodgy." He gestured toward the plush chocolate draperies that closed off the bathroom from the rest of the chamber. "Come, I'll tell you all about it once you're in the bath."

The bath itself was unlike anything Cylea had ever seen before, and a testament to the wealth of the Immortals if anything in the estate was. It was huge and twice as wide as necessary, like some oblong heated pool installed amid sprawling fields of cushioned luxury, each gilded edge polished to a high shine and every synth-rubber nozzle soft and durable, manufactured from materials of the finest quality. A touch, a gentle tap of Aerin's lacquered nails across a carefully concealed panel and the whole basin thrummed into quiet, purring action, alive with an eager electric tension that almost seemed to fill the room, to reach out and sooth the soul with its very presence.

Nanomachines in the water went to work immediately. Within minutes, tiny chemical factories had brewed a silky film of soap bubbles that rose on the surface of the water and filled the air with the cool scent of lavender and something exotic that Cylea couldn't place. Nearby, Aerin was already busy, smiling almost motherly as he went about triggering a series of strategically-placed neo-incense sticks and easily configured them for a high yield of scent with a quick, even twist of the point of a nail.

As the ambiance settled in around them and the last stick of neo-incense began to glow a pleasant shade of magenta, Cylea pulled in a deep breath, letting the ambiance draw her in. It was pleasant, almost comforting, the way every breath tingled the senses, full of mood enhancers that softened the tenseness still lingering in the air and untangled knotted muscles effortlessly. A smile was already pulling at the edges of her lips, spreading slowly as she dropped her clothes and widening into a more relaxed curve that creased its way across pink as she slipped into the water, the cold lines of pain, fatigue and tenseness finally melting, finally loosening and falling from her face like slack wax. When she closed her eyes, she felt the world lift its cruel, heavy talons from her shoulders and she drew in another deep breath, shuddering slightly as she let it out again to find herself suddenly more relaxed than she had felt in a long time, more relaxed than she could ever remember feeling before, and slipping deeper moment by moment. For the first time since she'd left the fleeting safety of Chow Fun, Cylea breathed, *truly breathed*, and felt safe, as safe as she'd had felt in Bao's arms, his chest rising and falling against her face, soft scent of musk and orange peel wafting along every breath... A silent, absent tear slid down her cheek at the memory, a tiny sliver of her heart breaking away, shed somewhere between buried pain and smothering ecstacy, shed and forgotten just as quickly.

"So talk to me." She managed a moment later, pulling in a lazy breath over words drawled and drawn out, her tone so casual and relaxed that it took her a moment to realize she'd spoken in German. Aerin didn't miss a beat, but responded immediately in kind, his tone and syntax crisp and flawless.

"What about?" Aerin's smile was secretive, amused. He hadn't caught the tear, didn't seem to know about Bao. Moving fluidly and with inhuman grace, he slipped in behind her head and began working her shoulders, kneading stubborn muscles into relaxed submission with his long fingers.

The weakest of contented laughs slipped through Cylea's nose. "Oh god, I don't know." Her eyes opened a crack. "What's in this water? I've never felt this good before in my entire life."

Aerin's smile widened slightly as he looked down, fronds of shimmering scarlet falling across his face.

"Mood enhancers geared to target every perceiving sense, even down to the vibrations and sounds outside the normal range of human hearing that are emitted by the multifunction nanites circulating among the bubbles and first few molecular levels of the water."

"Mmm." Cylea managed, leaving a peacefully absent silence in her wake.

"You asked earlier about Exeter and Castillo..." Aerin offered, letting it hang in the air like a question. Cylea stirred under his deftly massaging fingers.

"Oh..." She shifted and pulled in a long, deep breath, letting herself slip further into the water. "Ja... tell me about Castillo." Her smile softened, turned almost provocative. Another amused and secretive smile slipped across Aerin's face.

"You like him, don't you?"

Cylea pulled in another long, slow breath and held it, then laughed tiredly, eyes fluttering open.

"He's alright." She shifted, lifted one frothy hand out of the water in an absent gesture. "I mean, he's handsome... I like his hair." She turned slightly, just enough to catch sight of Aerin out of the corner of her eye. "I don't know, I mean, I like him, und he seems like a great guy, fun und sweet und intelligent und all..."

"But?" Aerin chuckled.

"But I don't really know him all that well, y'know?" Cylea made a resigned gesture. Aerin didn't need to know the rest, didn't need to know about Bao. "It's just too early to say."

"Mmm." Aerin nodded silently, tongue between his teeth, thumbs pressed in against knots of rebellious muscle.

"He's got the CEO thing down really well..." Cylea continued, trailing off absently. She shook her head, then gestured again carelessly. "But it seems like he's got this really spicy wild side..."

"He is the most unconventional member of the great Triumvirate." Aerin picked up, leaning over to give Cylea another silent nod as he worked. "That is one of the reasons why he and Exeter do not get along all that well."

"Exeter's one of those hard-asses who just doesn't have any clue what fun is, ja?" Cylea shifted under Aerin's fingers, let another laugh slip through her nose. "Makes perfect sense."

"Doesn't it?" Aerin laughed again, the tone so musical and feminine that Cylea couldn't help but smile. "He's a stickler for tradition and the worst of the Triumvirate when it comes to laxity." Aerin's fingers danced across Cylea's shoulders in a brief, unseen gesture. "And he can be incredibly dangerous if he decides he doesn't like you, so try to stay on his good side if you can."

"Ja..." Cylea breathed. "So don't make an enemy out of Exeter." She chuckled, her eyebrows sliding upward by the barest fraction of an inch. "Any tips I should know about?"

"Never call him by his forename." Aerin laughed again. "He takes it like the gravest of insults."

Cylea sat up slightly and turned toward Aerin, sheets of silken bathwater sliding down her chest. "Really?" She laughed. "Now I have to know what his first name is."

Aerin's smile turned mischievous, and he wiped his hands quickly. "His name is Elias, Elias Exeter."

"Elias Exeter?" Cylea echoed, snorting a quick laugh and shaking her head. "It seems too... I don't know... Old Western to me." She lifted a hand in the barest of gestures. "Like the name of a sheriff or some cowboy in some hokey old movie."

"He believes it sounds entirely too North American, and he despises practically everything associated with..." Aerin cleared his throat, adding the hint of an impression. "The Colonies."

"Mein Gott." Cylea closed her eyes and slipped further back into the bathwater. "I thought we were all one people here, y'know, *beyond* these stupid old ways of looking at the world." She made another quick gesture. "Didn't we just come out of the longest period of political correctness being so mainstream it was considered 'cool'? I swear, I haven't heard anyone call the North American District 'The Colonies' since I was in high school history classes."

"There are still recognized lines of race and region." Aerin pointed out. "It seems as if discrimination is a firmly integrated part of the human mind that cannot just be removed by programs and trends." Aerin stood, regarding Cylea calmly. "But we live in a time when there is relatively little violent discrimination, with most of what's left being perpetrated by the men and women of extremist groups like the Lonestar Secessionists or the DNPM."

"The Deutschland Neonazi People's Movement." Cylea sighed, slipping further back into the bath, her chin among the bubbles. "Ja... what a mess." She glanced back at Aerin. "Last thing I heard, they were on some national station, rallying in Berlin und marching in honor of Adolf Hitler's birthday or something stupid like that." She turned back to the water and closed her eyes. "They keep hoping that they'll be able to get a bunch of people who still identify strongly with their German heritage to unite behind them someday so they can do..." She blew out a disgusted breath and made a careless gesture. "Whatever it is they're planning on doing."

"We're lucky to live in a time when so many people feel that way about groups like the DNPM." Aerin crossed the length of the bath and stopped at the other end, turning to smile at Cylea. "Unfortunately, in the time when Exeter was a young man, racism and hatred were much more prevalent."

"But the world has been more or less unified for almost seventy years." Cylea sat up again. "I mean, wasn't Bolaji Washington's inaugural address of 2095 considered the beginning of the largest crackdown on discrimination in human history?" Aerin nodded and Cylea arched a questioning eyebrow. "Then just how old is Exeter anyway?"

"He was born in the late summer of 2058." Aerin turned and fetched an expensive-looking sponge from a nearby shelf the color of mocha and redwood, then flashed her a smile. "He looks pretty good for a man of a hundred and four, doesn't he?"

It took Cylea a moment to process the date. Castillo had said something about their oldest member being over two hundred years old, but... "Wait a minute, how old is Castillo then?"

"I wouldn't worry too much about that." Aerin grinned, walking back to the bath.

"Mein Gott, I feel like I'm surrounded by old people." Cylea laughed. "How old are you, Aerin?"

"Don't you know that it's considered impolite to ask a lady her age?" Aerin's grin widened.

"Lady?" Cylea shook her head, unable to find the words. "I..."

"It's alright. It's not important." Aerin crossed back to the tub, smile softening with a quick, dismissive gesture. "Technically, we House Derivatives are both male and female, blessed with the ability to change the shape and configuration of our sex organs at will, but as a whole, we generally prefer to be called 'she.' It separates us from the other, more brutish, distinctively more masculine Derivatives that handle more of the duties outside the manor involving force and other nastiness." Aerin smiled again, the smile so soft and charming it could have melted the ice off the face of Europa. "But you may refer to me as 'he' or him. For you, I will always be male, if it pleases you."

A mischevious smile crawled across Cylea's face. "So then you'll tell me how old you are?"

"Let's just say that I'm younger than you're likely to believe and keep it at that." Aerin laughed again and tossed her the sponge. "Now wash up. I'll go get your clothes and the tools for the ritual ready." He cocked his head and squinted at her playfully. "And I think something to eat is in order as well. It will be a long while before the ritual is complete, much less before the next meal is ready, and I'm willing to bet you didn't have lunch."

Cylea shook her head, smiling, and caught a slight nod from Aerin back in response. Then, in a flicker of curtain and incandescent skin, he was gone, leaving her watching the sponge absently as it took on water and slipped slowly beneath the surface.

Chapter 39: Man Made Gods

"Guardians of the winds of the North!" Cried one of the House Derivatives, hands thrown toward the sky, fingers splayed in the throes of religious ecstacy. Behind her, three more stood watch over each cardinal direction, eyes closed, faces upturned, arms held out at their sides. Aerin stood majestically near the center of them all, flowing silks shimmering a dozen paces from Cylea's wet skin. Every pale inch glistened smooth in the cool, scented air, naked but for a carefully wrapped towel that arced in beneath her bellybutton to cover her hips and legs, leaving anxious, delicate feet poking out beneath. She shot Aerin a nervous smile and got a soft, reassuring one back in response.

"Masters of permanence," The first House Derivative continued, breathing the words on a quiet, sacred breath, arms never wavering, eyes never opening. "Lords of breath and air and ice– come to us, come now, come and witness this our holy ritual, our sacred trespass into the realms of the ether." She sucked in a deep breath and the others joined her, each holding it like the essence of life as she finished: "In unified body, mind, and soul, be here now."

There was a collective sigh as her words were left hanging in the air, almost tangible and somehow charged, as if they had infused the very fabric of reality with some power that was just beyond the ability of the human eye to perceive, a power that seemed almost close enough, almost real enough to be touched. Cylea pulled in a quick breath, entranced as the next House Derivative threw her arms to the sky and cried her own invocation.

"Guardians of the winds of the East, Masters of nature!" She shouted, "Lords of land and earth and sea, come to us, come now, come and witness this our holy ritual, our sacred trespass into the realms of the ether. In unified body, mind, and soul, be here now."

There was another collective breath, another collective sigh, and then another House Derivative picked up the mantle of unseen energy and let her arms shoot skyward.

"Guardians of the winds of the South," she began, voice rich and almost as melodic as Aerin's. "Masters of impulse, Lords of blood and flame and passion," her voice turned suddenly silky, "come to us, come now, come and witness this our holy ritual, our sacred trespass into the realms of the ether. In unified body, mind, and soul, be here now."

A shiver passed through Cylea as the third House Derivative finished, each invocation adding more tension to the air, tension that built and moved with each inhale and each echoing sigh, collecting color she more felt than heard, streamers of insubstantial light that whipped and shimmered etherically. Her eyes darted for the fourth and final House Derivative as arms were raised to the west, the only direction that remained uncalled, the only direction not present in the circle of elements being forged out of spirit and willpower around her.

"Guardians of the winds of the west," Came the low voice, quietly confident, the voice of beauty and hidden thorns, "Masters of the realm of emotion, Lords of rain and water and the hidden depths of the soul, come to us, come now, come and witness this our holy ritual, our sacred trespass into the realms of the ether. In unified body, mind, and soul, be here now."

"Be here now." Aerin echoed amid the collective breaths and sighs, crossing the distance between himself and Cylea to take her hands gently in his. She swallowed, tried a smile, but it wouldn't stick. Her breasts quivered nervously in the cool air.

"Alekzandr and all the spirits tied one and another into the weave and flow of his generous spirit, be here now." Aerin continued, eyes locked with Cylea's, almost seeming to stare into the secret depths of her spirit, casting light into her, banishing shadow from everything she'd hidden there. She couldn't look away, couldn't have torn her eyes from his even if the world were burning to cinders around them. His violet eyes shimmered with life, with wisdom, with arcane secrets long forgotten by man and machine but remembered by the child of both, and she was entranced by every snap and fragment that flickered up from there to brush against her mind like sweet dew and flame. When it ended, she remembered to breathe, and it was like remembering how to do something from a past life. Each breath came slow, deep, and cautious, the half-gasping of a newborn.

"Witness this, the cleansing of this young woman's spirit, made clean as her body and mind have been made clean, and welcome the *Adamu* Cylea Engel Von Mitternacht into your heart and your home, even if her stay be but a short one." Aerin turned away suddenly, releasing one of Cylea's hands and throwing one arm elegantly skyward, lacquered nails shining, lithe fingers stretching, reaching.

"And be here now all the spirits of creation," He cried, grinning. "All the denizens of the ether who drive away the darkness to make way for the light and all those who drive away the light to make way for the darkness, for without one, the other cannot exist. The Ying cannot exist without the Yang, nor the Yang without the Ying, and without sacrifice there can be no achievement, no joy. We are creatures of both light and dark, creatures striving to find balance within ourselves, and when this balance is achieved, our souls sing out in joyous voices, creating balance in the world around us wherever we go. This is the godhood, for we are gods, made in the image of god to learn and grow and become creators like the spirits of the almighty. We are changers, and everything we touch can change." When he turned back to Cylea, it was as if the world suddenly shifted on its axis, reality twisting to bring his eyes in contact with hers again. Instantly, another House Derivative was at his side, offering a neat stack of folded white clothing.

"Take these clothes, offered freely and without condition, and find yourself among friends as true as family." Aerin smiled. "You have bared your flesh as you have bared your soul, and we have witnessed the cleansing of both. May Alekzandr watch over you as he watches over all the people of Eternity, until the day."

"Until the day." Cylea breathed reflexively, absently taking the clothes, her eyes never leaving Aerin's, even as his lips parted to allow the passing of the final word, that same "Amen" that had crossed Exeter's lips with all the air-tingling sincerity of the soul's most sacred exhale.
It seemed so long ago, another time, another life, one that came to an end and slipped into forgotten memory the moment she looked into Aerin's eyes, touched his soul, and felt her's touched in return.

It didn't matter how long ago it had been, Aerin was beautiful, so very beautiful, and powerful in ways she did not understand. His words fluttered through her mind like silver birds, lifting her heart and lighting fierce fires of passion and need deep within her that flared unexpectedly and leapt at the touch of his scent, at the shades of purple shimmering through his eyes and the hues of scarlet luminescing across the smooth sheets and wavy curls of his hair. *For you, I will always be male, if it pleases you.* She swallowed, forced away the thoughts, the words, the sensations, the feelings that boiled up, fighting for attention, for release. It all seemed too soon, too soon– Only two weeks ago she and Bao had been... had been... another swallow. Aerin continued to smile at her, and she silently wondered if he had noticed anything, if he'd caught even the slightest twitch or scent of the battle raging out of control across the burnt battlefield of her heart. God, the Immortals were all so... *perfect*.

Her mouth felt dry, and she bit her lip as Aerin turned away, voice resonating with a deep, soul-moving hum that the other House Derivatives took up just as quickly. One by one, their voices dropped melodically, arms dropping in unison until only Aerin remained standing, hands stretched to the sky, voice rumbling and rich, like the tones of an ancient mountain stirring from its stony slumber. He was the last to drop, and as his arms drifted earthward, the other House Derivatives knelt at their elements, quietly thanking each direction for its presence in the ritual, all while staying lower, closer to the ground than Aerin as he gave his own quick and quiet respects to spirit and the denizens of the ethers who had been called with the opening of the ritual. Slowly, steadily, reality seemed to unwind, to deflate and become relaxed until it felt almost two dimensional, somehow suddenly less crisp, less detailed, less *real*.

She glanced once at the clothes and let her towel fall to the floor. Her body felt like it was on fire, a pillar of hot light in a dull world, burning outward from within with the force of unignorable passion and need. She wanted Aerin to look at her again, wanted to watch his eyes as he took her in, wanted to see if they would linger.

She pulled the clothes on slowly, absently, working without caring and finding herself dressed all in white, every inch of fabric flowing and smooth, sheer as marble. In a moment, two Derivatives were at her sides, lithe fingers straightening her collar and the open, long sleeved shirt that went on over it. Tiny mists of perfume and perfume enhancers designed to augment the nanosterilized scent of jasmine that came through in her sweat danced across her shoulders, hung in the air like the fine iced fragrance of wildflowers and drifted down to sink into thirsty fabric. One of the Derivatives came up from behind her and worked her hair over with skilled hands and quiet-humming instruments until it looked perfect, a rough nanocosmetic job like the hair of a punk model in a lingerie silicon magazine targeting the gothic and raver crowds.

She smiled at Aerin as he came up to her and fussed momentarily over her nails, quickly smoothing them to elegant curves with a tiny file, and he returned the smile in turn, meeting her eyes easily and confidently. It was hard to keep her eyes off him, and getting harder with every moment she spent so close to him, but it didn't seem to bother him. He bloomed under her gaze, grinning with the attention and fussing over every detail like an artist trying to bring perfection to his canvas.

She basked in his angelic radiance as he worked, too euphoric, too drawn to him to do anything but smile until he suddenly shooed off the other House Derivatives and took her hands gently in his own, standing up full and tall, the image of otherworldly beauty and heavenly grace projected through silver film. Tense need and sudden, fleeting hopes dropped the smile from her face and she swallowed as he regarded her with a soft smile that could have brought light to even the hardest, iciest, most guarded heart-- staring into his eyes was like catching a glimpse of heaven, and the last thing she wanted to do was look away.

"Mmm." He began suddenly, amusement and pride playing at the edges of his lips. "You look absolutely stunning, Miss Cylea. Even the great goddess Aphrodite could not surpass your beauty."

She tried to speak, but there were no words. Her response was reflexive, uncontrollable. She leaned forward, and in one moment of electric tension and still flame, her lips touched his, pressed in and held him in a fierce, desperate kiss. Time stopped, reality fell away-- it was like kissing the very essence of heaven, and she couldn't let it go, couldn't draw herself away, and when their lips finally broke apart, her eyes refused to focus, refused to accept anything but the violet of his eyes, the curves and planes of his features. Her lips drifted apart, quivered. Even kissing Bao hadn't been so good, hadn't felt so right, so necessary... hadn't felt like *that*.

When her eyes finally did come back into focus, he was smiling softly at her, just the barest touch of dreaminess in his gaze. A hint of red lit her cheeks and she tried to speak, but Aerin silenced her with a gentle press of his finger.

"Hang onto that feeling. Nurture it, let it grow, let it be your light when all around you is darkness." He paused. "When two souls touch as deeply as ours just have, in a moment when the ether is alive with the elements and the very spirits of creation, the universe takes notice. There is a bond between us, between you and I, a bond of the spirit that can never be broken, not even by death." He squeezed her hands. "If you ever have need of me, for any reason, simply call my name and I will come to you."

She tried to speak again, but still could not find the words, couldn't express the depth of feeling that churned within her heart. There was only a nod, a smile, but Aerin seemed to understand, and he squeezed her hands again in response.

"Come," he said, putting the moment gently to rest. "I'll take you to the main dining hall. Before you meet with Alekzandr you must eat as he does, or did, when he walked among us as a man-- at the grand table of Eternity."

Chapter 40: A Shade of Incandescence

Castillo was waiting in the hallway outside Cylea's chambers when Aerin opened the door and he walked with them to the dining hall, wingtips whispering along plush carpet beside Aerin and Cylea's bare feet. Aerin smiled, seemed glad to have the other man's company, and the sparse chat they traded was easy and true, the idle conversation of friends. Cylea drifted listlessly after them, stalling a pace behind, silently watching Aerin, silently wishing they could be alone, that she could stare into the enigmatic depths of his violet eyes again and tell him exactly how she felt, tell him about herself, her life... ask him if he believed in love at first sight. Castillo turned back and flashed her one of his supermodel grins, but the smile he got back in response was halfhearted, almost forced.

It took every ounce of resolve she had to keep from quickening her pace, to keep from stepping up between the two men and reaching out and take Aerin's hand– she wanted to grab him, to thread her arm through his, kiss whatever part of him her lips happened to light on, and caress every inch of his skin in the kind of sensual worship his perfection seemed to beg for, seemed to need, seemed only too worthy of. She didn't want to go to dinner, didn't want to deal with Alekzandr or Castillo or Exeter or any of the other Immortals. She wanted Aerin to scoop her up in his arms, wanted him to carry her off and make sweet, passionate love to her in some lush garden or in some secret place where no one would ever find them. She wanted him so badly that it hurt, it burned, and his soft, gentle smiles only made it worse. She wanted to ask for a kiss, just one more kiss, just one more of those soul-touching kisses that would transport her to paradise and leave her reeling as it ended. She'd have stolen it outright if she'd had the nerve, but... she chastised herself, beat back the flames. *What about Bao?* The thought was probably the only thing keeping her from burying her face in Aerin's chest and begging him to take her right then and there, in the middle of the hallway, without a care as to who might walk by, who it might irk. She'd never felt so strongly about something like this before, never wanted someone so badly before, and it was a sweet, dragging torture, as physical and exquisite as starving to death on the doorstep of a gourmet restaurant on buffet night. His touch was the balm to sooth her wounds, the water to dampen the fire burning out of control in her heart. Bao would understand, she told herself– if Bao were here to see Aerin... she bit her lip as a cascade of new images flitted through her mind, images that pulled so strong on her psyche that she nearly missed a step and stumbled.

There were no words that seemed to fit. Heaven had nothing on Aerin.

The door to the dining hall came too fast. Every step had blurred together into a torturous eternity of gentle smiles and need, leaving her on the doorstep to something new, something profound that she wasn't ready for. She turned to Aerin, and for the briefest moment, their eyes locked, *connected*. She repressed a shiver, and he smiled.

It was too much. Castillo opened his mouth to say something, but Cylea was already crossing the meager distance between herself and Aerin, her hands lighting on his arms, dancing fleeting across velvet skin. His eyes were the last thing she took in as she leaned in and made to kiss him, but he turned away at the last moment, and her lips brushed across his cheek in a moment of bristling, denied electricity instead. He smiled again, but it felt like rejection, felt like a blatant dismissal of her needs. *Ravage me!* Her brain screamed, but she bit her lip against the surge and looked away quickly.

Aerin and Castillo shared a brief and knowing smile. She was acting like a horny teenager and they knew it, could see it, even had the nerve to think it was *funny*.

Cylea's cheeks colored again. She felt like an idiot– it probably wasn't the first time someone had fallen so hard for Aerin so quickly, but that didn't make it any easier, didn't make her want him any less. She pushed the thoughts away quickly, then squeezed her eyes against it all, shutting out the world.

When Aerin finally turned and walked away, she looked up at his retreating back and her heart sank. It was as if part of the room had left, as if an entire section of wall, furniture and lavish tapestry had been suddenly removed, leaving bleak and naked boards exposed in its wake– it felt wrong somehow, cruel. Castillo's hand landed softly on her shoulder, squeezing gently, and she looked up in response, eyes seeking his. She could see it there, behind the steel, in that depthless gray– she swallowed absently, but couldn't keep the smile from pushing its curve through her lips. It was so clear. *He understands.*

A suited, male Derivative opened the door to the dining room then, ushering them past like some sort of bulky living statue, his face as hard and emotionless as a granite bluff. Within, a huge table of sleek, polished mahogany stretched across intricate and gothic tiles of reflective cobalt-blue stone like a museum piece, glittering beneath the lights of a series of elaborate crystal chandeliers that looked like they were just as old and worth close to the same amount each-- a small fortune and then some. The lights caught Cylea's eye immediately, each shimmering, multifaceted gem of cut glass shining brilliant, tinged by a magnificent range of nanochromatic hues that held the eye and filled the dining hall with playful spots of faded rainbow.

Close to two dozen seats were pushed up to the table, but the space between each chair seemed to hint that it had been designed with more in mind. Elegantly dressed men and women filled most of the seats, trading jokes and low conversation with half-smiles and pointed gestures, a few absent glances and whispers rippling in among them as Castillo and Cylea stepped into the room, then fading again just as quickly under the impulse and whim of gossip and steady conversation.

Exeter and Mason sat facing the door, Exeter at the farthest end of the table, filling the last seat before the left arm of an empty, throne-like chair that sprawled out in the graceful rolling curves of a rich, golden wood with the symbol of the lotus engraved prominently across the monolithically high back. The throne-chair itself was incredible, an intricate work of art in wood, fashioned with the strength and girth of a grand pillar, one that stretched to support an elegant series of figures and faces playing out a celestial scene across the polished, wooden clouds perched at its highest peak before it dropped ruthlessly downward to crush the leering, ominous hordes of hell beneath its wide, Greco-Roman feet. both chairs to the right of the throne were empty, a pair of seats that faced Mason and Exeter across an expanse of table prepared for a meal that would probably be as elaborate and carefully crafted as the setting in which it was to be served.

Cylea lagged a pace behind Castillo as she followed him to the table, letting her eyes flick between the Immortals, slipping from one to another, studying them. These were the nobles that Castillo had mentioned on the cruise ship, they had to be-- the people who were part of Castillo's... or Alekzandr's flock. She swallowed uneasily.

Castillo reached out to take the seat across from Mason, leaving the seat at the edge and across from Exeter open. Following suit, Cylea reached for the open seat off the throne-chair's right arm, but as she reached for it, Exeter stopped her with a slow, warning hand.

"Generally, or should I say, *traditionally*, guests are seated in the empty chair at the other end of the table." He stated, then gestured past Mason and the Nobles to the foot of the table, where a seat that looked so simple as to be almost vulgar sat alone, clean but clearly unused for longer than anyone would probably care to admit. Cylea stared at it for a long moment. One of the Immortals cleared their throat in the dragging pause.

"Ah... here." Castillo began, breaking the moment with hurried action as he pulled out the chair across from exeter and smiled, gesturing for Cylea to sit. "Who needs tradition anyway?" Exeter glanced up, gave Castillo the barest of wary glances, but the glance was ignored. Alan was too busy making sure Cylea was comfortable and giving her encouraging, friendly grins that she was steadily more and more able to return and genuinely feel. Mason tried to hide her own smile by turning away and trading a few quiet words with the Noble next to her.

"So who sits in the big chair?" Cylea asked, trying to lighten the mood that Exeter seemed to be so good at darkening. "It's not Alekzandr's is it?"

"The empty seat at the head of the table is Alekzandr's, yes." Mason spoke up quickly, gesturing to the throne-like seat before Exeter had a chance to turn his eyes on Cylea and shoot her any kind of dark or disgusted glare across the plates and sharp silverware between them. It was clear he wasn't happy sitting directly across from an outsider like Cylea, even if she had undergone cleansing and looked like a fashion model or a Neuroline star on vacation. She shot him a friendly smile and got a dark stare of knitted brows and piercing eyes back in response.

"Keeping Alekzandr's place at the table and keeping it ready for him is part of tradition for us." Mason continued, smiling wryly and glancing over at Castillo in time to break apart the cold stare that was already forming between him and Exeter. "One of these days, the doors of this hall shall swing wide for him and he shall walk through to take his seat among us again." Her eyes met Cylea's and she grinned, her smile a perfect crescent of perfect, white teeth framed by perfect lips as luscious and rich as the ripest summer berries. "He is truly magnificent. I envy you, meeting him for the first time." Exeter looked up, face clearing as he nodded his agreement.

"Whose... I mean." Cylea paled, gesturing quickly as the realization hit her and trying to force the words to come. Her eyes flicked to meet Castillo's. "You weren't... um... saving this seat for anyone, were you?" She shifted uneasily, half-ready to stand.

Exeter arched a careful eyebrow and Castillo smiled gently as Mason gave her a dismissive gesture. "That seat belongs to no one. It really is not much more than a sad reminder, actually. In a way, it is good to see someone filling it." Mason smiled.

"We weren't always called the great Triumvirate." Castillo offered suddenly, attracting Cylea's curious eyes and smiling wider as he caught them. "Where you are sitting is where the fourth member of what was once the great Quartet sat before she moved on to better things, or so she no doubt believes." He looked away, eyes suddenly distant with memory. Mason seemed suddenly and entirely too interested in the table as Cylea's eyes tried to meet hers, but only Exeter would meet her gaze, his own eyes unwavering, soul-piercing. The smile faded from her face again, dropping at the corners with unease until she couldn't help but swallow. The pause was murderous, awkward to the point of stifling. Cylea swallowed again and opened her mouth, voice scratchy as she spoke, trying to make light conversation.

"Uh... really?" Cylea forced a smile as Castillo and Mason looked up. "What was... uh... y'know, uh... what was her name?"

"Aoi." Exeter answered quickly, eyes still fixed on Cylea. The pause began to settle in again. She glanced at Castillo, and slowly, steadily, he looked up to meet her gaze.

"Aoi?" She tried again. *Think, Cylea.* "Sounds uh... Japanese." She looked at Mason, and the other woman nodded, looking up again. "Was she pretty?"

"Beautiful." Exeter responded again, the word clipped to the barest statement of fact. Castillo looked up and gestured slowly with a fork.

"Doctor Aoi Tsuki Oshii was not only beautiful, but brilliant and possessed of a kind-heart as well." Castillo said, pushing away a sigh before flashing Cylea a quick grin. "I have to say, the seat seems to fit you well."

Mason glanced up immediately as Cylea blushed at the comment, but the look that Exeter shot the other man was all condescension and ice, a look ignored just as easily as the others that had come before had been. A chain of whispers rippled uneasily between the Nobles.

It took Cylea a moment to concentrate again. In the back of her mind, the name spun hot loops, scanned and rescanned as her brain searched for something to tie it too, something that would shed light on it. *Doctor Aoi Tsuki Oshii.* It sounded familiar, but she couldn't quite place it, kept feeling like it was lingering at the tip of her brain, just close enough for her fingers to brush against but not close enough to seize and force secrets from. A doctor? It was probably someone she'd seen interviewed on some late night BBH show– she couldn't remember. Her fingers touched the key at her neck absently, brushed across her mother's keepsake, as if it could somehow trigger a memory she'd forgotten. She silently mouthed the name of the Kanji. *Tsuki.* Her brows knitted. *Coincidence? What does it mean?*

"The good Doctor felt that her skills were not being used to their fullest," Exeter gave a quick, dismissive gesture, dispelling the last of the awkwardness suddenly, the slightest edges of a grimace pulling at his face. "So she gave up life extension research and the free reign sort of genetic and nanometric tinkering that we gave her lease to do here and joined some heavily guarded research and development program fully funded by none other than Ted Solomon instead."

"Last I heard, she was working with Doctors Wingates and Braxton on some new experimental lifeform program." One of the Nobles piped up suddenly, pushing into the conversation with a smile. The look Exeter gave him was disdain and mild interest all rolled into one. "Something having to do with engineering the perfect weapon or somesuch." He shrugged, folding his fingers in idly against the palm of his hand.

Exeter shrugged. "If you believe the reports. Fortunately, it doesn't look like Solomon is getting his money's worth out of the project. It seems Aoi, Wingates and Braxton have yet to create anything successful, much less saleable–"

"If you believe the reports." Castillo gestured quickly, attracting a careful glance from Exeter. "We've gotten a lot of conflicting information from our contacts in Solomon's labs during the past year." He and Mason shared a quick, absent glance. "I've heard some strange rumors about a secret field test of another new weapon, and something about Braxton disappearing, but..." He shrugged, held up his hands. "Well, as we know, rumors are just rumors, not solid fact." The smile Exeter shot him in response was sharp as razors.

Elegant wine glasses of clear, fluted crystal tinted with the barest hint of opalescent lavender broke the tension brewing in the air as House Derivatives descended upon the table like a flock of hungry butterflies, flitting from placesetting to placesetting, interrupting conversation with the porcelain clink of plates draped with elegant meats and simmering vegetables that steamed sweetly beside rich sauces and delicate garnishes. Exeter kept his darkly impassive expression throughout the entire process, and the House Derivatives gave him as much room as they could manage, but once the last of the food was laid out and the glasses filled with a light, floral wine, he was only too quick to dismiss them with piercing stares under arched brows and impatient waves.

"Exquisite creatures, aren't they?" Castillo smiled at Cylea as the last of the House Derivatives left. She glanced hungrily at the masterpiece of meat they'd left before her, then gave him a quick nod.

"Exquisite, indeed." Exeter scoffed, elegantly wielding his knife and fork like the tools of a surgeon on a Neuroline soap opera. "And equally disgusting in their own way– and not useful either, except as playthings for the *lesser levels* of our society." The disdain he put into the statement attracted a few careful glances from nearby Nobles. "Everything that House Derivatives specialize in that is not carnal in nature can be performed as well, if not better, by ordinary Derivatives." He made a quick, precise incision. "It would certainly cut down on costs and bolster our security if we replaced at least the table staff with the old standard, as opposed to these *domestic* creatures."

Mason was already shaking her head. "And who would you have perform the cleansing rituals? It is rather a personal ordeal to have to endure, and the House Derivatives excel at making the entire process more comfortable than probably anyone present could, including your *old standard*." She laughed and got a series of nods from further down the length of the table. "The old standard, as you put it, is useful, but still very basic. They have an entirely different energy about them, one that is more suited for the blatant and less for the sublime."

"Decadence." Exeter muttered. "Sometimes I think that it makes us weak." He made a quick, pointed gesture. "*Traditionally...*"

"*Traditionally* the house is to be tended by a staff of human servants hired by the house and paid extremely well to keep silent." Castillo spoke up suddenly. "*Traditionally* part of the budget goes towards a fund for petrol and thermoplastics. *Traditionally* the queen herself is invited to attend Sunday services at the chapel on the grounds." Exeter had stopped cutting, his eyes locked with Castillo's. Violent flame crackled and shot between them. "Shall I go on?"

"Boys, please." Mason interrupted suddenly. "Why must you argue so? Alekzandr chose both of you to take the place of his most trusted limbs because you think differently from one another, because he wanted your differences to augment each other, not because he wanted his household to be divided over petty issues." She smiled, and already the tense silence that had settled across the entire table began to drop away and fade into memory. "Alekzandr himself approved the use of House Derivatives and even meets with Aerin directly to confer on them and their role here in the Manor." She turned to Exeter, eyes impassive, cold as blue ice veiled by feigned curiosity. "You do not question the wisdom of the Ageless, do you?"

"No." Came Exeter's immediate reply. He forced more steel in his voice. "Never."

"I figured not." She gave him a broad grin, then turned her eyes on Cylea. "How do you find the food, my dear?"

"Excellent. Ja, just... really great." Cylea managed, then gestured to the food. "This is... they actually *cooked* this, right? With...erm... fire or... something?"

"They did." Alan grinned. "And, it came from a real cow, if you can believe that! It's even free range organic."

Cylea stopped chewing. In a way, it made perfect sense, considering the apparent wealth of the Immortals, but the sudden revelation that her meal was worth more than she usually spent on food in a month was enough to stun her appetite, if only momentarily. She felt like she should savor the meal more, truly enjoy it, take it in and commit each bite to memory, but she was too hungry. The meal went down faster and faster as her attention became more and more focused on the meandering dinner conversation passing between the three members of the Triumvirate around her. For once, for the first time since she'd come to the estate, she felt like she belonged, like she was that fourth, long lost member of what had been the Great Quartet, that she somehow made these three whole and was made whole in return. Castillo smiled, and she smiled back, genuine and full force.

"Disgusting" Exeter was saying, shaking his head and grimacing at the same rotund Noble that had spoken up before. The Noble smiled and spread his hands amicably.

"Come now, Exeter," He began, gesturing idly. A House Derivative slipped in from the shadows and gently kissed the back of his hand in immediate response, moving to run its lips across his neck and sensuously tease his ear with a nimble tongue. "Why deny the very thing that makes us human?"

"Because we are not human, *Porthos*, not in any ordinary sense." Exeter set down his glass, stressing the man's name as if he were a child in desperate need of discipline and sparing none of the disgusted look crawling across his face for the House Derivative, even as she squatted dog-like beside the Noble and allowed herself to be stroked. "Ordinary humans are weak, stupid, and have short, meaningless lives that they waste on petty concerns." He made a quick, slicing gesture. "Concerns like sexuality and vice."

"What's the point of living forever if you can't indulge the petty concerns of the common man at least once in a while?" Castillo asked suddenly, smiling mischievously. He had the look of a man who'd played this game with Exeter before, a man who knew the answer but kept asking it just to hear the response, the conviction in the other man's voice.

"Thinking like that is exactly the reason why Alekzandr encourages the members of the great Triumvirate to remain *celebate*." He looked pointedly at Castillo, "By refusing to indulge our greatest animal impulse, we are less inclined to indulge any of our other base impulses." He cocked an eyebrow at the other man. "As a member of the great Triumvirate, you should know this, Alan."

Castillo's palms went up instantly. "Oh, I do, Exeter. I was merely playing devil's advocate for the benefit of our guest." He grinned.

"Yes, well." Exeter paused, dabbing his lips quickly and efficiently with a napkin. "I'm sure she will get more than enough of an education out of this experience." He turned his eyes on Cylea. "You see, in short, by repressing the distracting and addictive urges closest to our animal psyche, we allow ourselves to be more in control of ourselves and the world around us." He gestured absently. "The animal within each of us always asks for more. Refusing to indulge at all keeps us from acting rashly."

She nodded quickly. It sounded plausible, but she didn't believe a word of it, and her mind was too busy spinning off on its own tangents again. *Castillo? Celibate?* She swallowed, and suddenly the need to see Aerin came back full force, her heart shooting into her throat. She set down her silverware and looked away, trying to organize her thoughts, trying to bring them back to the present and the conversation that was already leaving her behind. She looked up at Castillo, opened her mouth, but when her voice came, it was rough and dry.

"Castillo, I... uh." She paused, reddened a touch as Mason's eyes slipped across the table to her. Her half-eaten meal sat before her, forgotten.

Castillo didn't miss a beat. "I understand." He said quickly, giving her a soft smile. "Go ahead, I'll send for you later. You know how to find your way back to your chambers, don't you?"

She nodded quickly, silently, swallowing. Exeter was already talking with Porthos again, ignoring the little event that was unfolding between Castillo, Mason and Cylea.

Suddenly, she stood, and sparing them all a quick, fleeting smile, she turned and hurried back out, more self conscious than she'd ever felt before in her entire life. Outside the door, she met the vaguely curious eyes of a hulking Derivative.

"Ah... uh... female problems." She smiled sheepishly. "You know, in case... uh... in case anyone asks." He nodded understandingly.

She bit her lip as she slipped down the hallway. She couldn't move fast enough, couldn't get back to her room fast enough. She had to see Aerin, had to tell him how she felt. She needed him, needed him badly, and in that moment nothing else truly mattered.

She sucked in a quick breath, breathed a silent prayer that he'd be there, and pushed herself into a slow run.

Chapter 41: Throne of the Immortal Father

10:00 PM. Cylea rolled over and buried a restless sigh into her silken pillow.

It had been five hours, five boring, feverish hours of waiting, of drifting in and out of sleep, of needing and chastising herself for the needs that bounced around her head like a handful of rubber marbles. Words kept repeating themselves in her mind, Exeter's buzzkilling line: *Alekzandr encourages the members of the great Triumvirate to remain celibate,* and the words that flowed so strongly from Aerin's lips after she had kissed them: *If you ever have need of me, for any reason, simply call my name and I will come to you.*

She shivered. She wanted to call him, wanted to scream his name to the heavens and whisper it seductively until he came, but she didn't have the nerve, didn't have the gall to take him away from whatever else he might be doing on a whim, even if it was a desperate one. He had an effect on her she couldn't describe, an effect that was almost frightening– the perfection of the Immortals was invigorating, even intoxicating, and too much to handle. She was drunk on the feeling, drunk on the opulence that sprawled around her endlessly, every turn and nuance so perfect and immeasurably expensive that she felt like a desperate teenager in a rich CEO's private residence.

She licked her lips, forced the thoughts away and sat up, looking around the room for something to take her mind off Alan and Aerin, to take her mind off the everpresent wealth, but there was nothing. She sifted through a stack of BBH programs left on a nearby countertop next to the little silver pistol Yamazaki had given her, most of them Arizona Alhambra concerts, and finally slotted a stick of Chiba Tequila, the J-Salsa boy band that had topped the charts in their time and rivaled the Beatles as pioneers of pop, with more of their members under the dirt than above it. The stick was a concert from the decade when they were in their prime, and the cool, easy sound of the band helped her to relax, helped her clear her mind and gave her something to focus on that didn't involve the Immortals. It was the perfect distraction, and soon the outside world melted away around her– she was no longer alone, no longer a restless outsider lying in an unfamiliar bed with unfamiliar new clothes and craving the physical contact of physically perfect men and sinuous Arch Angels, she was part of a swaying mob, a face in the crowd, easily spotted and easily forgotten. She sang along with each lilting tune as if the words had come from some softer part of her own heart and not someone else's, and time passed unchecked into some nether region of her distant mind, gone forever, the dull grey of a blank datastick.

When the House Derivative finally came for her, she was oblivious– the concert had lulled her into a near sleep that left her hovering between the waking world and unconsciousness, floating through the flotsam and jetsam of the subconscious mind on a cloud of untouchable calm. The tap on her shoulder brought her shooting back, launched headfirst from the cool, comforting depths, and she sat up so quickly she nearly bowled the House Derivative over. Only fast reflexes put the House Derivative out of swinging distance before Cylea could reach for the straps to rip off the BBH and shoot the newcomer a groggy half-glare.

"I-I'm sorry, miss Cylea." The House Derivative took a deep, apologetic bow. "The Illumined– that is, Mr. Castillo, asked me to fetch you." She paused, giving Cylea a moment to process and return to the world of the living. "The Ageless, Alekzandr, wishes to meet with you now."

A cold feeling settled over Cylea and she swallowed. It was time, time to meet the man behind it all, behind all the wealth and decadence, the Ageless, the one everyone seemed so in awe of and saw almost as if he were a god– and perhaps he was, in his own right. *An audience with God,* she thought. It sounded like the title of a cheap 'soft written by some new-age technopriest, or a DJ who had fried his last sane brain cells decades ago. A tiny smile played across her lips. She felt like she might have laughed, if she hadn't been so nervous.

"If you'll just follow me..." The House Derivative offered her an arm, and slowly, almost hesitating for an instant, she took it, stopping only to give herself a quick once-over in the mirror that was more absent reflex than necessity. If she was going to meet a god, she decided, the last thing she wanted was to look like she'd slept in the new clothes his people had given her. The House Derivative smiled a slight, understanding smile.

The walk through the manor was short and alive with tension. Eternity was quiet– only a few Nobles still lounged about, spotting the halls like lazy sculptures, stretched across extravagant couches or working on tiny Neuroline-access programming headsets or trading small talk across steaming cups of coffee and tea. House Derivatives shuffled past in sudden, sporadic bursts, some stopping to refresh drinks or caress the waiting cheeks of tired Immortals. No one they passed was alone, no one left to feel the cold touch of lonely silence– no one except her. Cylea swallowed absently, pushed away the thought, and forced her eyes to the stretch of scarlet carpet stretching on before her. Every step she took was meaningful, putting her closer and closer to Alekzandr, feet whispering across fine carpet, clacking softly against smooth tile.

The huge staircase of dark steel and gothic tracery with its banister of thick ivory cream loomed up from the other side of a familiar doorway as they crossed into the manor's entryway, slipping across the dark and depthless floor to a small and unobtrusive hallway that meandered off the main foyer and into twisty, labyrinthine dimness. Comfortable and ever present white light gave way to tainted yellow as the floor turned to aged and pitted linoleum, the walls narrowing, pushing in to a gently arched roof of pavecrete spotted by flickering lights– lightbulbs, she noticed, real lightbulbs manufactured to fit the kind of ancient fixtures that had been so commonplace centuries ago.

Cylea couldn't help but stare– the hallway looked like the maintenance passage for access to the manor's utilities, the water or the sewer, or something the Immortals didn't want to see or touch, something they wanted to ignore. It seemed totally out of place sprouting off from luxury the way it did, and it didn't look like anything that might lead to anything worth seeing, much less the lair of a god, no matter how reclusive he might be. The House Derivative seemed to pick up on her thoughts and turned back to give her a sudden, reassuring smile, amusement playing at the edges like fire across excited elastic. Cylea's icy eyes were soft, impartial but active, taking everything in, searching for something that might explain the sudden change in decor. More linoleum passed on silently underfoot.

When the passageway dropped suddenly into darkness, the House Derivative stopped and pivoted through a graceful turn, delicate dancing feet never crossing that last threshold between feeble yellow light and darkness. Her face was a mask of playful smiles that flickered and faded one into another like the mischievous expressions of a frisky pixie, and her hands folded neatly into themselves at her waist, forming an elegant ball of fingers and faeriedust flesh that shimmered in the half-light like the surface of a mirror. She bowed gracefully, and her words came with all the apologetic reserve of a demure servant.

"You'll forgive me, Miss Cylea, if I cannot pass any further." She bowed again, quickly and elegantly, shimmering lavender hair falling across her face and shoulders. "The realm of Alekzandr is closed to such as myself." She gestured toward the darkened passage. "You'll find the Illumined, Mr. Castillo, in the light just ahead.

Cylea swallowed and glanced into the darkness, almost straining to see what lay beyond the invisible line the House Derivative refused to cross. It wasn't far, just a couple dozen paces of darkened downward slope before it seemed to open up again, eerie light the color of pale turquoise playing across the edges of another threshold, the threshold between momentary darkness and whatever secrets still lay ahead, waiting for her beside Castillo's reassuring presence. Her eyes came back to the House Derivative's face, skirted briefly across it. Neither moved, neither spoke– the liquid ambiance of distant and tiny, lapping waves filled the pause.

She hesitated for only a moment, then plunged headfirst into shadow, leaving the House Derivative at the top of the slope and making for the light ahead, eyes never wavering, resolve fashioned into a firm shield. All of Mason's talk about energy had put her on guard, and she cleared her mind of all thought as quickly as she could manage. She had no idea what to expect, but that was never anything new– it seemed like the best she could ever do was try to be prepared, to ready herself for anything and hope that everything still managed to come out okay in the end. If anything, the past few months had taught her that above all else, and she clung to it like a desperate mantra. *Hope for the best, expect the worst.* Another uneasy swallow.

"Welcome, Cylea." Came Castillo's sudden, echoing greeting, strangely deep and ominous as the passageway opened on a vast chamber of pavecrete and a pair of long, rectangular pools that stirred slowly with a shimmering, almost gel-like liquid the color of Carribean sea. He stood at the far end of the room, near the end of a seamless pavecrete catwalk and half a dozen paces from the massive face of a huge pressure door, his suit as immaculate and perfect as it had been the first time she'd seen him, his face graced with that same perfect smile.

Cylea smiled back reflexively, but the expression faltered and slipped as she took in the room and absently crossed the length of the slablike bridge– it almost came as a shock when Castillo took her hands in his own and squeezed them gently. She looked up, and her gaze met eyes already seeking hers.

"There is nothing like Alekzandr," he began, breaking the silence with the soft-gloved fist of a moment that felt almost holy, like time itself were obliged to pause and allow the passing of sacred knowledge in its wake. "There is nothing like his realm– there is nothing to compare it to, except perhaps the world of dreams, and there is no way to prepare yourself for what lies within. You must go with an open mind and an open heart– if you can do this, you will find that the wonders beyond these doors, beyond the Bridge and Heaven's Gate, will open themselves to you and will change the way you look at the world around you forever."

Cylea swallowed reflexively as the nervousness returned full force. One of Castillo's white gloved hands brushed against her cheek, just a gentle caress to comfort her made tender by another smile. She managed a smile of her own in response, but it was barely reflexive-- his eyes held her in the moment, held her heart, and she couldn't let go. Suddenly she understood, she understood Aerin, the physical attraction that drove her insane at his touch, and how she felt about Castillo, how the feelings rising steadily in her heart were more akin to those that had smothered her and Bao, feelings rooted somewhere deep within her soul, nurtured by a deeper need for someone, for the comfort of the heart's own truest emotion- love.

"Come," Castillo whispered as he turned, releasing her hand and the moment along with it. "No one likes to be kept waiting, least of all Alekzandr."

Cylea nodded quickly as a wide grin spread like smooth life across the lines of her face. A quick snap of his fingers, and the air beside him wrinkled and creased suddenly, falling away from the hard lines of a stern-faced Derivative, one starkly different from the others she'd seen. She watched as Castillo submitted to a quick retinal and print scan, taking in the red-painted shoulders and convoluted curves of armored fabric and bullet stopping gel that were part of the Derivative's bodysuit with silent interest. The rifle in his hands was totally unlike anything she had ever seen before, like something out of a BBH sci-fi flick about interstellar empires in the distant future, or maybe something that might make the headlines in some tech or gun enthusiast magazine as next year's hottest military piece. When he glanced at Cylea, she winced reflexively-- his eyes were like a pair of chrome discs, dark and soulless retinas lined by blue and gold and spotted deep within by lights of hungry red. They were the eyes of a vatgrown modified with techware to the fullest extent, his genetically enhanced body brimming with steel and silicon, more machine than man, a type V to be sure, packed with cybernetic enhancements years beyond anything available on the streets of Los Angeles. He was the kind of vatgrown that wholly qualified as an instrument, a tool that served a particular purpose and did so with all the finesse that was required of him, killing as cleanly and effortlessly as anyone else might smile.

Then, just as suddenly as he had looked at her, he turned away. Giving Castillo a quick nod, he slipped backward into shimmering nothingness, and the air itself seemed to fold in around him again, leaving a chill in his wake that hung frozen in the silence. Cylea's gaze drifted toward Castillo's and locked with his eyes again, finding warmth in their steely depths. In the pause, the massive pressure door cracked and sank back into the corners of the doorway, shattering the icy silence with the whirring vibrations of well-maintained machinery.

Beyond the door lay a smaller room, a close bunker of reinforced pavecrete and soft, indigo light set with another ominous pressure door. A few steps put Castillo past the threshold of the first door, and he ducked easily into an alcove, gesturing for Cylea to follow him. The instant she cleared the edge of the door, it slid closed and sealed behind her with a soft whir and the quiet clicks of immaculate locking mechanisms falling into place. She felt the room pressurize the instant the door was sealed, and her ears popped with the sudden change in pressure, dispelling some of the stifling thickness that hung heavy in the silence. A tiny fiberoptic camera slid down from a small rubber nipple in the center of the ceiling as she stifled a yawn and craned its long dark neck to take her in with one silent eye. She looked up at it, and it seemed to return her stare in turn, studying her like a specimen in a cage before silently turning to follow her back as she slipped into the alcove behind Castillo.

"Tight security." She chided. Castillo grinned, half-glanced back at her.

"Alekzandr's dome is designed to keep the Ageless safe at all costs." He began, punching a series of numbers across a keypad set into the wall of the alcove with steady efficiency. "We're still on the outside, but everything you see here is under his control, all extensions of his body, if you will."

Cylea nodded absently and glanced back at the door they had come through. "That Derivative out there looked different from the others I've seen..." She trailed off, turning back to him as the alcove reverberated with a low, buzzing tone.

"He is part of Alekzandr's elite guard," A small pad of polished steel slid out of the wall and Castillo pressed his hand against it. "He's what we call a Thanatos, a Derivative that has been specialized to handle just about anything that might come down here looking to drop in on Alekzandr without a proper invite." Cylea grinned as he finished. Another low buzz echoed through the room. "He won't be the only one of them you're likely to notice either, if you look– at any given time, there are ten or fifteen Thanatos patrolling everything between the last room we passed through and Heaven's Gate itself."

"You keep mentioning Heaven's Gate." Cylea pointed out, watching as a panel on the inside of the alcove slid aside, revealing a large, complex-looking key with a distinctively spade-shaped head. "I take it that's the last stop before Alekzandr's... realm?"

"And the last chance to retain your sanity before it sprouts wings and flies away forever." Castillo grinned, taking the key and twirling it on the end of his finger for a moment before his fist clamped shut around it. "Still game?"

There was no hesitation in her answer. "Always."

Beyond the second door, the Bridge stretched on through panels of pastel blues and soft whites like a horizontal column of glass mounted solidly at the center of a circular tunnel. It was stunning how long the whole thing was, how it subtly narrowed in at the end to give anyone crossing it a feeling of vertigo, like walking down across the face of a skyscraper and staring at the distant ground below but not falling, the laws of gravity themselves seemingly bent to man's will through the cunning use of elegant illusion.

"We are actually passing through the outer wall of Alekzandr's dome," Castillo began, leading the way across clear panels of glass-like material that looked textured and gave traction, but felt oddly smooth. "The Bridge itself is the only weak point in the entire structure, the only passage either into or out of the dome, which requires it to be one of the most heavily protected and guarded locales in the entire manor."

"Makes sense." She glanced at the walls, noticed the ever present eyes of cameras and small alcoves of unidentifiable electronics that tracked their every move across the Bridge. "So I guess there's more than just cameras und those custom Derivatives down here."

"Much more, yes– the Bridge is practically incursion proof." Castillo gestured at the walls. "You might have noticed that sections of the wall protrude slightly from between the panels and do so at decidedly regular intervals–" he pointed several out in turn as they walked, indicating stubby, steely lines like the sprouts of smooth new walls just waiting to spring forth and sever the Bridge as easily as if it were an unlucky thumb caught between the blades of a pair of cleavers. "The Bridge is lined with near to two dozen bulkheads which Alekzandr can seal at will in an emergency, and each section, once sealed off, is capable of being depressurized to a perfect vacuum, in case of instances of more violent incursion." He paused, letting the fact sink in. Cylea swallowed, pushed away the feelings of powerlessness and insignificance that tried to well up within her as Castillo continued. "You might also have noticed the silver panels in center of the ceiling of each respective section–" he gestured again, indicating another series of now-obvious things she had missed. "Each of these shields a pair of twelve millimeter, armor-piercing sentry cannons, capable of taking down anything that might try to cross the Bridge and not be affected by the bulkheads and the vacuum."

Cylea gave him a slow nod. "Sounds like he's thought of everything."

"He has indeed, or near to it." Castillo responded. "There are systems concealed in the workings that even the Triumvirate do not know about, systems capable of reducing even one of the Illumined to ash in an instant, or so I've been told." He shrugged. "Only Alekzandr truly knows for certain."

"Really?" She cocked an eyebrow at him. "What's the point in that? I thought you were all one big happy family."

"We've been betrayed by our own before." He said darkly, glancing at her. The look that he gave her sent shivers crawling down her spine. "We've learned to take no chances."

Cylea nodded and looked away reflexively, studying the walls. Castillo didn't seem inclined to offer anything further, and so the silence held, dragging on until Cylea finally spoke up, her eyes meeting his almost instantly.

"So what's the deal with the key?" she asked.

Castillo couldn't help but grin. "Most guests aren't interested in the more traditional workings of our security system."

"Well, I am." She caught his arm and threaded her own through it with the most playful smile she could manage. "So tell me."

Castillo's grin turned into a soft and contented smile as he pulled in a deep breath. "Very well." He gestured quickly with his free hand. "I take it that you already noticed the shape of the key, the way the head is fashioned after a poker card spade?" She nodded and he continued. "Each one of the Illumined, that is, each member of the Triumvirate, like myself, is assigned a suite from your average deck of cards." He gestured. "It denotes our area of expertise and rank, with each of our respective subordinates being of the same 'suite'." He paused, glancing at the passing ceiling. "The secret of the keys is that every poker deck has four aces, and that each ace is an identifier for Alekzandr and the records, logged the instant it's turned in the lock for Heaven's Gate. Only one key is necessary to pass into Alekzandr's realm, but all four at once will release the locks on his realm and set him free completely." He met her eyes again. "Of course, in his present state, releasing the locks would likely prove to be fatal, but one day, when the time comes that he is able to leave his prison, this... realm which binds him and keeps him alive, we will be waiting to release him and receive him into the world of the living once again."

"Sounds exciting." She lied. She felt the slightest tingling of Castillo's pride and hope, but it wasn't enough to make her feel as strongly as he obviously did. "So you're the Ace of Spades, ja? Didn't that Yakuza— Yamazaki, say something about that?"

"Mm." He nodded, smiling. "You noticed."

"Of course." She paused, then shot him a feisty grin "So who's the 'club' of Alekzandr's great Triumvirate?'"

"Exeter, of course." He grinned. "And the diamond is Mason's suite."

"Makes sense." She laughed. "Und the heart?"

Castillo's smile faded a little, softened. When he looked away, Cylea closed the negligible distance between them, pulling herself up and against his arm, eyes seeking his, face full of genuine concern.

"It's..." She faltered. She knew who it was— the fourth member of the Quartet, the one that had left the Immortals fractured and incomplete, the Doctor. "It's Aoi's, isn't it?"

"Yes," Castillo breathed, his manner as stiff and cold as a frozen corpse. "Yes it is."

"I'm–"

"No." He cut her off, shaking off the shackles of his own inner darkness with the traces of a smile. "I take solace knowing that perhaps one day we will be able to forget that sordid chapter of our history and the suite of the heart will be someone else's." He paused, and the smile spread wide across his face. "Perhaps yours."

"I don't plan to stick around that long." She laughed suddenly, pulling away just enough to meet his eyes. "I feel out of place here, you know? You're all so..." She fumbled for the words. "So perfect, ja?"

"And you feel out of place here?" He grinned playfully.

"I'm sure I'm no where near as beautiful as Aoi was." She grinned back, but regretted it the instant Castillo's own smile crumbled under the weight of her words. "I– sorry."

Castillo shook his head. "No, it is I who should be sorry. I've taken Aoi's desertion the hardest of anyone, and I've refused to look at it, refused to deal with the darkness it brings... and the pain."

"Were you two..." Cylea paused, considering her words. "You und Aoi were close... weren't you?"

"We had... a connection. An agreement." He gestured absently. "Mutual interests, if you will." He looked down, almost trying to hide the smile that played across his lips. "We were the only two of the Quartet who couldn't accept Alekzandr's idealized vision of celibacy among the Illumined."

She gave him a quick laugh. "It definitely makes me think twice about sticking around."

"In truth, it isn't all that bad– some sects of the clergy still practice it." He offered, shrugging. "I myself maintained my celibacy for several decades, but..." He shook his head. "Aoi was just too much to resist. We found one another absolutely irresistible, physically speaking." His eyes seemed to go out of focus, staring at some distant memory. "At the time it was just... something we needed, an urge to be dealt with, but I made the mistake of falling in love with her." He laughed ironically, eyes drifting back to meet Cylea's again. "I fell for the Queen of Hearts, or rather the ace, and I paid dearly for it– if I were an ordinary human, I'd likely still bear the scars of her handiwork etched as deeply into my skin as the scars that she left on my heart."

"Wow." Cylea managed, drawn into the moment. "She sounds... like a real bitch."

"No, merely an opportunist in the most extreme sense." He smiled again. "There was no malice in her eyes when she shot me, only determination."

Cylea couldn't help but laugh. "Do you think you'll make the same mistake again?" She paused, her smile flickering. "Falling in love, I mean."

The half-grin he gave her was full of promise and potential. "Hard to say. Time is a wondrous thing– it heals all wounds and reveals the secrets of the future as it sees fit."

"Ooh, cryptic." She grinned. "I've found that riddles are like men. They're fun to figure out."

The bottom of the Bridge came up on them suddenly then, walls drawing in to meet them and stifling their conversation as the sealed mouth of another ominous pressure door rose from the end of the passage like the face of a massive tombstone. It was different from the others they'd passed through before– the symbol of the lotus sprawled in raised steel across its smooth surface like some arcane imprint, radiating a presence that was tangible, permeable, as if it were a charm that kept the door from buckling under the weight of some ancient, unearthly energy that brewed and frothed beyond it. Cylea took it in with the curiosity and awe of a child, eyes transfixed by the ebb and flow of something she could vaguely feel but couldn't see.

"Heaven's Gate." Castillo broke the silence, his voice like the gentle tap of a silver hammer on fragile ice. "This is the last barrier between our world and the realm of Alekzandr."

She pursed her lips anxiously as Castillo gently pulled away from her and crossed the distance to the door, spade-key in hand. Four distinctive keyholes stretched across the face of the door, each marked with a different suite and waiting open like the mouths of silent lovers, hungry for their matching keys. The heart was the only lock jammed closed, with the jagged end of the key broken off in the lock. The spade-key turned smoothly beside it, then sunk into metal until its crown was flush with the surface of the door. Castillo glanced back at her, the traces of a smile still playing across his face.

Heaven's gate seemed to hesitate, whirring for a moment before it split open suddenly, seeming to take a piece of reality with it as it went, the fabric of time and space rolling back to expose the luminous inner workings that lay beneath. Chromatic lines of electric neon clashed in the threshold, then crossed suddenly and blossomed into a shimmering sheet of mother-of-pearl that hissed and spit like water thrown across a hot stove. Castillo grinned again, turning back to watch the wonder and uncertainty play alternating roles across Cylea's features, twisting her lips into unsure expressions. He caught her attention with a gesture, then gave her the most charming smile he could manage. "Well, ladies first!"

The look Cylea gave him was incredulous, and he only grinned wider in response.

Chapter 42: Our Father Who Art of Steel

Passing through Heaven's Gate and into Alekzandr's realm was like falling headfirst into an ocean of carbonated icewater.

The suddenness of the sensation caught Cylea completely off guard– she struggled to plug her nose, fumbling and gasping first with the shock and then desperately trying to close her mouth and keep her breath. The rising bubbles of cool gas shot across every inch of skin and cloth, scouring her, burning and rippling over flesh with frigid purpose. She tried to scream, tried to cry out before drowning darkness could close in on her, but the sound was lost somewhere between reality and the pocket of liquid void she'd found herself blinding struggling through. Death seemed close, looming up on wings of liquid asphyxiation, the black night coming in the icy embrace of effervescent ocean depths.

Castillo's gentle touch brought her rocketing back. At first, it didn't feel real, seemed almost out of place among the sensations of the frigid water swirling and frothing around her, the bubbles of cruel gas that forced themselves across tortured skin and into every orifice they could find, stirring in her sinuses like tiny insects... but it was gone, fading like the traces of a hazy nightmare. She blinked warily, then glanced up at Castillo, and he offered her a soft, reassuring smile in return.

"It's unpleasant, I know." He nodded. "But it gets easier and quicker after a while, I promise. The key is realizing that none of it is real. Heaven's Gate can read your deepest fears and make them into reality in the passing. You have to decide to step beyond the threshold, and it takes a great deal of willpower and experience to do so without guidance."

"You'll–" She breathed, eyes still wide from the struggle. "You'll teach me this, won't you?"

"We will teach you many things, if you give us your loyalty," He paused, gently putting one arm across her shoulders and pulling her close against him. She closed her eyes and drew in a deep breath, shivering as she greedily soaked up his warmth, desperate for the body heat. His smell was clean, comforting–

not sterile, but like the scent of fashion and high class, and each breath reached into her, soothed her, gave her something real, something *human* to cling to.

"But loyalty is something you must prove to Alekzandr." He finally continued, gesturing forward to indicate the greater world, the realm they'd stepped into when they'd crossed through the hell that had been Heaven's Gate. "That is, after all, his primary reason for wishing to meet with you." She pulled away slightly, just enough to meet his eyes, hands still pressed against his chest. He smiled softly in return. "There are worlds beyond the mundane that most only dream of. There are doors that are closed, places and skills and knowledge that are forbidden to those who walk the path of mortal man." His face became serious in the pause. "There are no doors that are closed to those who walk the halls of Eternity."

For the first time, Cylea turned and looked around her, *truly looked around her.* The world that unfolded around her on the wings of an ever present lavender mist was incredible, a landscape made all the more unbelievable and dreamlike by the tone and meaning laying behind Castillo's words. It all seemed so impossible, so far from the realm of reality that she had come to accept living off profits scraped from dirty deals in the Los Angeles underworld– everything in Alekzandr's realm was surreal to a degree that didn't seem possible, like something that might manifest in the strangest dreams to surface after a night spent watching Neil Gaiman films and paging through H.R. Giger portfolios. Every terrain feature was disturbingly organic, pulsing and yet strangely cleancut and regal– the sky seemed depthless, forever stretching to some impossibly distant edge of the universe, and yet it seemed alive and close at the same time, a membrane of purple flesh that pulled in breath after laborious breath, adding its own vacuous voice to the realm's unnatural ambiance.

Cylea shivered. Ice crystals hung in luminous, pale lavender fog like tiny wooden specters, twisting and morphing under the hard fingers of invisible hands, and the ground seemed all too eager to rise up and cushion her every step, silently growing to support her feet. At some far distant corner of the realm, among mountains like swollen fingers distorted by cokebottle lenses, the lonesome howl of some alien beast split the living air and hung with a tangible weight in the icy mists, frozen and distorted as it sang along the crystals like some hymn vibrating across prayer bowls and tuning forks. Silently, Castillo took her hand and led her forward into the mists and the soft, sprawling plains beyond, the crystals parting to let them pass and coming together again in their wake to sing the mournful songs of other souls cruelly chained to Alekzandr's realm.

Almost too suddenly, as if the world that spread out before them were much smaller, with a much greater curve to its surface than Earth, a grand cathedral with all the eldritch glory and gothic majesty of a forgotten temple rooted in the wet and abysmal depths of an abandoned hell rose up to meet them, massive door of charred black stone already swinging open in silent welcome. It was eerie, the way reality seemed to close in around them as they walked toward the cathedral, every step making the air more dense, more stifling. Once, she glanced back to see if reality really were narrowing into a tight little ball just outside their vision, but only the endless foggy horizon with its bloated mountains stared back, so full of wet purples and frigid mist that it seemed more alive than each piece did alone, as if all were merely part of some greater organism, a fleshy extension of Alekzandr's body. Cylea hugged her arms tight against her chest and repressed another shiver.

Walking through the door and into the darkness of the ebon cathedral was like being swallowed whole, and the whole being of the place seemed to rise up around them like the jaws of some gigantic beast, dark tiles pulsing underfoot, as soft and giving as living flesh and filled with a tangible fire of desperate hunger, desperate need. The air was moist, humid, with as many pockets of cold air as warm, and each drift filled with tiny shimmering motes that came alive as they brushed against exposed skin, holding the charge for the barest instant, then humming eerily as they dimmed.

The darkness thickened steadily as they stepped further into the cathedral, becoming as close and tangible as molasses, but Castillo fairly glowed in the cavernous night, casting off enough light to see by and illuminating the cracks and fractures in the nearby walls. He seemed so celestially radiant against the charred depths of those abysmal chambers and passages that she couldn't help but stare, and as he turned to meet her gaze, the smile that touched his lips was the embodiment of benevolence stolen from the very mouth of a god, a smile as brilliant and luminous and comforting as the purest dawn rays of a springtime sun. She half expected to see the faint tracery of grand, neon wings or some frozen explosion of chromatic fire sprout from his back at any moment, as if to reveal the true nature of the Immortals as servants of the divine, or perhaps even members of the divine themselves, a hierarchy of spirits or gods or angels guiding mankind along a rough path to some golden future that was still so far off, decades upon decades away and but a blink of a dusty eye to those beyond the flow of time, those like Castillo, his Triumvirate, and the Ageless, Alekzandr.

And I can be one of them. The thought came unbidden to her mind, bringing the cold and frozen sensations of death's regrets with it. *Not just under their protection—one of them.* Suddenly the Triads didn't matter anymore, the Yakuza, even the bounty on her head seemed inconsequential– a new life was unrolling before her, one full of promise, potential and possibility, a life where no door would be closed, no secret left unspoken or unread. The world would open itself to her, and Eternity would be her domain, the endless, ageless passing of time coalescing into one faded block of memories cushioned on elegance and the decadence of the Immortals. In Castillo's eyes, she saw her future and knew, in the very fiber of her being, that there was only one choice, one outcome.

"Alan."

The sound came on a harsh whisper that cracked the air like a sledgehammer hitting a windshield, the edge of something that was more a long, hoarse exhale than a call, and filled with mutterings that seemed out of place, as if the sound had trespassed through some other facet of reality and snared the very thoughts behind a hundred different voices before spewing them into the darkness on an eldritch wave of white noise. The darkness wavered with the impact of the sound, then stretched and collapsed entirely, breaking apart and shooting off into nothingness like the screaming bits of a popped balloon to reveal a massive colosseum of black steel and iron sand that stretched long to sheer and distant walls. The first thing she noticed was the throne, perched high and centrally among sloped terraces that could have been seats, but looked more like the steps of some garden fountain long since dried– and then she noticed him, the tall, austere figure already rising from the shadows of the grand and gothic throne like an impossibly ancient specter from some age so long forgotten by history that only his words might be capable of attesting to its existence. His electric blue eyes burned deep into her soul, his stare stern and piercing, almost reptilian, and as sharp and solid as the hardened length of a well-honed blade.

Castillo dropped to one knee immediately, head falling and eyes fixing obediently on the ground. It took Cylea only half a second to register what was going on, and then she was in the sand beside him, eyes averted, taking in each black and steely grain as obediently as Castillo. When the Ageless spoke, it was as if the very fabric of the universe coalesced into wet exhale and *breathed* his words into being, each syllable a labor of time that came and *was*, as slow and broken as it was precise– the voice of a petrified god.

"Rise, my children."

Silk the color of bruised viscera came free from the wall in wide sheets as Cylea looked up and watched Alekzandr descend stairs that came into being to catch his every step and winked out of existence just as quickly behind him. He was gaunt and severe, face a grim visage of age and distinction with all the curves and hard lines of a regal bloodline. Silk flapped in an unfelt breeze and brightened to a rich and bloody orange as he walked, twin streamers pouring from long slits in the walls to follow him and led steadily by the junction they sprouted from at the shoulders of his long, gold-trimmed robe. Light caught every obsidian edge and onyx rune set into the shadowy fabric as he walked, playing across the dark surfaces of rings etched with symbols that seemed otherworldly, like letters from some extinct alphabet long forgotten by mankind but remembered by the soul and the spirits of the ether.

"Alan, you've brought her." His eyes slid to fix on Cylea and he managed a thin-lipped smile that was oddly comforting, like the smile of an unfamiliar grandfather in someone else's family tree. "Good, good."

"Your grace." Castillo gave a shallow bow. Alekzandr spared him the barest glance, then held up two firm fingers and gave him a sharp, dismissive gesture.

"Leave us."

Another quick bow and Castillo turned to leave. Cylea glanced at him as he passed, and in the pause, she found an instant of reassurance in his eyes. When she turned back, Alekzandr had reached the ground and was walking steadily toward her, each step padding air an inch above the sand, as if he were making his way across glass or hovering on hidden suspensors. His eyes sought hers immediately, and when they met in stare, it was like receiving a transmission of his force of will– the man radiated... *something*, and she could feel it, could feel it projected through his intensely blue eyes and could almost see it diffusing into the cold air around him like latent warmth. She closed her eyes, pulled in a slow, deep breath, then opened them again, forcing her resolve and her confidence to harden around her heart like armor. *Be strong.*

"You have something you wish to ask of me." Alekzandr said as he closed the distance between them, stopping half a dozen paces from her, silk streamers rippling. "I can see it in your eyes."

There was much more than just *something*– there were so many somethings, so many questions– too many questions, all fighting for attention and spinning out of control as the chance to express them presented itself. Her mouth drifted open, worked silently. There were just too many things, too many– she closed her mouth again and exhaled slowly. One question burned bright above all the others, insatiable, demanding an answer that was firm and true, not tainted by glitter or bullshit.

"Why?" She asked suddenly. "Why me?"

"You do not trust Alan's answer." It was more of a statement than a question, spoken in a tone that was understanding, almost comforting. He nodded, and drew in a deep, rattling breath.

"I–" She paused, trying not to falter in her resolve. "It just seems too– I mean, what kind of benefit could really come from protecting me?" She shook her head quickly. "It just doesn't make sense!"

"Castillo may have talked about protection, but I have something more in mind." He said, eyes never wavering, never moving, like the stare of a stern statue. "They do not see it," He gestured past her, indicating the outside world. "But our exclusivity is rotting us from within like maggots in the belly of a corpse. Day by day, the Order grows weaker, more decadent." Flame stirred and rose behind his eyes, twisting angrily. "What it needs is a fresh infusion of life, of passion and fire, a fresh infusion of *power*." He clenched his fist emphatically, and the energy that came off him felt like a blast of hot air from an oven. "What the Order needs is someone young and vital." His finger stabbed in her direction like a bony stiletto. "Someone like you."

Her mouth stirred in the pause, restrained by hesitation. Alekzandr made a quick, sweeping gesture and continued.

"You are unique, Cylea. You have strengths and secrets unlike anything I have seen before in any human being in my many centuries of living, and I want those strengths and those secrets on my side." His gesture was powerful, solid, and rang out with all the force of a sledgehammer hitting the bell of a grand cathedral. "They're too valuable, too important to be lost to death or to heathens who don't have even the slightest inkling of worlds or *shars* beyond the basic material gains of their own petty little lives! Your abilities, the skills and strengths that make you unique, should be preserved, nurtured and allowed to grow."

She tried to talk again, but there were no words. Alekzandr pushed forward, taking a few easy steps toward her as he spoke.

"You are but a seed, Cylea, one that is young but holds so much promise. If the Immortals were likened to a flowerbed, then you would have the potential to become the most stunning flower in the entire garden, a bloom that would outshine any of the Illumined with more ease than you are currently willing to accept." He spread his hands before her amicably, wrinkled palms and spindly fingers turned up to the sky. "That is why I want you to become one of us. You will make us strong again."

She swallowed reflexively, meeting Alekzandr's stare for a moment, then looking away suddenly to stare at the dark sand again. Alekzandr closed the distance between them to a single pace.

"So tell me then, truthfully." Alekzandr spoke, and her eyes flicked up to meet his again. "Will you join us and walk the halls of Eternity as one of our own?"

She hesitated, lips moving for a moment before the words finally came. "I have to know who I am-- why I'm different." Her eyes hardened, knuckles whitening as her hands tightened into desperate fists at her sides. "I will, Alekzandr! I want to become one of you und walk the halls of Eternity as an Immortal!"

"Then allow yourself to be marked and raised to the level of the newly incepted." The smile that spread across Alekzandr's face was soft and proud. Cylea managed her own smile in response, but it was feeble and faltering. Alekzandr gestured firmly. "Kneel."

Bowing her head, she quickly did as she was told and dropped to her knees-- it took the Ageless only a moment to cross the last bit of distance between himself and Cylea, and in the silence he reached out to touch her, cold and bony finger rising and falling to trace intricate and invisible lines across her forehead and in the open air just above the wild tips of her hair.

"The lotus represents purity." He began, pale lavender light slipping into the room suddenly, glowing at the edge of her vision and pulsing with each line he traced. "It represents purity of the mind, of the body, and of the soul– it is the symbol of those who float above the currents made filthy by the ambitions of those blinded by material attachments and impulsive desires." He paused, finger pulling away as dusky purple light blossomed and filled the room, pouring into her eyes and forcing her to close them against its blinding radiance.

"The lotus is a symbol of creation, of divine godhood," Alekzandr continued, his voice the breath of a priest washed in the deepest waves of spiritual ecstacy. "It is the key to spiritual enlightenment, and the gateway to spiritual awakening. It represents all that is immaculate, and cleans away all that is tainted or impure." He paused and drew in a deep, shuddering breath. "Rise, my daughter, and be recognized as one who has been blessed by this household, by Eternity, and by my own hand." She rose slowly, steadily, and her eyes rolled open warily. The lavender light was faint now, gently glowing from the lines of a neon lotus that burned across the chest of Alekzandr's robe. She met his eyes, and he smiled gently again, then bit his thumb and pressed it into her forehead, smudging a dot and two quick lines of fresh blood across her skin. She closed her eyes slowly, head dipping.

"Thrice blessed, our mantle is now yours to carry as well." He breathed as he withdrew and took a few steps backward, flicking a few drops of blood into the sand before his hand disappeared into the depths of his robe. "Carry the mark I have left in your etheric field always and bear it like a blade before you. Darkness will always flee like shadow at the touch of your light, and the light of your spirit will reveal things otherwise obscured by the embrace of stagnant night." He paused, taking a quick breath before adding: "You are a subject of the Order now. Wear the title of the Immortal proudly."

She nodded once, quickly, eyes coming open to meet his again. "I will. I promise."

He gave her a quick, shallow nod. "Your training will begin soon. The newly incepted face many tests before they can advance to a higher level of caste, and our trust is something that you will work hard to earn. We may have your loyalty, but you must prove to us that it is genuine."

She nodded. "I understand."

"Then leave this place and walk back to the manor as one who belongs in Eternity and is not merely a guest tolerated by its walls. Time has no meaning for you, but be swift nonetheless— Alan waits for you at Heaven's Gate."

Cylea couldn't help but smile, and Alekzandr gave her a fatherly smile back in response. It was like being born into a whole new world and, looking on her new father with the eyes of an innocent, a single thought blossomed in her mind.

This is my new life, my new reality.

Epilogue

The clapping didn't begin until after Cylea had slipped out of the cathedral and gone sprinting toward Castillo at the edge of Alekzandr's realm. The Ageless turned and looked up, watching as the shadows parted to allow the passage of another man, a man whose immaculate white labcoat fluttered like Alekzandr's silk in some unfelt breeze.

"Cirrus."

"Isn't she just some kind of wonderful?"

"She is incredible." Alekzandr admitted immediately. "I actually felt a presence about her, a spirit, a true etheric field and a full set of focuses, of chakras, as if she really were of the *Adamu*, as if she really were human." He shook his head in wonder. "Incredible work, Doctor."

Cirrus grinned, his long, austere features stretching into a sharklike grin beneath his sharp nose and rectangular half-glasses. He had the aura of a genius about him, of a man who walked the line and indulged his insanity on brilliant whim, his pale blue eyes sparkling with a maddening light beneath lilting strings of wispy blond hair. "So then, I take it we have a deal?"

"Of course." Alekzandr nodded. "The Order is more than willing to administer your next phase of testing, considering the benefits."

"And the benefits are great." He grinned again. "I knew that a man like you would understand both the value and the importance of something like this."

"The Order could not have survived as long as it has if we were incapable of looking at the long term as well as the short term."

"Of course." Cirrus nodded, then gestured to the tracery of the lotus slowly fading across the front of Alekzandr's robe. "I'm glad to see that your people are still very much into the whole 'stay with what's pristine and touches you' honey-dipped flim flam you were all about when I first met you. Aoi was hoping something like this might come along to test the prototype's capacity for spirituality and feeling and all that jazz."

The smile dropped from Alekzandr's features and he made a sharp gesture. "Obvious disrespect aside, Cirrus, I'd refrain from mentioning that woman's name in my household again if you wish to have any dealings with the Order in the future." He looked away. "*That woman* betrayed me and she betrayed my Order. I have nothing but disdain for her."

"You know, she's talked about coming back..."

"Don't, Cirrus." Alekzandr warned, shooting the other man a solid, harsh glare. "We are both aware of the fact that she never intends to set foot in these halls again unless it is for the sake of her *precious experiment*." He bit the words off with disgust, then thought better of it and gave Cirrus the barest of nods. "Aoi is dead to me, but like a dutiful grandfather, I will see that Cylea is properly raised."

A sharp grin spread across Cirrus' face. "I have a feeling that she'll exceed even our projected expectations, Alekzandr." He made a quick gesture. "*Badda-bing, badda-boom.*"

"Like mother, like daughter, Doctor." Alekzandr admitted. "Like mother, like daughter."

* * *

Outside the mansion, an ominous black shape swathed in bulky black perched unseen among the branches of a tight grove of large and sturdy trees, rainwater rolling off the edge of his widebrim hat in tiny, frigid droplets. His dead stare never wavered, eyes never blinking. The neon lotus stretching across the face of the manor burned on into the grey night.

Instantly, a woman materialized out of the scant dimness next to him, silently stepping up to stand beside him. She was young, somewhere in her early twenties, with distinctively German features under short, wild hair the color of red gold. The rain didn't seem to touch her, and she didn't seem to notice the cold-- her skin was smooth and resolute, even where it was exposed beyond the edges of her scant, skin-tight outfit of red and black synthleather.

Slowly, she removed her dark sunglasses, her vibrant, clear blue eyes shining glacially over painfully pink lips bent into a stern expression, as stony and unruffled as any hunter's.

"They're both inside now, ja?"

Ginsley nodded, then pointed a dumb finger toward the manor. "Inside."

The young woman's mouth worked absently, chewing something. "Wonder why father doesn't just tell her what's going on." She glanced at Ginsley. "I mean, he told us."

Ginsley looked up and regarded her with a blank expression. She met his stare for a moment, then looked away and shook her head. "Mein Gott, talking to you is like talking to a wall." His elastic face stretched and he laughed quietly in response, face never moving.

The woman looked back at the manor and breathed a sigh. She felt cheated, felt anger at the inefficiency of the whole thing, the whole experiment, the whole process. *You're a military model,* father had told her, as if that explained everything. She spit in disgust. *In times like these,* she thought, *salivary glands don't seem like such a waste of bodily space.*

Ginsley had already turned his attention back to the manor. Both knew it was going to be a long wait, a long time sitting in the shadows outside the Immortal's estate and waiting for the orders that would send them darting off toward whatever destination awaited them next. For a moment, the young woman felt the barest pang of envy. *Must be nice not having to have to take orders from anyone.*

She dropped into a crouch and looked up at Ginsley, propping her chin up on her palm and forcing an irritated sigh through her nose.

"This whole thing seems like a big waste of time."

Ginsley only laughed again in response.

*   *   *

Aiko checked her watch. Forty-five minutes until the next flight out to Hong Kong.

She was sprawled across three seats, staring out the nearest window at the tarmac and watching the planes take off with tired, half-lidded eyes. Brent walked around the corner of an advertisement for nanocosmetic styling shampoo and smiled at her.

"Change of plans." He shook a pair of tickets at her. "I got a hot tip that says Cylea didn't skip to China like we thought."

Aiko arched an eyebrow at him and crossed her arms. "Yeah? Is she still in town?"

"No, she still left the district." He glanced down at a silicon newspaper he'd picked up from a vendor. "She's just in Europe– apparently she caught a cruise ship to the British Isles."

"That's random." Aiko sat up. "So why the British Isles? What's there besides rain and tourist traps?"

"Apparently someone with more clout in the crime world than the Golden Koi. Maybe a corporation." He shrugged. "I don't know. What I do know is that the bounty still stands, and that because the case started on North American soil, we've got permission from Anderson to chase her across every district and back again."

"Now it's just a matter of getting to her before the BTD and that smug bitch Kagami do."

"Relax Aiko." He sat down next to her. "Remember what the Doctor said about undue stress."

"Fuck the doctor." She muttered simply.

Brent smiled. "He might enjoy that." The glare Aiko shot him was dark and brutal.

In the distance, someone rattled on loudly in Mandarin.

* * *

Clouds slipped by like icy sheets outside the window of the BTD atmospheric transport, a field of white thousands of feet below with the surface stretched out like a texture map beneath it. Kagami regarded it silently through titanium-frame sunglasses, mulling over the printout sitting on her lap. *Three possible destinations–* it read. *Hong Kong under protection of the Golden Koi, Chiba under the alias of Kara Eisenhimmel (cosmetic surgery and enhancement), and London, under the protection of an unknown organization.* They'd already checked out the Chiba lead– it had turned out to be some rich banker's daughter who was trying to get out from under his thumb by getting a new face and a new identity, and Special Agent David Oberholtzer was working his own leads in China, which left Kagami to figure out where Cylea might have gone to ground in the British Isles.

It hadn't been the first time she'd had to chase someone into the European district– she had a few contacts in the underground, a few friends, people who *knew* things, but the case was getting old. She kept hoping that Bueller would pull her out it, give her something new to work on that required her *very specific* expertise. Chasing some low-life, low-ambition girl across the globe to slap her in a cell was Agent work, not something a Special Agent usually got assigned, and the risk of assignments like these always pissed her off. It didn't matter how dangerous an assignment looked, there was always a chance of getting hurt, and that was something she could never afford– she was special that way, unique among a sea of other Agents, a Special Agent without a single inorganic modification, a purebody, whose specialty was EMP fields and remote scramblers, not raver flunkies, even if they were magnets for shootouts and international syndicates.

She sighed lightly and rubbed her eyes, then managed a small smile. *Well, at least the FBI has no jurisdiction in the European district.* She thought. *No Brent, and no Aiko to deal with. Thank god for that.*

She glanced out the window again, and smiled as a face rose up beside hers in the reflection.

"Well, well. Long time, no see," The edges of her smile twisted in amusement. "How's business been, Mr. Yamazaki?"

Sneak Peek From Pink Carbide: Carbon Aria
Chapter: Rainy Night Revelations

The rain had gotten heavier, thicker. It fell in oppressive waves as the hoversedan plowed through the night, catching the endless hammering cascades and shrugging them off like a stout brick. Wipers flicked back and forth at full tilt. Damp air hung heavy and cold, the clammy humidity of a wet grave.

Cylea hunched back further into the passenger seat and drew her knees up to her chest, trying not to think about Castillo, about Aerin and Exeter, about Ginsley, about Gideon, or the red-winged techware valkyrie that had claimed to be her sister... it was easier to let her mind go to that cold, grey place instead, that place where the pain couldn't touch her, where it didn't even exist. The tiniest return to reality brought tears with it, made her pull in tighter, struggling to forget, to escape it all. A single word bounced slowly and endlessly through her skull like a sluggish bubble, as invulnerable and etheric as a tired ghost. *Why?*

Synth-leather squeaked as Kari shifted in the center of the back seat, sprawling out and leaning into the cushion, booted feet crossed and pressed hard into the door. Mason blinked, mouth working through tiny, silent consonants, eyes fixed blindly ahead into the darkness of the downpour, hands tight against the wheel.

"Where are we going?" Cylea managed finally, voice small and quiet, eyes absently staring through the streaming rivulets tracing cold lines across the windshield and off into the night as the dark world outside sprawled past, lush with tangled greenery. They were somewhere in Cornwall now, headed southwest along the old M-5 toward the sea, shooting through waterlogged lanes empty of cars.

"I..." for a long moment there was nothing else, just the icy silence that hung there, a thick specter of doubt, of fear, indismissible. Cylea closed her eyes as Mason finally finished. "I don't know."

"We need to find an Airport... or a harbor." Kari murmured from the back seat. "Something off the grid, off the network."

Mason's scoff came quietly. Her eyes flicked to the rear-view mirror and shot the other woman an incredulous look. "Something off the grid? Off the network? Alekzandr practically owns this entire island, Kari. He'll have everything in the district locked down and the ECC on high alert by now. Even if we did manage to steal something and get it off the ground, we'd likely be shot down by ECC or BTD interceptors within a few short minutes."

Kari leaned back a little further, shifted again, her face the image of calm resolve. "I know a few people. I can arrange a ship that'll get us to the east coast of the North American district and then we can hop through the underground networks there back to the West Coast Province." She paused. "I just need a secure port for my people to dock at, some place where we won't be *seen*. Know of a place?"

Mason glanced at her in the mirror again. "Perhaps, but why leave the district? Why would we take all the trouble to cross the ocean and then three-thousand miles of corporate controlled American land? Kari, I–"

"Listen, Sara." Kari fixed her with a dark look, ominous storm clouds boiling in her obsidian eyes. "At this point our options are severely limited. We need to take this chance because the best hope we have right now is Steven Welles."

"Steven?" Mason shot back, eyes flicking between the mirror and the road. "Of all the people and places... he's loyal to the Ageless, he laid the runes and sigils for Eternity..." She shook her head quickly, vehemently. "He'll turn us in the moment he learns where we are. We would probably walk in on him and Exeter *sharing tea!*"

Kari's eyes never wavered. "You don't know Steven like I do. Trust me, we'll be safe with him." Mason scoffed again, but Kari continued anyway, tone becoming an appeal to reason. "Welles isn't a member of the Order, Sara. He's *Illuminati.*

Cylea's eyes drifted open slowly. The name seemed familiar, lost somehow on memories that were hidden by the fog, the pain, the confusion. Mason sucked in a deep, careful breath. The name found her lips in a whisper. "*Illuminati.*"

"That's right." Kari nodded. "Welles is part of the brotherhood, and is only loyal to Alekzandr to the extent that it keeps him in the loop. We'll be safe with him."

Mason's mouth worked for a long while before the words finally came. "No... no. That's– that is not an option. No way. *No way.*"

"Why not?" Cylea asked, shifting over to glance at the other woman, eyes meeting hers in the briefest glance. Kari's eyes stayed hard in the mirror, meeting Sara's whenever her gaze wandered back there. Mason swallowed, voice taking on a sharp, uneven tone.

"No. No, we aren't going to deliver ourselves into the hands of the devil, into the hands of a bunch of... of hateful, *Satan-worshiping lunatics* bent on the corruption, subversion and the reduction of the human race into a race of slaves!" Her anger bubbled over, adding a harsh, biting edge to her tone as she finished. "I won't have it! We're going somewhere else."

Kari's gaze never wavered once through the whole tirade. When she spoke again, her voice was strong, level, no-nonsense. "The Brotherhood is not what you've been lead to believe, Sara. They no more worship Satan than the Knights Templar have ever worshiped a demon called Baphomet."

"Bull*shit*!" Mason spat. It was the first time Cylea had ever heard the woman curse, the first time she'd heard so much emphasis, so much rage and hatred blasting in Sara's words. "The Illuminati are the worst sort of people to get involved with. They're cruel and heartless, manipulative, vindictive... and they don't give a right damn about anyone who isn't a member of their little cult!"

"That right there is bullshit." Kari shot back, anger creeping into her tone. "Stop and think about what you're saying for a second! Who do you think spreads those lies? Have you ever asked yourself where all the accounts of the 'evil Illuminati' *actually come from*? Ever think about what organizations spread that crap or what their agendas might be?" She paused, "Here's a good one-- ever ask Alekzandr if he's ever had business relations with the Vatican? How about business interests in Jerusalem or with the Saudis? Maybe if he has any ties to the old Freemason bloodlines?" Kari's feet left the door and pressed hard into the floor as she sat up, meeting Mason's eyes stare for stare. "Sara, the founding fathers of the United States of America, which was the only truly free and sovereign nation until the unification act that created the North American Union *were Illuminati*– you can see it in their old money, the old dollars from the 20th and 21st century had the symbols of the brotherhood and the owls of wisdom all over them. History remembers them as Freemasons because they broke from Alekzandr's original stock of Freemasons out of disgust with the way he was running the world at the time. Heck, the whole revolution of 1776 was about getting away from the corruption and the grossly overbearing banking system Alekzandr had created in London and that the Immortals were using to turn people into debt slaves. America didn't even have income tax or the private central banking entity known as the Federal Reserve until the 1900's, and it wasn't until all the founding fathers were long dead and the Illuminati began to lose their grip on the American government that Alekzandr's agents started infiltrating the political ranks and working to corrupt the system that the Brotherhood had fought so hard to create."

Sara choked back a sob, grimaced hard as she tried to swallow against the pain, the rising tears. "Bullshit." She repeated. "I won't hear it. The Ageless..." She swallowed again, forcing herself on. "No! The Ageless... he's a good man, he loves us." She bit down hard, clenching her teeth. "He does... not... lie!"

"The Ageless lies all the time." Kari shot back. "He's a shriveled up old dictator that's been directing human affairs in one form or another since the beginning of civilization itself, and he's gotten very good at manipulating people because of it."

"No..." Sara pulled in a deep breath, shivered. "Kari, stop. Just... just be quiet."

"The truth hurts, I know." Kari said, leaning forward a little in her seat. "I can't imagine what it would be like to be in your situation right now, to find out that the organization your family has worked for in one form or another for generations is as rotten as they come." Sara sputtered quietly, and Kari's tone gentled. "If it makes you feel any better, you aren't the first of Alekzandr's aces to end up on the run from him. Adam Weishaupt was Ace of Spades in the mid 1700's, Ben Franklin was Ace of Clubs, and Jefferson was his close assistant as a previous King of Hearts, but all three saw the wasted potential of the human race in the way Alekzandr was running things, in the way he has destroyed or converted and consolidated every truly empowered individual that has ever crossed his all-seeing eye instead of letting humanity realize its power *en masse*, as individuals, the majority awakening to rule instead of the minority."

"Sounds like one hell of a story." Cylea managed.

"Yeah, it is, and there's a hell of a lot more to it, because when I say *every* empowered individual, I mean it." Kari's eyes were lit with intensity, the darkness there hot and impassioned. "There have been a lot of victims. The Brotherhood of the Illuminati is just one of them," she emphasized with a staunch finger. "Just one, in a fucking ocean of destroyed potential." She paused. "There have been literally millions more, people who were targeted during the inquisitions, the burning times, the Nazi genocides, the Jonestown massacre, the Waco siege, the hunting down of the Shi'ite Soldiers of Heaven, even during the quiet elimination of the Prophets of the Apocalypse in the streets of San Francisco in 2077... it's all the same, all orchestrated by one man and the order beneath him, all done for power and money." Kari gave Sara a harsh, grimacing smile. "It's enough to make anyone sick."

Mason was crying openly now, tears streaming down her cheeks, arms weakly clutching the wheel. Her shell was cracking, the resolve that had held her together breaking apart like an ancient wall suddenly shaken to the ground. Cylea could see it in her eyes, the way the purple shine there seemed desperate and beaten. The betrayal hurt, but the truth was like a thousand hot pokers boring into her soul, relentless and uncaring, forcing her to look at something she'd been taught to deny so hard that she'd never really realized it had existed until now, until it had been forced into the light and staked face-up in plain sight beneath the unyielding and incorruptible light of a new dawn. Kari's hand touched her shoulder, and she shivered, suddenly grateful that she wasn't alone.

"I... need to do some thinking." Mason finally managed, then glanced in the mirror and met Kari's eyes. "I don't know what to believe."

"Believe in yourself." Came Kari's level response. "You are the only person who knows what is right for you."

"I know a place." Mason managed. "There's a jetty not to far from here that belonged to my Grandfather... I– I haven't been there in years, but it should work for a quick and quiet getaway."

"Perfect." Kari gently squeezed the other woman's shoulder. "Thank you, Sara."

The barest traces of a smile creased Mason's lips. "Don't thank me. After everything that has happened, I think that it's safe to say that we're all in this together."

Be sure to check out the next book in the Pink Carbide series:
CARBON ARIA
On sale in 2009!

www.ingramcontent.com/pod-product-compliance
Lightning Source LLC
Chambersburg PA
CBHW032040240626
47154CB00003B/1013